SUZANNAH ROWNTREE

A Wind from the Wilderness

Watchers of Outremer, Book One

First published by Bocfodder Press in 2018

www.vintagenovels.com

First edition

ISBN: 978-0-9942339-2-9

Editing by L H Editing
Cover art by Seedlings Design Studio

This book was professionally typeset on Reedsy.
Find out more at reedsy.com

Books by Suzannah Rowntree

Pendragon's Heir

A Fairy Tale Retold series:
The Rakshasa's Bride
The Prince of Fishes
The Bells of Paradise
Death Be Not Proud
Ten Thousand Thorns
The City Beyond the Glass

Prologue

For most of their short walk, neither Lukas Bessarion nor his sister said anything, the air around them still silent and heavy with the news.

Although the sun had begun slanting toward evening, Lukas felt suffocated by the summer heat that still radiated from the limestone walls of Oliveta. It was a small town perched in the Syrian mountains above Antioch, a place for rich men to seek the summer breezes among their olive groves and oil presses. But no such breeze cooled this afternoon's bare and metallic sky.

And thy heaven that is over thy head shall be brass, and the earth that is under thee shall be iron, Lukas thought, gulping painfully.

Marta touched Lukas' hand, her sympathy prompting him to speak. "Where would *you* go, if you were me?"

At fourteen, Marta was two years his junior, but Lukas had always trusted her with the questions he did not dare ask anyone else.

"Would you go to Constantinople, with you and Mother and the children?" He looked down with distaste at the old, dust-stained tunic he wore. "Or back home with Father, to fight for Jerusalem?"

"He said it was your job to take care of *us*."

Lukas snorted. "He meant I should stay with Mother so she could take care of *me*." He paused, wiping his brow to clean away the dust that had collected there during the long day's journey into the

1

mountains. "He didn't let me ride with him to the great battle. He didn't let me stay in Jerusalem to help with the siege, and now he's sending me to Constantinople with you and the children while he goes home by himself."

Marta said nothing, her silence drawing more words from him.

"If no one stops this invasion, we could lose our *home*. I don't want to be sent away like a child. I don't want to be safe. I want to *fight*."

"Yes." Marta squeezed his hand in a gesture of understanding. "If I were you, I'd want to go home. To Jerusalem." She was silent for a moment before speaking again. "Do you have money for the baths?"

"Of course." Lukas shifted his bundle of clean clothes to his left hand and touched his pouch. "Will you?"

"Go home with you?" Marta's grey eyes widened. For a moment, she looked tempted. "I can't. Mother will need the help. Especially if *you...*"

She left the sentence unfinished, but Lukas read between the lines.

If he went home.

If he died in Jerusalem.

"He won't make you go, if you don't want to," Marta added softly. "Wait until tomorrow and ask him again."

Lukas pushed a hand through his hair with a sigh. Part of him still did not believe the choice he had to make. He was a *Bessarion*. A patrician of the old Roman order. He should be preparing for a glorious career fighting the emperor's battles on the borderlands...not being sent into exile while his father faced the invasion alone.

At first it was just raids. Arab heretic warriors eager to grab herds and crops and slaves. In the aftermath of the costly Persian wars, Palestine had only feeble defences and there was no choice but to bear it. Then one day it became clear that this was more than simply raiding.

It was an invasion.

By the time Emperor Heraclius had realised how serious the

situation was, the heretics had already captured cities in both Palestine and Syria. The emperor had come to Antioch with an army to face the heretics, and Lukas' father had ridden away to join them with half the fighting men in Jerusalem.

There had been an argument that day, too: Lukas had wanted to ride with them. He was trained to fight, he had wanted to help defend his home. But his mother told him to stay behind and Father had agreed.

Look after the city. Take care of your siblings. Listen to your mother. She knows these things.

Mother always knew. So he had not tried to argue. He had watched his father march away to the great defeat, then return alone with the stench of blood and fear on him and the news that they must flee to Syria.

"You really think he'll let me go home with him?" They emerged between two houses into the town's square and Lukas raised a hand to shade his eyes from the westering sun. In the evening light, the honey-coloured stone was warm as fire. Carts and stalls cluttered the open space. The dome of a modest basilica rose to the right, while a fog of steam to the left marked the location of the baths.

Marta laughed. "Let you? Of course. He's not one of *those* fathers. Ask him tomorrow, after the Council. Lukas, look, it's a market! I wonder what they sell here?"

Lukas grinned. "Come on, I'll buy you something pretty."

They wove among the stalls, browsing through foods, wines, scented soaps, and bolts of homespun. Marta led the way, her fingers trickling along the fabrics, nose twitching over the soaps, but she did not stop until they came to a stall selling second-hand odds and ends: jewellery, shawls, and embroidered tunics. Marta gave a little gasp, and reached behind a hanging shawl to retrieve something which blazed with orange fire.

"Lukas," she whispered, "it's *amber!*"

It was a smooth, polished ball about the size of both her fists, meant to be carried about in summer to keep the hands cool. Before Lukas could say anything, the shopkeeper emerged from the shadows of her stall and croaked, "I hope you're going to pay for that."

Her voice was so officious that Marta gave a guilty start.

Lukas wheeled around, putting his hand to his pouch. "How much?"

The woman looked skeptically from his travel-worn sandals to his dusty tunic, to the trickles of sweaty mud on his forehead. "A gold *solidus*."

Marta's breath caught. "Lukas…"

"I'm buying it," Lukas snapped, digging into his pouch. Just because they were wearing poor clothing, she assumed that they were beggars? But as his fingers explored the pouch, all the fight left him.

He extracted the coins. Five brass *nummi* and not even one silver coin.

The shopkeeper's snort was audible as she leaned across the counter and plucked the amber ball out of Marta's hands.

Lukas flushed. "I could have sworn…"

The woman rolled her eyes. "You're wasting my time. Get moving."

As they moved away, she muttered under her breath: something like *cheat the clothes off my back*.

Indignant, Lukas wheeled around, yanking his left sleeve back to reveal his forearm. A mark made of thick black lines was inked into the pale skin below his elbow: an *I* and an *X* superimposed upon each other like the six spokes of a rimless wheel. "I'm no cheat. I'm a Watcher, see?"

Her eyes flickered as she recognised the mark. "Watcher's Marks aren't money."

Lukas tried again. "Watchers do *justice*. A Watcher wouldn't try to cheat you."

The shopkeeper only laughed. "I've been bilked by plenty of Watchers, boy."

"Lukas! It's all right." Marta's face was red as she grabbed his elbow and pulled him away from the stall. "I need to travel light, anyway. At least there's enough for the baths."

Lukas pulled his sleeve down and dropped the coins into his pouch again, feeling dazed as his irritation receded. "I'm out of money, Marta. What happens when it's gone?"

"Father's got more."

"That's what I'm saying. Don't you understand?" Lukas pulled her to a stop. "There *is* no more. We *had* money. We had the house in Jerusalem, the vineyards along the coast, the flax in Petra…now we've got nothing. If the heretics win, that's the end of it."

Marta bit her lip, beginning to comprehend their situation. "We'll have to live in Constantinople somehow. We'll find the money…."

"No. I don't want to be a charity case in Constantinople." Lukas strode across the crowded square toward the bathhouse, forcing Marta to jog to keep up with him. "I'm not giving up on Jerusalem. We'll have to find a way. Maybe the emperor can't help us, but we've still got friends."

The Watchers' Council. That was why they were in Oliveta, after all.

Lukas gritted his teeth. "We'll find a way to get our home back. The Watchers will help us."

"I hope so." Marta looked doubtful.

"Why wouldn't they?"

"Something Mother said." There wasn't even the slightest breath of a cool wind, but Marta wrapped her arms around herself as if she was cold. "I heard them talking last night, when they thought we were asleep. Mother said she thought she shouldn't give the Message to the Council tonight."

"Why not?"

"Because she doesn't think they'll believe her. Because she thinks that once they hear what Father has to say they'll be angry."

Lukas slowed to a stop in front of the bathhouse's double entrance. "Has she…*seen* something?"

Marta shook her head. "No. Father asked. She said…she said tonight is dark. The air feels empty."

Lukas swallowed. The air felt thick and suffocating to him. "But that's a good thing, isn't it? If no evil is here?"

"Maybe." Her smile was strained. "Or maybe it hasn't come yet."

* * *

Barely ten minutes into the first Watcher's Council he had ever attended, Lukas began to wonder if it was an honour he could do without. His mother was right—the Watchers were offended.

"This is *your* letter, Presbyter John?" One of the Syrian Watchers flapped a piece of papyrus in the air.

In the dimly lighted church it was impossible to make out the script. "I did write the letter, yes." There was an edge in John Bessarion's normally mild voice. "And I've come to Syria to discuss it in person. As I promised."

In the shadows behind his father's shoulder, Lukas shifted his weight. If the blockhead with the letter didn't get out of his father's face…but the Syrian Watcher abruptly turned to wave the papyrus at the circle of men and women gathered in the lamplight.

"Shall we take a moment to recapitulate?" the Syrian boomed. "The heretics from Arabia have destroyed our army and are ready to complete their conquest of Palestine and Syria. The emperor has washed his hands of us and fled to Constantinople. Jerusalem prepares for a hopeless siege. And this is the moment Presbyter John chooses to declare himself an enemy of the Roman state?"

Lukas took a sharp breath, but before he could say anything his mother grabbed his elbow in warning. The next moment it was too late: the Watchers broke into angry dispute, their voices echoing in the dome above their heads.

"Order! Order!" The Presbyter of Syria thumped his white staff on the ground with each word. "Watcher Petros, you go too far. The

Presbyter of Palestine is here to explain his words. We'll hear him before passing judgement."

All heads swivelled toward the Bessarions as John began to chant.

"*O God, the heathen are come into thine inheritance, thy holy temple have they defiled.*" John took a breath, audible in the silence that fell upon the council. "*The dead bodies of thy servants have they given to be meat unto the fowls of heaven. How long, Lord? Wilt thou be angry for ever? Shall thy jealousy burn like fire? O remember not against us former iniquities: let thy tender mercies speedily help us.*"

Behind him, Lukas' mother used the corner of her veil to dab at her eyes.

Lukas stared at the ground. He wouldn't cry. He *refused* to cry.

"I was there at the great defeat," John went on. "Six days we fought, in a blinding sandstorm, till the heretics smashed us. I was there. I know that God fought for them. I know that this has happened to us for our sins."

"No one disputes that," said the Syrian Presbyter.

"Which means that we have *failed*," John said. "Now it lies in our power to undo our defeat. But our only hope is in repentance."

He looked into the faces of his fellow Watchers with a sigh. "Here, in the Council of Watchers, I am known as Presbyter John of Jerusalem. But in my ordinary life I am the Praetorian Prefect of Palestine, responsible for the peace and justice of the province. Responsible to enforce the emperor's commands."

His gaze fell to the floor. "As Watchers, we're supposed to see to it that justice is done with mercy, showing peace and humility to all men. Some of us run hospitals, some adopt foundlings, all of us feed and clothe the poor. I did these things also. And yet, as the emperor's prefect, I was expected to coerce and destroy. When the emperor resolved to cleanse the state of heretics, I obeyed. Jews, Monophysites, and Nestorians—I confiscated their property, I forced them to be baptised, I killed them when they resisted. I believed it was God's will. But then the emperor himself embraced the heresy of the Monothelites, and commanded me to persecute the orthodox with equal vigour.

"I couldn't do it. I asked myself: if it is wrong to destroy the orthodox, why is it not also wrong to destroy the heretics? For months I prayed, fasted, studied, and wept. But in the end, there was no way to escape the truth that I had sinned. That the emperor had sinned. That all of us had sinned in doing these things. In the eyes of God, the heretics had committed no crime, no strife, no sedition, and we had murdered them."

"Blasphemy," one of the Watchers shouted from the shadows. "Merely by their presence in the land, the heretics pull down judgement on our heads!"

"One moment, brother. Presbyter John, what proof do you offer for this imagined crime?" Petros demanded.

"The wrath of God." John's voice was weary. "I said that God fought against us in the battle. I will tell you who else fought against us. In the moment of our need, a division of our cavalry went over to the enemy. Monophysite heretics each one of them, not a man among them who would not gladly strike a blow against the Empire. We could have reconciled them through love, but we persecuted them through fear. Is it any wonder that they turned to destroy us?"

This time there was only silence in the aftermath of his words.

At length, a Watcher from Mesopotamia moved forward. "The Presbyter of Palestine has given us much to think about. I suggest that we postpone future discussion until the next Council."

Lukas could keep silent no longer. "*Next* Council? We came here for help! We're in the middle of an invasion!"

"Not now, Lukas," his father muttered.

"That's an excellent idea, Nicephorus," the Syrian Presbyter said hurriedly. "If there's no dissent…"

"*I* dissent!" For the second time that day, Lukas pushed up his sleeve, revealing his Watcher's mark. "And I have the right to do it. Don't you understand? We don't have the time to delay. By next year's

Council we'll probably be *dead.*"

Nobody looked at him. In the agonised silence, the truth hit him: by next year they probably *would* be dead, and the Council was willing to bet on it. Anything rather than face the truth of his father's words. *Cowards.*

"Nevertheless," someone else chimed in smoothly, "this is an issue that shouldn't be decided hastily. I support an adjournment."

"Then it's decided," the Syrian Presbyter said, sounding relieved. "Let's move on. Call the Messenger."

The silence that followed was an embarrassed one as the Watchers realised who their Messenger was.

John turned uncertainly and looked toward his wife. "Rahel?"

But Lukas' mother was unperturbed. She turned to where Marta stood in the shadows holding little brother Paulus by the hand and perching their youngest sibling on her hip: three-year-old Elisa, her eyes huge and sleepy in the lamplight. Oblivious to what was happening, Elisa popped two middle fingers out of her mouth and hid her face in Rahel's neck.

Rahel carried the child onto the council floor.

"Let me forgo the Message tonight." She bent down, setting the startled Elisa on the floor. "The child will speak."

Lukas understood the gambit. After tonight's disagreements, any message Rahel gave would be subject to doubt. If it came from Elisa, however, there would be no doubt it was genuine.

If it came from Elisa.

As Rahel straightened, Elisa burst into tears, grabbing onto her mother's leg.

The Syrian Presbyter had to lift his voice to be heard over her wails. "Are you sure of this, sister?"

Rahel put her hand on the child's head. Astonishingly, the crying stopped. Elisa buried her face in the folds of her mother's dress.

"I have the right to appoint my replacement, Presbyter. I appoint Elisa Bessarion."

The Presbyter looked at her sceptically, cleared his throat, and said, "Elisa Bessarion, I name you Messenger for the Council of Watchers. If you have the words, speak."

Elisa did not let go of her mother. Did not move.

"This is useless," one of the Syrian Watchers harrumphed. "We need a better substitute. Let me send for a slave."

Elisa mumbled something.

"Hush!" Rahel lifted a hand.

Chubby fists still knotted into her mother's dress, Elisa turned toward the Syrian Watcher and spoke.

"Heart of stone!" she said. "Even the ancient Jews must release their slaves at the end of seven years. But you have kept yours years upon years with no recompense, no reparation. There are even some that you have maimed in anger."

The Watcher's mouth dropped open; his face paled. The hairs lifted on Lukas' arms. The voice was so firm, so articulate—so wrong, coming from his baby sister.

Elisa turned. "If you will not confess your sins, they will be exposed before all." She pointed. "*You* have dealt cruelly with the strangers which God has sent you to welcome and protect. *You* have dealt treacherously with your wife. *You* have made false accusations of heresy for the enrichment of your own coffers."

The Watchers fell back, jostling to avoid the pointing finger.

"You have the witness of your own hearts against you," the un-childish voice continued. "You have had warning after warning and you have refused to heed them. Therefore the guardianship of these provinces is taken from you and given to John Bessarion and his heirs, in whom there is no deceit. The Council of Watchers is disbanded."

For three heartbeats, no one said a word. Then Elisa began to cry again, and the Council went into an uproar.

It never occurred to Lukas to question the message. "Let's go," he muttered to his father as Rahel scooped Elisa into her arms and rejoined them. His mother's face was pale; Elisa did not quiet her wails, and everyone in the shadowed church was shouting or arguing or shaking their fists. By instinct, Lukas moved in front of his family to protect them.

"No." John looked as dazed as if the church had caved in and fallen on him. "This will need to be discussed."

"I should take Elisa home," said Rahel.

"Yes…" John blinked his shock away. "Yes. Lukas, will you…?"

He nodded tightly and led the way down the shadowed nave, eager for fresh air and quiet. Outside the church door, Rahel stopped to shush Elisa, wrapping her shawl more closely around both of them. Lukas breathed deeply. The suffocating heat of the afternoon had finally dissipated, leaving the August night warm, clear and speckled with a thousand stars. The light of the moon was so bright that he could still see faint colours in the tessellated pavement of the basilica's courtyard. Beyond the courtyard walls, the night was perfectly quiet, perfectly peaceful.

Coming to Oliveta had felt like coming to the ends of the earth. It was a small slice of Paradise, far removed from war and defeat.

Why must the Watchers be so unreasonable?

Elisa's crying hushed, giving way to shallow, heaving little breaths. Lukas turned to his mother. "It's that bad, is it? Receiving a Message?"

She looked worried as she led him out the courtyard gate and into the main street of the town. "No. I don't know what could have upset her this much."

A few lights shone from some of the villa windows, signalling where a merchant or clerk sat up late entering oil yields or olive weights into ledgers. The road was even and well-kept, and the moon was bright enough that they could still walk without lamplight.

"What now?" Lukas asked. "Do we start a new Watchers' Council?"

"I don't know. But I'm afraid of what this means."

"Which is?"

"As Watchers, we are supposed to do justice and love mercy. Like salt preserves meat, so the Watchers preserve us from the divine wrath. But if the Watchers are as bad as this—if the Council is so corrupt that it must be abandoned, then there's no help for us. The time of wrath has come."

Lukas chewed his lip savagely. "No, it hasn't. You can't mean that. Jerusalem has not fallen. We are still Watchers."

She did not answer.

"Well, if the heretics want our homes, they're going to have to kill us first."

A torch burned outside their destination: the largest villa in the town, where the Syrian Presbyter had loaned them rooms. Rahel hitched Elisa onto her hip and lifted her fist as if to knock.

Instead, she gave a stifled groan and fell against the door.

"Mother?" Lukas grabbed for her, but only managed to pull her shawl askew. "Mother, what's wrong?"

She slid down onto her knees, her body hunching over Elisa's. "Mother!" Lukas caught her head between his hands, looked into wide unseeing eyes. "Can you hear me?"

Rahel groaned again.

Lukas lifted his fist to bang on the door, but then she grabbed his wrist with surprising strength.

"Lukas. We have to leave. Now." Her voice was firm and clear.

The hair lifted on the back of his neck. He would never get used to having a prophetess for a mother.

"Tell me what you saw."

She climbed to her feet, pulling Elisa close. "North into the olive groves, Lukas. There's no time."

"I'm not moving."

"Then I must go alone." She turned and walked away from him.

There was no reasoning with her in this mood. Lukas ran after her. "Is there danger? What about the others?"

"I saw soldiers." She moved purposefully, as if she knew where she was going. "They were killing everyone, burning the rest. And worse."

12

Her words froze Lukas in place for a moment, forcing him to run to catch up with her. "Heretics?" The Arabs held Emesa, not far south. It was a long strike from there to Oliveta, but not unimaginable.

"Lukas, please," Rahel said.

They came to the edge of the village. Beyond, gardens and olive groves slanted across the plateau. Shadows congregated thickly beneath them: welcoming, concealing. There was no sound to suggest an imminent attack.

She really means to do it, he thought dazedly. *She'll really walk into the shadows and leave Father, Marta and Paulus to their fate.*

"I have to warn them."

She turned then, catching his arm. "There's no time! *Please!*"

Mother always knew. But no matter what the risk was, they were his *family*.

Lukas pulled free of her grip and turned back to Oliveta.

"I'm sick of running away."

* * *

On the south side of the village, at the gate to the basilica's courtyard, he paused to listen. If there was any sound of attack in the distance, there was no hearing it over the thunder of his pulse. Still, he knew better than to doubt his mother's visions.

He pelted into the courtyard and came face to face with his father and siblings.

"They told us to leave," Marta said. From the set of her mouth, he could tell she was seething.

"Forget them," Lukas gasped. "Mother's had a vision. Heretics. A raid."

Instantly his father wheeled around and began hammering on the church door. "Heretics! Heretics! Raise the alarm!" he yelled.

The door remained closed. No footsteps came to open it.

John fell back, his voice a hoarse whisper of disbelief.

13

"They've locked us out."

Lukas tasted bile. "But we're Watchers! We have the Mark! Can they even *do* that to us?"

His father wheeled around, throwing out a hand to them. "Lukas. Marta. Take Paulus and run for the hills. Find your mother. Go to Antioch and get a ship for Constantinople. *Don't return.*"

Run away. Again. Lukas fought the words back. "What about you?"

"Don't wait for me."

It was too much. "I'm staying with you."

"Lukas, no—"

"First we ran away from Jerusalem. Now we're running away from Syria?" He clenched his fists. "I'm a *Bessarion.* I'm a Watcher. I'm a Roman knight. And you haven't let me strike a single blow for the cause. Do you think I'm a coward? Do you want us to run until we're nobody at all? *No.* I'm going to stay with you. I'm going to fight."

In the silence after his words came the sound he had been dreading, rolling through the night time streets. Hoof beats, like distant thunder.

"Lukas!" John put a hand to his own head. "I'm not staying to fight, boy! I'm staying to give you a chance! Take your siblings and go!"

"No." Marta spoke. "Not unless you come with us."

"Where's Mama?" Frightened by their words, six-year-old Paulus seemed ready to burst into tears. "Is Elisa all right?"

"Don't be scared, chicken." But Marta's voice shook.

John surged forward, gripping his elder children each by the shoulder. "I should have told you. I know who this is. I know why he's here. He won't stop until he finds me. You have to leave me. Go to Antioch. Go to the basilica, and..." His voice trailed away as his eyes went beyond them.

Shivers crept down Lukas' neck. He turned.

It was only a man wrapped in a black cloak, but he stood only a few paces away from them under the courtyard arch. So silent was he that he might have risen like a shade from the tessellated pavement.

More shadows clustered beyond the arch of the gate. Beyond, slamming doors, shouts and cries told of Oliveta's rude awakening. Inside the courtyard, silence fell.

"Abba?" Marta whispered.

"I am not here to fight, John Bessarion." The man in the cloak spoke accented Greek. "You know why I am here."

John stepped forward, putting out a hand to keep his children back. "I know."

The cloaked man moved forward a step, and with a flash in the moonlight he brought his naked sword out from its hiding place. The steel whispered to a halt within a hair's breadth of their father's eye. "If you are wise, you will surrender the weapon without resistance."

Lukas felt his pulse speed up. His mother's vision, his father's acceptance… They had made him more afraid than he had ever been in his life. This was no ordinary heretic raid.

He slid a hand to his belt. The fool that he was, he had left his sword at the villa. All he had was a knife. It would have to do. Lukas looked at Marta and found he did not have to say anything. She let go of Paulus, slid a hand under her shawl, and exchanged an infinitesimal nod.

"Lukas," his father said sharply. "Don't be a fool."

He took his hands away from his belt. Only he saw the flash of disappointment in Marta's eyes. She said nothing, but did not let go of her own blade.

The heretic leader made a silent gesture and the handful of men at the gate ran forward. Two stood by the church door. Six more surrounded the Bessarions, levelling their spears.

If I live past tonight, Lukas swore, *I'll never be parted from my weapons again.*

"Where are you hiding it?" The heretic leader turned back to John, the brittle calm in his voice threatening to snap at any moment.

"Knowing I held such a thing, do you think I would willingly put it in the hands of my enemies?"

15

Someone screamed in the street outside, and was abruptly silenced. Little Paulus gave a sound like a sob, and Marta freed one hand from her shawl to pull his head against her.

"You have not destroyed it," the heretic said. "I should have known, if you had destroyed it."

"No, I have not destroyed it. Perhaps I might. Perhaps it is a thing too dangerous to exist."

"You will not. You need it too much."

"But you do not," said John. "The armies of your heresiarchs have conquered Arabia and most of Syria. The armies of the orthodox have perished. So, what brings Khalil ibn Hassan post-haste from Emesa, through miles of enemy territory, with only a handful of men to retrieve it? Answer me that. Then, perhaps, I will know how to answer."

The heretic smiled. "He who has the strongest weapons holds power over men. But you spin out the time to no purpose, John Bessarion. Now lead me to it."

John said nothing.

Heartbeats passed, and Lukas began to believe that his father and Khalil were locked in a battle no one else could see. The night was cool, but Lukas began to sweat, sensing the heresiarch's power in the spear points that held him motionless, in the echoes of pillage that hung in the air.

John smiled.

It was a mistake. Khalil's mouth tightened. "Kill his children," he breathed.

The spear points closed in tighter. John's smile vanished.

"Touch them and I promise you'll never find the weapon."

Khalil halted his men with a lifted hand. Sweat trickled down Lukas' temple.

Oliveta was awake now, shouts and screams echoing in the night air. Behind, the door of the basilica opened: a Watcher demanded to know what was happening. There was a sound of shouting

16

and scuffling as the heretics forced him back inside, and the door slammed again, locking the Watchers within. Lukas' last hope trickled away.

He could have been out on the hills with his mother, helping her reach safety. She had been right, as always: there was no time. But what difference did it make? He could not have abandoned his family. They were all he had left.

Another of the heretics entered the courtyard and spoke to Khalil in his own tongue. The heresiarch turned back to them, his face solemn. "The town has been searched. There is no sign of the weapon." He paused. "Tell me where to find it, and I'll spare your children."

"Don't tell him," Lukas hissed. *He who has the strongest weapon holds power over men.* This weapon, whatever it was, could be their last hope.

He could die in peace if he knew the orthodox had some way to fight back.

But his father did not hesitate. "How can I trust you to keep your word?" John asked.

"You can trust me to kill them if you refuse."

Again, the air thickened between the two men as their wills strove for mastery—but this time John Bessarion faltered.

"It isn't in Oliveta," he said. "I left it in the heart of Antioch, hidden with the bones of my old tutor, the Patriarch Anastasius. Look for it in the great basilica—if you dare!"

He began to laugh. The sound was overwrought, almost hysterical.

Until now, Khalil had spoken softly, smiled courteously. Now, denied his prize, he seemed to transform before their eyes. Baring his teeth, Khalil hissed something in his own language and threw himself on John, pummelling and kicking. Marta gave a horrified shriek, and Paulus began to sob in pure fear. As Lukas stepped forward, a heretic's blade nestled itself against his ribs.

His father dropped to his knees and curled over, shielding his belly and head as best he could. For a horrible moment there were no sounds but heavy blows, Khalil's snarls of rage, and his father's pained gasps.

There were tears of pure terror on Lukas's cheeks.

At long last, the church bells began to ring the alarm. The Watchers inside must have taken this long to confer among themselves and come to a decision. Much too late. Oliveta was remote, the nearest villages much too small to provide anything like help, if the sound even carried that far.

But the tolling bells seemed to restore Khalil to his senses. He drew back, ran a trembling hand through his hair, and shouted a command over his shoulder.

John uncurled, his voice ragged with pain. "Rage all you want, it will not open Antioch's gates to you."

"No," Khalil agreed.

Behind him, the gate darkened with people. They stumbled under the arch, sobbing and limping: the citizens of Oliveta. Their captors backed them against the wall, packing more and more people into the cramped space. Raiders at the church door broke it open and hauled the Watchers out. Others lit torches, flooding the courtyard with baleful red light.

Khalil turned to John with a hard smile. "I am prepared for this hour. Are you?"

The torchlight showed his face clearly for the first time: smooth skin, a firm mouth, a short dark beard—a face young and in its own way handsome. But the heavy-lidded eyes burned.

"Rage may not get me into Antioch, but power will." The hot eyes narrowed at the assembled townspeople. "Those who inhabit the waste places, the silences of the desert, know that there is power to be found in destruction. But the ritual requires blood and perversity. I do not know if there is enough in this whole town."

A sound of horror escaped Marta. Then her arm swung out and something like a dart of light left it. Khalil slid aside and Marta's knife arced through empty air, clattering harmlessly on the pavement.

One of the guards reversed his spear and struck her behind the knee. Marta crumpled to the stones with a gasp of pain. Khalil looked at her and for a moment he seemed almost amused, before one of his men held out a brush and pot.

The tessellated pavement beneath their feet radiated out in colourful geometric patterns of tile and glass from a central medallion. Khalil dipped the brush into the pot of white paint and began to trace lines upon the ground. A diamond that enclosed the central medallion, four lines to each cardinal direction, then a pattern of his own: symbols of the ancient pagan mysteries, and words in a flowing script Lukas could not read.

An orange light grew stronger outside the courtyard. Some of the captives cried out in renewed anguish or protest. Heat and the sputtering hiss of flames crowned the courtyard walls.

They'd set fire to the town.

Lukas' gut clenched.

They were killing everyone, burning the rest, his mother had said. *And worse.* What worse was there?

Khalil finished his pattern and stepped into the centre. Four circles completed the design at each point of the compass. At his signal, the guards seized Lukas and the others and forced them each into a circle at one of the points: Lukas to the west, Paulus north, John east, Marta south.

The man was a sorcerer. That was the *worse.*

These were powers he did not comprehend. Lukas watched the same realisation dawn across Marta's face and his father's. Paulus was hysterical. The guards had to hold him down to bind his hands and feet.

Lukas endured it in silence. A terrible, numbing despair fell over him. Evidently the others felt it too. Trussed up, unable to move. Abandoned by the emperor. Denied by the Watchers.

If only he could be sure that his mother had escaped.

But she did, he realised. He would doubt anything, but he would not doubt the words Elisa had spoken in that weird calm in the circle of Watchers. The guardianship of Syria and Palestine belonged to the Bessarions now. That meant Elisa. She had to have escaped.

Khalil leaned over each of them in turn, marking them on the forehead with a finger dipped in paint. "There are many *djinn* in the deserts and mountains, from the hairy jackals that inhabit lost cities, to the Pestilence by Day and the Destruction by Night. For a sacrifice, they will give me the power to destroy Antioch. You have sealed your fate, John Bessarion." Then he spoke three time so that all would understand his meaning: once in Greek, once in Syriac, and once, finally, in his own language.

"Kill them all."

Lukas could never remember exactly what followed the words. It was as though his memory could not bear to record it.

There was a great deal of screaming.

At the centre of the geometric pattern, Khalil began to chant. Lukas did not know whether the heretic spoke his own language or some forgotten tongue of power, but he felt the words crushing the breath from his lungs. He could never remember whether he saw or only imagined them: gigantic words, words like stones, words like labyrinths, hanging in the air above him.

A hot wind whipped through the town. The red light grew as the flames of the town streamed skyward to become a pillar ascending to the heavens, a pulsating column of unbearable heat. The sound was already unbearable, but now it took on sharp edges, a rattle and clink like bones and blades. In the wind, shapes appeared, the chatter of wings, the howl of beasts. Around and around they rushed, descending like a maelstrom, like burning furies.

His voice rising to a climax, Khalil thrust out his arm, baring the skin. A shape black and birdlike settled upon it. Ribbons of blood laced across his skin as its talons sank into the sorcerer's arm. The bird of prey screamed, but its voice was a woman's, its head a harpy's head as it leaned down, its awful red lips parting to touch Khalil's.

Across the sigil, Paulus began to convulse, vomiting and sobbing. Lukas tried to call his name, to tell him that it would be all right, but the hot wind stole the words from his throat.

In abject panic, the little boy began to inch away.

Amidst the surrounding fury, Lukas sensed a sudden fervid joy. "Paulus!" he screamed. "Stay inside the lines!"

Khalil had his back to the child. The heresiarch's guards had fallen back, shielding their eyes, hardly less frightened than Paulus himself. On knees and elbows, mouth open in a wail of fear, Paulus wriggled through his circle, smearing the still-wet paint.

The circle is broken! The words spoke not to his ears but to some inchoate sense which he used now for the very first time. *The circle is broken! Mother, let us feed!*

Khalil's voice faltered. The bone wings above snapped and clattered. The harpy screamed, and so did the sorcerer.

Utter blackness fell.

Chapter I.

Anatolia, AD 1097

Ayla knew that she would die at the hands of a Christian, but according to her father's foretelling, this would not happen until the third day of the month Zulqida in the year 490. Six months from now. There was comfort in knowing the exact date of her death. It meant she did not have to worry about now.

It meant that the Greek boys blocking her way did not scare her in the slightest.

"Hey, Turk." One of them settled his hands on his hips as more dropped to the wooden quay from the road above, blocking her retreat. "What have you got in the bag, eh?"

"The emperor of Rome." Ayla eased the bag off her shoulder onto the quay, shooting a quick glance to where her ship lay a hundred paces further on. It was just far enough that the crew would not notice their cabin boy being waylaid by street trash on the way home from the market.

Fine. It was nothing she had not dealt with before.

"Oh, funny." The same boy spoke again. Taller and uglier than the rest, he was obviously their leader. He did not sound amused. "Let's take a look."

He reached out for the sack. At the same moment, someone grabbed her from behind by her short-cropped hair. Ayla briefly considered drawing the knife she wore tucked inside the waistband of her trousers, then decided against it. She did not need to kill anyone. Not for a sack of oranges.

As the hand in her hair tightened, Ayla let go of the sack and grabbed the wrist of the boy behind. A step back, a twist, and she had his arm locked painfully behind his back. He released her hair with a yell of pain, and she shoved him toward the stone embankment dividing the quay from the road above.

He smacked into the stones and collapsed with a groan.

She had moved too fast for the other boys to do anything—but she had distracted them from the sack. Turning back to her, their leader's eyes narrowed to ugly slits.

"You little rat. No one messes with my little brother."

Ayla took a sharp breath. Just her luck. Now she was *really* in trouble.

But only if they could catch her.

An open stretch of water beckoned to her right. She was a bad swimmer, but it was her only way out, speckled and streaked with refuse as it was. Ayla lurched sideways, but the Greek boy must have seen her eyes flicker that way, noted the moment of calculation as she decided what to do. He grabbed her by the arm and yanked her back to the quay, slamming her back against the embankment.

He was faster than she was. Stronger. His fist poised to strike.

Her father's foretelling promised she would not die for another six months. It did not promise she would be *safe,* nor that she would reach her death unharmed in all the ways a helpless girl could be.

Just as she braced for the impact, a voice halted the fist. "Excuse me, fellows. I am the prefect's son. What town is this?"

The newcomer slithered unsteadily down the rocks and landed on the quay beside her, holding the rocks to keep himself upright. The boy with the ugly face looked him up and down and drawled a curse.

Ayla looked at him hopefully. *Gorgeous. But drunk. Convenient anyway.*

"Who are you, rich boy?" the ugly Greek growled.

"I told you, I'm the son of the prefect of Palestine."

"And I'm the emperor of Rome. There's no prefect in Palestine, son."

The rich boy just looked confused.

"Maybe he means the Turkish prefect," another of the boys sneered. "Is that it? You one of the filthy *beys*, huh? This a friend of yours?" He jerked his head toward Ayla.

"I don't know what you mean. I want to know what town this is." He straightened, looked down his nose at them. His accent was strange to Ayla—and he talked like someone in an old play.

The boy holding her growled. "All you need to know is this is *my* town. My ground, understand? You stay off it."

The other Greek flushed red. "You will tell me the name of the town, slave!" he barked. All high breeding and offended dignity. She could have told him it was useless.

Ayla's captor took his fist from her head long enough to make the sign of the fig at the newcomer.

Ayla took her chance and whipped her head forward, catching the boy in the jaw. Pain exploded as her forehead made contact, but she was expecting it: he was not. He lost his grip on her and Ayla slid aside, picked up her sack of oranges, and scurried down the quay toward the ship.

Filthy Greeks. They're all the same—dumb and violent.

Behind her, the rich boy's voice lifted in protest that was suddenly cut off with a groan.

Don't get involved. Don't—oh, hell. Ayla turned.

She had left the Greek louts smarting and madder than hornets. Rather than chase her, they had evidently decided to take it out on the newcomer. Their leader sank a fist into the boy's gut. Without a sound, he doubled up, staggered backward two steps, and toppled into the water with a resounding splash.

The Greek boys laughed, clustering on the edge, looking over.

The water smoothed out. No sign of the newcomer. That must

have been a crippling blow. He was down there, helpless, and none of them were going to save him.

Ayla sighed and lowered the oranges again. She wore a twisted blue-and-orange cord around her waist where most people assumed it was a badly-made belt. With one yank, it came free and she dipped her hand into the pocket where she always kept a handful of smooth pebbles.

She aimed low.

One of the boys yelled in pain as her first pebble struck his bare leg, breaking skin and drawing blood. Ayla already had her second stone in the sling's pouch. "The next one goes in your eye," she yelled, speeding the sling to a striped blur.

At that range, she could kill at least one of them before they got within striking distance. None of them wanted to take the chance. With shouted insults, they pulled themselves up the embankment and ran.

Ayla checked that they had vanished into the town's bustling streets before racing back down the quay to where the newcomer had vanished into the water. A few bubbles broke the water, telling her where to jump. She found the boy twisted into a knot near the bottom and dragged him to the surface, grabbing hold of the slippery quay posts to pull their heads above water.

"Come on. Breathe," she told him.

He wheezed painfully, then coughed up saltwater. "I—can't."

"Filthy Greek pig-boys," Ayla said. She switched to Turkish to abuse them at her leisure while the boy gasped and wheezed. "You breathing yet? My arm hurts."

He shoved at her and broke free, getting one pale hand onto the planks of the quay and hanging there, looking like death. "Better without you crushing my lungs."

"You're welcome, Greek." Ayla rolled her eyes and hauled herself out of the water.

Once she had landed him on the quay, like a great pale ungainly fish, gasping mouth and all, she was able to see the boy more clearly. Her first impression was correct: if his voice was not enough to show it, his clothes proved he had definitely come from money. He was clad in multiple layers of white linen, beautifully embroidered at the neck and wrists, and much too flimsy for a chilly April morning like this one. With dark curls, even white teeth and a rather full mouth, he was nearly as pretty as a girl, and certainly no more than a year or two older than herself. From the stains and rips mussing his clothes, the puffy eyes, and the bruises already formed on his arms and knees, he must have had a pretty wild night.

Oddly, he did not smell of wine. Maybe the smell of the harbour had overwhelmed that particular stench.

"Never been in a fight before, have you?" Ayla unwound her sling from the wrist where she had stored it for safekeeping, and fastened it around her waist again.

Despite his discomfort, the boy shot her a withering look. "I'm a trained cataphract."

"No idea, sorry."

"Heavy cavalry. I fight with a spear on horseback."

She twitched an incredulous eyebrow.

"At least, I would if my father let me."

Ayla could not help laughing at him. "S'pose that's why you don't know beans about scrapping. Your folks must be rich. What are you doing down here? This isn't your part of town."

"If you told me where *here* was I could tell you."

Ayla glanced up the embankment, where rocky slopes embraced the narrow harbour on two sides. A cleft between the hills led northeast toward the city proper. They had built the port suburb wherever they could find footing on those tumbled rocks, and planted cypresses and junipers on the rest. "This is Myra. Or its port, anyway."

"Myra." He whispered the word in evident shock. "Saint George! What am I doing in *Myra?*"

"Must have had quite a night."

26

"To put it mildly." He dropped his forehead onto his knees and his hands shook as he linked them around his shins. "That's impossible. What's your name, boy?"

Ayla might not fear death, but she was not fool enough to dress like the girl she was, nor to use the name she had been born with. "Kismet." A twisted grin. "So you might say you've been saved by Fate."

"Fate?" The Greek looked up at her in quiet desperation.

She rolled her eyes. "That's what the name means. Kismet. Fate. You'd know it if you weren't a stuck-up Greekling."

He took no notice, instead digging into the purse he wore on his belt. His fingers scrabbled loudly inside and he came out with a single brass coin. He looked at it despairingly. "Saint George. Barely enough for a bath. What am I going to *do?*"

A bath? She shouldn't be sitting here—she should be collecting her oranges and heading back to ship. Still, even if he was not drunk, this Greek was irresistibly helpless. One brass coin in his purse and he thought of paying for a *bath?*

"You got folks somewhere, right?"

"They're in Syria. I think."

"That's four days by ship."

"Impossible," he said again, dully.

"You want to argue with me? I've just come from Antioch on that ship." She pointed. "Four days. Four nights. Myra."

"Saint Lukas and Saint George," he muttered. "How do I get to Syria on a single *nummus?*"

"Kismet!" The yell came from further down the dock, where the ship was moored. Ayla glanced up to see her shipmate catch sight of her and throw up exasperated hands. "High tide!" He beckoned her and returned to the ship.

She looked back at the Greek. He had buried his face in his knees again and was muttering what sounded like prayers.

Not my problem. Not my responsibility. The thought made no impression on her. *Bigger things to worry about. Only six months left.* That got closer.

Still.

She slapped him on the shoulder and said, "Maybe I can get you home, if you're willing to work."

"Work?" He stared at her as if the suggestion was an indecent one.

"God have mercy, Greek. No one's going to pay you to sit on your lily-white—"

"On your ship?" he interrupted. A spark of hope flared in his eyes. "You're going to Antioch?"

"Not right away. We're going to Constantinople first. But then, yes—she'll head back to Antioch. You're lucky Ahmed is short-handed."

"Ahmed?" He frowned. "That's a heretic name."

Greeks. Ayla took a slow breath and counted to three before she let it out. "Look, Greek, I hauled you out of the water, I'm trying to get you home, and all you can do is complain? You haven't even thanked me."

He stared at her for a moment. To her astonishment, he reddened. "I'm sorry. You saved my life, Kismet. Thank you."

He said it so sincerely that she did not know how to react. Instead, she stood, clearing her throat. "Come on. We're about to sail."

Ayla retrieved her oranges and led the way up the gangplank. Silently dripping, he followed her down the quay.

The ship was a compact, Roman-style galley with two masts, one amidships and a much smaller one jutting from the prow. Up on the poop deck, leaning against the rudders, Captain Ahmed stood to supervise the ship's departure. Ignoring the first mate's instructions to unfoul some lines, Ayla dropped her oranges near the hatch which led to the hold and led the Greek boy to the poop deck. "Captain? We still short-handed?"

She had known Ahmed for all of four days, since approaching him on the docks of Antioch's port town, Saint-Simeon, to ask for work.

She had no idea what he would say, but he grinned at her easily around his silver toothpick. "Depends. This one looking for work?"

"He's a Greek. Don't know if he'd be any use, but he needs passage."

She waved the boy forward, but her heart sank as he stood before the captain. Ahmed was half a head taller and built like a barrel; by comparison, the Greek boy looked about as much use as the toothpick..

"How old are you, boy?" Ahmed switched from Turkish to Greek to ask the question.

"Sixteen."

"You look healthy."

A touch of red hauteur returned to his cheekbones. "My health is irrelevant, captain. Either Constantinople or Antioch, it doesn't matter where you take me. My father has powerful friends in both cities. There will be no trouble paying my passage."

Ahmed looked amused, but to Ayla's surprise he made no objection. "Luggage?"

The Greek spread his hands. "None."

Again, the captain made no comment, just a grunt of assent. "Enjoy your passage to Constantinople, m'lord." He lifted his voice. "Cast off!"

"Kismet!" the mate shouted again.

Nodding to the Greek, Ayla slid down the ladder to the main deck and cleared the rigging lines. While one of the hands reeled in the mooring-line, the mate leaned over the rail, shoving them off with an iron-tipped boathook.

Ayla spun the hempen lines through her hands like she was a fine lady spinning thread. Under her breath she chanted: *"God! There is no deity but Him, the Alive, the Eternal. Neither slumber nor sleep overtaketh Him."*

At first the ship barely seemed to move. Then, slowly, the tide teased it away from the quay and into the long inlet of the bay. Ayla finished clearing the lines and stood up, wiping her hands on her trousers, her tongue still pattering over the well-remembered verses.

"Unto Him belongeth whatsoever is in the heavens and whatsoever is in the earth. Who is he that intercedeth with Him save by His leave? He knoweth that which is in front of them and that which is behind them, while they encompass nothing of His knowledge save what He wills."

"Anchor!" Ahmed called.

It was just a stone with a hole bored through, but it was enough to hold them. Over it went. The ship drifted on for a moment; then an almost imperceptible jerk told them it had reached the length of its rope. Ayla took one of the rigging-lines.

"His throne includeth the heavens and the earth, and He is never weary of preserving them. He is the Sublime, the Tremendous."

Another deckhand joined her, gathering up the line, testing the wind with a licked thumb. Two more ran for the foremast.

Slowly, the ship swung around, nosing into the wind.

"Raise the anchor! Hoist sails!"

In came the dripping length of rope, the stone itself. Then the square sails bloomed like roses. Ayla heaved her end of the rope and fastened it to the cleat. With sails unfurled, the ship seemed to come alive, to breathe, almost. Ahmed took the rudder and turned them toward the open sea.

The mate strode up the deck toward the poop. "Get those oranges stowed," he snapped at Ayla. Then he raised his voice, asking in booming Turkish: "What's the story with the Greek, captain? Can he pay?"

Ahmed's eyes flicked sideways. The boy stood by the rail staring at the receding shore, hugging himself and shivering. "Can you pay, Greek?" he asked in the same language.

No answer, of course. The Greeks were generally too stuck-up to soil their tongues with barbarian words. Ahmed gave an amused grunt and turned back to the mate, his voice dipping. "He's a stray, clearly. Nah. I'll wager he fetches ten times more as a slave than a passenger."

A slave. All the satisfaction of helping a lost stranger turned to ashes in Ayla's mouth.

The captain lifted his voice. "Kismet! Where are you, boy?"

She had been crouched down near the hatch, her hands on the sack of oranges. She realised Ahmed did not realise she was above deck, or he would hardly have told the mate that he saw the Greek as cargo.

She did not move.

"Kismet!"

She scrambled out from behind the cover of the locker under the mainmast, hoping he would assume she had been in the hold.

"Take the Greek below and get him some dry clothes before he catches his death."

The captain had switched to Greek, letting the boy know what he was expected to do next. Slowly, looking half-dead with exhaustion, the boy descended the ladder and ambled toward her. Ayla glanced at the shoreline. They were just coming out of the narrow port, the shoreline dropping away on either side. Open water lay ahead. She was no swimmer herself. What were the odds the Greek could make it to land now in the shape he was in?

Well, that was fate. She knew her own fate was to die young. And now she knew that the Greek's fate was slavery.

Sometimes, she wished she could forget.

As always, a foul bouquet of aromas rose to greet them as they descended the ladder into the hold. Inside, bales of cargo and boxes of supplies were stacked fore and aft of the mast. A constant sloshing told of foul water in the ship's keel and huge pale patches of mildew crawled across the hull.

The Greek looked at it all with a grimace of distaste.

A few hammocks swung from the underdeck, loaded with personal belongings and forgotten about now that the weather was fine enough to sleep in the cleaner air above decks. Ayla rifled through one, found a bundle, and tossed it to the Greek. "Should be something in there to fit you. They're Abdul's, and he'll probably squeal, but the captain'll fix him."

The Greek caught the clothes, but he did not move. "You're all so good to me."

She could not look him in the eyes for a moment. "Can't get paid if you're dead when we arrive."

"Who are you? I thought I'd heard all languages before, but I can't place yours."

She snorted softly. "You really never heard anyone speak Turkish before?"

The Greek shook his head. "Why are you doing this for me?"

"Wondering the same thing, to be honest. Maybe I like your face."

There was a bruise forming on his cheekbone. He prodded it with careful fingers. "Right. It's a work of art."

She was still trying to figure it out for herself. Maybe it was not his face so much as the look in his eyes. *Guileless.* She was not used to that. She was used to bullies who thought they could get what they wanted by hitting her.

At least he had spared her that, blundering in when he did. Once they'd got her pinned down, they might have figured out she was a girl. Ayla did not fear death, but she had nightmares about that.

"Those Greeks wanted my blood. I got some of theirs." She spat into the bilge. "Ran his head into the wall."

"Why?"

"I know their sort. Cowards. Knew they'd run."

"They weren't running when I came up."

"Mm. So I s'pose I owe you." She bit her lip. Fate was fate. But if you knew your fate, then at least you had a chance to make the most of it. "Listen, Greek. Don't let anyone know I told you this, but I messed up. You shouldn't have come aboard."

He blinked at her in confusion. "Why?"

"I should have known the captain wouldn't take on a lily of the valley like you without a guaranteed return. He plans to sell you once we get to Constantinople."

"*Sell* me? What? How? Why?"

She smiled wryly. "Well, a good-looking halfwit like you? Some fine Greek lady would pay a lot to keep you around."

His mouth dropped open. "As a *slave?*"

"As God wills it."

"But I'm not a slave!" Outraged, his voice lifted.

"You will be."

"How do you know?"

"Heard the captain tell the mate when they thought I wasn't listening."

He lifted a shaking hand to his forehead. "This is...this is *wrong.*"

"Yeh, it's a pain. Didn't mean to get you into this mess, but how bad can it be? You'll have food, clothes *and* a roof over your head." More than most people had.

"They'll make me a *eunuch.*"

Ayla nearly laughed. Being rich must make you a special kind of stupid. Whoever this Greek was, he had probably owned slaves himself. Including eunuchs. And he was only just now imagining what it must be like?

Maybe he was just putting it on. Nobody could *really* be that naive.

"They'll never get away with it," he said finally. "I was telling the truth, I *do* have powerful friends. My father's the prefect of Palestine."

"What's a prefect?"

He looked at her as if she was stupid. "The prefect is the emperor's governor in Palestine."

"What's Palestine?"

"It's a province. You know. The capital city is Jerusalem."

Ayla frowned. "The emperor doesn't have any governors in Jerusalem."

He looked at her warily. "All right. My father was the governor there until two weeks ago at the latest."

She lifted her eyebrows. "The *emperor's* governor? As in the emperor of Rome?"

"Yes. Emperor Heraclius."

Ayla could only stare at him. "You don't mean Emperor Alexius?"

Confusion and exhaustion chased each other across his face. "No."

"God is great," she breathed. Then, on a breath of suspicion: "Are you mocking me?"

"Saints and angels! Why would I mock you?"

"Because it's impossible. Emperor Heraclius lived at the time of the Prophet. Hundreds of years ago, when Syria first fell into the hands of the believing."

He stared at her, aghast. "Impossible."

"That's what I'm saying."

He dug his hand into his purse again and pulled out the brass coin to hold it up to the light. Then he thrust it at her. "Read this coin. What does it say?"

She took it, tilting it to catch the light streaming through the hatch above them. There were two figures in Greek imperial regalia on one side of the coin, and a cross on the other. There were also some words. "I don't read," she said, offering it back to him, "but this isn't a coin I've ever seen before."

"It's got the emperor's name on it. Heraclius. Here, see?" He looked at her pleadingly.

"The coins say Alexius now."

He was silent for a long time. Then: "What month is it?"

"The Greeks call it April."

A gulp. "I see."

"You all right, Greek?"

He ignored the question. "And Syria? Who rules it now?"

"My people. The Turks."

He looked as if he was about to be sick. "You mentioned a prophet."

"Mahomet, peace be upon him."

The Greek folded to the deck, burying his face in his hands. "Heretics," he groaned. "You're heretics."

Ayla rolled her eyes. "Greek? You've got bigger problems than this."

34

"Go away," he said raggedly. But as she turned to leave, the Greek called out to her again. "Last night I was in Syria, Kismet. In the mountains above Antioch. It was August. Heraclius was emperor." He looked at her with eyes almost blinded by despair. "What's happening to me? Am I going mad?"

Chapter II.

The man with a grudge against the emperor of the Greeks must shroud it from sight long enough to penetrate the walls, gardens, gates, guards, and eunuchs that divided him from the world. The man nursing a grievance must carry it shrouded in reverences and genuflections, in smiles and simpers. The man wishing to force a quarrel must carry it cold, cold as the next day's ashes, into the light and the incense and reignite it as hot as it ever had been.

Raymond of Saint-Gilles, count of Toulouse, was a man of cold tempers, and now, after half-an-hour's wait, he was as icy as the English sea.

"The God-led emperor invites the count of Saint-Gilles to his presence."

Saint-Gilles had been leaning on the spear he used as a walking stick, contemplating the water-clock in the vestibule. Now, he wheeled toward the summons, his four attendants falling into place on either hand. It was almost impossible to see the gilded Greek official who'd called his name against the equally gilded doors leading into the emperor's throne room.

As the doors unfolded, the unique woody timbre of eunuchs singing burst against him. Inside the imperial audience-hall, the air was heavy with incense. A golden jewel-box of a place, the octagonal hall was crowned with a dome of mosaics and teeming with gem-crusted courtiers, both gleaming in the light of the ornate hanging lamps.

What did they see in him? A lean, battered old man who had lost an eye? He had something worthy of their respect nonetheless: he had an army of Provençal chivalry. Saint-Gilles squared his shoulders and strode into the hall.

At the far end—what he would have called an apse if it had been a church—an enormous and forbidding icon hung, Christ Pantocrator with one hand raised in blessing, the other in judgement. Below it, a blaze of gold light burst from behind a filmy curtain as inner doors cracked open. Then the curtain itself was drawn back like a veil. The singing voices reached a crescendo and cut off, leaving only a ringing silence.

This *was* a church, he realised. The rood screen had been opened, but instead of altar and Eucharist, it revealed the emperor himself enthroned on a high platform below the Christ Pantocrator.

At that moment, the official leading him prostrated himself on the floor of polished green porphyry. From his previous audience with the emperor, Saint-Gilles knew he was expected to do likewise. In the midst of such overpowering splendour, it took a conscious effort of willpower to stiffen his spine, ignore the murmuring onlookers, and stalk down the porphyry aisle.

Saint-Gilles took care not to fumble as he climbed the two steps that led up to the rood screen. With only one eye, he was not always sure of his heights, but he would die before he showed any weakness before these people. It was quite possible he would die anyway, at the hands of a very polite and well-dressed assassin. Saint-Gilles might be taking a risk, but he was no fool. He had weighed that possibility before coming, and deemed it worth the risk.

The emperor's gigantic English guardsmen shifted as he approached the brass rail before the throne. As one, the hafts of their massive battle-axes slammed on the floor, barring his way. Saint-Gilles came to a stop almost close enough to smell their breath. He took no notice of them, fixing his eye on the man behind, the man on the throne.

Saint-Gilles had been a warrior all his life, and in his own dominions he wielded the power of a king. He would not permit these Greeks or their tame Northmen to intimidate him.

"Justice, my lord," he growled.

Alexius Comnenus, emperor of the Greeks, who called himself the emperor of Rome, wore a gold crown dripping with strings of pearls. Between the gems his face was incongruous and startling: the full dark beard, the dark, weathered skin of an old campaigner, and the coldest, brightest eyes Saint-Gilles had ever seen.

Alexius said something in Greek, and the English men stood aside. Nodding to his interpreter, the emperor sat back. The interpreter bowed deeply and began the ceremonial greeting.

"In the name of the Father and the Son and the Holy Ghost, my God-given majesty welcomes you, Raymond of Saint-Gilles. How are you, my son? How is the young son of my son? How is the countess?"

"What if I told you they were dead?" Saint-Gilles bit.

That got the interpreter's attention. He wheeled to the throne. Alexius leaned forward as the interpreter translated. His reply was tediously long in coming: "Dead, my lord? What news is this?"

Saint-Gilles held his gaze. Let him learn who he was dealing with. "They live, my lord, and are with me. No thanks to you." He stuck his thumbs into his belt. "*You* urged me to leave my people and hasten to Constantinople. I assumed that in my absence, my followers would be safe from injury. Evidently I was wrong."

He half turned, beckoning to one of the knights behind him. Bleary-eyed and mud-splashed from the road, the man came forward, pulling a piece of parchment from his pouch.

Saint-Gilles shook it at the emperor. "My vassals write to say that they were attacked by *your* troops, my lord. They speak of terror and desperation, of the danger to their women and children, of the deaths of great princes. Men of *my* blood. Men of *my* household, who trusted my word and were betrayed. You strike at them, you strike at me." He threw the letter down like a gage on the steps below the emperor's feet. "I summon you to justice, Alexius Comnenus."

As the interpreter finished translating his words, Saint-Gilles kept his eyes on the emperor's face. Alexius' expression was tightly controlled. *Well, you did not cling to the imperial throne for so long if you could not hide a knife behind a smile.*

The reply, when it came, was brief. "I gave no order for any attack."

He had expected as much, but he refused to back down. His authority as a count depended on his ability to protect his people...and God knew there was little else to justify his rule. "You're denying responsibility?"

"Your own troops plundered my people. Had I asked you for justice, what would you have said?"

"As I told you, I put a stop to that when I found out about it."

Alexius was impervious. "As will I, now that I have your information."

One of the Englishmen bent down to pick up the parchment, and offered it back to Saint-Gilles. He took it, permitting himself a sour smile.

"I see your design, my lord. I have refused your pact, and you will destroy my people for it."

The day before yesterday, at his first meeting with the emperor, he had been asked to do homage to Alexius in exchange for passage across the sea to Anatolia and some form of military support once he got there. Nothing else: no land, no power. It was a miserly arrangement that would have muzzled him and his people while they did the emperor's work. He had turned it down out of hand.

He had not imagined the emperor would resort to force.

Alexius was unruffled by the accusation. "On the contrary, my lord. Your people met only with the danger they sought of their own accord." He leaned forward, his fingers linked. "I hoped to make you my vassal, Saint-Gilles. I still hope it. Why should I destroy your troops?"

"Then give me justice."

Alexius was silent for a moment. "You have summoned me. Very well, let judges be convened to try this matter."

Saint-Gilles tasted triumph. "And the hostage, to guarantee my people's safety until the decision is reached?"

At that question, officials clustered to the emperor's side, waving their hands as they argued. One of them was evidently a Frank—a tall, fair-haired man with the shoulders and the big veined hands of a fighter, who spoke in fluent Greek. Saint-Gilles smirked at the contrast between the Western warrior on Alexius' left and the Greek general on his right: a soft-bellied man draped in silk, so vain that he wore a gold nose strapped to his face to replace the feature he had lost. *Tatikius,* he recalled. Alexius' half-Turkish foster-brother, a eunuch who had somehow become the emperor's most trusted general.

They said he had lost the nose in battle. Saint-Gilles would sooner have guessed it was an amorous disease. No matter—Tatikius would make an apt hostage.

The gold-nosed general and the Frankish knight made a last exchange, then straightened to attention as the emperor spoke.

"You shall have the hostage you ask, Raymond of Saint-Gilles." Even in translation, the words rolled with condescension. Alexius motioned toward the Frankish knight. "I will deliver into your hands my well-beloved vassal, Bohemond of Taranto."

For a moment, Saint-Gilles could not even speak.

Bohemond of Taranto? He had never met the man but he knew him by repute. The Norman count who'd invaded Greece twice and made Alexius look a fool each time. The man so penniless, he had poached knights from his brother in order to take the cross.

This was his hostage?

"You must be *joking*. The purpose of a hostage, my lord, is to hazard the life of one who is *dear* to you."

Bohemond's lips quivered in the beginning of a grin, but he said nothing.

40

"I speak in earnest," Alexius retorted. "The count is my vassal now. He has taken the oath you refused."

"You are mocking me," Saint-Gilles spat. "Why not hand over your general, there?"

Bohemond interposed. "Don't translate that," he said to the interpreter in French. "Tell him the count is willing to accept me as hostage."

"I am *not*," Saint-Gilles protested, but the interpreter was already speaking. Alexius smiled and answered, lifting two fingers in a gesture of benediction. The interpreter repeated the formula of leave-taking. Bohemond turned and bowed to the emperor. Clearly the audience was over.

Bile filled Saint-Gilles' stomach, but he held his peace. Clearly the emperor meant to make a fool of him. The lives of his people now depended on whatever fragile alliance existed between Alexius and Bohemond, but he could not fight for them without knowl-edge—knowledge that only Bohemond could give him.

"What was the meaning of *that* interference, count?" he growled as he and Bohemond retreated into the vestibule of the water-clock.

The South Norman count gave a smirk and a shrug. "Raymond, Raymond, 'it is hard for thee to kick against the goads'. This is the *east*. Men have subtle minds here; they don't think or fight plainly."

"So? I'm a soldier, not a horse-dealer."

"As you like it, but you're not in Toulouse any more, count. Alexius is no peer of ours, and he'll never treat us like equals. Better to take what small concessions he gives."

"We'll see about that." Saint-Gilles ironed his lips shut. "Where have you been lodging?"

"Outside the city walls, at the monastery of Saint Cosmas and Saint Damian."

Saint-Gilles scowled, taken aback. "How strange. So am I." If he had known Bohemond was also a guest, he would have spoken to him sooner.

An escort of the emperor's burly, axe-wielding English and Norsemen waited for them on the outside steps and the chance to speak freely was over. Forming up in two ranks, they led Saint-Gilles, Bohemond, and their small entourage through the grounds of Constantinople's Great Palace. Sprawled across the slopes of the tallest hill in the city, the palace was a complex of halls, chapels, baths, and offices which itself occupied enough ground for an entire town. Every surface seemed to shimmer or glitter. Floors of polished porphyry or marble, walls that sparkled with the intense colours of glass and gold-leaf mosaics. Icons and silks. A silent congregation of statues and a garden of melodious clockwork birds.

Saint-Gilles wondered if this was what Eden looked like before the Fall of Man.

Their horses awaited them in the courtyard that fronted the Great Palace's main gate at the crest of the hill. Beyond, an open square bordered with pillars and punctuated with soaring columns led to a wide avenue stretching down into the city streets. Towering houses marched side-by-side as far as the eye could see, the clutter of their walls and roofs broken only by trees. Patches of lush greenery promised more gardens and hinted at the presence of water cisterns. The escort broke their way through the congested streets toward the city's western wall. Even beyond the palace, the people and animals looked well-dressed and better fed. Saint-Gilles studied them in wonder. Like any city, Constantinople must have its beggars. Christ had predicted that the poor would always exist. But here, even a poor man could be wealthier than some of the nobles in his own army.

One heard stories, of course. Constantinople and her emperor were legendary. But nothing really prepared one for the truth.

Their escort shepherded them to the Adrianople Gate, or rather the series of gates that took them through the massive triple wall of the city. Beyond, a sprawl of suburbs, monasteries, and orchards fanned out for another half-mile or so, but the guards bowed their farewells, contented that they had done their job and escorted the dangerous Franks safely beyond the wall.

Saint-Gilles kicked his horse into a canter and quickly shook off the clustered suburbs. On the slopes beyond, a brown blotch like an enormous bruise marked the ground, pockmarked with hoof prints, scarred with latrine trenches. Saint-Gilles would know the marks of an army's passing anywhere, but what he wanted to know was why the campground was empty. If Bohemond was still in Constantinople, where were his men?

"Come and speak with me," Saint-Gilles told the count as they dismounted in the monastery's outer courtyard.

Bohemond cocked an eyebrow. "Permission to step into my rooms and let my household know about the new arrangement, my lord? I'm your hostage, after all. No doubt you'll be shifting me into your own quarters where you can keep an eye on me and whip off my head if Alexius disappoints you."

Saint-Gilles gave him a flat stare. "I'm glad you find the situation so amusing, my lord. But no. As far as Alexius is concerned, you are not a hostage. You are a calculated insult. Stay in your own rooms and go where you will."

Bohemond pursed his lips. "You wash your hands of me? Don't be so hasty. I flatter myself Alexius does have *some* interest in my welfare."

"Yes, but is he for or against it?" Saint-Gilles beckoned. "Right now, all I want from you is some answers."

Bohemond shrugged and followed him into his rooms. Wine, cheese, and a bowl of fresh cherries waited on a table near the alabaster-paned window. Saint-Gilles threw the shutters open. Beyond, the back wall of the guesthouse dropped sharply to a green lawn that sloped toward the inlet named the Golden Horn. From the window, he could just make out a large black bird of prey perched in a mulberry tree, one bright eye cocked in his direction, and a distant monk at work in the herb garden to the left.

Saint-Gilles withdrew his head and nodded toward the wine. "Pour us some, will you?"

Bohemond had only just picked up the flagon when a connecting door opened and Elvira rushed in.

"My lord," she said hectically, and then stopped in confusion when she saw Bohemond.

Saint-Gilles folded his arms. "Count, I *beg leave* to present my wife."

Elvira looked at him as if he had slapped her, and Saint-Gilles cursed himself for the jab. His third and least comprehensible wife was less than a third his age, a bastard of the King of Castile's, and far from home. If only he had held his tongue long enough to see her face, he would have known something was wrong—

William. Instantly, Saint-Gilles shifted toward her.

Before Saint-Gilles could voice his concern, Bohemond moved smoothly forward and captured Elvira's fingertips, his voice deepening by half a tone as he greeted her.

"Countess. A pleasure."

Thinks he's God's gift to women, Saint-Gilles thought irritably. "You wanted me, my lady?"

"It's William." Her hands fluttered out to catch his sleeve, then pulled back without touching him. "He's sleeping now. But the journey was too much for him, my lord…he isn't feeding, I'm certain he's losing flesh…"

It was uncourteous to keep a man of Bohemond's rank waiting, but William was only his second living son. "Give me a moment," he told the count, softly opening the door to the connecting chamber.

Elvira tiptoed in after him. The three-month-old child lay in a cradle near the countess' bed, watched over by a tired-looking nurse. Saint-Gilles looked down anxiously at the thread on which the future of his house might hang and asked himself if he had been mad to bring a pregnant wife on a long and dangerous pilgrimage like this.

"It's not teeth?" he whispered, trying to tell if the child's cheeks were red.

Elvira's mouth fell open in confusion and she looked at the nurse, a capable Provencal matron. She shook her head. "Too soon for teeth."

"He needs rest," Elvira said. There were dark hollows under her own eyes. "We've been on the road five months already…"

Five gruelling months, most of them through winter, had taken a toll on all of them. Saint-Gilles saw the solution immediately.

"We won't risk his life. When we travel on, you should stay in Constantinople with the babe."

Even in the dim room, he could tell how unwilling she was. "With the Greeks?"

"You shall have a guard, and a house of your own…"

She wilted before his eyes, head hanging, fingers twisting. "What's the *matter?*" Saint-Gilles hissed in exasperation.

"I wanted to visit the Holy Sepulchre," she gulped. "For my salvation."

"Dear child, it's dangerous."

"You *promised.*"

"Yes, devil take it, I promised, and so did every other man with a wife or a sister or a dear old dad who wants to worship in Jerusalem. Now I've got all these helpless people on my hands, and it's my duty to keep you all alive somehow. Saint Faith! I can't save them, but maybe I can save my son. If he can't continue, he must stay here."

"Shh!" the nurse warned, but it was too late. William stirred and wailed.

Saint-Gilles threw up a hand with a huff of frustration. "Now I've done it."

But Elvira caught his sleeve. "If we could only stay here in Constantinople for a month or two before moving on. *Please,*" she begged. And then, quietly, "You *promised.*"

He had, and no one had ever heard of him breaking his word. *"Only if he improves,"* Saint-Gilles snapped, and beat a hurried retreat.

Bohemond was sitting by the table, looking at his reflection in the blade of his dagger. "Ah, there you are. I trust the child is well."

"He will be," Saint-Gilles said shortly. He stuck his thumbs into his belt, wishing he could not still hear the babe's wails. "This forced march to Constantinople was too much for him. But if I'd left him with the rest of the army at Roussa, who knows if the Greeks would have left him alive?" A chill shot through him as he thought how close he had come to leaving them behind to be cared for by his knights. He sank into a seat. "Saint Faith, to think of all my poor people, like sheep without a shepherd…"

"How many do you still have?"

Saint-Gilles rubbed his chin "There's no telling. Several thousands of armed knights, each with a following of four or five able-bodied men, at least. But it's the others that keep me awake at night: the women and children, the old and infirm…"

"And you let them come?"

"How was I going to stop them following me? They're all like my countess—fearful for their souls, and bound to visit the Holy Sepulchre."

Bohemond leaned his elbows on the table. "And your soul, count? Does it trouble you?"

Saint-Gilles swivelled his head to see out the window. "You and I are knights, count. We have been good knights, but perhaps it's made us evil men…"

"Toulouse," Bohemond said softly. "From what I hear, you came by it none too honestly."

Startled, Saint-Gilles swung around to look the count in the face. Never in his life had anyone spoken to him so plainly. No one but himself. The inner voice was with him now:

Thief. Usurper.

He clamped his teeth on the angry denial that welled up inside him and pretended Bohemond had not spoken. "I have always wanted to serve Christ, count, but they told me I should have to become a monk, and I…"

"Would make a very bad monk." There was a sympathetic twist in Bohemond's mouth, and not a trace of mockery in his eyes. "Isn't it so?"

"For fifty-five years they told me I must choose one or the other. Never both—until now." Saint-Gilles shook his head. "Both! Serve Christ, atone for my sins—and remain a knight! What a time to be living! No, I won't turn monk. I'll die in harness, here in the east."

Bohemond slid a glass of wine across the table. "To living loud, and dying well."

Saint-Gilles drank and set the cup down again gently for fear of breaking the delicate confection of coloured glass. "What do you think of my chances of getting justice, count? As opposed to, say, a knife in the back, or nightshade in my wine one of these mornings…"

"That depends on whether you're willing to do homage."

"To Alexius?"

"Why not?" Bohemond gestured with his cup. "I know, the attacks. But you had refused the oath even before you heard about those."

Saint-Gilles savoured the complex flavours of the wine. It was in perfect shape: a smooth rich taste exactly balanced between dry and sweet, with no hint of any additional ingredients. "Because then I should be bound to keep it, no matter what harm it might do to my people. Because I have sworn an oath to Christ, to fight for him in the Holy Land, and I will take no other oaths to any other lord until this one is fulfilled."

Bohemond lifted a sardonic eyebrow.

Saint-Gilles grinned. *"And* because I can't bear to take orders from a gold-plated *Greek*. Yes. That too."

Bohemond breathed in the wine's bouquet. "All the others have taken it, all the great princes who have come east on the pilgrimage: Vermandois, Blois, Flanders, the Duke of Lorraine…"

"And Bohemond of Taranto."

Bohemond grinned wolfishly. "I've invaded Greece twice already. They believe I'm the Devil himself. Of course I took the oath. What the Greeks don't know about poisons and conspiracies isn't worth knowing."

Saint-Gilles did not need reminding. "And the others? Why did they submit?"

"You heard Alexius. He posed the same ultimatum to the others. No oath, no transport across the sea to Asia. No chance of seeing Jerusalem." Bohemond took a mouthful of wine. "They *tell* me Duke Godfrey even attacked the city."

"No! Not from *outside?*"

"Where else? Yes, from outside. During the winter."

"I like his spirit."

"Pfft. From what I hear he's a meek man, and not much of a manager of men. It's his brother, who's got his ear…"

Saint-Gilles searched his memory. "Baldwin of Boulogne?"

Bohemond nodded. "There's the one with fire in his belly. Godfrey's a second son; he was never meant to be a duke. He earned his title through serving greater men."

Saint-Gilles nodded thoughtfully. "A follower, and not a leader, then. Did his brother take the oath?"

There was a flicker of amusement in Bohemond's eyes. "No."

"Hmm." Saint-Gilles paused. "Shame he's gone to Asia, then."

Bohemond did not pursue that thought. "They're waiting for you, you realise."

"You think I should take the oath?"

"I think you should realise Alexius means what he says. Either you'll have to take the oath, or…"

"Or what?"

Bohemond lifted his eyebrows. "Or you'll have to take the city."

Was the man serious? Saint-Gilles wondered. *Attack those triple walls?* Come to think of it, Bohemond had already set out to try it. Twice!

Defying the emperor and subduing the city was, if nothing else, an enticing opportunity for immortal fame. But he had vowed to go to Jerusalem. He could not afford to get bogged down in Greek politics.

Besides, he was supposed to be fighting the pagans, not fellow Christians. He would never be able to explain *that* one to the papal legate.

"I see," he said after a moment. "You think I should take the oath for the sake of getting to Jerusalem."

Bohemond did not answer at once. Instead he said, "Wasn't the papal legate travelling with you?"

"Adhemar of le Puy? Temporally speaking he's a vassal of mine, so he's with the rest of my army." Saint-Gilles rasped his chin. "He tells me he lost a cousin in the fighting. God help us…"

"Well, I'd bet my Flemish destrier against any stake you like that when he gets here, the good bishop will tell you to swear."

"Not unless this matter of the attack is settled. This touches my honour." If he could not protect his people, they had every right to abandon him.

Usurper. Thief.

Saint-Gilles pursed his lips and turned back to the window, his mind running back and forth over the problem.

"Seven princes with seven armies, all travelling to Jerusalem. And because we arrived at the rendezvous separately, Alexius was able to subdue each of us separately. If only we'd arrived together…"

But there was no helping it. If four of the princes had already taken their oaths and crossed into Asia, then he must take his stand alone.

"If he gives me justice for my people," Saint-Gilles said, "then I will think about taking the oath. But, by the Virgin! Not without it."

Chapter III.

Pssst. Greek." A hot, anxious whisper tickled Lukas' ear. "Wake up!"

He *was* awake. He had been awake for hours. At first, he had tried to pray. Now he was going around and around in his mind, trying for the thousandth time to find some way out of the horrifying truth.

He had survived the raid on Oliveta—but somehow he had been transported hundreds of years into the future and hundreds of miles away from where he had started, all in the space of a single night. Tomorrow they would arrive in Constantinople, where these foreign heretics would sell him into slavery. Probably to someone who, in the old days, he would not even have stopped in the street to talk with.

The old days, the good days, when he was a Bessarion in Jerusalem. After so many hundreds of years, who would remember that name? Who would help him? Lukas could only think of one person who might care, one person who might follow him through the ages from his own time.

Khalil, the sorcerer.

Was that all he had to look forward to? A short, miserable life of slavery cut short by his family's murderer?

He had always believed that everything happened for a reason. *Despise not the chastening of the Lord, neither be weary of his correction.* But Lord God, what was the reason for this? What was he supposed to do next?

A finger jabbed him in the ribs and another damp whisper blew into his ear. "Greek?"

Lukas groaned. "For heaven's sake, Kismet. It's the middle of the night."

"Keep your voice down, you idiot! I'm trying to help!"

"Then let me sleep."

Another spiteful jab. "You want your freedom? You have to take it. *Now.*"

Lukas cracked his eyes open. Overhead, the April sky was a star-flecked dome. He was lying near the foremast, far enough from the rest of the crew to escape both the sound of their snores and the coming and goings of the changing lookouts.

Kismet was just a dark shape kneeling beside him.

In the seven days since he had joined the ship, Kismet had never mentioned his captain's plans to sell him, and Lukas himself had done his best to forget it. For the first few days, a bout of seasickness had ensured that. Since he had recovered, his mind had gnawed on the problem like a starving dog on a bone. By now, he was ready to despair.

"My freedom," he whispered into the dark. "And what will I do with it? Starve?"

"God be merciful, Greek. Forget I said anything. Lie there and whine some more! You've done nothing else since you got here!"

The boy's contempt stung him. Lukas sat up, trying to see his face. "Why should I bother with anything else? Everyone I know is probably dead."

There was a space of silence before Kismet spoke again, tight and cold.

"Then you ought to avenge them."

Avenge them.

If Khalil was coming for him, then the least he could do was prepare himself.

It was as if a piece of himself that had been missing suddenly locked

51

back into place. He was not whole again—he would never be whole again—but now the clouds had lifted, and he could see the horizon. Lukas unspooled the blanket from his legs and sat up "Show me," he said.

"Can you swim?"

He had grown up on his family's country estate near the coast, spending long, hot summer days getting brown in the water.

"I can swim."

Kismet took his hand and pulled him to the rail. From the prow, a lantern hung to warn other ships that they were passing, but the night was already faintly lit by the stars. He could just make out the racing sea and the white foam curling from the keel as they raced before the breeze.

Kismet put his mouth to Lukas' ear. "This is the Hellespont. It's the closest we'll be to land until we reach Constantinople, and you'll be locked safely below deck when that happens." He pointed north. "That's Greek territory." He pointed south. "That's mostly Turkish territory. Take your pick, but you'll be better off on Greek ground."

The Hellespont. Lukas knew of it. Specifically, that someone named Leander had died in it on a night much like this one.

The thought did not terrify him. Not if the land on the other side of the water held freedom and a purpose.

"All right," he said. "Thanks, Kismet."

Now that he was ready to go, he felt oddly reluctant to leave. Everyone he knew was dead. Everyone except this ruffian of a heretic.

"Nice knowing you, Greek." The boy, too, seemed wistful.

Lukas bent down to pull off his sandals, but as he did so a movement caught the corner of his eye.

He looked up and froze. A shadow loomed just beyond the heretic boy. Lamplight from the prow flickered briefly on the man's face as he pounced. Kismet yelled, grabbing for the knife at his belt, but the deckhand had the advantage of surprise. He managed to pinion the boy's wrists and shouted for help.

The lamplight—that's what had betrayed them.

"Jump, you cucumber!" Kismet hissed as his captor dragged him back from the rail.

Footsteps echoed from the other end of the deck. Lukas grabbed the rail, but looked back. "What will they do to you?"

"Jump!" the boy screeched.

He looked at the water. Purpose. Freedom. It was not as if Kismet was part of his family. But he owed his life to the boy, maybe even his freedom. He couldn't just leave him.

Lukas turned and launched himself after Kismet. If he could trip the deckhand, he might get them both free just long enough to jump the rail—

Too late, a scuffle of motion warned him of danger. A heavy body hit him, slamming him painfully to the deck. Cumbrously, his assailant got up, grinding a knee into his breastbone. Hands slapped at his belt and confiscated his knife.

More ship hands clustered around them. Dizzily, Lukas heard Kismet's voice protesting in his own language. He tried to make out some of the words, but in the last week he had only managed to learn the Turkish for *yes, no, Greek,* and *food.* Captain Ahmed shouldered through the crowd towards them, lofting a lantern of his own and speaking with a rumble of laughter. Lukas heard the word for *Greek* several times. Kismet spat defiantly, and the other hands laughed.

"What's happening?" Lukas wheezed.

No answer. Kismet's voice rose to a high wail, begging and pleading, but the captain's only reply was a dismissive order as he stalked away.

Kismet's panic was catching. Something was wrong. Were they going to kill him? Were they going to cut his throat? Why had he not jumped overboard when he had the chance? Lukas clawed at the weight on his chest—

They picked him up, one gripping each elbow, and dragged him toward the hatch leading below deck. *You'll be locked safely below deck before we reach Constantinople.* "No," he shouted, twisting in their grip, but they showed no mercy, heaving him over the hatch to dangle swinging and kicking over the long drop.

A blade tickled his neck and he stopped struggling. Then one of them let go of his elbow and he grabbed for the ladder with a yelp of fright. Not a moment too soon. They dropped his second elbow, letting him slam against the ladder.

Where was that knife? What if he charged up the ladder—

Above, Kismet was still crying and begging as they positioned him over the hatch and fed his feet into the opening. The Turk's desperately flailing feet connected with Lukas' head and he saw stars. Then Kismet slithered down onto him, grabbing for his shoulders, the ladder, anything that could be clutched at. The hatch slammed, its bars stark against the faint starlight. Its bolt rattled and Kismet let out a scream, lunging upwards to hammer on the trapdoor.

There was no answer but the slap of waves on the hull.

Chapter IV.

Ayla stilled, panting.

No. No. God have mercy, no.

I didn't come all this way for—this.

Something wriggled under her foot. "You're standing on my hand," said the Greek.

Ayla caught a shuddering breath, shifted her weight and shinned down the ladder.

"Ahmed," she gritted. With an angry shriek she lashed out at the big, soft bales of cargo.

"Kismet?"

She whirled on him—not that it made any difference in the dark. "What is it now?"

"What happened up there? Why are you—"

"Going to sell both of us," she growled. Her throat tightened, her eyes stung. *God, have mercy. I can't have this now...*

"Saints...I really got you in trouble, didn't I?"

"Not your fault, Greek." She gasped for breath; it sounded too much like a sob, too frightened, too vulnerable...but with it, the words spilled out, and she couldn't stop them. "Turns out he knew all along. Didn't tell anyone. Didn't want me to be *damaged* before we got to market."

It was the Greek's silence that dragged her back to the present.

No. *No.* What was she saying? Ayla froze.

Too late.

"Saint George," the Greek blurted. "You're a *girl.*"

55

They'd taken her sling, but she still had her knife, mainly because she wasn't stupid enough to ever let them see it. Ayla snatched it from her waistband and went into a crouch. "Touch me, and I'll cut your throat."

The Greek said blankly, "But you act nothing *like* a girl."

"Yeh, well, that's a luxury for rich people. When you live on the streets you can't afford it."

"Is your name really Kismet?"

No sound of movement. As far as she could tell, he was still clinging to the ladder with eyes as big as coins.

Ayla gritted her teeth. She couldn't trust him. He'd wait till she was off her guard, and then—

But everyone who had once known her real name was dead or far away. And it would be nice, even just for a moment, to pretend she *could* trust him. It wasn't as if he was very big, or even good at scrapping.

"Ayla," she said gruffly.

"That's a nice name." He still hadn't moved. "Can...can I come down now?"

Her hand tightened on the hilt of her knife. "I meant what I said. You try anything, and I'll kill you."

"I believe it."

"All right, then."

"Thanks." He gave a whistling sigh and collapsed onto the deck. His voice came from a respectful distance, unafraid, unsuspicious. "Kismet—Ayla—I'm sorry about this, I swear. I'm going to get you out of here, all right?"

"Not your fault, Greek." God have mercy, if she had to let a spoilt Greek save her, she really *was* doomed. Ayla stared into the bleak darkness and spat another curse. Six months left. Less. She couldn't die a slave. Where was the honour in that?

The Greek interrupted her thoughts. "Lukas."

"What?"

"That's my name. Lukas Bessarion."

Ayla wiped her sweaty palms on her trousers and tried to keep the tremor out of her voice. "Good for you. Now be quiet. I need to think."

She crawled onto a cargo bale and tucked her knees into her chest, whispering. *"God! There is no deity but Him, the Alive, the Eternal..."*

In the dark, there was no other sound but the Greek's steady breathing. She heard him muttering under his own breath. Saying the prayers of his people, maybe. As time dragged by, he began to snore softly.

The sound stirred something deep inside her, in a place that had been locked and closed for years. There was no faking this: he trusted her. The Greek was guileless, and stupid, and she wished, oh, how she *wished* she was still like that. The memory was bright, and far away, like a tiny window painted in gold: the time when she had people to love, nothing to hide, and nothing to fear. It was only a child's wish. The truth was, she was a prisoner, and she had everything to hide, everything to fear.

As morning came, a little light struggled into the hull through the small ventilation ports just below the upper deck. Lukas still sat with his back to the rungs of the ladder. Ayla uncurled herself from her sleepless perch, stifling a yawn.

"Should have known Ahmed would doublecross me, the pig. Should have known when I heard him talk about selling you."

Lukas grinned half-heartedly. "How bad can it be, being a slave in Constantinople? You'll have food and clothes. That's what you told me."

"Yeh, but I'm not a whiny iris like you. Besides, I'm a Turk. Can you imagine how they'll treat me?"

He stiffened. "Yes, well, maybe your people should have thought of that before they invaded us."

"Why should they care?" Ayla snorted. "No one gives a damn what happens to me. 'Cept me."

Lukas sighed. "No one gives a damn what happens to me either." He looked up at her suddenly, trustingly. "Except *you.*"

She blinked at him, then changed the subject. "You don't know anyone in Constantinople?"

"No one." But then he stilled in realisation. "By the Virgin, that's who'll help me! I'll go to the Greek Watchers."

The Watchers? Ayla's stomach knotted. "God have mercy! What do you want to be mixed up with them for?"

He shot her a wary look. "Why shouldn't I?"

"They're infidel sorcerers. Very powerful. Very unpredictable." She swallowed hard, trying to block the memories. "Very, very dangerous."

"What makes you say that?"

"I just know, alright? I..." She stopped herself. "I just *know.* Be careful, yeh?"

There was an awkward silence.

"All right," he said finally. "I will. But it all depends on whether we can get out of here. Do you know what's inside the bales?"

"Flax fibre."

"See? It's a sign. *A bruised reed shall he not break, and the smoking flax shall he not quench: he shall bring forth judgment unto truth.*" Even in the dim light he seemed more alive than she had ever seen him before. He pointed upward. "Is this the only entrance?"

"Only one our size."

"Tools? Weapons?"

She rolled her eyes. "You couldn't have been this quick off the mark last night when I was trying to help you?"

"You were in trouble. I couldn't just leave you. Don't be afraid," he added. "I don't believe either of us was meant to be a slave. I've got to find my way home, and you..." He lifted an eyebrow. "What do you have to live for?"

"Me?" She had nothing to live for. That was the problem. She was looking for something to die for. Still, she had to tell him something.

"I've got…an uncle, living in Constantinople. Thought he might give me something to do."

He nodded. "Right. Neither of us was meant to be a slave. So what weapons do we have?"

"Only my knife, unless…" Ordinarily, she would want all the weapons in her own hands. But now, against every instinct, she was beginning to trust him. "They ought to keep a boathook down here. There."

It was a six-foot length of oak tipped with iron, and as he retrieved it from the shadows, the Greek twirled it in his fingers and grinned. "Perfect. Once we dock, how do we get out?"

Ayla stared at the crowded shadows, trying to think. "It can't be opened from inside. So we'll have to get them to open it."

Lukas blinked. "How?"

"You just gave me an idea." She touched the bale beside her. "But you're not going to like it."

Chapter V.

Before Lukas joined Ayla on the ladder, he had made sure his Watcher's mark was completely covered, cinching his left sleeve at the wrist with a strip of canvas so that it could not ride up. Ayla seemed to have a grudge against the Watchers, and if they were going to escape, they needed to trust each other. For now, he would just have to keep his mark a secret.

For a moment, Lukas wondered what kind of magical powers she thought he had. *Infidel sorcerers?* If only.

He gripped the boathook and felt his way up the ladder. After a long, uneventful day, the time had finally come to act. Three hours ago, the ship had cast anchor in a huge harbour on the south shore of Constantinople. Now, with the sun down and the ship sleeping, they would have to take their chance or die as slaves.

Ayla stood above him on the ladder, peering through the grille of the trapdoor above. "You ready, Greek?"

"As ready as I ever will be." He stood back to let her down, handing her another scrap of canvas and a handful of the flax fibre.

Ayla dipped her canvas into the bilge water beneath the low deck. "Any last words?"

"This is mad, and we're both going to die."

"If it's any comfort to you, I know I won't."

"You're right. That is a wonderful comfort."

She flicked water at him. "Would you rather be a slave? Because I can arrange that, you know."

"Better to die tonight." Lukas dipped his own canvas into the water and slapped the wet, reeking rag over a pad of linen fibre on his mouth and nose. The noisome water quickly seeped through the flax to his face, but he prayed it would save his life.

Ayla tied hers loosely around her neck and went aft to the bale they'd opened. The *crack! crack!* of tinder and flint seemed to reverberate like a drumbeat. Then, a tiny yellow glow threw her crouching figure into sharp relief.

She blew on the fire once, twice—and got it into the clouds of loose fibre they had teased apart and strewn through the aft of the ship. Ayla jumped back with a yell of fright as the flames took.

There was no pretense in her screams. "Fire! Fire! Help us!" She swarmed up the ladder, beating on the hatch. "Fire!"

Lukas crawled after her, pounding on the hatch with the boathook. As the flames howled through the loose flax, the heat was unbearable. Even through his mask he tasted the acrid grit of smoke. Shouts and footsteps thudded across the deck. *Oh, Saint George,* Lukas thought. They had wagered everything on the possibility that the crew would open the hatch before jumping ship.

A wave of scalding heat hit them as the fire found something it liked, perhaps the lantern-oil. "Don't breathe in!" he shouted to Ayla.

"Help us!" she screamed.

The hatch slammed open. With a string of profanities, Ahmed grabbed Ayla and yanked her out. Lukas scrambled up after her, dragging the boathook behind. The captain scruffed him as well and threw him to the deck. Up here it was dark, with only a faint smell of smoke and the hissing growl of the fire below to warn of danger. Dark shapes converged on him, but Lukas was ready for them.

He rolled to his knees, bringing the boathook around in a deadly swing that caught the closest ship hand on the knee. The oak shaft thrummed in his hands and the sailor collapsed. Hands fastened on his shoulders from behind, but he rammed the butt back and up under his elbow until they released him with a grunt of pain.

Lukas charged to his feet. Ahead, the lights of Constantinople sparkled beyond the water. He dropped his left hand to the ship's rail and vaulted over—

A wordless scream. *Ayla.*

Instead of letting go, his fingertips found the rounded edge and gripped. *Whump.* He slammed against the hull and hung there, gasping. No time to feel the pain. He kicked his legs for momentum and managed to get his right hand onto the rail without losing grip on the boathook. Straining, Lukas hoisted himself back over the rail, onto the deck.

By now, smoke filled the air and an orange light glowed within the hatch. Coughing and choking, Captain Ahmed dragged himself up the ladder. Beyond, Ayla struggled between two ship hands.

The captain clearly had no doubt how the fire had started. In a flashing silver arc, he drew the long knife at his belt and swung toward Ayla.

Lukas sprinted.

The captain shouted in Turkish, his knife hissing through the air. Lukas gripped the boathook near the butt-end of the shaft, lunged almost to the deck, and drove forward. The boathook was not sharp, but the iron point punched through skin and bone with barely a tremor.

With a hollow grunt, Captain Ahmed wavered to a stop and folded to the deck. The men holding Ayla stared at him, their faces painted with horror in the hellish light. Lukas got to his feet again. He yanked at the boathook and felt an awful, squelching crunch. Caught between two ribs, it would not move.

He had lost his weapon, again.

The deckhands were too terrified to notice. With yells of fright, they released Ayla and dashed for the rail. A moment later the two of them were alone on the burning ship.

Ayla took a shaky breath, staring at the dying man. "To God we belong and to God we return," she breathed. Then she raced for the aft cabin.

Lukas followed her across smoking boards that warmed his feet. "Ayla, no! We have to jump! Now!"

She paid no notice, disappearing into the captain's cabin.

"Ayla!" He slammed the door open behind her, but she was already on her way out, clutching her sling and pouch. "Up," she gasped. As the flames broke through the main deck with a hungry roar, they caught each other's hand and fled up the poop-deck stairs and over the rail.

From that height, the water hit them like a wall. Lukas surfaced sore and gasping for breath. Further toward the city lights, bobbing heads on the water's surface marked where the other deckhands swam for shore.

"Quick," he gasped to Ayla. "They're sure to complain to the Watch. We should get ashore and lose ourselves."

She seemed not to hear him. Instead, she latched her arms around his neck in a strangling, panicked hold. "Stay with me! I can't swim!"

She dragged his head under the water. For some reason his mind was finding it difficult to focus, but the cold water shocked him awake again. He surfaced, spluttering. "All right! All right! Hold still. Remember Myra..."

"Myra wasn't *deep!*"

He grabbed her by the shoulders, gave her a shake. "Calm down. Calm down. Look at me. You got us out of that hold. You didn't burn, and you won't drown. You can do this."

The panic slowly faded from her face. "I don't drown," she whispered. "Not tonight."

"Not while I'm here. All right? Hold onto my wrist and kick."

She gulped, let go of his neck, and latched onto his wrist.

"Kick," Lukas told her, but she was back in action now, both kicking and striking out with her free arm. He steered them away from the city, toward the long mole that sheltered the port. It was nearer than the shore and would also lead them well away from the other deckhands.

The black bulk of the mole rose before him, crowned with a high wall. Atop it, lights burned at intervals. Lights meant people. People were probably city guards. His mind was unfocusing again, but he had a feeling that this was important…

"Greek!" Ayla said sharply. "Are you all right?"

Focus. Focus on the lights. Focus on swimming. It was so cold. He was so tired. Lights. People. Danger. If only he could remember why…

Stone grazed his shins and he pulled himself gratefully onto the rocks, shuddering in the autumn wind.

Chapter VI.

L ukas climbed up the huge stone footings and dragged himself, wet and shivering, to the solid ground. Ayla followed, shushing him as he collapsed onto the packed earth.

It was as if all the strength had left him. He bowed his head onto his knees and wept. Lukas felt bruised all over, his throat still scratchy with smoke. Worst of all, his hands still felt the vibration of grating bone, though the boathook was far behind them. He wrung his hands together, trying to erase the sensation.

Ayla fell to her knees in front of him. "Lukas," she hissed. "What's wrong?"

He gulped soundlessly. "I never killed a man before."

Her hands found his face, lifted his head to stare blearily at the shape of her against the stars. "Right, I need you to calm down. We still have to get into the city. Walls and gates to deal with. Breathe."

When she pulled him to his feet, he found he had the strength to stand. Wordlessly, almost mindlessly, he followed her down the length of the mole. At the end of it a gate awaited them, a massive tunnel piercing through the city's immense wall. Lukas watched fuzzily as Ayla produced gold from somewhere and the gate swung open.

"Beware the Watch!" the guard whispered as they passed. "If they find you wandering during curfew, they'll birch you!"

Beyond the gate, the streets were dark as pitch. Lukas stumbled on in a waking dream, hearing Ayla's muttered commentary without understanding the words. Finally they stopped, and Ayla crawled into a low space ahead of them.

"In here," she whispered, and he groped his way into the low crawlspace below a set of wooden steps.

The ground was hard and cold, but after so many nights of sleeping on a wooden deck under the stars, Lukas was getting used to it. A little warmth crept through his sodden bones as Ayla huddled up beside him, and Lukas' mind drifted out of focus for a while. When he woke, it was bone-cold and still dark. Beside him, Ayla was murmuring something in a language he did not understand.

After a moment she whispered, "You awake, Greek?"

Last night, in the hold, she had hissed at him to keep his distance. This morning she snuggled against his side, his only source of warmth. The change puzzled him, but maybe it would be awkward to point this out.

"What are you reciting?" he asked.

"*Ayat el korsi,*" she said, "the Throne Verse. It speaks of the greatness of God above all others."

"You say it often."

She shifted restlessly. "Twice a day. It grants protection from the evil of *djinns.* Spirits."

Lukas couldn't resist: "I thought a pure heart did that."

"You Greeks. You're all so smug and condescending."

"And *hungry.*" He sighed.

She gave a strangled snort. "Now you know what it's like for the rest of us."

He had been hungry before, of course. One fasted for Lent and Advent and the rest of it. But then, one always knew the food would eventually come.

"Is any of that gold left?"

A movement in the dark as she shook her head. "Gatekeeper took it all. He guessed who we were. Ship was still burning."

"Where did it come from, anyway?"

"Captain's cabin."

"But that's *stealing!*" As a Watcher, he could not steal—not unless he wanted God to abandon him.

"He started it," she pointed out. "Stole us, didn't he?"

And then he, Lukas, had stolen the man's life. If taking a man's gold was wrong, then how much worse was it to take his life unjustly? Lukas wrapped his hands together, shivering.

Ayla's thoughts must be running similarly. "S'pose you know something about scrapping after all."

"Not enough." If he was going to survive long enough to avenge his family, he needed to be stronger than this. "I've only been trained. I was going to be a cataphract, but..."

She grunted. "I saw you run for the rail that first time. One man against two. Wish you'd show me how to do that."

"It only worked because they weren't paying attention. If they'd been ready for me it would have been different."

"S'pose. Still, it was a good scrap."

"I wish..." His voice trailed away. What else could he have done? Ahmed would have killed her.

"Don't pity him. You saved my life. Twice." She let him think about that for a moment and then added, "Thank you."

"You saved mine first. I'm glad I could do the same for you."

Otherwise he might have felt obliged to repay the favour some other time, to some other heretic. Maybe not all of them were madmen like Khalil, but he did not want to owe the others anything at all.

"No one has ever done anything like that for me before." Ayla's voice was soft.

If she had been his sister he would have patted her hand, but he didn't want to overstep. Instead he waited until she sniffed once or twice, and said, "What time is it?"

"Getting grey."

They lay in silence. Lukas rubbed his arms in an attempt to warm himself, to no avail.

"S'pose we'll be saying goodbye soon," Ayla said.

"Do you know where to find your uncle?"

"Got a name. That's all."

"How will you find him in this place?"

"Start by looking for some of my people."

"What happened to the rest of your family?"

She was quiet for so long he thought she would not answer.

"Only if you want to tell me," he added.

"It's all right," she said after a moment. "Father died. Mother couldn't keep me. So I lived on the streets in Antioch."

"Saints. I'm sorry."

"Could've been worse." She did not say how.

"I can't think of *anything* worse. Your mother threw you out?"

"Would have been different if father had lived. But no. I left because I chose to. Easier on the others if there was one less mouth."

"I can't imagine having to make a choice like that."

In the dark beside him, Ayla shrugged. "Family is everything, yeh?"

Overhead, a little grey light seeped through the slats of the wooden landing. Lukas stared at it. *How many of us are left? Did Mother escape with Elisa? Is my father dead? What did he do to anger Khalil, anyway?*

Am I the last of the Bessarions?

Am I alone, too?

"Yes," he said softly. "Family is everything."

And he had to find his way back to them. Even if he could not save them. Even if only to avenge them.

"Get some more sleep, if you can." Ayla burrowed into his side. "No point moving until the city's awake."

The next time he woke it was day in earnest and Ayla was still asleep next to him. With the sun's rising, the morning had warmed. He shifted away from her and got up on one elbow to peer into the street.

Through the slats of the wooden steps, a narrow road was visible, sloping down between high tenement walls toward the harbour, where a thin slice of water sparkled in the sun. Behind, the road curved uphill, breaking into stairways where the ground rose sharply.

The smell of frying fish drifted toward him on the breeze. Far above, a door slammed and Lukas peered up to see washing fluttering from crisscrossing lines between balconies.

Ayla jerked awake. "Greek? Oh, there you are."

"We made it," he whispered. "We're in Constantinople!"

Ayla peered up the street. "I've never seen such a clean street. No wonder I couldn't find anything to wrap us in. How do the beggars live?"

"There are charities for them. At least there used to be."

"What, for all of them? This *is* the richest city in the world."

Lukas watched her as she studied the street. Slanted brown eyes, full lips, a rounded face—how could he have mistaken her for a boy? Washed and properly dressed, she would almost be pretty.

"Look at this," she murmured.

Lukas transferred his gaze to the street again. A small band of four priests in fine vestments followed a Greek guide down the street toward them, lifting their fine robes out of the muck that gathered in the central gutter. Pale-skinned and clean-shaven, the men were clearly barbarians from the West. One of them, a tall, spare old man, wore the cross and ring of a bishop.

Not far from Lukas' hiding place, the bishop turned to his guide and said in Latin, *"This* is the way to the Hospital of Sampson? Are you sure?"

"It's a short cut, my lord." The barbarians were so tall that their guide had to crane his neck to look at the bishop. "Traffic's so bad on the Mese, that…"

The bishop interrupted him. "They told me the hospital was near the church of Saint Sophia. I did not think the church was by the sea, and yet I see water." He pointed down the alley toward the harbour.

Lukas slewed his head around and saw four more seedy-looking men shift away from where they stood half-concealed in stairs and doorways. With apparent laziness, they drifted toward the barbarians.

Ayla nudged Lukas. "Feeling hungry?"

"Yes, but…"

"We save the Christian's purse, might be something in it for us."

"There are *five* of them!"

"Bet I can do it."

Lukas grabbed her wrist. "No! Don't get involved in this."

She rolled her eyes. "Look. I know this kind of scum. You just have to scare their leader, and the rest will follow, right?"

In the alley, the bishop tightened his grip on his staff as the Greek ruffians confronted him. Most of them had long knives, while one carried a serviceable club. Behind the bishop, his priests clustered together.

"I would have paid you well to guide me honestly," the bishop told the guide.

"Not as much as you *will* pay, barbarian." The guide stepped away from the westerners and pulled a knife from his belt. "Hand over everything. Your men too."

The bishop stood his ground.

"I am the personal representative of Pope Urban of Rome and a guest of the emperor. Are you sure you have chosen wisely?"

"Less talk, more gold," one of the Greeks growled in his own language, and the guide repeated it in Latin.

The bishop sighed and spoke to the priests in a barbarian language. Lukas did not know the tongue, but it sounded familiar. If you lived in Jerusalem, sooner or later you heard every language in the world.

With apparent meekness, the priests dug into robes and unbuckled purses.

"Now," Ayla whispered. "Back me up!"

Before he could protest, she hopped out of their shelter and strolled toward the Greeks. Lukas scrambled after, stifling a groan for his bruised and cramped muscles.

"Hey, boys." Her voice deepened, but it was the most feminine sound he had yet heard from her. "Going to keep *all* of that?"

They turned as Ayla sauntered up to the Greek who had asked for gold. He only gave her a flat stare in return, evidently seeing no threat in the young Turk.

Without warning, Ayla shot out a hand, grabbed and jerked. Drops of the Greek's blood spattered the bishop's white vestments. With a howl, he staggered back, clapping a hand to his bloody head.

Ayla let out a whoop, whipped around and threw the Greek's ear in the guide's face. Then she drew her own knife.

"You going to do the smart thing?" she hissed.

Swearing, they grabbed their one-eared leader and ran. Some of the oaths hanging in the air were Lukas' own.

Ayla shot him a smug grin over her shoulder. "See? Worked."

"Saint George! Are you crazy? You'll get yourself killed one of these days." His hands were shaking. She had almost got *him* killed, and she was just laughing at him.

"Some day. But not today."

The barbarians stood gaping, still holding their purses in their hands. When Lukas and Ayla stepped toward them, the bishop held out his without a word.

Ayla accepted it.

"You can't do that!" Lukas gasped.

"Can't eat good deeds either." Ayla rifled within and came out with two silver coins. "This will get us breakfast."

She handed the purse back to the bewildered bishop and tossed one of the coins to Lukas.

"Oh heaven," Lukas said helplessly. Switching to Latin, he said, "My lord, I beg your pardon. My friend is…trying to help."

The bishop looked from Lukas to the purse and back again. Slowly, his brow smoothed. "So I see."

"Please, you can put your money away. We don't want it."

"There's more if you can guide us to the Hospital of Sampson," the bishop offered.

"I'm sorry, my lord. I'm new to the city myself."

"You can speak their language?" Ayla cocked her head. "What's he saying?"

The bishop drew his black mantle aside to fasten his purse to his belt. As the fabric moved it revealed a weapon: a short broadsword, wide, flat and wickedly pointed. As the other priests rearranged their robes, more weapons showed. A glint of steel at the bishop's neck revealed that he was wearing a mail shirt.

Armed priests? Lukas swallowed, noticing what he had previously missed: the breadth of the bishop's shoulders, his hands big and scarred like a warrior's. Not at all like a scholar or a priest.

Ayla looked puzzled. "God have mercy, Lukas, why didn't they fight?"

"What does he say?" the bishop asked in Latin.

"He wonders why you let those rascals take your money instead of fighting, my lord."

The bishop touched the sword at his side with those warrior's hands. "Well, it is only a purse, a small matter to spill blood over. I am a priest of God and Holy Church. I did not come all the way from France to shed the blood of my fellow Christians."

France. These barbarians must be Franks then. Lukas strained his memory. Surely he *had* seen Franks visiting Jerusalem in the old days. They must not be pagans either, since they came to worship at Jerusalem, and now had a bishop.

A bishop who spoke like a holy man, yet carried a sword.

"Your Latin is good," the bishop said when Lukas had translated his words to Ayla. He rearranged his mantle to conceal the sword. "Have you any other languages, boy?"

Lukas shrugged. "Greek, Syriac and Armenian."

"Ah!" The bishop glanced at his priests, lifting a meaningful eyebrow. *"But my God shall supply all your need according to his riches!* My lord the count of Saint-Gilles wants a faithful man to provide interpretation of such languages. If you speak them as well as you do Latin, there may be a place for you in his household."

A place? As a *servant*? Lukas opened his mouth and then shut it again, trying to find a tactful way to refuse.

Ayla jabbed him in the ribs. "What's he saying, Greek?"

"He wants me to work for his lord. As an interpreter."

"Wonderful!"

"I can't." He turned to the bishop. "I'm sorry, my lord. I have...a journey to make."

"I also have a journey to make. Perhaps our paths lie together."

Lukas grimaced. Unless the bishop was also trying to turn back time by centuries, that was *very* unlikely.

Ayla nudged him again. "What do you mean you can't? Are you crazy? You'll starve otherwise."

The bilingual conversation was making his head spin. Meanwhile the bishop said, "The count and I are travelling to Jerusalem."

Jerusalem! That made him pause. While he struggled for thought, one of the priests glanced at the sky and tapped the bishop's elbow.

"My lord, remember the Watchers."

The Watchers?

The bishop turned back to Lukas. "I have a meeting to attend. An interpreter of my own might be useful. Come with me now and make your choice about Jerusalem after."

The Watchers! Lukas did not hesitate this time. "Done."

The bishop blinked at his easy capitulation. Meanwhile, Ayla must have guessed that they'd reached an agreement. "Good choice, Greek. Beats asking the Watchers for help. Well, I suppose this is goodbye."

Lukas turned to her with a sudden pang. "Are you leaving?"

"Got to find my uncle."

"Will you be all right?"

She shot him an incredulous look.

She was not his sister Marta, he reminded himself. She was bred on the streets and knew how to forge her way. If he doubted that he only had to look at the blood on her hands.

"Let me know how you fare. Meet me at Saint Sophia…tomorrow at noon." The great basilica was the only landmark he was sure of finding in this immense city.

She pursed her lips. "All right. Stay gold, Greek."

"Be safe, Kismet."

He stepped back. But before she left, he had to ask it.

"Wait. Why *shouldn't* I go to the Watchers?"

Ayla had already turned away from him. Now, she glanced back over her shoulder. The smile on her face did not reach her eyes.

"Because if you did, I'd have to kill you."

Chapter VII.

Perched on a cornice above the Constantinople alley, a black vulture watched the Frankish bishop and the Greek interpreter head north.

A bird's mind was a feeble thing, easily suppressed. Deep underneath the alien compulsion that drove it, the bird was nervous. It was meant for mountain peaks and towering firs, and it was uneasy skulking along city rooftops like a tame pigeon.

Yet there was nothing it could do. Another spirit had entered it, peering through its charcoal-coloured eyes at the humans below.

The girl is mine, she mused. *The sigil marks her forehead. Fresh and full of life. A feast that soon approaches.*

But the young Watcher bears my stamp on his brow too. How? Surely I would have known if someone had dedicated a Watcher.

The bird launched into the air, its white-tipped wings beating laboriously as it climbed into the higher currents. *Surely there was something familiar in the Watcher's face.* At this age, memory rose slowly, like bubbles moving through oil. When this one surfaced, the shock almost unseated her.

Oliveta.

For an instant, the iron control slipped. The vulture's consciousness resurfaced, aware of little but terror, hunger, and overwhelming relief.

Only for a moment, until the alien consciousness clamped back down, and it became little more than a feathered puppet.

Ah. Now I remember you, young Watcher. Well now, this changes everything...

The vulture had climbed high enough now to coast on the wind—still too close to the rooftops for comfort, but the passenger inside its mind cared little for its comfort. The bird sighted the massive dome of the Christian temple and slid down the wind toward a small building in the streets beyond.

The passenger held on until the roof was too near to miss. The physical realm was like a book: full of knowledge encoded in sights, smells, or sounds. But one needed material senses in order to read it, and the vulture's mistress had none of her own.

The bird recovered its senses barely in time to swerve aside and avoid a collision with the building's chimney. As its passenger let go, she felt a momentary dislocation as she returned to a mode of existence that did not know gravity, sight, or hearing.

A cursed half-life. She envied the favoured creatures that bodily inhabited this world. She would tear them to pieces if she could.

She descended like a bolt through roof, floors, and furniture, halting just above the marble floors at the ground level. Her surroundings were cloudy and insubstantial to her, the murmur of voices little more than an underwater echo. But she could sense the creatures' spirits around her. The building teemed with them.

Imagine what I could do if I had a proper alliance with one of these creatures. If Oliveta had worked...

Perhaps I can still profit from that day, now that the young Watcher is here.

She drifted through the building, searching. This was where the Frank and the Watcher were heading, but none of the creatures she wanted was here. She saw the spark of life burning low in many of them, and shuddered. *Hospitals.* Instead of devouring their weak, the damnable children of earth wasted treasure and risked pestilence in a futile attempt to prolong their existence.

She knew she should not tarry, but the temptation was too delicious. One of the low-burning sparks was clouded with sickness. Not enough to kill a strong man, but deadly to the weak. She took three arrows from the quiver at her belt and stabbed them into the spark as she passed. It flickered and came free of its body.

She did not bother to see which way it went, instead loosing the arrows swiftly from her bow. She spread the infection where it would do most damage: the room where some of the creatures recovered from wounds, the vestibule where they sat waiting for treatment and the room of mothers who had suffered in giving birth.

She smiled. She had a particular…*regard* for childbirth.

By now, she had located the creature she wanted in a smaller building next to this one. She slid through his wall and almost fell into his dream. She had trouble dealing with waking minds, but dreams were an open door to her, especially those of a Watcher with a decayed and hollow Mark. She settled on his chest as light as a feather and slipped into his mind.

The creature sits at a desk, scratching with a pen in a ledger. The ledger's numbers are wrong, and the creature feels the sweat on his forehead. The money isn't there—no matter what he does, the sums don't add up. Someone was going to discover that he had been skimming gold. Damn that silkworks, he ought to have known it was a bad investment. If he could just obscure the numbers—

But he can't. His hand won't move right. The pen writes nothing but the truth and then, in the blink of an eye, it writes his sentence for theft.

She smiled. It was tempting just to sit there and enjoy the guilty dream. But there was work to do.

The door slams open and a young boy enters, a Syrian Mark inked into his bared left arm and a flaming torch lifted high in his right hand.

"This is the thief," he tells the soldiers behind him. They drag him away from his desk and the boy reads out the sentence written in the ledger. "Presbyter Didymus, I sentence you to be taken into the street, where your good works shall be burned before your eyes."

"No," gasps the thief.

But they are outside already, watching the hospital as light blazes from one window, then another.

The young Syrian emerges from the door, a malevolent grin spreading across his face.

"I've come to destroy all your lies."

The dream burst like a bubble, expelling her from his mind.

Chapter VIII.

oly saints, they get younger every year, Saint-Gilles thought as he watched the solemn blond giant dismount.

Duke Godfrey of Lorraine walked forward and ponderously embraced him. "I hope I find you in good health, my lord."

"Can't complain." Saint-Gilles extracted himself from the duke's arms and motioned him to enter the tent. He was living under canvas again now. Two days ago, the remainder of his army had arrived from the mountains of Greece, and he had shifted his household from the monastery of Cosmas and Damian to the field outside where his army was camped.

He had watched them arrive with a mixture of pride and grief. The long march from Provence had been hard on everyone. His knights were down-at-heel and dirty, the common people ragged and starving, and many of every estate nursed wounds or illness.

He was a seasoned warrior, not a nervous boy, but it frightened him to be so far from home. The sheer distance, the loneliness, the uncertainty of having neither walls nor friends to hide behind. The wretched Greeks had already sprung on them like wolves. Seeing the tattered remnant had only renewed his outrage.

Inside the tent, Godfrey straightened, pulling off his gloves. "And your countess. I hope she is in good health."

"Likewise."

"And..." evidently the duke was straining his memory. "You have a child, I believe. Young..."

"William, my lord."

"How old?"

"Three months."

"Ah. And how is he?"

"Recovering well from the journey." With the army delayed in Constantinople, William's health seemed to be returning. The duke nodded vaguely and tucked his gloves very deliberately into his belt. *Now, at last, we'll get to the point.*

Instead the duke said, "And the weather has been good for you on this side of the sea?"

Saint-Gilles took a deep breath and told himself to have patience. Evidently the duke was trying to be polite, but the insincerity was galling. Godfrey did not care a fig for his Provençals, or his wife, or his son.

"Do you mind if we get down to business, my lord?" He motioned to the duke to a seat at the table. "I'm aware you didn't cross the sea to make small talk, and I'd like to hear what you have to say."

Godfrey blinked. "Oh. I was going to ask after the lord bishop."

"Adhemar? He's in the best of health now. Now, my lord—"

"Forgive me," the duke added. "I meant, perhaps he should be here also. After all, he is the Pope's representative on this pilgrimage."

"I'm afraid he's gone into the city, my lord. If you'd sent word sooner, I might have kept him here to meet you."

"I see." Godfrey seemed momentarily at a loss. Saint-Gilles laughed inwardly. He understood now why Bohemond had called the duke a poor manager of men. But the duke himself would be easily managed. He would be no trouble.

"Sit down," Saint-Gilles said crisply, "and let's have it out, my lord. It's about this oath, isn't it?"

"Well, yes, in fact, it is." The duke sat, clasping his hands, every movement tight and controlled. There was fruit and wine and cheese on the table, but he left them untouched. For a moment he only stared at them, still as a stone. *You're not going to like this,* his hunched shoulders said. *Please don't lose your temper.* When the duke actually spoke, with much preliminary throat-clearing, he only said, with desperate finality, "I'm here partly on my own behalf, but also partly for Vermandois, Flanders, and Bohemond."

Like Godfrey, the three princes he named had already sworn oaths to Alexius and had their people ferried to the Asian shore, ready for the march east.

"Go on," Saint-Gilles said.

"Our men have been waiting in camp for months now. The weather's good, and we can't afford to wait. You know how armies spoil for lack of action."

"You want to march on?"

Godfrey nodded. "We want to take Nicaea."

Nicaea was within striking distance of Constantinople, the city of the first great council of the church. Now a Turkish sultan had his capital there. It had been the crown jewel of the Greek empire, and Alexius had been trying to recapture it ever since the Turks took it sixteen years ago.

Saint-Gilles had to admit it was a logical opening gambit. Nicaea was the gate to Syria. While the Turks held her, the road east was closed. And yet…

"There was a pilgrimage last year, they say. Alexius ferried them to the Asian shore, and rather than wait for the rest of us, they marched on Nicaea." Saint-Gilles searched the duke's face. "You know what happened next."

"Yes. I have seen the hill of their slain." Godfrey twisted his fingers. "Still. Together, we have enough men to attempt her. Best to strike now, and give our people something to do. We're aware of the dangers, and we would sleep easier if you were with us, my lord. That's why I'm here."

So that was it. Saint-Gilles tightened his lips. "You want me to swear the oath to Alexius."

"What else can you do?"

"It is impossible." Anger propelled Saint-Gilles to his feet. "The

81

wretched emperor lured me away from my people so that his troops could attack them in my absence! Then, when I went to remonstrate with him, he gave me *Bohemond,* of all people, as a hostage! And finally, to cap it off, his judges decided against us! They were every *one* of them his sworn men. I have no hostage, no justice, and now no way to get it." He stopped pacing and faced Godfrey. "No man of spirit would make such a submission."

"Yet put yourself in the emperor's shoes," Godfrey urged.

Remembering the gemmed purple slippers Alexius wore, Saint-Gilles barked with laughter. "I wouldn't be seen dead in the emperor's shoes. And I wouldn't make such an oath as he demands to *any* man, not even the King of France. He wishes to receive every city or fortress that submits to us, and he promises nothing in return!"

"He promises help. Food, siege engines, men."

"He promises the bare minimum." Saint-Gilles snorted. "No. I tell you it is impossible. But no fear: he doesn't want me outside his gates any more than I want to stay here. Sooner or later, he will send us on our way."

"And if he doesn't?"

"Then I'll twist his arm until he does."

Godfrey looked as if he was sitting on thorns. "Surely you don't intend an attack on the city."

"Like yours, you mean?"

Godfrey actually blushed. "I have sinned in shedding Christian blood, my lord. I'm here to beg you not to do the same. Come over and help us fight the Turks. They're our real enemy."

Saint-Gilles was silent for a moment. Attack the city? Until now, he had not seriously entertained the idea. But what if it did hasten Alexius' capitulation?

Godfrey cleared his throat. "Have you spoken to Bishop Adhemar about it?"

Saint-Gilles restrained himself from rolling his one good eye. "The bishop is my personal friend."

Godfrey looked blank. The duke of Lorraine was clearly not the most brilliant mind among them.

"He advised me to swear," Saint-Gilles snapped, "but that's easy for a bishop to say. A bishop is not a count. A bishop is supposed to turn the other cheek, but a count must obey the demands of knightly honour. That means avenging my people. If I can't guarantee their safety, why should any of them follow me? I tell you the answer is no."

Godfrey sighed and stood up. "I'm sorry to find you in this mood, my lord."

"Don't worry. It's just a matter of time and pressure, and then we can all march on to Nicaea together. Have patience."

"Ah," said Godfrey. He had taken his gloves from his belt, and now he tucked them back again. "I ought to have told you. For all the reasons I mentioned, it's been resolved to set out for Nicaea at once. We begin tomorrow."

"Tomorrow?" Saint-Gilles choked back a curse. "Look, you can't do that. Won't you at least wait for Normandy and Blois?"

Word was that Duke Robert of Normandy and Count Stephen of Blois were still on their way to Constantinople. But Godfrey pursed his lips. "They can join the siege when they arrive. If they should be late...well, no man can complain if his tardiness robs him of honour."

With that parting shot, he bowed and departed. Saint-Gilles yanked his chair away from the table and slumped down, chewing his lip. Outmanoeuvred, by Saint Faith! If the other princes meant to march on Nicaea, that changed everything. While they advanced boldly to battle and glory, he would be sitting idly outside Constantinople, a laughing-stock.

There was no way to salvage his honour, except to force Alexius' hand. Attack the city? In his mind's eye he saw the massive triple wall. Madness! He would get no further than Godfrey had. Not without twice the number of men.

Deferring the question, Saint-Gilles summoned two knights of his household and set out to make the rounds of the camp. It was another beautiful, clear spring morning, with just a hint of summer's warmth in the air. Constantinople sprawled across the hills southwest, its domes and spires shining with reflected light. Beyond, the Sea of Marmara was a glistening silver road to the east, to Jerusalem, where he had vowed to worship.

Between it and himself stood the walls of Constantinople.

Saint-Gilles leaned on the spear he used as a staff and stared toward the Asian shore. His vow to Christ called him east, but knightly honour kept him here, trying to avenge his people's wrongs. He was a divided man, torn between two worlds. He had always been a divided man. Perhaps he had only himself to blame: if he had shown more integrity in the past, then he would not have to justify himself as a ruler now.

"It's so close, isn't it?" Lord Galdemar Carpenel strolled out of the camp to greet him, chewing on an exotic golden stonefruit which the Greeks called an apricot.

Saint-Gilles ignored the fruit's delectable aroma. "I wish I was over there, and done with this place. With Alexius. With Bohemond."

Galdemar gave a rich chuckle. "Count Bohemond is no fool. Did you hear? They say he sent his men across by stealth."

"How's that possible? The Greeks are watching the sea like hawks."

"It was at the Hellespont, at the other end of the sea." Galdemar pointed his apricot west down the Marmara. "They say his followers wanted to avoid doing homage."

Saint-Gilles heaved a sigh. He ought to have thought of the same thing. It was impossible now, of course. He could not cross at Constantinople, and it was too late to steal away and cross elsewhere.

He would have to think of something else.

Galdemar accompanied him on his circuit of the camp. As they turned north, a bright flutter caught Saint-Gilles' good eye, a red banner making its way down the road that led from the monastery of Saint Cosmas and Saint Damian.

"Speak of the devil," Saint-Gilles said as the tiny entourage left the road and angled toward them.

It was Bohemond, riding a beautiful, vicious-tempered black horse that fought him every step of the way and only succeeded in showing off his horsemanship. The count dismounted springily and met Saint-Gilles with outstretched arms. "Just the man I came to see! Pardon my coming unannounced like this, but now I've been your hostage, I feel like one of the household."

"Evidently," Saint-Gilles said drily. "What brings you here, my lord?"

Bohemond unpinned his cloak and threw it to the squire holding his horse. "To tell the truth, I'd hoped for a private word."

He was not the first this morning. The Norman count had to know that Godfrey had already come.

"Where's the duke?" Saint-Gilles asked.

Bohemond pointed at the water traffic on the Golden Horn. "On his way back to Asia. I'll be following as soon as I'm packed."

Saint-Gilles narrowed his eyes at the distant vessel. So it was really happening. They meant to leave him behind.

He turned back to his people. "Galdemar, stay with us. The rest of you, fall back." To Bohemond he added, "My lord of Carpenel is a friend and advisor. You may speak your mind before both of us."

Bohemond glanced toward the camp. "And Bishop Adhemar?"

"Don't worry. I'll pass on to him anything you say." Saint-Gilles led them across the road, down the grassy slope, and through a gap in the hedge that admitted them to the orderly rows of the monastery's vineyard. The hubbub of the camp, with its voices, animals, and ringing anvils, died away behind them, muffled by wind and hedge.

Saint-Gilles turned to Bohemond. "Speak."

Bohemond smiled, his teeth a white flash in his sunburned face. "Godfrey tells me you are determined not to take the oath."

He was sick of defending himself. "What does it matter to you?"

"I've pledged my support to the emperor in this affair. If you continue to defy him, I'll be obliged to act on that pledge."

Saint-Gilles scowled, fists clenching on his spear. "What, by force of arms?"

"That's usually implied in such an oath." Bohemond spoke apologetically.

"Why take it, then?"

"I had to. The Greeks have never forgiven me for my past…excursions. They don't trust me. As long as the Greeks host my army, I'm their hostage. Whether anyone says the word or not."

"Hogwash! If they were really holding you hostage then they *would* have said the word, believe me."

There was a short silence broken only by the hum of bees investigating wildflowers growing in the turf.

Bohemond said slowly, "Trust me, I understand why you refuse to take the oath. It's obvious that Alexius wants to profit from our labours. We'll spend our blood taking cities, but he'll enjoy them. I did what I had to, but I don't relish telling my men that we'll get nothing out of it. Oh, yes. I understand."

Saint-Gilles grunted. "It's not the paltry reward that holds me back, it's the emperor's treachery to my people. What would we do with land, anyway? All of us have vowed a pilgrimage to Jerusalem."

"To liberate it from the pagans, yes." Bohemond half-smiled. "Isn't that the goal? Say we win the Holy City. That belonged to the emperors once, too."

"That will be a problem for you, my lord. Not for me, because I've taken no oath."

Bohemond clicked his fingers. "Then you see what I'm getting at!"

Saint-Gilles blinked. "No, I don't."

"I mean that it's hardly in your interest to take the oath. Raymond Saint-Gilles, King of Jerusalem! How does *that* sound, ha?"

"Blasphemous." Saint-Gilles spoke acidly. Only Christ could be king in Jerusalem. But of course, Christ would require an earthly representative to actually guard the city. A count. Raymond Saint-

Gilles, count of Jerusalem... "Come to the point, my lord. I'm listening."

Bohemond stuck his thumbs in his belt. "You and I can help each other."

"With what?"

"You understand that I cannot be *seen* to be helping you," Bohemond added. "I've taken every oath Alexius pressed on me, but my men crossed the sea without me. My nephew Tancred has the command of them now, and he's sworn no oaths to Alexius. None. If he took it into his head to bring the men back and combine forces with you..."

"I thought so," Saint-Gilles said with sour satisfaction. He understood now. Understood, and laughed inwardly.

"Pardon me?"

Saint-Gilles waved a hand. "No, go on. I want to hear it. How will you bring all your men over?"

"Fishing and merchant vessels on the Asian side. Tancred tells me they aren't closely watched. He can land his men west of the city one night and be under the Land Walls before Alexius hears of it."

"You have this planned in detail." Saint-Gilles ironed his lips shut.

"Thanks to your determination, I've had the time to think it over. My men could never take Constantinople on their own. I'll wager there's not a better-seasoned army in the pilgrimage, but this calls for numbers as well as experience. With both our forces combined..."

He could hold his tongue no longer. "You want me to help you conquer Constantinople."

Bohemond did not hesitate. "You'll be well paid for it."

"By our Lady, not a penny!"

"My lord?"

Saint-Gilles stepped closer. "Did you really think I would join you in this?"

Bohemond took a step backwards and laughed. "Why not, my lord? It would release you from this stalemate. And think of Constantinople! She will replenish your coffers a hundred—a *thousand* times over."

"You must think—"

"There is no loss she cannot repay."

"You must think I am a *merchant*," Saint-Gilles bellowed. "Money? Is that what you think of me? That a little gold will tempt me off the path I have sworn on the price of my *salvation* to take? That because I will not sell my honour to the emperor, I will sell it for the plunder of a Christian city? Holy Mother Mary! *You made an oath!*"

"And I would never break it, my lord!" Bohemond had the gall to look offended. "That's why Tancred—"

"You are breaking it with every *word.*"

"I thought we agreed that the oath was unreasonable."

"Unreasonable?" Saint-Gilles reigned in the impulse to strike him. *"Unreasonable?* The time to think of that was before you bound yourself to it! This is treason, and you think I will hear it? Dog!"

The Norman count flushed, putting his hand to the gloves tucked into his belt. "Calm yourself, my lord!"

"How dare you! *I am calm!*" His voice echoed from the distant monastery walls. Bohemond whipped the gloves from his belt.

"My lords." Standing by the gap in the hedge, Lord Galdemar jerked his head in the direction of the road. "Is it your wish to keep this conversation private?"

The servants.

Pale with anger, Bohemond stood rigid with his gloves clenched in his fist. One more word, and the count's fist would fly. One more word, and they would be enemies, honour bound to the feud.

One more word, and he badly wanted to say it.

Instead, Saint-Gilles stepped back. "I have a vow to keep," he said bleakly. Somewhere in the last moments it had become clear what he must do. Here was something worth more than honour. Curse it! "I must go to Jerusalem for the good of my soul. No matter what happens once I get there, no matter what honour demands, if nothing else it demands I keep that oath. Adhemar was right. I cannot fight

Alexius, so I must submit. I will offer him an oath."

Not of homage. He still could not bring himself to that, but certainly an oath of non-aggression. Saint-Gilles took a deep breath, trying to let the bitterness drain out of him, but he allowed himself one parting shot. "Thank you for coming, my lord. You have without a doubt shown me the right way."

Bohemond smiled and began to pull on his gloves. "I praise God for it, my lord! I'll send to Godfrey at once with the good news."

His voice rang utterly sincere. Saint-Gilles stared.

Bohemond smirked. "Did you think my suggestion was made in earnest, count? You would have had to conquer Alexius before you changed his mind, and I did not think you had considered that question fully. I thank God I was the means of recalling you to your senses. Now, shall we be friends?"

Whatever else was afoot, Bohemond evidently meant to keep up at least the appearance of good faith.

"I am a man of honour," Saint-Gilles growled. "If I take an oath, I shall keep it."

"I expect nothing less, my lord."

Saint-Gilles narrowed his eyes. "Then yes. We shall be friends."

As Bohemond remounted his horse and pranced back to the monastery, Galdemar watched with wry admiration. "Careful, my lord. I'm no simpleton, but that count makes me feel like a babe in arms. I'll wager he's fought the Greeks so long he's nearly become one of them."

"I'm not afraid of any of them," Saint-Gilles growled. "I'm an old wolf with wits of my own."

Nevertheless, as they completed their circuit of the camp, Saint-Gilles wondered which of the two men he had met just now was the true Bohemond.

Whichever it was, both were formidable.

Chapter IX.

After leaving Lukas with the Franks, Ayla found a main road and headed west. The man she was looking for would never be found among the palaces and villas that sprawled across the high ground to the east. No, if he was here, it would be somewhere in the clutter of shops and tenements that clogged Constantinople's poorer districts.

A baker's boy directed her to a small marketplace near a large cistern in a part of the city called Paradiseion. Among the stalls there, it didn't take her long to find the Turk he had promised: a leather-worker sporting long tribesman's braids.

Plague it! Ayla hesitated as she caught sight of him. She was a Turk of Antioch, a subject of the Shah of Baghdad. This was obviously one of the half-nomad Turks of Rum, the freshly conquered Roman provinces in Asia Minor. With bad blood between the Shah and Rum, Ayla didn't want to ask this stranger for anything.

Yet his face lit up at the sound of their native tongue. "Well met, little brother! How can I help you?"

"Do you know where I can find the Vowed?" Ayla asked.

"The Vowed?" He lifted an eyebrow. "What do you want with one of them? Troublemakers, every one."

Then I should fit right in, Ayla thought. "I've got a message for the Vowed. From my father."

Disguised as a boy, most people mistook Ayla for much younger than her fifteen years. The leatherworker shrugged, accepting her explanation.

"Go down that street until you find a wine seller. The man you are looking for lives on the second level of the house opposite."

Ayla thanked him and headed down the narrow street as it writhed between shabby, slouching tenements. Across from the wine seller, steps led up the outside of a house that looked as though it might have been built by Methuselah himself. Ayla trod lightly as she ascended the rickety stairs and thumped on the door with her heart in her mouth. Now came the moment of truth.

The door didn't open. Instead, a muffled voice called her in. Ayla lifted the latch and slipped into the stuffy warmth.

After the brightness of the morning, she was almost blinded for a moment. As her eyes adjusted, she saw a large, bare room furnished only with shutters to keep the light out and a bedroll that took up one corner. The man sitting cross-legged on the pallet laid down the pestle and mortar with which he was grinding herbs.

"What do you want, girl?"

Girl. The hair prickled on her forearms. He'd seen through her disguise with no trouble at all. She closed the door behind her and stood with the length of the room separating them. "I want to speak to the Vowed. You are one of them?"

"Yes."

With the door closed, only a thin ray of light lit the room, slanting in between the shutters of one window. It showed her a man with pale skin and a black beard, his head swathed in an indigo-dyed turban. Something about his looks prompted her memory to replay his words, and as she identified the accented Greek, her fingers hooked into the cord that circled her waist. "You're an Armenian," she challenged.

"I am Armen of Kars, the Vowed, and you should know better than to waste my time."

He could be lying. She had expected a Turk like herself. But if there was one thing you learned living in Syria, it was not to judge people by their blood. If she'd forgotten that, she would never have saved the Greek boy's life, and if she had never saved the Greek boy's life, she would not be standing in this room.

She let go of the sling and stepped forward cautiously. "My father was Ilkay of Antioch, the Vowed. He often spoke of his brothers, the Acolytes of the Mountain, those who had been given divine power to heal and to prophesy."

Armen's face might have been drawn in the sand for all the expression it gave.

"Did you know my father?" Ayla prodded.

"I knew him."

"Did you know he was dead?"

"All the Vowed are dead," said Armen.

All? Ayla put a hand against the wall to steady herself, and then inched forward another step, trying to get a better look at the Armenian's face. "All? You're the *only* one left?" She drew a shaky breath. "Curse those Watchers."

Armen began grinding his herbs again. "Is that all?"

"No." She inched forward again and sank into a crouch. "Teach me. Let me join you."

The grinding in the pestle stopped, and Armen looked into her eyes for the first time. "You're just a girl. What makes you think you'd have the gift?"

"Gift?"

"Would God give a woman the gifts of healing or prophecy? Only men can be Vowed. Only men ever have."

"Maybe it's time for that to change."

Armen snorted.

"My father thought of the Vowed as his brothers," Ayla said, "the children of one father. That makes you my uncle, and now you tell me you're the very last. What happens if you die?"

"I don't plan to die."

Ayla stared at him, but he was looking at his herbs. "Please. I watched my father die, and I know that the Watchers won't be happy till they've hunted down and slaughtered every last one of his brothers. You may not think you need me, but you do."

Armen smiled grimly. "So you will keep the light alive for the next generation, will you?"

"No." She dropped her gaze, no longer sure of herself. "I'm going to die in less than six months. When I was born, my father prophesied the exact date over my crib. No one can do anything to thwart fate, but when I realised how little time I had left, I made a vow. Before I die, I'll do something to make my father proud when I meet him beyond the grave. Before I die, I want to serve God like he did. I want to bring back the Vowed to continue his work."

Armen's eyebrow lifted. "Within six months?"

Ayla flushed. "I have to do *something*. Maybe I'm not meant to be a Vowed. But I want to do something for them before I die. I thought you would have some use for me."

Armen sat very still and looked at her. Slowly, he reached inside his robe and drew a knife. Ayla watched, mesmerised, as the blade came nearer and settled cold and ticklish into the hollow behind her jawbone.

She stared the Vowed in the eye and said, "You can't scare me. I know I don't die today."

The knife pushed, tracing a line of fire through her skin.

Ayla stifled her gasp of pain. He was only testing her.

"This is childish," she said.

He grabbed her wrist, fingers probing her pulse, eyes studying her face. Then he let go and lowered his knife. He did not speak at once. Instead, he handed her a reasonably clean scrap of fabric and a box of salve for the cut.

As she took it, Armen went to the window and threw open the shutters, staring out into the bright street.

"Yes," he said finally. "I can use this courage."

Chapter X.

W atch out!" Lukas grabbed hold of the barbarian bishop and hauled him aside, moments away from blundering into a street vendor's brazier.

Letting out a relieved breath, Lukas released him. "Forgive me, my lord."

"Forgive *me*," said the bishop. "I wasn't watching. It's...overwhelming."

The main road of Constantinople was a wide boulevard paved with stone and crawling with people. Labourers, fishermen, and street vendors rubbed shoulders with merchants, soldiers, and eunuchs. Just across the road, a silk-shrouded litter had come to a halt and a noblewoman in a gown of stiff metallic brocade was leaning out to speak to a passing officer—a massive, axe-wielding barbarian in a shirt of steel plates. The street, like a vast river, flowed downhill behind them. Beneath the enormous tenements on each side, garish shop awnings and signs advertising a thousand different wares shrieked for attention.

"So this is the Queen of Cities," the bishop added, undisguised awe on his face. "Have you ever seen its like?"

The question was not directed to Lukas, but he shook his head all the same.

A street vendor directed them toward the Hospital of Sampson. Their path led uphill along the boulevard, heading east past magnificent basilicas and pillared forums. As they climbed higher, the street vendors became fewer and the houses began to look more luxurious.

Trees peered over walls, and gardens peeped through arches and gates.

"Should we ask for directions again, Greek?" the bishop asked.

Lukas shook his head. "The sherbert-seller said we'd find the Hospital in a street behind Saint Sophia. We can't miss Saint Sophia. Holy saints!"

"Quid estne?"

Lukas stared at the magnificent tetrapylon crowning the street's end. A quadruple archway hung with icons and topped with statues, it formed the gateway to another huge forum. He swallowed. "This is the Milion. Every road in the Empire is measured from here. My father described it to me many times."

He led them through the glistening stone interior into the forum beyond. Marble pillars outlined its oblong perimeter. A row of columns marched down the centre, beginning with one bearing an immense equestrian statue of the emperor Justinian. Directly ahead, an enormous icon of the Pantocrator stared challengingly at him from a massive brazen gatehouse that bristled with gold, gems, and statues. Beyond, he knew, lay the Great Palace.

To their left, dwarfing the forum, pillar upon pillar, arch upon arch, a very mountain of stone crowned with one immense dome resting upon massive buttresses—that, beyond a doubt, was Saint Sophia.

Lukas' mouth dropped open. He would be afraid to enter such a place for fear of being crushed. One of the priests crossed himself. Once more the bishop breathed, "What is it?"

"Saint Sophia. They say it's the largest dome in the world."

"I can well believe it."

"They say it was built in just six years." The knowledge tumbled out of him in a flood. "They say it includes pillars from the temple of Diana of the Ephesians. They say the emperor Justinian offended every architect in the empire by asking two mathematicians to draw the plans."

"They say the light is different there than in any other church in

95

the world."

Lukas looked at the bishop in surprise.

The barbarian smiled. "I've heard much of this church."

"It's because of the windows under the dome, my lord. The light flows through all of them at once. A ring of pure light."

"You know a great deal about it, Greek."

A dull pain thrummed in his ribcage. "It was my father's favourite place in the world. He always promised to take us there."

The bishop waited for him to go on, but Lukas could give no more explanations. After a moment, he broke the silence himself. "If you want to see inside, the Patriach has promised to show us around tomorrow. You'd be welcome to attend us."

Lukas nodded without answering. That would depend on what he learned from the Watchers, but in any case, he would meet Ayla there tomorrow. Still following the sherbert-seller's directions, he led the barbarians past the mountainous basilica and into the street behind. It was easy to spot the hospital. There was a queue of people in the building's porch, most of them evidently very poor, waiting to see the doctors. As they entered, the bishop dipped into his purse and distributed brass coins among the waiting people, murmuring blessings in Latin.

"It is good work the Watchers are doing here," he observed as they crossed into the vestibule.

Many more indigents were waiting inside, nursing every kind of ailment. A priest was waiting to lead them through a corridor bisecting the building, to emerge in a spacious garden beyond. Just inside the open door, he stopped and spoke in Latin.

"The Lord Presbyters are waiting, my lord. But only Watchers are permitted inside the garden during the meeting." He looked Lukas up and down from his filthy feet to his salty and unkempt hair. Lukas' face heated as he realised how he must look—and worse, smell.

"But I'm a Watcher too!"

"This meeting is between the Imperial Lord Presbyters and the

Watcher from France, boy. The general meeting of the Watchers' Council is not for another six months."

"But you have to help me." Lukas unwrapped the strip of canvas from his sleeve and shoved the fabric back to reveal his Watcher's Mark. "I am Lukas Bessarion, and I've come all the way from Syria to speak to the Watchers here."

The priest's breath hissed. *"Syria?"* He looked as if Lukas had kicked him in the gut.

In the silence, the bishop spoke quietly. "My own business has to do with Syria. If this boy is really a Syrian Watcher, I'd like to insist on his presence."

The priest grabbed Lukas' arm. "He bears the Syrian mark. He'd better go in. They'll want to hear him."

Mystified, Lukas followed the bishop and his entourage into the garden, a place of green peacefulness and the burbling coo of doves. The priest led them past the central fountain into the dappled shade beneath a gnarled old olive tree where the Watchers sat in a circle. There were only five of them, bearded old men sitting at their ease on chairs carved from ivory with wine and dried fruit at each elbow.

One chair, of a rather humbler make, awaited the bishop.

"Watcher," one of them greeted in Latin, bowing his head but not rising. "Welcome to Constantinople. I am Presbyter Didymus of Constantinople, and these are the Presbyters of Thrace, Macedonia, Thessalonica and Optimatoi. Be seated."

The bishop had bowed to each of the Greek Presbyters in turn. Now he cleared his throat and addressed them. "I am Adhemar Monteil, a humble Watcher of the Council in Provence."

Presbyter Didymus gave a soft snort of laughter. *"Only* a Watcher, my lord?"

"Within the Council of Watchers, we are all equals."

"Yet we remain ourselves, Watcher Adhemar. Or, should I say, Bishop Adhemar of Puy-en-Velay, the legate and personal representative of Urban of Rome?"

The bishop bowed his head. "That is correct. I bring letters of commission from the Watchers of France, but I have come at least partly in my legatine capacity as well." One of the barbarian priests handed Adhemar a folded parchment, which he passed around the circle of Watchers to Presbyter Didymus.

Didymus did not open the bishop's letter at once, instead sniffing as he looked the bishop up and down. "You travel with this Frankish horde, then, Watcher?"

"Yes, Presbyter."

"Some say that the whole Frankish nation is migrating in a body to Asia." Didymus lifted an eyebrow. "Others say that their real aim is to capture this city and with it, the whole empire."

The bishop gave a tight smile. "On the contrary, Presbyter, I assure you. Only a portion of our people were moved to make this pilgrimage, and we truly seek Jerusalem."

"But why?" The Presbyter of Thrace spoke for the first time. When Didymus looked at him, he ducked his head deferentially and said, "Whatever help the Watcher seeks, we will be in a better position to judge it if he explains the purpose of this pilgrimage."

Adhemar bowed slightly. He had still not taken his seat.

"Our mission is one of liberation," he said softly. "Two or three years ago, the lord Pope received a message from your emperor requesting knights to help him reconquer the ground so recently lost in Anatolia. By this means God awakened the pope's mind to the plight of the eastern church and the oppression of the holy places, where Christ was crowned King and of which he died possessed. These places are now trodden underfoot by the pagans. The churches are left to disaster and disrepair. And our own poor pilgrims who travel to the holy places for the good of their souls have been abused, plundered, imprisoned, and even killed by these Ishmaelites.

"We are Christ's servants, his vassals. If we owe it to our temporal lords to protect their people and property, how much more do we owe it to Christ? For this reason we have all solemnly sworn to travel to his sepulchre in Jerusalem, to drive out the enemies that infest it, and to worship him there."

"He's lying." The Presbyter from Thessalonica hissed in Greek. "They're only here to grab what they can get in the way of land and money. I saw them myself, pillaging every town and village along the Egnatian Way."

"Presbyter, I'd remind you to speak in Latin as a courtesy to the Watcher," Didymus said smoothly in that language.

"It's a legitimate question," put in the Presbyter from Thrace. "With all respect to the Watcher from France, how can we be sure that this is the real reason? No doubt the Watcher himself is honestly concerned for the liberation of Jerusalem, but he travels among thousands of fierce and sinful men. Does he speak for all of them? Why should such sinners care for their souls?"

"Perhaps the honourable Presbyter has answered himself," Adhemar said softly. "The life of a knight steeps a man in sins, many and dark and difficult to absolve. The lord Pope has promised a remission of penance to anyone who makes this pilgrimage for the sake of his soul alone. There is a great thirst in our lands for forgiveness, for redemption. I am not greatly surprised by the response."

Lukas' scalp prickled in awe. So this was the meaning of the bishop's journey to Jerusalem. Yet this was not just one man's journey: this sounded like an army. It sounded like a new epoch of the world.

Presbyter Didymus said, politely: "The ways of France are so different to the Greeks as to be nigh incomprehensible to us. I thank you for your patience, but you have yet to explain what you desire from this council."

"Any help you can give! Arm your vassals and join us in our march. Bring healers for our sick and provisions for our poor. Be our Watchers, the righteous men for whose sake we should be preserved even though we entered Sodom itself."

The Presbyters glanced at each other uneasily, and Didymus cleared his throat.

"Unfortunately, my duties keep me here at the Hospital of Sampson."

The bishop seemed to shrink in on himself. "I beg your pardon. You have good work, excellent work, to do here."

"But anything else…"

"Healers," the bishop said eagerly. "Medicines. Money, or grain, either is as good as the other. I don't ask for myself, but for charity, to keep the poor alive. And beyond that, there's something only you can give me, Presbyters. Information about the Watchers' Councils in Antioch and Jerusalem. We'll need their help if we're to succeed. Who should I speak to? Will you give me letters of accreditation for them? I've asked my own Council in France, and I've spoken to old pilgrims. But none of them can tell me anything about the Watchers in the East."

Presbyter Didymus let out a sigh. "Nor can I, Watcher. I grieve to be the bearer of bad news, but rumours have reached us in Constantinople. We gravely fear that there are no more Watchers left in the East."

Lukas stared. "What? *None?*"

Everyone turned to him. Adhemar looked hopeful, the Presbyter from Thessalonica coldly disapproving, Presbyter Didymus puzzled, with a crease between his brows.

"There may be a handful left," Didymus said majestically. "Certainly there are known to have been Watchers in Antioch when the Turks retook it fourteen years ago. But there was some manner of…disturbance. Their Presbyters were killed, the Watchers scattered. There is no Council there now, and there has been no Council in Jerusalem for even longer. That is all we know."

Adhemar sank into the chair provided for him, looking as stricken as Lukas felt. "If this is true, then the whole East is in danger. Lukas—"

"We will of course make a donation, for charity's sake," Didymus interrupted. "And we'll seek out at least one trustworthy surgeon to travel with you."

"I thank you." The bishop spoke absent-mindedly. "May God establish this city more firmly on your good deeds for it. But there's hope for Syria, surely. Lukas Bessarion, you are a Syrian Watcher. What news from the East?"

There was a sharp crash: Didymus had upset his wineglass. His cheeks paled. "Syrian?"

Seeing that he had their attention, Lukas held out his arm, pushing the sleeve above the elbow. "I'm a Watcher of Jerusalem," he began.

The Presbyter of Macedonia looked at him with something like hope, but he said: "Impossible!"

Lukas could tell that he wanted to believe, and that gave him courage. "What I'm about to tell you may seem like madness. But please listen before you judge. I came to ask for your help. I—I had no idea there were no Watchers left in Syria."

They looked confused. He should start at the beginning: the night when Oliveta burned.

Lukas cleared his throat: "In the reign of Emperor Heraclius, my family and I left Jerusalem and fled north to Syria to meet with the Watchers there…"

By the time he finished the story, the whole council was staring at him, mystified.

"You expect us to *believe* this?" the Presbyter from Thrace challenged him.

Lukas shrugged helplessly. "If I was trying to fool you, I would have invented a better story. I hoped you would know what happened to me, and how I can find my way back."

Adhemar cleared his throat. "Strange things have been known to happen. Think of the Seven Sleepers."

"But four hundred years and hundreds of miles?"

"Wait, Presbyter." Didymus stared at Lukas, his fingers white on the arms of his chair. "Do none of you know his tale?"

No one spoke.

"The annals of the Syrian Watchers say that in the reign of Heraclius, right before Antioch fell—"

Antioch fell. The Presbyter went on speaking, but Lukas had stopped listening. Oh, Saint George! From his conversations with Ayla, he knew that all of Syria and even much of Anatolia was controlled by the heretics now. His own city of Jerusalem had fallen long ago. But the sorcerer, Khalil, had had a specific goal in mind. He had wanted a weapon which Lukas' father had hidden in Antioch, and he had performed that ghastly ritual of blood and fire in order to get the power to retrieve it.

Antioch fell. Just over two weeks ago—before Oliveta—Lukas had *been* in Antioch. That battle was still ahead of them. He had been determined to fight rather than see his province conquered…and in a night of sleep, in the blink of an eye, it was lost. He *had* to find his way back. Whatever the weapon was, Khalil must have it by now, but if Lukas could return to his own time, he might prevent that from happening. If he could get the weapon before Khalil did, he could *fight,* so that this terrible future never came to pass.

But time was not on his side. The longer he delayed getting home, the more time Khalil had to find him and finish what he had started in Oliveta.

"Young Watcher?"

The Presbyter was speaking to him. Lukas jerked to attention. "I'm sorry?"

"I asked the name of your father."

Lukas straightened in pride. "John Bessarion, Presbyter of Jerusalem."

The Greek Presbyters recognised the name. "Holy Virgin!" one of them yelped, and Presbyter Didymus crossed himself.

Lukas' face heated. "What's wrong with my father?"

Presbyter Didymus stood up, looking pale. "You have gained access to this Council under false pretences, young man."

For a moment, all he could do was gape. Then he thrust out his

102

arm again, trembling. "I have not! I bear the Mark!"

"Presbyters, please." Adhemar jumped up and put a hand on Lukas' shoulder. "This young man is here as my guest."

Didymus pressed white lips together. "He's lying to us, my lord. Either that, or he actually is the son of the heretic John Bessarion."

"My father was no heretic," Lukas shouted. "It was the rest of the Council that was justly disbanded because they would not hear his rebuke!"

"Lukas," the bishop warned.

"Your father betrayed and killed the Syrian Council! Do you dare to come into this council defending his name?"

Lukas shoved the bishop's hand from his shoulder. "I know that the Messenger spoke the truth in disbanding the council at Oliveta. The guardianship of Syria and Palestine was given to John Bessarion and his heirs. That means that *I* am the Watcher's Council now. Do *you* dare to gainsay me?"

There was a moment's incredulous silence. From the branches of the olive tree, a small silver gong hung with a wand of the same material dangling beside it. Now, almost purple with rage, Didymus grabbed the wand and struck a crashing blow. With a hoarse croak, an enormous black bird unfolded its wings and mounted into the sky from its perch in the tree above, flapping so loudly that for a moment everyone in the garden stared in amazement. *A black vulture*, Lukas realised, blinking. What was such a bird doing in a city garden?

Didymus wiped a fleck of spittle from his beard and said hoarsely, "Will you leave or will you be removed, Lukas Bessarion?"

There came a sound of running feet. Didymus made a sign, and Lukas turned just in time to see the priest who had ushered them into the garden turn and race back into the hospital. The hair prickled on his arms.

"Lukas." Bishop Adhemar gripped him by the shoulders. "You had better wait outside."

The bishop's words made him mulish. "Are you kicking me out, too?"

Adhemar's voice dipped. "I'm trying to find answers about the Watchers in Syria. I can't get those answers if this meeting ends now. Nor if you disappear."

Footsteps interrupted them. The attendant priest reappeared in the garden, followed by four armed men. Didymus pointed at Lukas, his voice high-pitched and shaking. "Take this man into custody!"

"I hope you have his Mark defaced!" added the Presbyter from Thrace.

His Mark! Till now, Lukas had been hot with rage, but the Thracian's words acted like a douse of icy water. He had already lost his home, his family and everyone who might have known him. The Mark was the only thing he had left.

He ran, springing over a low table, sending wine flying. Presbyter Didymus yelped, grabbing for his arm, but Lukas sent him sprawling. Ahead, an enormous Judas-tree in purple bloom overhung the garden wall. He scaled it like a monkey, fear lending him agility. One of the guards got a hand on his ankle, but he kicked wildly and got free. Then he shinned along an outthrust limb, dropped from the branch to the coping-stone of the garden wall, and swung himself down on the other side.

Behind him in the garden, Lukas heard a rising cacophony and the thudding of feet. Didymus was yelling at the soldiers to go around by a gate. Above, Saint Sophia towered on his right. He was in a cul-de-sac leading out into the crowded square in front of the basilica.

He had to find some kind of shelter before the Watchers could find him and destroy his last link with the past. Lukas bolted.

Chapter XI.

On the outside, the basilica of Saint Sophia was like a small, dense mountain of stone, yet inside, it seemed so light and insubstantial that at any moment it might float away. Windows pierced the whole bulk of the great church, letting in enough light to make it sparkle like the inside of a lantern. Gigantic mosaic saints and emperors peered down at Ayla, their calm and detached gaze eerie and unsettling to one unaccustomed to seeing the images of people. For a long time she stood with her head craned back, feeling as though she was about to fall *up,* up into the airy gold heavens and float away with them.

Then Lukas Bessarion hissed her name in her ear. She had to look down, down a long way before she found herself inside a body that seemed no bigger than a grasshopper within the endless space.

"Ayla," Lukas repeated. "Follow me. Hurry!"

He turned, keeping his head down, and scurried behind a set of pillars dividing the main space of the church from a conch-shaped niche in one corner. Ayla followed rather reluctantly. There was so much to look at—she caught a glimpse of seraphs painted at each corner of the main dome, a knot of triple wings bursting like a bud into flower, of people going to and fro on galleries high above. She had never been inside a Christian church before. Now she wanted to explore.

"This place must have been built by *giants,*" she whispered as she joined him in the niche.

"I'll tell you all about it someday."

"What have you been doing? You look...different." She studied him, trying to figure out why.

"I do?"

"You've washed your face," she realised.

"Oh." He cleared his throat. "Actually, I visited the baths. I couldn't stand my own smell any longer."

He edged around the pillar and peeked into the main space of the building. Ayla followed his gaze across the endless expanse of polished marble floor to a far pillar where the Frankish bishop and his entourage stood talking to some Greek priests.

"Hiding from someone?" she asked, bemused.

Lukas put his back to the pillar again and blew out a harried breath. "Things didn't go well yesterday. The Watchers tried to arrest me. Do you see that man standing between the bishop and the patriarch? I had to climb over his garden wall with guards hanging onto my ankles."

"That's a Watcher?" The hair on Ayla's neck lifted at the sight of the Greek sorcerer and her fingers itched for her sling. "I can take care of him, you know."

Lukas threw out his hands. "No, no, no! You can't throw stones in here, it's the house of God!"

More to the point, it would probably get Lukas in trouble, and unlike herself, he wasn't guaranteed to live. Besides, she had a bigger purpose now. Ayla shrugged, folding her arms.

"All right. So what you're telling me is, you *paid* for a bath? With the coin the bishop gave us for saving his purse? The coin you were going to buy food with?" She paused just long enough to laugh at the expression on his face. "You are the *strangest* boy, Lukas Bessarion. What's wrong with seawater?"

He looked sheepish. "I've fasted before. I've *never* been so filthy in my life. Besides, I slept on the streets last night as well and I couldn't face cold water." He shivered. "What about you? Did you find your uncle?"

106

She'd slept well last night, tucked into the corner of an abandoned rooftop. Armen had given her enough money to buy food and equipment. Better still, he'd given her work that mattered. But she couldn't tell Lukas any of that.

"I found where he used to live. But he's already gone. No one could tell me where."

He looked sick. "Ayla. I'm so sorry."

Lying to him was more uncomfortable than she'd expected. "Not your fault, Greek. Looks like we're still in the same boat. Why did the Watchers try to arrest you?"

Lukas rubbed his left forearm. "It's a long story." He looked sheepish. "Actually, they called me an apostate and a heretic."

"Ha!" Ayla smothered a laugh with her sleeve. "Greek, you have no idea how much that means to me."

He gave a sickly smile and once again slid around the pillar to look at the priests. Still chatting, they looked almost ready to put down roots.

"Are the Franks trying to arrest you too?"

"I don't know. Probably not." Lukas sighed. "I think the bishop wants to help."

Ayla chewed on a nail, nodding thoughtfully. "If he offers you a job, you should take it."

Lukas curled his lip. "I wasn't born to be a servant."

"Wake up, Greek. No one's going to throw money at you for doing nothing." She bit off a fingernail and spat it onto the floor.

"Don't be such a barbarian," he snapped. "Of course I don't expect to live for nothing."

Ayla felt her face grow hot. Barbarian? How was she to know that rich people didn't bite their fingernails? She hid the hands behind her back. "So work for them then, you cucumber. What else is there?"

His shoulders slumped, acknowledgement of the truth in his eyes. "I just…wish I had a choice."

She swallowed. When she spoke, her voice was diamond-hard. "If we ever have a choice, it's usually between servitude and death."

His eyes clouded, and he pointed at the scab on her neck where Armen had cut her. "What happened, Ayla?"

"Someone thought he'd try my metal. I had to make my choice."

"You chose death?"

No, she had chosen servitude. She couldn't tell him that, but she did have to say something.

"You're different from anyone else I know, Lukas Bessarion. I wish..." She didn't look at him. Just waited for him to speak.

Lukas said, "Come with me to Syria."

This was it. This was the thing she'd been dreading since yesterday, when Armen told her what to do. He was guileless and trusting, and she would use him as her tool.

Her voice was only a scratchy whisper. "Why?"

"I have to find my way home. And quickly, before..." He sighed. "The man who sent me here, the sorcerer. I have to find answers before he catches me, and if there are any answers to be found, they'll be in Syria."

"I mean, why do you want me to come?"

"Oh." He blinked. "So I can keep you safe."

God have mercy, he was so innocent. She managed a weary laugh. "Do you command the wind from the wilderness? Are you the master of Fate, Lukas Bessarion? No? Then don't make any promises to me."

"But I can't stay in this city; they want my blood. Bishop Adhemar said he could find employment for a Turkish interpreter. You said your uncle's gone, so why not?"

If only there was some other way. But she needed work in the Frankish camp. And in order to do her job properly, she'd have to forget how much she liked this Greek infidel.

She heaved a sigh. "All right. Why not?"

She wasn't expecting him to smile, but the wide grin transformed his face. She pretended to grin back. "You should smile like that all the time, handsome."

"I'll try." He leaned around the pillar and stiffened like a dog at point. "Look."

* * *

Finally, the Greek clergy and Watchers were bidding the Frankish bishop farewell with ceremonious bows and kisses. Lukas waited until they had turned their backs before beckoning to Ayla and hurrying across the marble floor to where the bishop stood watching them go.

"My lord," he hissed as he and Ayla came within hearing. Adhemar glanced at them and his face lit up. At the same moment, however, someone called the bishop's name in a voice far too loud for a church and Lukas was brushed aside by a retinue of men.

There were four of them, tall clean-shaven men in freshly-scoured chain armour and splendid cloaks. The bishop greeted the leader with surprise in the northern language which they evidently shared, but he quickly threw out a scarred hand toward Lukas.

"I see you, Lukas Bessarion. Don't go."

Before this onslaught of big, pale, armoured Franks, Lukas had had a thought of slipping behind the nearest pillar again. Now, although he stood his ground, he felt himself sweating a little as four heads swivelled toward him.

Lukas fingered his chin, glad he'd taken the opportunity to bathe and shave this morning.

"This is Raymond of Saint-Gilles," said Adhemar, "Count of Toulouse, Duke of Narbonne, and Margrave of Provence. He is the friend I told you of. He wishes to hire an interpreter for his journey to Syria."

The count was a tall, lean, grey old man. A scar seamed his face, intersecting what had once been an eyeball but was now only an empty drooping lid. The eye that remained, however, was bright and unimpressed. He looked both Lukas and Ayla up and down, then said something curtly to Adhemar and headed back toward the doors. For a moment, a breath, Lukas' heart plunged.

"He says we'll discuss this business outside. Follow us," said Adhemar.

They almost had to run to keep up with the Franks' long, purposeful strides. Thankfully, Presbyter Didymus was nowhere to be seen when they emerged from the basilica's porch into the grey Constantinople morning. The count slowed, feeling his way with the butt of a spear to navigate the step at the entrance.

Beside him, Ayla stiffened with a little indrawn breath. Lukas glanced at her and saw that she was staring up into the sky above the pillars of the forum. Silhouetted against the clouds, climbing heavily into the air with laborious sweeps of its wings, was a black vulture.

Under her breath, Ayla began muttering her twice-daily litany. *It grants protection from the evil of djinn,* she had told him. Lukas felt the hairs prickle on the back of his neck, but before he could ask her why she chose to recite it now, the count spoke and the bishop translated.

"He asks what languages the two of you speak."

Lukas listed his four languages and Ayla's two. The conversation that followed was very unwieldy. Ayla could speak to him in Greek, and he could speak to the bishop in Latin, and the bishop could speak to the count in Frankish, but no more than two of them could use the same tongue. The count wanted to know if Lukas and Ayla were willing to undertake the dangerous journey to Syria and whether they would be prepared to learn Frankish within the next few months. As the count told them how much he expected to pay them, Lukas began to wonder if the man ever blinked. Whilst waiting for the simple messages to travel from one end of the translation chain to the other, Lukas inspected the Franks, from their finely-knit mesh armour to the stirrups on the horses that waited with an escort of the Varangian palace guard in the courtyard beyond.

"The count asks why you were hiding in the church just now," the bishop said.

Lukas blinked, turning his full attention back to the conversation. *Saint George, help.*

"You were there yesterday," he said pleadingly. "The Greek Watchers say I'm a heretic and set their guards on me. That's the only reason I'm in trouble with them."

He watched the count's face as this was translated. To his amazement, Count Raymond barked a short laugh and clapped Lukas on the shoulder.

"He says you're exactly what he needs," the bishop told him, but the count was already speaking again.

"I need someone whose fealty belongs to me," Adhemar translated. "Someone I can trust. In this city translators are thick as flies on a carcass, but they're no use to me if their loyalties belong to Alexius. What do you say? Are you ready to leave your emperor and serve me instead?"

Leave the emperor's service? He, a Bessarion? When his family had served the Roman emperors for *generations.*

But the emperors had abandoned Syria, he reminded himself. On the same day that his family left Antioch for the Council at Oliveta, desperately hoping to find a way to save their province, Emperor Heraclius was running away in the opposite direction, no longer willing to defend them.

That was more than four hundred years ago now. Lukas swallowed. "I'm ready."

When this was translated, the count held out his hands expectantly, a span apart.

"He is ready to accept your fealty," Adhemar said softly. "Kneel and put your hands between his."

Lukas was utterly confused, but he obeyed, kneeling on the stone pavement and letting the Frankish count clasp his hands. They were warm, callused, and hard.

"Are you willing to become completely the count's man?" asked Adhemar. "Do you pledge your entire faith to your lord against all men who might live or die?"

Saint George. It was like watching a door swing shut on him. For a moment, Lukas wanted to pull his hands away and run. But where? What other choice did he have?

He swallowed hard. "I do."

The count's grip on his hands hardened, pulling him to his feet and, before he knew what was happening, into a raspy kiss. Then he was released. The count was grimly smiling. The bishop was holding out an exquisite reliquary, asking him to take an oath. Dazedly, Lukas fumbled through the words after Adhemar.

"I swear upon this relic of the holy Silvio that I will always be a faithful man to my lord and to his successors."

The bishop turned toward Ayla. Her eyes were huge.

"What just happened?" she asked.

His head was spinning. "It…seems like a kind of adoption ceremony."

"I thought we were just getting a *job.*"

"You'll have to make an oath to serve him completely."

She thought about that for a moment, looking at the count who stood waiting, holding out his hands.

"Well," she said at last, "if he's going to feed me, I don't mind."

He had to help administer the oath to her in a language she understood. She swore on the bishop's relic without a word of protest and submitted to having her cheeks ceremoniously kissed.

As the count turned away to mount his horse, Ayla pulled a droll face. "What have we got ourselves into, Lukas? This had better be worth it."

"I think it will be." Lukas turned back to look at the Frankish warriors, examining them more closely this time. "Do you see their armour? I've never seen anything like it. And look—they *all* have stirrups to their saddles. Those were new in my time. I don't even know what *that* is." He pointed at a contraption one of them hefted to his shoulder, a very short bow mounted on the end of a wooden shaft.

"So much has changed since my time. New armour. New weapons. If I can learn from them…"

If he could learn from them, maybe he would not be so helpless next time. For a little while, he had forgotten. But now, again, he felt flesh and bone rasping on the shaft of a boathook, and shivered. He didn't want to be a killer, but maybe it was better than standing helpless, watching his people die.

Ayla was not listening, her eyes still fixed on the sky, and a black speck that rode the high winds.

The bishop beckoned them to follow. The escort of Varangians forged a path for the Franks through the bustling crowds of the Mese and turned right to skirt the hills of the city, before finally to emerging at the Gate of Charisius. Unused to travelling by foot, Lukas' legs ached by the time they passed through the massive triple gate into a patchwork of suburbs and small farms.

Here, the Varangians turned back and the Franks seemed to breathe a collective sigh of relief. A hum of talk began among the priests, the armed men lowered their short cross-mounted bows, and the count dismounted, beckoning the bishop to walk beside him and talk. Lukas scanned the countryside, looking for the Frankish camp.

Suddenly, Ayla grabbed his elbow.

"God have mercy," she muttered under her breath. "Is *that* it?"

Straight ahead of them was a sprawl of canvas which at first Lukas had taken for a crowded slum, a shanty-town. Even at this distance, the settlement seethed with people and animals. Lukas' mouth went dry. The whole population of Jerusalem could barely make a crowd like this. They were like a swarm of flies. They were like a plague of locusts.

No wonder the Greek Watchers had been worried.

Ayla's grip on his arm tightened. Again, she muttered: "What have we got ourselves into?"

* * *

Outside the city, the one-eyed count was pleased with himself.

"You'll be proud of me, old friend," he said. "I have been to see the emperor."

"You made the oath?" The western bishop looked surprised.

"I made *an* oath. Not the one Alexius wanted. I didn't render homage, but I promised to respect his people and possessions in the land where we are going to make war."

"And he accepted?"

"Yes. Honour is satisfied, my followers will be protected and I can stop watching my back for assassins. As soon as it can be arranged, the emperor will have us ferried to Asia."

"I'm glad to hear it." The bishop brightened. "We didn't come east to fight with our fellow Christians, you know."

"I wish the emperor had the same convictions." The count clenched his jaw. "I'll keep my oath, Adhemar. You know me well enough to know that. But I don't trust Alexius."

High in the air, riding a current of the southwest wind, the black vulture could not hear their conversation. But her eyesight was keen enough to see their faces, to read the movements of their lips.

She adjusted the angle of her wings and cut through the air toward the city. When the Paradiseion came in view, she folded her wings and swooped toward a shabby tenement where a man in an upper room worked hard, grinding herbs.

At the last moment, the spirit riding the bird flew free, gliding through the wooden shutters and coming to a smooth halt poised above the dusty floorboards.

Armen saw her and jumped back, his hands forming the sign against the evil eye, but the visitor did not flinch.

"The time has come," she told him. "Cross the sea and find the sultan."

Chapter XII.

I told Godfrey not to besiege Nicaea without me," Saint-Gilles growled. "Did he listen?"

"My lord," the duke's messenger pleaded, "tell me what answer I should give the army of God."

Saint-Gilles glared at the man with his good eye. Behind him, the long column of the Provençal army had come to a weary halt. Horses rested their feet and nosed for grass, while foot-travellers downed their packs and slumped gratefully into the dust. All day, they'd stumbled along the ancient, overgrown mountain road that led from Nicomedia to Nicaea, with the mid-May sun beating down upon them. Now the sun was low, its slanting beams a golden herald of the approaching night.

"How far to the city?" Saint-Gilles snapped.

"A full day's march." Lord Galdemar looked predictably unhappy; he had already asked to make camp half an hour ago, pleading hunger. "We'd have to march all night, and probably fight in the morning."

The bishop shook his head. "We can't drive the people all night. Not after a day like this."

Saint-Gilles chewed on the news. According to the messenger, when Godfrey, Bohemond, and the other Franks reached Nicaea at the beginning of May, a week and a half ago, the city's sultan was in the Anatolian hinterlands waging war on another tribe of Turks. He had taken all his men with him, leaving a garrison of just one thousand men to man the city's walls. Massively outnumbered by the besieging Franks, the remaining Turks had naturally opened negotiations.

Yesterday, however, discussions were cut off. The Franks had waited to hear from the city, in vain, until a captured Turk had provided the reason. The sultan had returned and brought his army with him. Tomorrow morning he would launch a surprise attack from the south hills. The Franks had not yet surrounded the city completely, and the sultan clearly intended to fight his way into Nicaea with reinforcements through the unguarded south gate.

If the pilgrimage could not take Nicaea, the journey to Jerusalem would be unthinkably dangerous. Saint-Gilles pressed his lips together.

"We can do it," he said with some force. "Polignac!"

The standard-bearer kneed his mount closer. "Yes, my lord?"

"Call a rest. No one is to pitch camp. In three hours, we march to Nicaea."

There was a blank silence from those close enough to hear him speak. One of his vassals cleared his throat and said, "My lord, we've been marching all day—"

"What of it?" Saint-Gilles barked. "Did you think we were on a pleasure trip?"

In the mutinous silence, Adhemar cleared his throat and raised his voice. "Should these Turks think that the knights of God are to be trifled with?"

"Should we hang back from the battle while our comrades win glory?" Galdemar boomed. "To Nicaea! Tomorrow we break our lances on the Turks!"

That broke through their fatigue, reminding them of their purpose. Someone cheered. Polignac sounded the halt, then trotted along the column calling out Saint-Gilles' instructions.

Galdemar gave a rich chuckle. "You can give orders, Saint-Gilles, but you're terrible at putting the heart into a man. It's just as well you have us with you."

"To manipulate their passions? To prevent them counting the cost?"

The prospect of a full night's march had him feeling every bit as cranky as his men. Saint-Gilles dismounted onto aching legs. "Yes. You're indispensable."

The pilgrims marched all night, whipped to a punishing pace and held to it only by their lord's willpower and Galdemar's encouragement. Saint-Gilles watched the stragglers fall by the wayside and prayed that he would see them again, but he dared not leave a cohort of knights behind to protect his unwieldy flock of non-combatants. A large concentration of unarmed people might only attract the enemy's attention to an easy target. They must, as far as possible, stick together and draw all the Turks' wrath upon a well-defended body.

All night, their path wound downhill to flatter ground. As the sun rose and the road broadened, Saint-Gilles put his army in battle array. First a steel ram of knights, then the baggage and non-combatants in a column behind them. Finally, the foot soldiers, flanking the column on both sides.

He rode down the column and back again, pausing to speak to one rider.

"Is William in his crib?"

"Yes, my lord." Like many of the other ladies on pilgrimage, Elvira wore a mail shirt and conical helmet in case of attack, but a child of William's age was too young to bear armour. Instead, Saint-Gilles had had one of the carts fortified to provide safety.

"Make sure the child and his nurse remain undercover," he warned her. "And if the Turks attack, I want you in there too."

He changed his easy-going palfrey for a warhorse and returned to the front of the column. From then on he drove them at an even quicker pace. As the road descended and the morning light grew, the plain opened before them.

Nicaea was a fortress city, ringed by a many-towered double wall and defended on the west by the immense Askanian Lake. It lay in the midst of a green countryside threaded with mist, but even from a distance, the attackers' camp on Nicaea's north and east flanks was clear to see. The pilgrim armies scarred the land like leprosy. No wonder the Greeks believed whole nations had come from the west.

The Frankish camp was already awake. As the Provençals inched nearer, men waved and shouted in welcome. Saint-Gilles did not have to order his men to march faster; they had stopped yawning when the city came in view, and even the horses picked up their feet at the scent of water. Slowly, the great column trickled past the city, past the massive Frankish camp, and halted at last on the open ground before the city's south gate.

A flat shore to the west led to the lake itself, a vast expanse of silver fringed with dry brown reeds. The far shore was lost to view. To the north towered the mountains they had just crossed, their peaks shrouded in snow and cloud despite the approach of summer.

By this time, the city's defenders had seen them. Within the walls, trumpets sounded.

Saint-Gilles gave the signal to make camp and rallied his knights to face the south hills, not a moment too soon. Behind a bristling wall of steel, the baggage train lumbered to a halt and began to unpack.

The trumpets on the city walls finished their shrill alarm. Then there was silence.

Drums pounded in reply.

They thudded like a heartbeat in the south hills, as if the land itself had come to life. Saint-Gilles shook the weariness from his head and divided his forces. He hastily threw a line of footmen around the nascent camp to protect it, then mustered his knights in a tight body facing the hills.

"Stick together! Don't let them separate you!" he ordered.

"Do you hear the enemy?" Galdemar sang out. "Here he comes in high spirits, exulting in the certainty of victory and bringing ropes with which to lead us bound into Khorasan! But we are the men of Provence! Protected on all sides by the sign of the Cross, and glorious in earthly weapons! There will be hard fighting for the Turks today!"

The drums pounded on. Then a low rumble began and built to a mighty thunder, horses' hooves echoing in the hills. There was movement at the mouth of a valley, a flash of colour among the trees and scattered farmhouses.

The Turks were coming. They must have been lying in wait in the hills, watching for the moment at the end of his long march when his people were most vulnerable.

Saint-Gilles' head was buzzing from sleeplessness and he knew the men could feel no better, but the sound of the oncoming storm seemed to recall life to man and beast. Around him, horses fidgeted. One neighed its defiance, and another joined him. The line frayed as some plunged forward a pace or two, eager for glory...

"Stick together!" Saint-Gilles gripped his spear tighter, his hands beginning to sweat. His son and wife were behind him in the unfurling camp, his dearest friends at his right hand and his left. *"Hold the line!"*

In Constantinople after swearing his oath, Alexius told him how the Turkish horse archers would shred heavier troops with floods of arrows before administering the coup-de-grace via massed charge. Yet the sky remained clear. Saint-Gilles held his men in check until the Turkish charge was within two bowshots of his own lines. Horsemen all of them, their war-cry shrilling to the heavens, riding too fast to use their bows.

Did they know they were facing the best knights of Provence?

Alexius had told him that the Turks were masters of ambush. When charged, they would open ranks or even pretend to run—only to turn and close around their scattered enemy, or lead them into a trap.

Perhaps that was what was about to happen.

Only one way to find out. He shifted his sweaty hands inside his gloves, then signalled Polignac to let the leash slip.

The trumpet blared. With a sound like thunder and a shout rippling up and down the line like pelting water, the Franks surged forward.

"Saint Silvio for Toulouse!" Saint-Gilles howled, shaking his spear above his head. His warhorse broke into a slamming gallop and the ground between the two armies melted away. Their meeting rang like the hammer of a dragon slayer's forge. Saint-Gilles picked a target and struck down with his spear. His whole arm jarred as the blade punched through armour, flesh, and bone. As the body fell away behind him, his spear rose, and he sought a new target.

Chapter XIII.

Ayla felt numb. Beyond the line of footmen, the mounted Franks tore into the ranks of her people like a knife through silk. No—more like a hammer through butter. Their war-horses were little taller than the wiry steppe ponies ridden by the Turks, but they were still twice the size: barrel-chested, stumpy-legged, and completely unstoppable.

The Turks withered before them.

"Holy Virgin!" Next to her, Lukas stood transfixed.

"God have mercy," Ayla whispered.

As the Frankish knights crashed into her people, their foot soldiers and camp followers yelled encouragement. Buffeted by the noise, by the aggression and carnage, Ayla only wanted to shrink into the ground and disappear.

Lukas, however, looked as though he had received a revelation. Before they'd left Constantinople, he'd bought a stout iron-shod staff for the journey. Now, he threw it to Ayla and wheeled around.

"For the love of God, a spear! A sword! Does no one have something *sharp?*"

Within the baggage train was an enormous crowd of women, children and priests, those too sick and frail and elderly to fight. They only stared at Lukas in bemusement. As he doubled back on her, still pleading for someone to give him a weapon, she stuck the staff between his feet and tripped him facedown into the grass. "You're speaking Greek, wiseling," she said bitterly. "They don't understand you."

"Can't remember their word for *spear*. Give that back!" He grabbed the end of the staff and pulled himself to his feet. Before either of them could speak again, a burly Frankish foot soldier bore down on them, shouting and motioning them toward the frontline. Ayla didn't recognise the words, but the meaning was clear. As able-bodied men, they were expected to join the battle.

Ayla froze. Armen had never told her what to do if this happened.

Lukas yanked the staff from her grip. "Stay behind me." He grabbed her elbow and steered her toward the line. "I'll take care of you, all right?"

All night, they had trudged painfully behind the count's luggage cart at the very rear of the march. In the new shoes she had bought in Constantinople, Ayla's feet were a mass of blisters and she knew that Lukas' were not much better. Nevertheless, he shouldered his way to the very front of the line with his eyes blazing and his knuckles white on the oaken staff.

More chaos broke out to their left. Ayla wheeled around. Another cohort of Turks were flooding down from the hills to the east. The Franks camped east of Nicaea charged, yelling. They tucked their spears below mail-clad elbows, and with a rending crash, ploughed into the Turks. The two armies became one thunderous maelstrom, the Franks' long silver shirts flashing among the more colourful over-tunics worn by the Turks.

So many Franks. Her mouth was dry. Her first few days amongst the Provençal army had been bad enough, surrounded by rowdy Franks who dreamed loudly of getting revenge on her people for the wrongs done to their prophet. Somehow, she'd failed to realise that the Provençals did not represent even half their numbers.

Nor the destruction they could unleash in battle.

Ayla pulled her sling from her waist as her hand automatically dipped into the pouch at her belt. She had to do something for her people, but what? Surrounded by so many Franks eager for combat, it was enough of a battle just to breathe.

122

In front of her, Lukas still looked as though he was seeing a vision.

"They're *magnificent,*" he yelled. "Ayla! Did you ever see such fighters?"

The Franks had shredded the Turkish charge to a standstill. Now, the battlefield was a confused melee of men hacking, horses kicking, swords flashing.

"God have mercy, Greek," she choked. "Those are *my* people they're killing."

He stilled, then threw a look over his shoulder. "Oh, Saint George. You shouldn't be here. Get back to the carts."

The thought of being separated from him made her panic. "No! They'll just send me back. I'm staying with you."

He turned. "Tell them you're not a Christian and they'll let you—"

The line of foot rippled in expectation. Out of the chaos of the battle, three Turkish horsemen emerged galloping for the Frankish foot, swinging their swords into the sky. One looked her directly in the eye.

Realising what was happening, Lukas began to turn, but it was already too late. He was off-balance, unprepared. She would live, but he would die in front of her.

She didn't think. She could only act. Her sling thrummed and a stone punched through the Turkish rider's throat. His sword dropped, his hands went up, and then he was rolling on the grass while his riderless horse swerved aside and collided with another Turkish rider. Ayla paid no attention to the struggle on each side as the Franks repelled the half-hearted charge. She could only stare, sickened, at the Turkish rider's dying form. Blood bubbled from his throat and lips as he gasped for air, until finally he lay still.

Her stomach churned. *What did I do?* Her whole body felt numb. *One of my own people. How was he to know...*In front of her, Lukas seemed oblivious to what she had just done. He hadn't even seen her snap off that shot.

Slowly, Ayla realised the Turkish charge was giving way. The

Franks pushed them back toward the hills, gradually gaining momentum. The slow advance turned into a flood as the cursed Franks urged their massive lumbering animals into pursuit.

The battle was lost.

Ahead, Lukas let out a roar of victory and punched both fists into the air. He seemed to have gone mad, possessed by devils.

"Run," he yelled. "Run back to your own lands, you dogs!"

Cheers rolled down the line like the braying of wild animals. Then as the shouting died down, one of the skinny Frankish peasants nearby slapped Ayla on the back and pointed at the dead Turk, shouting to the others. The Franks around her began to cheer.

Lukas turned to her, his face changing as he looked from the Frank, to the corpse, to Ayla...

Ayla threw an elbow at the peasant, unsettling his grip on her shoulders. Through tight lips, she said to Lukas, "I killed one of my own people for you. Aren't you happy?"

"Ayla..." The triumphant frenzy had left him, but she couldn't stand to hear anything else.

"Don't speak to me." She wound her sling around her wrist and turned to shove her way back through the line, breaking through just in time to vomit all over her new shoes.

She crawled under a cart, wanting only to hide. Ayla had attacked people before. Turkish or Greek, it had never mattered to her in the past. She'd burned Captain Ahmed's boat to the waterline without a second thought. But she'd never killed a man fighting for a cause she believed in, certainly not to save the life of a sulky Greek patrician who'd got himself in the way and then let his mind wander.

She gritted her teeth in frustration. Why did he cheer the Franks? Didn't he know who she was? The Franks weren't *his* people any more than the Turks were the ones who'd taken his homeland all those centuries ago.

Why did he have to be a Christian?

Her anger ebbed, leaving her feeling drained. She shifted her aching head on the still-fresh turf and listlessly traced the joins in the cart-bed above her. *Use your brain, Ayla.* Lukas Bessarion was a Christian, a Greek, a gullible fool. Useful, but nothing more, and certainly not a *friend.* She squeezed her eyes shut, but it didn't keep her tears from escaping.

Under the cart, Ayla cried until sleep took her.

* * *

Ayla's head was still aching that night when she crept out of the tent which housed Count Raymond and his followers. She waited until Lukas' breathing beside her was as deep and even as everyone else's, then slid out of her blanket and picked up the bundle of personal belongings she used as a pillow.

Outside, the slivered moon shed only a faint light on the Provençal camp and in the aisles between the large, circular pavilions, it was almost impossible to see. Ayla navigated by feel and memory, careful not to blunder into the latrine trenches or horse pickets. She could only pray that nobody's dog would catch her scent and yell the camp into wakefulness.

She reached the west edge of the camp without incident. An expanse of flat pasture stretched along the south wall of the besieged town, sloping down to a white shore at the edge of the moon-gilded lake. It was difficult to see anything clearly except for the water. If she stayed close to the ground, it was likely that no watchman would see her pass.

She sank into a crouch.

Behind, a guy-rope thrummed as someone or something blundered into it.

Ayla whipped around. But she saw nothing.

Curse this feeble moon! There could be someone crouching almost close enough to touch, but she would never see him. Ayla closed her eyes and stilled, willing her thundering heart to slow.

No sound of movement, not even the rasp of crickets. No sound of breathing, not even her own. Still, anyone could keep quiet a few moments. Ayla opened her eyes, shifting her gaze a little to the right of where she thought she'd heard the sound. She counted a thousand heartbeats before relaxing.

Probably a scavenging animal.

Ayla slung her bundle onto her back. On the other side of the open ground was the lakeside, fringed here and there with slender trees. She sighted the clump of saplings she had chosen that afternoon and went toward it at a crouching run. She was sweating by the time she reached it, but still no alarm had sounded. Gratefully, she slid through the shadows and eased down the shore into the lake

It was good to feel cool water around her feet. Going slowly, Ayla pushed her way through a curtain of reeds. The water rose to her knees, then receded again as she climbed onto a soft, marshy islet hidden among the rushes.

First, she took the opportunity to wash herself in the shallow water where the islet dipped back into the lake, working her way through all the prayers she'd missed that day as she did so. Since joining the Franks, she hadn't had the opportunity to make the daily prayers as often as she should—the Frankish bishop had warned her that it might be dangerous to make a public display of her religion, and although she wasn't afraid of death, she didn't want to draw attention, either.

God must know why she hadn't been praying, but she was going to die five months from now and she couldn't afford to spoil her chances of heaven. She could only hope her hasty prayers would be enough.

Finally, she reached into her bag and pulled out Armen's bowl.

Made of solid silver, the bowl was etched deep with geometric patterns and calligraphy. Ayla had never owned anything so valuable in her life, and the knowledge that it was hidden at the end of her bag still troubled her sleep. She had suggested using a tin bowl as a substitute, but Armen insisted that silver was crucial.

She dipped the bowl full of water and kneeled down to peer at the shimmering surface. For a long while, it was only a bowl of water.

Just as she was beginning to wonder if she had forgotten some vital step, a yellow light began to glow within its depths, spreading through the water like a stain. Then Armen was looking at her, his face watery and vague through the ripples.

"Armen," she whispered. "Can you hear me?"

"You will address me as 'my lord'." His voice was muffled by the water but still audible.

Ayla resisted the temptation to roll her eyes. "Got to Nicaea, my lord, and camped on the south side of the city. Bad news: the Franks have already defeated a Turkish attack."

"I know," Armen said coldly. "I have been putting breakables out of the sultan's reach all afternoon."

"You're already with Kilij Arslan?"

"This will work best if you allow *me* to ask the questions. The Franks had knowledge of the attack. Do you know how?"

Ayla nodded. "They say the sultan's messenger to the garrison was captured."

"Foolish risk." Within the wavering water, Armen put a hand up to his chin. "What position have you gained within the camp?"

Since joining the Franks, she hadn't risked using the bowl. Armen had told her to wait until they reached Nicaea to begin contacting him; the Franks needed time to trust her.

"A Greek I know got me a job with their leader, Saint-Gilles, as a Turkish interpreter. I live with the rest of his household in his own tent."

"Excellent! You have the language?"

"A few words only, but I'm learning. What do you want me to do?"

"Watch and listen."

"What else? Aren't we going to destroy them?" In her eagerness, she shook ripples across the face of the bowl. By now, she'd learned that these people meant to take Syria, Palestine, all of it.

"No. You will report to me every night at the same hour. During the day, you'll do as the Franks tell you and seem as harmless as possible. That's all."

Ayla bit back her protests. Armen wouldn't have entrusted her with the silver bowl if he didn't think her information would be worth it.

"I can do that."

"If the Franks reach the East, then they will bring more Watchers with them. I want to know which of the Franks are Watchers and how they spend their time. I want to know everything that happens during the siege. Sooner or later, you will give us something we can use to destroy them." Armen paused. "One more thing. This Greek friend. Is he…dear to you?"

Ayla fought back an unexpected wave of panic to answer as smoothly as she could.

"He's nothing to me, my lord."

"One day," Armen said, "I may ask you to kill him."

The bottom dropped out of her stomach.

"This is war, and you are a soldier in it. Watch yourself. Do not let yourself feel."

She moistened her lips. "I'll bear that in mind, my lord."

"Tomorrow, same time." Armen lifted his fist, releasing a trickle of powder into the bowl. The light went out as if blown like a candle. Only a cloud in the water showed that Armen had been with her. Salt, she determined, putting a grain on her tongue.

Her head still ached. She stared listlessly into the water a moment longer, then dumped it back into the lake. Kill Lukas? The only friend she had?

If she had any sense, she'd pitch Armen's bowl into the lake and make her own way back to Antioch.

And die five months from now with nothing to show for herself.

God, why did you make the world like this?

She wiped the bowl dry and stowed it back into her bag before wading back through the reeds. She was halfway up the white shore, just inside the shadow of the trees, when some sense warned her that she was being watched.

The indistinct shape of a man sat at the top of the slope.

* * *

Lukas flinched as the girl hissed, dropping the bag and grabbing for the weapons at her belt.

"It's all right, Ayla. It's me." He called out just in time to stop her spring. "I—I didn't mean to frighten you."

There was a long, breathless silence. Lukas swallowed loudly. He should have known not to let her see him.

"What are you *doing* here?" she growled at last. "What did you see?"

"Nothing," he assured her. "I wasn't trying to watch you bathe. Just making sure no one bothered you."

"Cucumber!" She bent to pick up her bag. "Don't even think about doing that again. Could have gutted you. I got on just fine without you on the streets of Antioch for five years, thanks."

She stomped up the bank toward the camp. Lukas felt like kicking himself. He ought not to have let her see him. But now that she had, he had no excuses.

"I wanted to apologise about this morning," he blurted.

The words pulled her to a halt. "Why try? I know where your loyalties lie."

Watching the Franks destroy the heretics this morning had gone to his head like wine. They seemed to him like warrior angels, and he had not even thought of feeling sorry for the enemy until he saw Ayla's face as she ran away from the battle-line. Maybe he still didn't feel sorry for them.

But Ayla was all he had.

"Just because our people are at war, doesn't mean we have to be."

A hollow bravado rang in her voice. "They aren't *my* people.

Different tribe. Different sultan. Get it right."

"Ayla, these Franks are just a way home for me. But you? You're the only person I know I can trust. You..."

He sighed, feeling all the weight of his loneliness settling on his shoulders again. "You're the only family I have."

She turned toward him, just a dark shape in the night. Something about the catch of her breath made him wonder if she was crying, but her voice was still a growl.

"We're not family. I have no family. *Your* people, your precious Watchers saw to that. I was nine years old when they killed my father. Can *you* replace him? Can *you* bring back the lost years?"

For a moment, Lukas was speechless. *This* was why she hated the Watchers? "There must be some mistake," he said after a strained moment. "The Watchers I know—"

"A *mistake?*" Her voice became an enraged squeak. "Lukas, I saw it with my own eyes!"

The Watchers weren't supposed to *kill* people. They were supposed to be advocates and donors, not executioners.

His father's words that night at Oliveta, echoed in his mind: *We could have reconciled them through love, but we persecuted them through fear.*

Saint George, maybe it was not so incredible after all. Maybe the Watchers really were capable of murder.

Lukas swallowed. All this time he had thought of the Turks simply as heretics, as enemies. Now all he could see was a lonely girl and the father she had lost, and he knew how *that* felt.

"You must have loved him."

Her voice softened. "My father had a *gift,* Lukas. People would come to him with the most horrible wounds and diseases. After five minutes with him, they walked away, sound and healthy. I can't even begin to count how many lives he saved. That was the man your noble Watchers murdered in front of our eyes."

"I'm so sorry."

"Don't be. It's not your fault." Ayla sniffed loudly. "But these Franks…Lukas, do you realise that there are Watchers with them? Do you know what it means to look into their faces and wonder if one day they'll do the same to me?"

His Watcher's mark burned on his forearm. That was the other thing he had come to tell her. But now, at the moment of decision, he couldn't find the words.

In the weeks since he had washed up on the shores of this distant future, Ayla had become his one point of reference, his fixed star. Until today, he had almost forgotten that she was a heretic. He had forgotten she had as much reason to hate his people as he had to hate hers. Until today it had never occurred to him that she would choose her own people above him.

Ayla did not consider him an enemy, but if he told her about the Mark, that would change. There would be no chance of reconciliation. He did not know if he could bear that. Instead, he touched his arm to make sure that the sleeve covered it.

"You killed someone for my sake. I know what that costs a person." He swallowed, rubbing his hands on his tunic. "I can't imagine what it feels like to kill one of your own."

"It was instinct. Stupid of me. Won't happen again."

"I thought maybe we could do something for him. Give him the last rites of your people. If…if you want."

She did not answer at once and Lukas wondered if he had offended her again. But when she spoke, he realised that she really was crying this time.

"Yes. Please. I'd like that."

She put the bundle down again and got him to stand facing toward the morning's battle-field. Haltingly, she translated the words into Greek so that he could understand them.

"In the name of God, the infinitely Compassionate and Merciful. Praise be to God, Lord of all the worlds. The Compassionate, the Merciful, Ruler on the Day of Reckoning. You alone do we worship, and You alone do we

ask for help. Guide us on the straight path, the path of those who have received your grace; not the path of those who have brought down wrath, nor of those who wander astray. Amen."

"Amen," Lukas echoed, hoping that was right.

"God forgive him, God forgive him."

She paused. Lukas repeated the words after her.

"To God we belong, and to God we return."

"To God we belong, and to God we return," Lukas echoed. He waited for her to go on, but she seemed lost for words.

Instead, she reached out and touched his hand.

"Thank you," she said gently.

As they stole back to the camp, Lukas still felt the Watcher's Mark burning on his skin like a brand. Once they reached Syria, he could say goodbye to Ayla and go in search of the Syrian Watchers. Until then, he would keep his Mark covered. Ayla need never know.

Chapter XIV.

Saint-Gilles looked Count Baldwin of Boulogne up and down, trying to get the man's measure. Like his brother, Duke Godfrey, Baldwin was tall and fair-haired, but his eyes were almost dark enough to be black. Saint-Gilles found the contrast disconcerting. In the lamp lit tent, Saint-Gilles could see his own reflection in those shadowed eyes—and nothing else.

So this was the man who had incited the docile Godfrey to attack Constantinople.

"Your brother won't be joining us, count?" Saint-Gilles glanced around the tent, noting that apart from a single attendant, the place was empty.

"Not tonight." The count gave a slanted smile. "My brother…may take some convincing on this."

Saint-Gilles was mystified, but chose not to show it. Behind, another figure shouldered through the flap.

"Phew!" Bohemond uncloaked noisily. "It's too warm for this cloak-and-dagger business. Why the secrecy, count?"

Baldwin came forward with a cup of wine for each of them. His black eyes glittered. "What I have to show you may change the whole course of this pilgrimage. I wanted to sound out the two of you alone."

"Sounds portentous." Bohemond wafted the wine under his nose and his eyes gleamed appreciatively. "Samian muscat! No finer vintage anywhere. You honour us, count."

Baldwin refused to be distracted. "You must be wondering why I

133

asked you to come, and no others. It's simple. The three of us share something in common. All of us have defied Alexius and lived." He paused. "What if I told you that your oaths were already absolved?"

Saint-Gilles tightened his lips. "By whom?"

Baldwin strode to the flap of the tent.

"By heaven, my lord. We have received visions." He yanked the flap back with something like a juggler's flourish. The man who entered at the count's signal looked and smelled as if he had never seen the inside of a proper dwelling-place, let alone a bath-house. A barefooted, half-starved ascetic. Saint-Gilles gave a non-committal grunt, and wished the bishop was with him. Adhemar was wiser than himself when it came to vagrant prophets.

Beside him, Bohemond chuckled.

Baldwin waved at them. "Tell the counts what you told me, Roger."

Stringy hair hung in the man's eyes, but he glared at Bohemond.

"I will not speak to scoffers. My lady's words are not for him."

Baldwin purpled. "You'll speak as I bid you, creature."

"Wait, wait." Bohemond grinned, clearly enjoying himself. "Let us test the prophet first. Let him tell me how many coins I have in my purse here."

There was silence. Saint-Gilles watched the ascetic's face. Maybe he could do without Adhemar, after all. Bohemond seemed more than capable of unmasking a fraud.

The man straightened. "Twelve, all gold stamped with the emperor's image."

For a breath, Bohemond stared. "Huh."

"Are you satisfied?" Baldwin folded his arms.

Bohemond put down his cup. "I beg your pardon, count. I am all attention."

Roger the ascetic looked at them with a gleam of triumph. "I have received visions. Three times I have been visited by a messenger of heavenly light. Three times she gave me a message for the princes. You have sinned! In three weeks of siege Nicaea has not fallen because you have made an alliance with the Greek heretics. Have you not travelled east to avenge Christ's death on the unbelievers? Separate yourselves from the wretched Greeks, and you will triumph!"

"Did this messenger identify herself?" Saint-Gilles asked.

"I tell you she was a heavenly angel. She cried, *Woe, woe to the—*"

"Just a moment." Saint-Gilles leaned forward. "It's important to verify these things. What made you think she was an angel? Can you describe her?"

"She was surrounded by light. More lovely than any mortal woman. And her wings were like an eagle's, black as ebony."

"I've never heard of an angel having black wings." His scalp prickled. "And Adhemar tells me that the lord Pope considers the Greeks to be brothers, not heretics."

"What are you suggesting?" Baldwin's jaw bulged stubbornly. "The angel says that if we sever ourselves from the Greeks, we might become mighty lords in the east."

"Indeed?" Bohemond lifted an eyebrow.

That was all it took to set the prophet off again. "Indeed, you scoffers! Obey my words, and you will receive lands and honours in Syria, in Khorasan, and in Persia! Disobey, and you will perish!"

Saint-Gilles stood up. "I'd be happy to discuss this at more length with Bishop Adhemar, but I don't like it." Brusque words, but the man would go on and on if he was encouraged. "We could end up at war with Alexius if we followed this advice. I find it hard to believe that *that* is God's will. It's possible this man needs a few square meals, not obedience."

The ascetic would have responded, but Baldwin silenced him with a gesture. He looked at Bohemond. "And you, count?"

The Norman count gave a lazy chuckle and stood. "My days of terrorising the Greeks are at an end. I made my oath to Alexius with all good faith and so far I've profited by it. I'm with Saint-Gilles. You should give this man a feed and see if his…condition improves."

Baldwin's black eyes narrowed. "Very well, but don't forget what

135

you heard tonight. We could all be emperors."

"Thank you, my lord. I won't forget." The words were solemn, but laughter danced in Bohemond's eyes.

Outside Count Baldwin's portion of the camp, Saint-Gilles looked at Bohemond. *"We could all be emperors,* indeed! I don't trust that young man."

Bohemond laughed. "A *child* would hide his ambition better."

"Our vow is to reach Jerusalem, our intent to aid Holy Church in the east." Saint-Gilles narrowed his gaze on Bohemond. *"Any* prince who wants to do things differently will have to deal with me."

"And with me," Bohemond added soothingly. "As for this prophet, I can get him away from Baldwin easily enough." The count unbuckled his purse from his belt and tossed it into the hands of his attendant, a silent Norman manservant. "Take that to the vagrant seer named Roger, who we met in Boulogne's tent just now. Tell him it's his if he'll change his allegiance and follow me instead. Do whatever it takes."

Was Bohemond was more concerned to stifle Baldwin's ambition—or to further his own? Saint-Gilles permitted himself a tight-lipped smile. Either way, he must be careful not to underestimate the Norman count. Bohemond, like Alexius, was a master of the devious politics of the east, where wars were fought as much with wits as with weapons.

"A black-winged angel," Saint-Gilles muttered as Bohemond's servant retreated into the camp. "What do you make of that, count?"

Bohemond shrugged. "What should I make of it? I'm a count, not a theologian."

They said farewell and parted, Bohemond toward his camp north of the city, Saint-Gilles toward the south. All the way back to his tent, he walked with his thumbs stuck in his belt, head bowed.

Was something evil at work in God's army? Saint-Gilles shook his head. *Impossible.* It could only be hunger and delirium.

Yet before he slept, he lit a taper in the chapel tent and prayed for the army's protection.

Chapter XV.

Lukas was scowling at his book when one of the squires lumbered through the flap of the bishop's tent, grabbed his steel helmet, and jammed it onto his head.

No trumpets had blown, and there was little sound in the Frankish camp but the steady thudding of siege engines. Evidently they were not under attack.

Which meant that something else was afoot.

Lukas slammed the book shut. It was a Frankish psalter which the bishop had loaned to him in an attempt to improve his grasp of the language, and for the last hour it had been scrambling his brain. "Bertrand! Where are you going?"

Bertrand was a squire of the bishop's, a tall, hulking young kinsman of the Monteil family who cared for the bishop's armour and weapons and fought as part of his bodyguard.

By now Lukas knew that Adhemar himself rarely elected to fight, but like many of the Frankish non-combatants, even churchmen and ladies, he had a knight's training and was a competent leader in battle. Just another of the strange Frankish ways. Barbaric, some of the Greeks called it. Lukas didn't know about that. He would rather be victorious than civilised. And the Franks! What warriors they were!

Bertrand fitted his kite-shaped shield over his shoulder, tightening the leather strap. "Some of the young men are having a—a passage of arms." He had switched from Latin to Frankish for the last few words. "With the North Franks."

"A passage of arms?" Lukas was unfamiliar with the idiom.

"A friendly fight. To keep us in training."

Lukas jumped up so quickly he almost knocked the bench over. "There is going to be training? May I come?"

For days now, he had spent every spare moment haunting the Frankish squires and blacksmiths, constantly asking *why* and getting underfoot. He wanted to know how they made their weapons, how they trained their hoses, how they repaired their armour. But most of all, he wanted to know how they fought.

He wanted to be ready if—*when*—Khalil came for him.

Already on his way out the door, Bertrand paused. "The lord count doesn't have work for you?"

Lukas might have liked the squire better if he was not constantly reminding him of his lower rank. "This *is* my work. The more time I spend talking to your Frankish people the better I can translate for the count."

Bertrand shrugged and resettled his helmet so that the nose-piece lined up between his eyes.

"All right. You won't find it easy speaking Frankish with that lot, though. The North French dialects are hard for the best of us to understand."

Outside, the June sun dazzled Lukas for a few seconds before everything swam back into its proper place. A month ago, when they'd arrived, the fields surrounding Nicaea were green with spring growth. Now the grass was hard and brown. A permanent dust-cloud hung over the Frankish camp, stirred up by innumerable feet.

Yet despite their long assault, the city seemed no closer to falling and the road to Syria was still closed. With the Askanian Lake washing Nicaea's western walls, the garrison was still able to receive supplies and reinforcements while it waited for its sultan to return.

As always, Lukas spared the city's massive wall a sad glance. Studded with towers, it was clearly visible beyond the sprawl of the camp. By now its stone was scarred black from fire and white from missiles, but it stood firm despite constant bombardment. From the battlements where the fighting had been most fierce hung strings of Frankish corpses, dragged from the moat with long, sharp hooks and displayed, rotting and crow-speckled, as a defiance to the besieging army.

It was in this city that the Nicaean creed was written when the Arian heresy was rebuked. How could a city like this fall into the hands of the heretics? Had its Watchers completely failed in their task?

He had to return to his own time, to find a way to prevent these terrible losses before they occurred. He had to get back to Syria. But to open the road, Nicaea must fall.

As he followed Bertrand past Count Raymond's tent, Ayla came into view carrying a bundle of firewood. She threw it down by the tent's entrance, wiping her hands on her trousers, and watched him and Bertrand wordlessly.

Since that first night by the lake, Ayla had become a silent, hard-working presence in the camp. Each night she slipped away to the lake to bathe. Each night at Vigils, between the greater and lesser sleep, he watched for her return. It was only with him that she seemed to be herself, given to talking and laughing. Lukas knew why, without having to ask. As reluctant as she was to admit it, the Franks frightened her.

"Kismet!" he called. "We're going to watch the sparring. Do you want to come?"

As far as the count and his followers knew, Ayla was still a Turkish boy named Kismet. Lukas wondered if they were blind. Her hair had grown a little in the past month, she always kept scrupulously clean, and in the count's service, she was eating well enough to put on some weight. She looked prettier each time he saw her. He did his best not to stare openly as the two of them followed Bertrand to a level area east of the city.

On its border a crowd of idlers were gathered. Peasants and

servants lolled on the grass, their heads shaded with hoods, straw hats, and turbans, their chatter a cacophony of tongues. Frankish, German, English, Greek, Armenian—it was like the Tower of Babel. But above the commotion rose the bell-like ringing of swords and the thud of hooves as the knights in the field sparred each other or tilted at quintains.

Bertrand skirted the field to a spreading sycamore maple. In the black shade beneath it sat a company of young Franks among a litter of weapons, shields, food and drink.

"Bertrand!"

Lukas recalled seeing the knight who had spoken in Count Raymond's company. He looked the squire up and down, laughing.

"Now for the honour of the Provençals, welcome. These men of Blois don't stand a *chance*."

Blois. Lukas mentally sifted through the letters he had translated, looking for connections. Count Stephen of Blois had arrived with Duke Robert of Normandy at the beginning of June, the final princes to join the pilgrimage. These men must be among his followers.

One of the North Franks laughed. "Pride is a sin, my friend, and goes before a fall. We still have Evrard in the field." He pointed at two warriors nearby, busy sparring with sword and shield. Back and forth they went, the sun gleaming off their mail shirts like the scales of a snake.

Lukas chose a place to sit on the dappled border between shade and sun, and Ayla plopped down beside him. "I've got one," she announced. "It goes like this: *I have a bagful of walnuts I can never finish counting.*"

In the last few days, they had begun playing riddles to pass the time. Ayla was a never-ending fount of them. Lukas groaned, wishing he had never asked about Turkish games.

"Walnuts?"

"Remember, if you go without answering for three days then you have to spend a whole day clucking like a chicken."

According to Ayla, silly forfeits were the most important part of the game, although Lukas was not entirely sure he believed her. He brushed a fly from his forehead.

"Your riddles are so hard, though. Why are walnuts so important to you, anyway? What do Turkish people think about when they see walnuts? Do you have legends about walnuts? How can I guess a riddle with walnuts in it when I don't know what walnuts *mean* to you?"

"Oh." Ayla tapped her mouth with a forefinger. "Good point. Well, for my people, walnuts are a medium-sized nut resembling the brain, which is difficult to get out of its shell—"

"You're a walnut." Lukas elbowed her in the ribs, not too hard.

"Ow!" She was laughing. "Come on. It's easy. I'll give you a hint."

"Don't you dare." Lukas frowned at the sparring knights, and chewed his lower lip. *A bagful of walnuts I can never finish counting...* He frowned. "Wait a minute, you never answered my last riddle! And it's been three days!"

"Ah, curse it. You remembered."

"You *cheated.*"

She was still laughing. "Yeh, so? I forgot the riddle."

"So did I." Lukas frowned. "No, it's coming back. *A tiny animal, I am not edible; my name consists of three letters only; should you take away the first of my letters, I'd be a large one, and ready for eating.*"

"God have mercy. That is the most *ridiculously* Greek riddle in the world."

"Ah, but you've still got till Compline to answer it. After that...the chicken."

"Bully." She fell silent, occasionally whispering under her breath.

Lukas watched the Frankish knights, until her whispers died away and he sensed that she was watching him. These days he was always acutely aware of Ayla, as if she was tied to him by an invisible thread. He glanced sideways. As he caught her eye, he saw her teeth clamp down on the soft lower lip.

He wondered what it would be like to kiss her.

Saint George! Where did a thought like that come from? She was—she was his friend, yes, but a *heretic*.

He riveted his gaze on the knights again. *Pay attention, Lukas. You have to learn from these people, remember?*

Ayla spoke softly. "You wish you were out there with them."

He glanced back at her and wished he hadn't. It was not just the hot summer day—his cheeks were afire. "If I had my rights, I would be. I'm not a scholar, I'm a noble. I was born to fight, not to pore over books and bandy words."

"Try telling the count that." Ayla snickered.

"I tried to tell Bishop Adhemar."

The bishop had not been impressed. *Anyone can destroy things,* he had said, *but only a man of peace can build the future. We need interpreters, not more crow fodder.*

"He didn't understand," Lukas summarised.

"Yeh." Ayla shrugged. "So you'll have to wait till you get back home to kill some heretics, right?"

"Saints, Ayla!"

"Cook took me with him to buy grain today," she said abruptly, before he could go on, and Lukas sensed that the change of subject was the closest thing he would get to an apology. She dug into the turf with her fingers. "Something was happening in the north camp."

Count Bohemond and his Normans were encamped north of the city, right near the market where Greek merchants kept the Franks supplied with food. Lukas had run errands there himself. "Oh yes?"

She slid him an empty glance. "They were hanging a girl."

"What for?"

"Taking a Turkish lover."

"A Frankish girl?"

"Yeh."

He knit his eyebrows, trying to guess why she would bring this up. "Are you afraid?"

"Just curious. I didn't know you Christians did that too."

"Did what?"

"Killed girls, for honour. Even if it's not their fault."

"I…" Lukas thought about it for a moment. "I don't think it's about honour, for us."

She shot him an inquiring look.

"For us it's about…pleasing God, I think. If we have fornication and infidelity in the camp, we'll lose our battles like the Jews of old. So the sins are purged out, and everyone feels safe."

"Do you think you can predict God's actions like that, then?"

"Well, it's about justice, isn't it? God following his own rules."

She lifted an eyebrow. "And this is one of God's rules?"

"I don't know." Lukas looked down at his hands. "My father was a judge. He used to say there were many verdicts given in God's name that were nowhere justified by his law. He used to say it was the duty of—"

Of Watchers, he almost said. It was the duty of Watchers to safeguard holy justice. But at that moment there was a shout from the knights sitting under the tree. At the same instant, a squire kneeling at the edge of the field whistled through his fingers. Cheers and gleeful applause mingled with hoots and groans.

"Evrard! Evrard! Le Puiset!" chanted the North French.

On the field, one of the knights lay in the dust, his sword thrown from his grasp and the other knight's sword tickling his nose. Lukas hissed in annoyance. He had only looked away for a moment, but he'd missed the victorious knight's manoeuver.

This was ridiculous. How was he going to learn by watching? He needed someone to teach him the Franks' way of fighting.

Under the sycamore tree, Bertrand readjusted his helmet and replaced his defeated compatriot on the field opposite the victorious Evrard. The cheers hushed as the defeated Provençal flopped down in the shade, and the fighting began again.

Ayla rubbed her hands gleefully. "Bertrand's going to win this one."

Next to the bishop's gigantic squire, the knight Evrard seemed slender as a twig. "The North Frank may not be strong, but he's quick," Lukas pointed out.

"But it's his second fight at least," Ayla pointed out. "Must be tiring. Basic scrapping."

For a while they watched the fight in silence, but Lukas couldn't seem to focus on the combat.

"I'm sorry you had to see that. I'm sorry you have to fear for your life."

Ayla did not look at him. "I don't," she said very quietly. "I believe my death will mean something."

Out on the field, her prediction came true. Bertrand made a sudden movement, so fast Lukas saw only the blinding flash of his blade. The North Frank stumbled and Bertrand lunged for him, hefting his sword for the *coup-de-grace*. The umpire whistled shrilly.

The Provençals yelled and hooted.

"Your turn, Robert!" someone called, and one of the North Franks stood up, pulling a leather hood over his head and settling his helmet atop it. On the field, the fallen man rolled to his feet and pulled off his helmet and steel coif. Under a damp thatch of fair hair, the Frank's gaunt and bony face was shiny with effort.

"Well struck," he gasped, holding out a hand to Bertrand. "I don't believe I know you, sir knight."

Bertrand did not take the hand. Instead, he stepped back and bowed. "Bertrand Monteil, squire to the bishop of le Puy."

The smile on Evrard's face froze. "Squire," he repeated.

"Ooooohh," jeered some of the Provençals in chorus. Even the North Franks laughed.

The knight could not possibly flush any redder. Abruptly he turned his back on Bertrand and stalked back into the shade.

"Begging for mercy, are we?" called one of the Provençals.

"It's the heat," Evrard said stiffly. "I'm counting on you to avenge me, Robert."

The North Frank laughed and headed onto the field.

Unlike the other men scattered in the shade, the defeated knight wore not only a shirt of mail to protect his body, but also mailed leggings, mitts, and coif. Much wealthier than the others, Lukas decided, as the other knights shuffled deferentially out of his way. Maybe that's why he was so touchy about his dignity.

As he flopped down onto the dry grass, Evrard caught Lukas' eye. "Holy Stephen, it's hot. Get me something to drink, fellow."

Just like that, his clothing and lack of weapons had proclaimed him a servant. And just like that, this Frankish knight could order him around.

By rights, he should be one of them. Not that it was any good trying to convince them of it. At home, people *knew* the name Bessarion. It was not simply the name of a half forgotten heretic, but a guarantee of honour and nobility. But this was not home. Lukas got up, picked up a water-skin, and handed it to the knight.

"Here, my lord."

Evrard glared at him. "Holy Virgin! Who taught *you* your manners, boy?" The water-skin hit Lukas in the chest. "Find me a cup and try again."

Lukas stiffened. "Don't you have your own servants, sir?"

By this time all the knights were looking at them in various stages of bemusement. To his relief, Evrard decided to give up.

"Imbecile," he muttered, reaching out and yanking the water-skin from Lukas' hands again. He poured the water straight down his throat, and made a face. "Tastes like lake and leather," he remarked to his friends. "Haven't we any ale left? Small beer? Wine?"

"No, it's all gone," a North Frank said.

"Aren't these Greeks supposed to be supplying us?"

There was a harsh *clank* from the field as the knight named Robert buffeted Bertrand's helmet and knocked it flying. The umpire whistled. Bertrand retreated, mopping his forehead with a sleeve, and another of the Provençals got up to face Robert.

"I thought Count Stephen bought a whole cartload of wine last week," Evrard said.

"There's good water in the lake here, so he said to leave it till the water gets scarce in the desert. Don't want to get the bloody flux, do you?"

A grimace. "Trust me, when I came to suffer for the love of Christ in this hellish country, I counted on getting the bloody flux. Didn't count on being roasted alive in my armour, though."

The other knights laughed. Lukas smiled mockingly, and spoke to Bertrand in Latin: "This man complains too much. I do not think he will live long in Palestine."

Bertrand gave an incredulous snort of laughter.

Then, to Lukas' horror, the knight rose up on his elbow and glared daggers at him. "I'm sorry," he said in fluent Latin, "did you speak?"

Devil take it.

But Lukas wouldn't back down now. "Well, it's the truth. I know Judaea. If you can't bear the sun this far north, how will you survive in Jerusalem?"

Evrard sat up. His face was still red, this time from anger which drew the skin tightly across his cheekbones. "Who the hell are *you?*"

"I am a knight like you." He was, too. He was a member of the equestrian class. As noble as anyone else here.

He had never seen anyone so taken aback as the North Frank. For an instant, the man looked shocked. It was unpardonable, of course, to treat a fellow knight like a servant.

But before anyone else could say something, Bertrand spoke. "He's just Count Raymond's Greek interpreter, my lord."

"I *am* a knight!" Lukas jumped to his feet. "Try me! Give me something to fight with, and we'll see who stands the sun longest!"

Some of the knights could evidently follow enough of the Latin to understand his challenge. Hungry for new entertainment, some of them began to cheer: "Fight! Fight!"

One of the North Franks held up a sword. "Here, Greek!"

Triumph washed through him as he put out his hand for the weapon.

But Evrard snapped out in his own language. "Imbeciles!" He let out a stream of North Frankish too rapid for Lukas to understand and silenced all of them. Then, he turned scornfully to Bertrand. "Take this fellow away, Monteil, since he can't conduct himself properly."

"My lord, forgive me." Bertrand gripped Lukas by the arm. "Time to go, Greek."

Lukas looked at the knight who'd offered him a sword. Suddenly, this wasn't a game anymore. He *was* of the knightly class. If he could prove it, then maybe they would give him real weapons. Maybe they would teach him. Maybe this was why God sent him here—to learn what he needed to save his people.

It was more than that. It was as stupid as wanting to kiss Ayla, but he wanted to be their friend. Their sword-brother.

He spoke in slow, careful Frankish. "Why? Is this man afraid to fight me?"

If he didn't already have everyone's attention, he had it now. There were a few seconds of utter silence. Then the knight peeled himself off the ground and rose slowly to his feet.

"Saints *above!*" he roared. "I'll beat you myself for that!"

Bertrand only hesitated a moment. Then he stepped back, lifting his hands. "He asked for it, count."

Count? The bottom fell out of Lukas' stomach.

The Frank stepped forward, toe to toe with him. Lukas swallowed, realising that the gauntness of Count Evrard's face owed more to his natural features than his physical condition. The man he had taken for a simple knight was four inches, several pounds' worth of muscle, and maybe five years' worth of experience ahead of him. Lukas gulped, aware that he was not wearing any kind of protection.

The count suddenly drew back his fist to strike and Lukas could not help flinching.

He dropped his fist with a contemptuous laugh. "Apologise, and

I'll let you go without hitting you."

There were sniggers from the other knights. Lukas felt a wave of heat rush to his face. Having deliberately insulted the count, he must now be humiliated to restore his dignity.

"Do it, Greek," Bertrand said. "For heaven's sake..."

He was a fool. He was such a fool.

The count lifted his fist again. "You're out of time, Greek."

"All right. I take it back!"

"In Frankish."

Lukas fumbled through the words. They were all laughing at him. With a grim, satisfied smile the count lowered his hand and turned away. "The coward can't even take a blow," he told the others.

"Effeminate Greeks," someone laughed.

Lukas' face heated again, and he clenched his fists. But before he could say a word, Bertrand grabbed him by the arm and dragged him away from the sycamore tree.

"Let go of me!" Lukas hissed, struggling uselessly to get free. "I want him to hit me!"

"Don't be a fool!" The big squire yanked Lukas around to face him, white-lipped and furious. "Are you happy? Picking fights with your betters! Is this how you repay the lord count's charity?"

"I only wanted to spar with him! I'll show him who's effeminate!"

"Count Raymond took you off the *streets,* Greek. He gave you every *single* stitch you wear. Do you realise that there are people starving in this camp?" A shake. "Do you?"

"That arrogant toad wouldn't even shake hands with you! Let him hit me! I'll show him what I'm made of!"

Bertrand's lip curled. "All right."

Pain exploded along his jawline and Lukas staggered to the ground.

He rolled to his elbow with something akin to a whimper, putting a hand to his aching jaw. Bertrand stepped back, unclenching his fist. Next to the squire, Ayla grimaced in sympathy, but made no move to help him.

"I know my station." Bertrand spoke very softly. "I'm not going to fight my superiors to change it, and neither should you. You owe every bite in your mouth to the count's good favour, and unless you want to starve, you should remember that everything you do reflects on him."

This time, the words got through to him. His rage seeped away, replaced by a cold fear. Count Raymond was his only chance of getting back to Syria and finding the answers he needed.

"I'm sorry," he growled.

"*Sorry* isn't going to help you. Not unless you're willing to accept what you are." Bertrand did not wait to hear more. He slung his shield over his shoulder, then turned his back on them, heading back toward the Provençal camp.

Lukas took Ayla's hand and reeled muzzily to his feet. "But I'm *not* a servant."

He was perplexed when she responded with a laugh. "You got to stop this, Lukas. Might as well bang your head on that wall."

She jerked a thumb toward the city.

"I just want to help my people," he said with a catch in his voice.

"You will," she said simply. "But you got to stop whining about what you deserve, all right? They don't know who you were. They just know what you *are*. So far all they've seen is a lily of the valley. Pretty but useless."

Cucumber, whiny iris, and now lily of the valley. "I wish you'd stop comparing me to plants."

"Then you better stop acting like one." She laughed, poked him in the chest with a forefinger. "Better prove yourself first."

Against his will, she drew a smile from him. *Kiss her,* said part of his mind that was becoming harder to ignore. Did she read the look on his face?

Ayla backed away from him. "Think about it. I've got firewood to cut and riddles to solve." She hurried off in Bertrand's wake.

Chapter XVI.

Above Ayla, the cold stars swam in an infinitely deep blue sea, drawing off the heat of day.

She had crept out of the Frankish camp many times before, but still a nervous sweat trickled down her body as she moved at a crouch among the long grasses and clumps of saplings lining the lakeshore. For one thing, she was actively disobeying Armen's orders. For another, the long summer dusk was not yet dark enough to fully hide her. If any of the Franks were making an evening trip to the lake, whether for water or to bathe, they would certainly see her.

She refused to listen to her fears, instead focusing on the next dash—a long, open stretch of grass leading down toward the city walls. She'd have to cover a bowshot's length without anyone from the Frankish camp seeing her. Briefly, she considered lying down in the grass and waiting until the night became dark enough to hide her.

But an hour from now it might already be too late. She wasn't here to stay safe, Ayla reminded herself. She was here to help her people fight. No matter what Armen wanted. Heart already pumping, she rose to her toes and fingers, crouching like a runner at the start of a race.

Go.

She was a deer. She was a hound. She was a bird. For a moment all she could feel was the exhilaration of speed. Her bare feet made barely a whisper in the dry grass. Dark mounds littered the grass around her, rank with the smell of blood: Frankish men and horses that had fallen in the day's fighting. She must have covered a quarter of the distance, and no challenge from the Frankish campfires. Half, and no sound. Two-thirds, and...

The air hissed and an arrow sprouted from the ground at her feet. Ayla gasped, twisted in the air, and hit the ground hard, rolling into the smallest target she could manage. Another arrow hit inches away from her head.

"Who's there?" someone called from the wall above her. The voice was Turkish.

Mingled relief and shock thudded through her, and for a moment, Ayla couldn't speak.

"Answer, or we shoot!"

"Friend! I'm a friend," she called back, as softly as she dared. The Frankish siege-engines were not so far away, and even a soft sound carried well.

Her Turkish was her passport. "Come up to the water gate," the voice ordered.

Where the walls of Nicaea kissed the lake, an unwatched gate led onto a narrow strip of shore where boats came and went at spindly jetties. Ayla lay where she was for a moment, thinking. What if she did present herself at the gate? Most likely she would be ordered within the walls to speak to the garrison commander. They might even refuse to let her out again. She was defying Armen by coming at all, but she couldn't imagine what he would say if she let herself get shut into Nicaea.

Besides, in another hour she was supposed to report to him.

She got up and bolted into the shadow of Nicaea's wall, nearly tumbling into the stagnant stream that filled its fosse. "Hey! Are you still there?"

"I told you, proceed to the water gate," the voice repeated officiously.

"I can't. But you have to know something. The Franks have been undermining your citadel. If you don't believe me, just wait and see.

152

They're going to fire the mine tonight and attack at first light."

"How do you know this?"

She knew because Lukas was terrible at keeping secrets. Count Raymond had spent most of the day and countless lives manoeuvering his siege machine—a big, tortoise-shaped shelter—up to the foot of Nicaea's wall. While the Franks put on a show of storming the wall, their sappers were digging into the citadel's foundation, shoring up the passage with huge beams of wood. Hours ago, the count had sent Lukas to inform the other Frankish princes of what was going on, summoning them to prepare a dawn attack once the wall was breached.

Lukas, of course, was eager to see the city fall. Each day Nicaea stood was one more day's delay in the journey to Syria. He'd returned to the Provençal camp this afternoon hoping for a quick victory. It wasn't difficult to wheedle the information out of him.

But it felt too much like betrayal.

"Don't worry about how I know it, just *tell* someone," Ayla snapped. "They might already have set the fire."

More voices hummed on the walls. It sounded as if someone was arguing with the officious voice. Whether they took her warning seriously or not, she'd done her best. Ayla wheeled around, caught her breath, and dashed back for the shore.

It was getting darker now. Overhead, the stars provided little light and the waning moon had not yet risen. Ayla was halfway across the grass when something grabbed her ankle and she fell, helplessly, onto a soft body that expelled a gust of foul air.

Ayla yelped in terror. For a ghastly few moments, it was as if the thing was clinging to her, embracing her. Every ghost story, every nightmare she'd ever had rioted through her brain as she fought herself free.

Then a hand fastened on her shoulders and yanked her to her feet. Someone hissed a question in a language she only half understood.

Franks.

Four dark shapes surrounded her. Ayla reached for her knife, but she already knew it was useless—the Franks were twice her size and one of them had an unbreakable grip on the scruff of her neck. Belatedly, her mind absorbed their words.

Her name. They wanted to know her name.

"Bertrand," she lied. It didn't matter if they believed her or not, just so long as they didn't find out that she was Turkish.

"Bertrand, hm? Who do you belong to?"

"No one."

"Come on, everyone belongs to someone. Who's your lord?"

"None of your business."

"Quit it," someone else put in. "We can't stand here till the Turks start shooting at us."

The hand at the back of her neck gave her a shake, then pulled her to one side. "You ought to be ashamed of yourself, stealing from men who've died for the name of Christ. Come on, make yourself useful. You can pull the cart."

He let go of her neck and guided her hands to the wooden shaft of a hand-cart. Ayla scented blood and ordure, and immediately understood. These men were here to collect their dead for burial under cover of night. Thankfully, they'd taken her for a looter, not a spy.

As Ayla helped drag the cart across the bumpy field, the Franks communicated in whispers and only when necessary. Some of the bodies they came across were of horses or livestock that had wandered into the kill zone that surrounded Nicaea, but those were left to be collected either by their owners or by looters. One by one, the human corpses were heaved onto the cart.

Ayla's back was aching by the time one of them whispered, "That's it for this side. Let's get back to camp."

The five of them bent their backs to the cart. Ayla slipped to a rear corner, where she hoped she would be overlooked. As the city wall faded into the darkness behind them, one of the Franks let out a nervous chuckle.

"Holy Virgin, Simon! I thought you were grabbing for a ghost back there."

"Huh! I knew it was a looter. Ghosts don't make footsteps."

That set them all off telling ghost stories. They had seen pale lights in the burial-grounds at night. They knew someone who had seen a dead squire walking through the camp three days after he'd been buried. They knew someone who knew someone who had heard the Devil and the Archangel Michael rolling dice for the soul of Raimbold the Bastard.

Ayla was moving her lips, reciting her litany against the djinn and nearly ready to scream when one of them spoke again.

"Here's something I saw with my own eyes: Three nights ago, I saw a woman walking around the walls of Nicaea and singing. A beautiful woman, you understand? But there were black feathers growing out of her skin. When I called out, she turned into a bird and flew away. Saint Silvio! I thought she was going to peck out my eyes."

The litany died on Ayla's lips. *Not just any birds. A vulture.*

It is Her.

She's here.

She forced back the panic. It was full dark now, and they were almost in the camp. Ayla let go of her corner of the cart, lagged behind the others, then darted for the tents.

"Oi!" A hand fastened on her sleeve, yanking her to a stop. "Where are you sneaking off to?"

"Let go of me!" Ayla lashed out in a blind panic. It must be time to meet with Armen by now. She had to tell him what she had just learned. She had to find out what to do about it.

About *Her.*

"Now, then," said the Frank, annoyed. It was the one who'd caught her in the first place, the one named Simon. Ayla whipped around and tried to bite into his hand, but he saw her coming and grabbed her by the hair. "Now, then, let's get some answers out of you, my springald." He turned her face to the light of a nearby campfire. "You're no Provençal. What are you, hmm? One of those wretched Greeks?"

His fists clenched painfully in her hair. Ayla swallowed. Armen would be livid if she let herself be caught. Before she could think of a way out, one of the other Franks made a noise of surprise.

"I know who that is! It's the count's Turkish interpreter."

"A Turk!"

What would they do to her if they guessed she was an enemy?

"I belong to the count! I appeal to Count Raymond!" Ayla yelped.

The men looked at each other, and Simon's hand slackened a little.

"Wait here," Simon told them. "I'll be back as soon as I've taken him to the count."

He shoved her ahead of him into the camp. Ayla's heart pounded. Was she walking into the lion's mouth? The count saw further with one eye than most men did with two. Maybe it would have been better to keep her mouth shut and take her beating.

The count was still awake, the lights burning when they reached his tent. Simon spoke to the guards at the flap and they were beckoned inside a moment later. Still dressed in full armour, battered and bloody from the day's fighting, the count and his household were sitting down to a belated meal.

Anxiously, Ayla scanned the faces that turned to look at her from each side of the table. Lukas wasn't there, and she sagged in relief. He was the one who'd told her what the Franks were up to. She didn't want to see the look on his face when he realised how she had been using him.

She prayed he would stay away, and breathed deeply, trying to get her panic under control.

The vulture is here. I have to warn Armen.

I'm going to survive this.

Simon finished explaining her suspicious behaviour to the count, who now swivelled his head, birdlike, to fix his one good eye on her.

"Well?"

That was all he said.

Ayla threw her shoulders back and marched to the end of the table, fishing inside her pouch. Out came a greasy, not-quite-fresh chunk of horse meat. That was followed by three silver coins and a rather small and battered reliquary, odds and ends she had pilfered in the dark from the bodies on the cart. A gold chain came from around her neck, and the culmination of the collection, a big ruby signet ring, had to be slipped out of her tunic.

One by one, she set them down on the table and looked the count in the eye. "Thought they might be worth something, my lord."

Then, she held her breath.

The count narrowed his eye at her and sipped his wine. "Do I not pay you enough?"

"Enough to live, my lord. But I'd like to improve myself."

"These belong to the kin of the dead." Count Raymond motioned toward the trinkets. "And theft is a whipping offence among us, Turk."

Ayla swallowed.

"So." The count straightened. "I will not tolerate a second offence, understand? Take them away, Simon."

He wasn't going to punish her. Her loot had convinced him that she was guilty of nothing more than theft, and the relief almost made her knees wobble. Maybe luck was on her side, after all.

As Simon reached for the trinkets, the count lifted a finger.

"Not the meat," he added. To Ayla's astonishment, his eyelid dropped in a wink. "If the owner didn't collect his animal's corpse, I can't stop the diligent from making a profit on it."

Ayla's hands were shaking. As she reached out to grab the meat, a rumble and a tremor shook earth and air alike.

"The citadel." Count Raymond almost knocked his chair over as he stood.

They jostled eagerly out of the tent. By now it was fully dark;

there was no way the Franks could make an assault tonight. Ayla slid behind the partition into the sleeping-quarters and grabbed the bundle with her silver bowl.

She'd done everything she could to save the city. Now she had to warn Armen. Sticking to the deepest shadows, Ayla headed back towards the lake.

In her hiding-place among the reeds, she dipped the silver bowl full of water. Instantly, a light shone in its depths. "My lord?"

After a moment, Armen moved into view. "You're late."

"I'm sorry. But I have news." Ayla sank her voice to a whisper. "Lilith is here. The Poison Mother."

"What makes you think that?"

"The black vultures. The Franks have seen her too—in both her forms. Some of them were talking about her this evening. She was circling the walls."

"Leave her to me. Don't go looking for her."

"No fear." Her hands were shaking again, making the water in the bowl ripple. She already recited the Throne Verse twice a day. If only she knew it was working!

"And the siege?" Armen prompted.

"That's the other thing. The count has undermined the citadel. We just heard part of the wall collapse."

"A breach?"

She moistened her lips. "He's going to attack at dawn."

Armen's face was in shadow, as difficult to see as ever. "What about the other Franks? Is this a concerted attack?"

"I don't know."

"You should have found out. There's strength in unity, girl. So long as the Franks don't act together, we have a chance."

"I warned them."

Armen didn't answer at once. When he did, his voice was flat and quiet. "What?"

God have mercy, she was as bad at keeping secrets as Lukas was.

"I waited till it was dark, and went up to the wall and warned them."

"Stupid girl!" Through the muffling barrier of the water, Armen's voice sharpened. "I told you to do nothing! You are far more valuable reporting the Frankish plans than you are taking messages to the garrison. What if they'd caught you?"

They *had* caught her. And it was the sheerest luck that she'd got away with it.

Ayla swallowed. "I still have a few months left. I knew I could do it. If Nicaea falls, the Franks will march on Antioch next. Am I supposed to do nothing?"

"You're supposed to do your *job*. And if you can't do that, then you're worse than useless. Don't ever disobey me again."

Salt clouded the basin, cutting off the light.

Ayla fumed silently. Cursed renegade Armenian. Did he *want* to see Nicaea opened to the Christians? Did he want to see the Franks at the gates of Antioch?

The doubt, once awakened, tugged insistently at her mind. Armen might be Vowed, but he was no Muslim. What guarantee did she really have that she could trust him? He'd told her nothing about his plans, not even who they were really trying to help.

He is still Vowed, she reminded herself. He'd been one of her father's closest friends, and he'd promised to help her earn a place by his side in the afterlife. If nothing else, family loyalty demanded her unquestioning obedience.

Stupid girl...worse than useless. Suddenly, Ayla hated herself. Just tonight, she'd disobeyed her overseer, robbed the dead, betrayed the trust of her best friend and broken her vow to the count. Those last two shouldn't bother her, but they did. They weighed down her conscience like stones. And soon, she'd be dead. She would have to answer for every last fault.

Only four months. Her stomach contracted.

Hastily, she washed herself in preparation for all the prayers she had missed that day. She performed them in painstaking detail this time, not omitting a single recitation.

The slivered moon had risen by the time Ayla headed back into the camp at Vigils. The count's sleeping-quarters were empty while he attended the nightly prayer. Like her, these Franks knew they faced their death. Like her, they wanted to make the best of their chances at heaven.

Something moved in the darkness.

Not empty. Ayla froze.

"It's just me," Lukas whispered. "I wanted to speak to you."

Her stomach roiled, partly from euphoria that he'd been thinking of her—and partly from the old dread of what she might have to do to him one day.

Ayla swallowed. "Where were you all evening?"

"Running messages. Trying to coordinate the attack tomorrow. You should hear the wrangling. All these Franks are *obsessed* with their own dignity."

Do not let yourself feel. Ayla dropped her bundle down next to her bedroll and began fumbling for her blanket. "Amazing. I don't know *anyone* like that."

That shut him up, but only for a moment. "There are a lot of vultures around here." His voice was thoughtful. "Any idea why?"

Ayla's stomach knotted, but she kept her voice steady. "None. Shouldn't you be outside praying?"

"I wanted...I heard you got caught looting."

"So? I'm not a saint."

"I wanted to warn you. They see you as the enemy, Ayla. Please...be careful. Don't draw attention to yourself." He reached out, squeezing her hand. "I want you to see your home again in safety."

Long after the Franks returned and rolled themselves into their blankets, Ayla lay rigid, staring into the darkness.

When she finally slept, she dreamed she was crawling agonisingly across a chasm, on a bridge thinner than a hair and sharper than a sword. The palms of her hands and her knees were sliced to the bone.

A hot wind bellowed up from the blazing depths, puffing sparks over her and threatening to topple her. Ayla swallowed, her mouth so dry that she heard a clicking in her throat. She regained her balance and reached forward with bleeding hands. The end was in sight. Safety.

Then *She* came, gigantic and stinking, wings unfurled, talons outstretched. Ayla screamed, but nothing could save her. The claws sank into her body as though she were no more than a field-mouse, and she lost her grip on the bridge—the bridge that was her only hope, her only salvation.

For an instant, she looked up into the vulture's screaming mouth.

You are mine, girl.

The steely beak slashed down.

Terror kicked her into waking. Ayla lay for a moment staring into the grey canvas overhead, clutching a hand to her thudding heart as the phantom pain she'd felt in her dream faded away.

"To God we belong, and to God we return," she whispered.

It was years since she'd had one of *those* nightmares. They were all different, but they all ended the same way.

You are mine, girl. Don't think you'll make it across the chasm to heaven. You'll fall into the fire. And I'll be waiting.

Her head was pounding, her eyes gritty, and her throat dry. The sleeping-quarters were empty. Muttering the Throne Verse under her breath, Ayla got up and stumbled outside in search of water to drink.

Outside, the camp was already awake and busy. *The assault,* Ayla realised. She ran out into the camp's main thoroughfare, trying to catch a glimpse of the walls.

The Nicaean citadel, never very straight to begin with, had slumped down at a crazy angle. In the dawn light, Ayla could see that the outer wall was destroyed, a heap of rubble burying the entrance to the Frankish mine.

Beyond, the gap was already filled with an immense barrier of stone and timber.

They must have worked all night.

Feet tromped down the road toward her. Count Raymond and his household. Ayla darted aside, hiding between two tents, but a chill ran down her spine as she saw the anger on the count's face. At the entrance to his own pavilion, he turned to Lukas.

"Take this message to the other princes: there will be no assault today. Someone has warned them."

Chapter XVII.

M y lords, at this rate Nicaea will never fall." Duke Godfrey's voice was apologetic. "My brother Boulogne and I agree that there needs to be a new strategy."

The pilgrim lords held their council under the trees today, on a hilltop south of the city. Rainfall this morning had cleared the air, leaving a blue sky and bright sunshine in place of yesterday's stifling clouds. With a cup of clear white wine at his elbow and his favourite hound curled into a slumbering coil at his feet, Saint-Gilles was easy in body. In spirit, he seethed with frustration.

"I'll tell you what's wrong with our strategy," he growled. "We're divided, when we should be working together. If we made a concerted attack..."

"Then we'd still have to take the city by storm." Baldwin of Boulogne interrupted from where he stood lounging against a tree. "I say we starve them out. Force them to surrender."

"If we cut off their supply through the lake, they'll have to offer terms," said Godfrey.

"If we attack together, we could have the city *tomorrow*," Saint-Gilles insisted. "Even without a breach in the wall. Their garrison is small and their walls are long. We can spread them thin, take them by storm..."

A loud snort interrupted him. "If they thought so, they'd have surrendered already."

Baldwin had had a chip on his shoulder ever since Bohemond poached his mad seer. Saint-Gilles swung his head toward Adhemar and mouthed the word, *Puppy!*

The bishop sat with his capable fingers steepled under his chin. "He has a point, my friend. If we can convince them to make terms we can save countless lives on both sides. Let's hear the count's suggestions."

Baldwin bristled. "I need no one's permission to speak."

"The bishop represents the Pope himself," Saint-Gilles snapped. "Show respect!"

"All due reverence." Baldwin nodded in Adhemar's direction with a smile that did not reach his cold black eyes. "But I was speaking to you, Saint-Gilles. Who gave *you* authority over the rest of us?"

To his surprise, the other counts nodded their heads or murmured agreement.

Well, then.

"Since you ask, it was the *Pope.*" Saint-Gilles used his spear to hoist himself up. On his feet, he swung his head to look each of the other princes in the eye. "Before preaching the pilgrimage, Pope Urban appointed *me* to lead those who would make the journey."

Baldwin's jaw bulged. "How is it that the lord Pope never told *us* about this?"

"Do you doubt my word?" Usually, strong men flinched when he used that tone. But that was at home, in Provence, where he was lord. It had less effect here in Anatolia, and on Baldwin of Boulogne it was no good at all.

Saint-Gilles levelled his stare at the others. "I have the right to be your leader, but even now, I would not insist if the need was less pressing. My lords, you ought to hear me, for pity's sake if nothing else. Our people are trapped here under the walls of Nicaea, subject to disease and starvation. How many of our poor have already starved to death for the name of Christ? And have you forgotten the Turks? They surely haven't forgotten us. While we sit here and twiddle our thumbs, they have all the time they need to raise an army."

Adhemar looked at him thoughtfully, stroking his top lip with a stubby forefinger. Bohemond put away the jewelled dagger with which he had been cleaning his nails and leaned forward, his lips slightly parted.

Baldwin looked as though he had smelled something bad.

"If you won't recognise my authority, you should recognise my position. I'm older than the rest of you, I've fought the Saracens in Spain, I've lost blood on pilgrimage to Jerusalem." He tapped his empty eye socket. "And I'm a man of my word. I don't make pretty speeches, but I *will* get you to Jerusalem safely, along with the rest of my people, God help me. What do you say?"

"I say you are right, my lord." Bohemond jumped to his feet, put a hand on Saint-Gilles' shoulder, and flashed a smile at the council. "We need a leader, and what better choice than this good old man?"

There was an adamant silence. Saint-Gilles permitted himself a grim smile. Evidently, they would accept any danger, any difficulty, rather than submit themselves to his command.

He could not blame them too much. He had been equally unwilling to submit to Alexius.

"What about the lord bishop?" Count Stephen of Blois turned to Adhemar. "As the Pope's representative, perhaps he should lead us."

Adhemar looked startled. "I'm a churchman, my lord, not a tactician." He turned to a member of the council who sat a little way back, tracing the bridge of his artificial gold nose with one pudgy forefinger. "How do you advise us, my lord Tatikius?"

The emperor's half-Turkish foster-brother blinked and focused on the Franks as if returning from a mental absence. The eunuch general had recently arrived from the imperial court with an entourage that included a hunting cheetah and a pair of the emperor's Varangian bodyguards, immense blond Norsemen who carried battle-axes nearly as tall as themselves.

All three of them stood by his chair, watching the Franks with feline disdain.

Tatikius gave a very Greek smirk and said in reasonable Frankish, "The God-led emperor is in Pelekanum like a good father, watching over your affairs from afar. If we speak of experience, of wisdom, or of integrity, he excels you in these as a giant excels pygmies in stature. If I were you I should entrust the conduct of this siege to him."

Saint-Gilles snorted. "That's absurd."

"There, I agree," Boulogne said.

"I mean no offence," Saint-Gilles added hastily.

Tatikius smirked again. "None taken, I assure you."

"I intend to keep my oath to Alexius, but I have already asked him if he was coming to the Holy Sepulchre, and he refused. We need a leader for the duration of the whole pilgrimage, not just for this siege." Saint-Gilles turned back to the Frankish princes. "And that is what I can offer you."

There was another unwilling silence.

"In my dominions, I have the power of a crowned king," growled the count of Flanders. "Why should I take orders from *you?*"

"*I* am the brother of the King of France." The arrogant, high-pitched voice could only belong to Hugh of Vermandois. "You're all his vassals, and in his absence I claim precedence!"

A babel of protest arose. Only the look of dismay on Adhemar's face helped Saint-Gilles keep his temper. "It's no good heading off to the Holy Sepulchre on your own," he murmured. "You promised to stick with us."

Adhemar smiled wryly. "More's the pity."

Saint-Gilles lifted his voice in an attempt to make himself heard. "How can we fight the Turks like this? I understand that all of us are accustomed to supreme rank and unquestioned authority. But something more important is at stake here: our vows to Christ and the lives of our people!"

"Why not go on taking all decisions in council?" Until now, Godfrey had not spoken. "We are peers and brothers, after all."

"And have a committee meeting each time someone wants to move his tent? God help us!"

"If we chose anyone, it wouldn't be you," Baldwin growled. "You don't even have the right to rule your own people. Much less the rest of us."

Saint-Gilles felt his face slowly redden.

Usurper. Thief. He could not find the words to speak, but to his amazement, Bohemond did.

"Is *your* conscience so clean, Boulogne? The count is doing his penance like an honest man, as are all of us, by travelling to Jerusalem." His grip tightened on Saint-Gilles' shoulder. "It's as the bishop said. We must choose our leader for his ability, not for his holiness."

Bohemond's support was as welcome as it was unexpected. Saint-Gilles gripped his shoulder in silent thanks. Maybe he had misjudged the count.

"Saint-Gilles is right," Bohemond continued. "*Someone* must determine our battle plans. Otherwise, believe me when I tell you we are all dead meat. We *must* choose a leader."

"*Thank* you." Saint-Gilles glared at the other princes. "Maybe it doesn't have to be me, but *one* of us must lead."

Bohemond looked at Adhemar. "We don't have the Holy Father with us, but we have his representative. My lord bishop, will you choose a leader from among us?"

The bishop looked startled. "Me?"

"We all trust and respect you," said Bohemond. "I, for one, will abide by your choice."

Duke Godfrey stood up, clearing his throat. "As will I."

"And I." Count Stephen of Blois jumped to his feet.

"I will *not*." Vermandois spoke with nasal outrage. "With all reverence, the bishop is Count Raymond's vassal. It's all very well to speak of penance, but what guarantee do we have that the man who usurped Toulouse isn't looking to usurp some other realm?"

"You have my word." Saint-Gilles' lips tightened. "What do you say, Adhemar?"

But the bishop hesitated.

Saint-Gilles forced himself to wait. He had not the slightest doubt

167

of what Adhemar would say. The bishop was his friend, his sworn man, and the Pope's confidant.

Yet still he hesitated, staring at his feet with what Saint-Gilles suddenly recognised as misery.

Then he looked straight at Saint-Gilles, and Saint-Gilles *knew.*

"Adhemar?" he said in bewilderment.

The bishop shook his head. "I cannot do this. I cannot ordain a leader when we are so divided in our trust. Godfrey is right. Until everyone can agree, we must continue to take our decisions in council."

Saint-Gilles could not believe his ears. "Adhemar," he began again, but no one paid any heed to him.

Duke Godfrey cleared his throat diffidently, but he sounded relieved. "I will abide by the bishop's decision. And further, I think that no one could ask for more than this without declaring himself to be a high-handed troublemaker."

"Hear, hear," said Vermandois.

"All this is very well," Baldwin of Boulogne interrupted, "but now we are back where we started. What about the city?"

Bohemond stepped away from Saint-Gilles, a sparkle lighting his eyes. "As it happens, I have a plan."

Saint-Gilles fumbled his way back to his seat and subsided heavily. *Adhemar,* he thought, *mine own familiar friend.* Suddenly, a wave of homesickness hit him. In his bones, he could feel every inch of the weary distance that separated him from his home.

If he could not trust his own friend and vassal, who could he trust?

Bohemond was explaining his plan to an eager audience. "We must put ships on the lake, of course. We can't blockade them by land, so it must be by water. If the emperor will lend us the ships, we can carry them overland to the lake."

Next to Saint-Gilles, Adhemar leaned closer, looking worried. "My friend. I'm sorry."

"*Why? We need* this."

"Do we?" Adhemar tipped his head toward the other counts, sinking his voice so low that Saint-Gilles had to lean closer to hear him. "Power is a two-edged blade, Raymond. Even if one man *could* command this whole immense army, I'm not convinced that he should."

"You think I'm incapable? Or untrustworthy?"

"My friend…"

If selling all his possessions and going to die in the east was not enough to erase his sins, what was?

Suddenly, he just wanted to get away from them all. "I've had enough of this." Saint-Gilles erupted from his chair and clapped Bohemond on the shoulder. "It's a good plan, count. Tell me what I can do to help."

Then, with his hound and his servants at his heels, he stomped down the hill.

Chapter XVIII.

The panic gripping Lukas' guts was familiar. At first he thought he was back in Oliveta, but this time he knelt on lush grass instead of the tessellated pavement outside the basilica. The red torchlight was hardly bright enough to light his surroundings, but he could easily make out the body lying on the ground in front of him.

It was Ayla. A red star marked her forehead, dripping down onto her cheeks.

Panic squeezed the air from his lungs.

"No," he tried to say, but the words would hardly make it past the stiff barrier of his lips. "No, no, no."

"Lukas." She opened her eyes and reached up to touch his shoulder. "Wake up."

He could only stare.

"Wake up," she said again, shaking him harder. "The count wants you."

He jerked awake and knocked his forehead against the underside of the cart which he'd crawled under, exhausted, just minutes before. He collapsed back onto the grass with a groan, then turned his head.

Ayla peered under the cart at him, little more than a silhouette in the thickening darkness. "Getting worse, aren't they?"

Lukas grunted. Since Oliveta he had been haunted by nightmares. Sometimes he relived those awful moments in the basilica courtyard, or hid as Khalil hunted him through the camp. Sometimes he dreamed of finding his family again, only to discover that no matter how fast he ran, no matter how loud he shouted, he never could close the distance between them.

In the last week, Ayla had begun haunting him too.

"You should tell me about your dream. Maybe I can interpret it for you."

"No," he said firmly.

"What if it turns out to be important? Dreams have meaning, you know."

"I know what it means." Lukas rolled out from under the cart. It meant that on top of everything else, he was now worried about Ayla. It must have been that story about the hanging. He stretched wearily. "What time is it?"

"Somewhere between Vespers and Compline. Oh, and it's been three days. You still haven't answered my last riddle."

Despite himself, Lukas had to smile. Difficult as they were to solve, he was grateful for Ayla's riddles. They were like an escape to simpler times.

"Oh." He rubbed his eyes, trying to think. "No! I *had* the answer just this morning. But I've forgotten it again."

Sunrise that morning found Greek ships on the lake. Serene and arrogant, they had bellied forth with the dawn wind, sweeping down from the west and anchoring just out of bowshot from the city walls. Nicaea was surrounded.

Even so, she refused to yield. The Christians attacked immediately after Prime, a coordinated attack launched from both land and water. All day, as the fighting raged, Lukas was kept busy running messages around the city to the other Frankish armies, sometimes to the Greek camp which had pitched last night between the Provençals and the lake. When he wasn't needed, the sergeants kept him busy taking water to the thirsty men or helping carry the wounded to makeshift infirmaries where Greek physicians and Frankish monks did their best to ease their dying moments.

By the time the fighting stopped at sunset, Lukas had no strength left for anything but sleep. But at some stage during the day, he had *done* it—he had solved the riddle.

Ayla gave a whoop. "One hour, and you're honour-bound to play the fowl."

"Red but not an apple; layered but not pastry. Devil take it! I *had* it. Come on, you can give me credit."

"No, I can't. Maybe it was the wrong answer."

"Take pity. I might have to translate for the count."

"Into chicken. Ooh, that would be awkward." She grinned wickedly.

"Fine. I'll just have to remember it by Compline. Did you wake me up just for that?"

"No—"

"Don't tell me the count wants me to run another message for him. I think I'd rather lie down and die."

"Lukas…" Her grin flashed in the half-light. "I think the count wants you to run another message for him."

He groaned. "Lead on."

She hurried him toward Count Raymond's tent much too fast for his aching bones. Inside, the count was still on his feet, barking at Lord Raymond Pilet about horse pickets. As he turned to follow the knight out of his tent, the count spared a glance for Lukas and Ayla, and a single word.

"Eat."

Bread and meat were on the table. Lukas grabbed a bannock of bread and a collop of the tough gamey mutton that smelled like heaven. He was wiping greasy fingers on the last of the bread, his stomach growling around the long-desired food, when the one-eyed count returned.

"I could send a priest." Count Raymond's chaplain followed him into the tent. "But his looks would give him away at once."

"Not to mention his voice. We'll try this one." The count fixed Lukas with his good eye. "Can I trust you, Greek?"

Lukas gulped his last mouthful and stood up, bristling. "You made me swear fealty to you, my lord."

Precious little he had got in return. Each day, the count worked him to exhaustion doing menial tasks each day. Having his good faith doubted only added to the insult.

"Then it's time to prove your worth." The count threw himself into a chair, running both hands down his haggard face. "Listen, Bessarion. We need someone to spy on the Greeks for us."

Spy on the Greeks! Lukas opened his mouth, but the count forged on inexorably.

"This afternoon, one of our people saw a Greek boat rowing to the water gate. We think they could be dealing with the Turks behind our backs. I want you to go into the Greek camp and learn everything you can. Be back by Vigils to report. By that time I should have returned from the council meeting, but if not, come find me in the count of Blois' tent." The count stopped, searching his face. "What do you say, Bessarion?"

Lukas swallowed. "They are my own people."

"Do they feed and clothe you? Do they shield you from your enemies? *I* am your people now. If you cannot do as I ask, I will release you of your oath and you will be free to leave. Well?"

Lukas was hot with anger. But if he left, what would he do? Where would he go?

"I'll do it."

The count leaned forward. "Then remember your oath, Greek. If you break it, you won't just feel heaven's wrath. You'll suffer mine as well."

Before he realised what he was doing, Lukas lifted his chin and gave the count glare for glare. "And if I keep it, it will be for the love of heaven, not for the fear of you."

The count turned his head in a little sharp movement like the challenge of a bird of prey. Lukas braced himself for an eruption. To his surprise, the count laughed.

"Hah! That's the spirit." The count slapped his shoulder and stalked out of the tent pulling on his gloves.

As the tent flap closed behind the him, Ayla pulled a face. "That one thinks himself so great-hearted," she whispered in Greek. "Reminds me of you."

Lukas ignored the jab. "I meant to sell him my service, not my soul."

Ayla shrugged. "What other choice is there?"

Death or servitude, she had once told him.

Lukas shook his head, slinging his staff across his back. "Better is it not to vow, than to vow and not pay. Well. It's too late now."

Outside, the night was clear. A fresh breeze blew from the lake. Two thousand Greeks were camped along the shore with their gold-nosed general, the light of their campfires making it difficult to see the lake beyond.

Lukas hesitated, watching them. His father had fought for the emperor at Nineveh, at Yarmouk. He had always been so proud of that legacy. He had always wanted to follow in that path.

And now here he was. And no matter what he did next, this was the moment that made him a traitor, either to his oath, or to his family.

He started across the gap into the Greek camp, aiming for a dark passage between two tents. He was nearly there when something shot between his legs and tripped him.

The dark shape of a sentry blocked the stars, and the cold blade of a spear tickled his chest. "Go on, Frank. Give us a reason."

Lukas threw up his hands. "I'm not a Frank! My name is Lukas Bessarion. I'm a Greek and..." devil take it, why had he not come up with an excuse? "I was coming to see my brother."

"Which company is your brother with?"

Saint George. Lukas tried a name at random. "He's with the Smyrna troops..."

"He's lying," said another voice at once. "Nobody from Smyrna here. Take him to Kari."

They pulled him to his feet and marched him to the centre of the camp. Lukas could have kicked himself. He was trained as a cataphract, not a spy. It stood to reason that if he betrayed the count it would be through incompetence, not faithlessness.

He needed to find a way out, and quickly.

Outside the Greek general's tent, a palfrey and a small escort waited to accompany him to the Frankish council of war. To Lukas' surprise, the man waiting at their head whetting his axe was a Varangian. Norse, English or Russian? Lukas could not tell, but there was no mistaking the first-rate weaponry or the icy northern features.

"Kari?" he said when the sentries spoke to him. "That way."

A second Varangian was just finishing his evening meal beside a nearby campfire. The sentries marched Lukas up to the light and stood to attention.

"Caught this fellow sneaking in from the Frankish camp, sir. He's got a strange accent, sir, and some cock-and-bull story about a brother from Smyrna."

Lukas felt desperate. Varangians were not only tasked with protecting the emperor's personal safety, they also investigated cases of treason and conspiracy. If the emperor had loaned two of them to General Tatikius, it was a sign that the emperor was taking the Frankish threat very seriously indeed.

It was a sign that he was about to be in deep trouble.

The Varangian wiped his pale beard on the back of an enormous hand. "Smyrna's occupied by the Turks, boy. Thought everyone knew that. Where are you really from?"

He could only save himself with the truth. Maybe later there would be an opportunity to find the information the count wanted, but first, he had to convince this Varangian he was on the emperor's side.

"My name is Lukas Bessarion. I'm a Greek from Jerusalem and a member of the household of Raymond of Saint-Gilles. I've got news for General Tatikius."

"What news?"

He almost blurted it out, but an idea had taken shape in his mind.

"I won't speak to you. Only the general."

The Varangian yawned. "Follow me, then."

Although Lukas had grown up in luxury, he was unprepared for the gorgeousness of the Greek general's tent. Gilding shone everywhere. The lamp hanging from the tent's centre was a magnificent glow of blue and pearl-coloured glass, and in its diffuse light, the dark figured silk of the tent's lining glittered with silver threads. From its bed among the cushions, a cheetah's jewelled eyes blazed with reflected light.

Tatikius was just pinning his cloak to one shoulder when the Varangian motioned Lukas to enter.

"This man says he comes from the Frankish camp with a report, my lord."

The eunuch general swivelled to stare at him. "Did Count Bohemond send you, fellow?"

"No one sent me, my lord. I've come because the empire claims my loyalty."

The general's eyes narrowed with curiosity. "I'll hear it. Speak quickly."

He would be more cautious this time than he had been in the Hospital of Sampson. "Do you know the name Bessarion?"

"It's a noble name," Tatikius said. "An old family."

He did not seem to have heard anything against it from the Watchers. "It's my name, and yet I'm reduced to serving the Franks as an interpreter rather than starve in the streets." Lukas swallowed. "If I give you this information, do I have your word that I won't lose by it?"

Tatikius did not blink. "Name your price."

"A horse, armour and the weapons of a cataphract."

"Done. If your information is good you shall have what you ask and a purse of gold to go with it."

The general waited, scratching his great cat's ears. The cheetah's eyes closed in bliss and a husky purr left its throat.

Lukas drew breath and stopped. His whole body tingled with a sense of warning. *Danger.* He glanced behind, to his left. The Varangian stood motionless to attention.

Tatikius was growing impatient. "I am waiting."

It was his one chance to regain his freedom—to be a fighter again, not a servant. Lukas forced himself to speak. "The Franks are suspicious. One of them saw a boat of yours going to the Nicaean water gate. They suspect you may be in negotiations with the Turks, though they don't know for sure. They sent me to find out."

"And you came to me instead."

Only because he had no other choice. "Yes."

"What did you say your name was?"

"Lukas Bessarion."

Tatikius pressed his thin lips together thoughtfully. For a moment, his jowls worked. Then he said to the Varangian, "Left forearm."

Not until the northerner grabbed his left wrist did Lukas realise what was happening. He reached for the staff on his back, but the Varangian was both faster and tougher. A foot slammed into the back of his knee, collapsing him to the carpet. At the same moment, his left arm was twisted behind his back, the sleeve yanked up. Padding as silently as his cheetah, Tatikius circled Lukas and stood behind him.

The Varangian spoke. "This is the Syrian Mark, my lord."

"I thought so. Presbyter Didymus was searching all Constantinople for this fellow." Tatikius sighed. "I'll deal with him tomorrow. For tonight, slash his mark and have him watched."

Lukas' stomach clenched. "No! You're making a mistake! I'm not a heretic!"

Tatikius chuckled. "A curiously specific denial."

The Varangian yanked Lukas to his feet, capturing his other arm and twisting both behind him with what seemed to be deliberate brutality. Whining with pain, Lukas stumbled out of the tent in Tatikius' wake. As the Greek general swung into the saddle, the bodyguard propelled him down an avenue of tents away from the city.

Dear God, what were they going to do with him?

Lukas had no opportunity to think. Behind him, the sound of hoof beats carried Tatikius and his escort away from the camp. Instantly, the punishing grip left Lukas' wrists. The Varangian grabbed his shoulders and hauled him into a narrow walkway between the rows of tents.

"You're Syrian," he hissed. "You're a Syrian Watcher. Why does the Presbyter want you dead?"

Lukas tried to twist, but the hands on his shoulders tightened. "Keep walking."

It made sense. Most of the army would be inside their tents by now, falling asleep. With only thin canvas between them, the best privacy would come from moving as they talked.

"Didymus thinks I helped destroy the Syrian Watchers," Lukas whispered. "But it was the Messenger who took away their office and gave it to my family. I don't know what lies they've told about me, but I'm no heretic."

"I know."

The flood of relief almost choked him. He yanked again on the guiding hands. "You *know*? Who are you?"

"Not so loud. I'm a Messenger too." They reached another thoroughfare, dark and abandoned.

"Then you can tell the Presbyters I'm not a heretic!"

"I'm sorry, boy. The Presbyters won't hear the likes of me any more than they'll hear you. They're powerful men, and they've got the general in their pockets."

Lukas swallowed. "Please let me go. I have to go back to Syria. I have to make things right."

The Varangian shoved him across, into another laneway. "Things are worse than you know, Lukas Bessarion. There are no Watchers in Syria any more. And without Watchers, they'll be destroyed."

"Who?"

"Not who. *What.* Antioch and Jerusalem."

Hair prickled on Lukas' neck. "The whole cities?"

"Only one thing can save them. A Watcher. Go back to Jerusalem, Syrian. Save her."

"I will. I will. As soon as the road opens." Go back he would, far enough back that he could prevent this disaster from ever happening.

"Good." The Varangian grabbed the staff from his shoulders. "I'm going to put you under guard, but your watchman will fall asleep by midnight. Don't harm him as you escape."

A little further, and the Varangian steered him onto one of the oblong tents. Inside, a lamp burned, revealing that the tent was stacked high with boxes and bundles of supplies. The sleepy-eyed sentry nodded dully when the Varangian ordered him to watch a prisoner for the night. Together, they tethered Lukas' wrists to a tent-pole with cord, but before the Varangian left, he quietly slipped Lukas' knife back into his hands.

As the tent flap fell behind him, Lukas felt a stab of loneliness. At last, a Watcher who accepted him. Would he ever see the man again?

He drew up his knees and laid his head back against the box behind. Exhaustion descended again. *They're powerful men, and they've got the general in their pockets.* Against the might of the Greek Watchers, what could a lonely and friendless wanderer do? They had thrown him out as readily as had the Syrian Watchers at Oliveta.

For a moment, he had imagined that he could find his rightful place amongst the Greeks, after all. And now that too had failed.

He had to believe there was a way back for him. He had to believe that he would live to see Syria again, that once the time was right, a way would open for him to go home, find his family, and save his people. Two months already he had been stranded in this terrible future, looking over his shoulder and jumping at every shadow, but surely, *surely,* Nicaea could not block the road much longer.

His attention jolted back to his surroundings when someone

tripped over a guy-rope outside. There was a faint hiss of blasphemy as whoever it was stumbled away to find a latrine trench. On the other side of the tent, the sleeping guard shifted, then resumed snoring.

With the knife ready in his hand, it only took a moment to free himself. Lukas returned it to its sheath, retrieved his staff, and slid like a wraith through the tent flap. Beyond, the night was lit only by stars. Now he had to get away somehow, without disturbing either the Greek or the Frankish sentries.

The Franks! Devil take it, what was he going to do now? The Greeks had disowned him. He couldn't survive on his own. That only left one option—Saint-Gilles. He must complete his mission. But how? He was supposed to be gathering information, and all he had done was get himself captured.

He was no good at reading the night sky, but he felt sure it was still the right side of Vigils. With any luck, he had been asleep less than an hour. If anything was happening between the Greeks and the Turkish garrison, it was almost certain to take place now, during the greater sleep. And it would involve the water gate. Lukas turned west.

Unlike the Frankish camp, the Greek camp was set out in neat, logical rows that took him directly to the lakeshore. He dropped to the ground and lay flat in the shadow of the last tent for a while until one of the Greek sentries plodded by. When the man had faded into the darkness, he pelted forward, rolled down the sloping white shore, and hid himself in the nearest clump of reeds.

From here he could scan the dappled surface of the wider lake. Not even the thin sliver of the new moon hung in the sky, but the stars were bright enough to shed a faint light. The Greek ships were great hulks of shadow opposite the city, lit by dim white lanterns hanging from the prow of each. Sails folded and anchors cast, they brooded like enormous sleeping waterfowl. The city itself was only a big black shadow on the shore with dim lights dotting its battlements. It was impossible to see the water gate at this distance. He would have to get closer. Lukas slipped through the reeds to deeper water, rolled onto his back, and began to swim silently to the north.

It was a long way, but Lukas had spent almost every summer of his life at the Bessarion estate on the coast south of Jaffa. For years on end, he had almost lived in the water. Slowly but surely, he pulled past the Greek camp and watched the city wall angle closer.

The Greek ships, closer now, were eerily silent. The white shore seemed empty. Not far away, the shape of a jetty opposite a light burning on the wall showed where to find the water-gate. Lukas waded ashore.

The lamp above the gate shed a faint circle of light on the shore. Lukas was getting to his feet when he saw a shadow detach itself from the gate and run toward him.

Silently, Lukas dropped to his knees. He must have made a sound, for the figure halted. From this angle, it was only a featureless outline against the light. Slowly, it drew a knife. Then, with only a soft intake of breath as warning, it sprang at him.

Lukas grabbed at his staff, but its makeshift strap clung to his soaking shirt. Instead, he threw himself aside. His attacker's stroke went wide as Lukas hit the ground. He pushed himself off again and backed away, still yanking at the strap. The knife fighter wheeled and got on the other side of him, melting into the darkness and disappearing.

Getting him silhouetted against the light.

Lukas backed toward the water gate, all his senses jangling. The soft ripple of water on the shore interfered with his hearing, but if the attacker had run, he ought to have heard the footsteps.

A blade flashed in the darkness.

Lukas got his staff free just in time. A blaze of pain scored his lower belly, but the blade fouled in his tunic, only scratching him. As he swung out with his staff, a figure emerged from the darkness and snared it in the crook of an elbow, inside Lukas' guard and close enough not to be bothered by the mismatch of their weapons. Back went the bladed right hand.

You can be stabbed half a dozen times in the space of a heartbeat, a voice from the past said inside his head. Lukas let go of the staff, grabbed for the wrist just as it slammed home.

His hand closed on the arm, halting the blade within a whisper of his belly. At once the wrist twisted through the hinge of his thumb. A foot slammed into his ribcage, catching him before he got the chance to tense his stomach. Lukas staggered back, bending double. His own staff caught him between the legs and tripped him. Now the light over the gate was blazing directly into his eyes, blinding him.

A heavy weight dropped onto his chest. The blade flashed again. Blindly, he parried it with his forearm. The knife sank into the ground next to his shoulder.

But the weight of his attacker on his chest went oddly still. A hand grabbed him by the chin, turning his face full into the light. *"Lukas? God ha' mercy, Greek! I nearly killed you!"*

"Ayla?"

"Get up! Someone's coming!" She rolled off him, grabbed his hand, and pulled him to his feet.

Lukas resisted her attempts to drag him into the shadows. "What are you *doing* here?"

"Sparing your idiot life!"

But he knew the true answer. All his weariness returned like a stone on his chest. *Saint George, she was in the tent when the count spoke to me,* Lukas thought. She had heard the count's suspicions that the city was about to surrender. She had been to the water gate.

She was a Turk. She was working for them.

Something splashed in the shallows nearby. From the darkness came a muted flash of gold and the creak of rowlocks. A boat. That could only mean...

"Stand your ground or we shoot!" The challenge was in hushed Greek.

Beside him, Ayla whispered a curse.

Lukas grabbed her arm. If she was working for the Turks, and if the Turks were negotiating with the Greeks…

"Ayla," he whispered frantically, "you can't hand me over to them. They want me dead."

A keel grated across sand. Eight shapes loomed out of the darkness and ventured into the light, advancing in a cautious half-circle, spears and swords ready. One of them carried bundled standards in his arms.

Greek standards. Once in the city, they would mark Nicaea as the emperor's property.

Lukas brought his staff to guard.

Ayla shot him a sideways glance. "Are you sure about this?"

"There's a price on my head. They'll hand me over to the Watchers. Please."

There was no time to say anything else. "Who are you?" one of the Greeks challenged.

Lukas backed against the wall. "Our names are none of your business."

"Stand down, Greek. Your loyalty is to the emperor."

"Not anymore."

"Shoot them," said their leader.

Lukas' heart stopped as one of them lifted his bow. An archer. Saint George! He hadn't reckoned for that. These Greeks could pick him off at a distance—

Ayla moved, a graceful blur of speed, snapping off a shot with her sling. The archer dropped his weapon and crumpled with a grunt of pain.

"Run!" she yelled at him.

Lukas found his wits and charged for the man nearest the south wall.

He was trained for this. He parried the Greek's sword blow with one end of the staff, then swung it back to knock the man's feet from under him. He followed that with a long jab to the stomach of the

183

next assailant. As the blow connected, so did a stone from Ayla's sling. The unfortunate man crumpled, opening a way along the shoreline.

Ayla grabbed his wrist and they ran.

A low whistle sounded from behind, but it was the sound from in front that stopped them. Hundreds of feet, crunching on the hard shore—the unmistakeable sound of soldiers marching in time.

"The reeds," Lukas breathed. As the footsteps ahead jostled into a run, they plunged down the sloping shore and slid into the water. A moment later they were crouched in a thicket of reeds, listening to whispered oaths and the chaos of running feet.

Ayla's breath was in his ear, laughing. "Think they'll find us?"

He turned toward her and their noses bumped. Her fingers tightened reflexively in his, jolting euphoria through his veins. *Kiss her,* said the voice inside. *Quickly, before—*

He crushed her close with his free arm, banged his nose against hers and then found her lips as a gurgle of delight crossed them. Her fingers laced into his wet hair as he tried to pull away. He had never kissed anyone before. How was it done? But she pulled him back, kissed him again, slower this time, sweeter...

—before you remember what a bad idea this is.

Lukas broke away. All the heat rushed to his face, leaving him shivering with cold.

"Ayla," he whispered.

Fingers still clutching his hair, she gazed toward the city. "Look!"

Under the light of the water gate, the shore was thronged with Greek infantry. As the gate itself opened, they began sorting themselves into a column to enter.

"Must be a good hundred of them." The elation drained out of her voice.

Lukas grabbed her shoulders. "Ayla. Tell me what you know."

She was invisible in the dark, but her voice was bleak and bitter. "Isn't it obvious? Nicaea is handed over to the Greeks."

"But why are *you* here?"

There was a cold silence. "Same as you. Trying to stop it. Trying to keep these madmen away from my home."

He pulled her unresisting hands away and sat back on his heels. "Saint George, Ayla. You've been spying for the Turks."

"They're my people, aren't they?"

He swallowed, trying to choke back the sour bile in his throat. "I trusted you. The count trusted you."

"God have mercy, Greek, is that my fault? Did you think I would turn my back on my own people? Who do you think I am?"

"They would have sold you into slavery."

"Ahmed was *one man!*"

He was still holding both her hands. She tried to yank them out of his grasp, but he tightened them. "You told me yourself nobody gives a damn about you. Who are these people of yours? What have they ever done for you? At best, they've watched you starve. At worst, they would have sold you like an animal."

In the dark, her unsteady breath broke into a sob.

"Ayla, you deserve better than this. Your father was a great man. You should be a lady. You should be a *queen*. Why serve them?"

At that, Alya shoved him in the chest, nearly toppling him. "My *mother* is in Antioch, Lukas. My *sisters*. What happens to them when the Franks arrive?"

That took his breath away. Somehow, he had never thought of Ayla still having *family* in Antioch.

She gave a bitter laugh. "Do you think I am like you, to abandon my people the moment it suits me?"

"Saint George! Is that what you think of me?"

"I'm sorry, did I hurt your feelings?" She spat. "Maybe you'll think of that next time you tell me to abandon my kin."

She flailed to her feet and charged recklessly for the shore, not even bothering to be quiet. Further up, the water gate was just closing on the last of the Greek soldiers.

Lukas staggered to his feet. "Ayla, wait!"

"Find someone else to dry your tears, Greek." She tossed the words over her shoulder as she reached the shore and vanished into the dark.

Chapter XIX.

Lukas collapsed into the reeds again, tasting the bitterness of her betrayal. He had trusted her. He had *kissed* her. And all this time, she had been spying on them.

No.

My mother is in Antioch, Lukas.

She had not betrayed him, she had been faithful to her own people. She was doing the same for them as he was trying to do for his. He couldn't reproach her for that.

Could he really reproach any of the Turks for it? They might be heretics, they might be invaders, but they weren't madmen like Khalil. Maybe they were just...*people,* with mothers they worried about and fathers they grieved for.

Muffled sounds reached him from the direction of the water gate. Greek boats, their lamps burning, drifted close to the reeds. Searching for him.

Lukas slithered through the reeds into deeper water and began to swim, the effort pumping warmth into his shivering body. *The count.* He still had to make his report.

Oh, Saint George. What was he going to say? What if Tatikius told the count that his Greek interpreter had tried to betray him? In truth, he *had* betrayed him. The excuses that were so convincing an hour ago melted away in hindsight. He was worse than Ayla, breaking his oath in a moment of greed and panic. He had no right to condemn her.

He remembered the sound of delight she had made as he pulled her into his arms. He shouldn't have done it, but he could not seem to make himself sorry for it. Ayla was so much more than the girl he had always dreamed of. She was fire and rock. She was kindness and grit.

Once they reached Syria, he would have to leave her.

The thought hit him like a fist in the gut. For an instant, all he could do was float numbly in the water, watching the stars spin. He could never have stayed with her. At home, he would have to marry someone from his own class. Ayla was no match for a Bessarion.

Maybe it was just as well that she was angry with him.

Lukas came ashore well south of the Greek encampment and cut through the fields and copses toward the larger, more chaotic Provençal camp. A sentry dozing over the embers of his fire challenged him, but waved him through on a few words of explanation.

When Lukas reached the count's tent, the servants, yawning over knucklebones in the lamplight, told him that the count had not yet returned from council. Lukas groaned. It had to be at least a mile northeast around the city walls to where the council was being held, and by this time he was exhausted. He thanked them and left, picking his way through the round Frankish tents, evading latrine trenches and armour-trees until he found his way to the ring of bare ground that circled the city walls, the closest thing the camp had to a thoroughfare. He spurred himself to a weary jog.

Finding Count Raymond should be easy. He only had to look for a big tent where the lights were burning. The tricky part would be getting him out of the meeting without falling afoul of Tatikius.

When he reached the centre of the North Frankish encampment, he found two equally large and fine pavilions glowing with light.

The nearest rang with voices. Outside, a huddle of squires and horses waited. Lukas headed toward it and announced, "I'm looking for the count of Blois. Is this his tent?"

He was gaining ground in the Provençal dialect, but the squire replied with a stream of thickly-accented North Frankish and a shake of the head. Lukas only recognised a couple of the words: "count" and "busy."

"Yes, I know he's busy." Lukas spoke as slowly as he could, fumbling for the unfamiliar Frankish words through a fog of weariness. "But my count wants to see me."

The man shook his head again, motioning for Lukas to leave.

Something like panic took hold of him. The news was urgent; he couldn't wait all night.

"The count sent for me," Lukas repeated. Before the squire could stop him, he yanked open the tent's flap and stepped in.

Inside were nine or ten knights, in full regalia except for helmets. Their conversation fell silent as they met his eyes and Lukas' heart slammed into his throat. There was no Count Raymond, no Bishop Adhemar, and none of the other princes he had seen from afar.

He was in the wrong tent.

At the table's head, facing him, sat Count Evrard of Le Puiset, the man he'd fallen afoul of at the sparring-field. In the harsh lamplight, his face looked like a death's head.

Evrard spoke softly. "It's the little Greek."

Lukas backed. "I'm looking for Count Raymond of Saint-Gilles. I'm sorry—"

"Seems like your manners haven't improved." The count got up with a tipsy laugh, circling the table for him. "I should have taught you a lesson the first time."

Lukas threw back the flap and ran.

In his haste, he knocked one of the squires down. Behind, Count Evrard shouted. Just as he thought he was clear of them, a hand gripped the back of his tunic and yanked him to a halt like a dog on a leash. For an instant, he reached helplessly toward the distant lamplight in Count Stephen's tent. Then they spun him round to face Evrard.

Or at least, Evrard's fist. Lukas never saw the blow coming. It crashed home just below the ribs, catching him on the tender spot where Ayla had kicked him earlier. He folded onto the ground with a grunt of pain. Hands grabbed him by each arm and dragged him away from the tent to clearer ground.

When he staggered retching to his feet, he found himself standing in a ring of armed men with folded arms and a terrifying delight on their faces.

"Let me go." To his horror, he sounded as though he might cry. "I have an urgent message for Count Raymond! He's expecting me."

Count Evrard circled into view, rubbing his knuckles and still smiling. "Not so fast, my boy. Count Raymond is occupied with more important things right now."

Lukas clenched his fists. Instead of replying to the count, he yelled at the top of his lungs.

"My lord—"

The count backhanded Lukas across the face. He staggered back and fell heavily to the ground, but anger washed away any sense of caution as he pushed himself to his feet. If he only had a weapon! Even his staff would do, but he had left it in the Provençal camp, sure that it would only slow him down.

At least, this time, he could take his beating with courage. Lukas spat blood. "I can promise you that if you keep me from seeing the count, you'll regret it."

"Threats!" Again, the wine-soaked laughter. "Know what I think of your threats?"

The count moved again, but this time Lukas was watching. When Evrard's fist swung, he stepped back, ducked, then dove in while the count was off-balance. He caught the bigger man around the waist and managed to throw him. For one instant he straddled his enemy, coiling his fist back for a blow to the arrogant Frankish face, but it never fell. From behind, someone caught his arms and yanked him off Evrard.

The count climbed to his feet, not too steadily.

Just then a voice called from the direction of Count Stephen's tent.

"Ho, there! What's all this commotion?"

Before Lukas could reply, someone clapped a hand over his mouth.

"Nothing of any importance," Evrard called. The voice seemed to accept this explanation; at any rate, no one appeared to help him.

The count punched him in the gut again, knocking the breath out of him. Lukas collapsed, gasping, but the Franks gave him no respite. Count Evrard grabbed him by the scruff of the neck and began to haul him along the ground.

"You presume too much, Greek. You need to learn your place." The count gave him a shake that crashed his teeth together, and the taste of blood seeped into his mouth. "This is where you belong, peasant."

The ground seemed to open beneath him. A whiff of foul air struck his nose as he tumbled forward. *No*, he thought, but it was already too late. He plunged into the soft and stinking mess of a latrine trench.

Tipsy laughter shook the camp.

Lukas struggled to his knees, wheezing for air.

"Let this be a lesson to you," said the count.

The trench was lined with jeering, laughing Franks. Lukas struggled to his feet, letting the filth drip off him. His body was a knot of pain, but he drew himself up to his full height regardless.

"I know my place," he rasped. "I am as well born as you are, if not better. I am what I am, and nothing you can do will change that."

He pinned the count with a defiant stare. One by one, the others stopped laughing.

"Holy Virgin, Greek, I've a mind to—"

One of the other knights caught his arm. "Enough, my lord. Take no bait from the braggart."

Evrard stared at Lukas. Then his shoulders slumped and he laughed contemptuously, as if angry with himself. "More than enough, I think." He turned and headed back to his tent with the others.

With the threat gone, a wave of nausea hit Lukas and he doubled over, retching again and again. It was so many hours since he'd eaten that he brought up nothing but bile, but the convulsions left him weak and shivering, outraged in every fibre of his being. He had been in fights before, but he had never been pummelled like this by men who gave him no chance to fight back.

The knights were gone, but their servants and hangers-on still lined the trench, laughing and mocking. *This is where you belong, peasant.* As if he was worse than a dog.

Lukas gritted his teeth and squelched his way out of the latrine. The Frankish peasants held their noses and backed away to avoid touching him, but as he shook his dripping hands and shuffled toward the lit pavilions, a pair of tough-looking sergeants barred his way.

"Oi! Where do you think you're going, boy?"

He would have given anything to be heading in the opposite direction, toward the clean water of the lake, but he had failed Count Raymond once already tonight. Lukas spoke through clenched teeth. "I have a message for my master, the count of Toulouse."

The Franks exchanged glances.

"Look at yourself. You're covered in filth." Slowly, the man who had spoken rolled up his sleeves.

Another levelled a spear at him, forestalling his sideways dodge. "You're not fit to be seen."

"Please," Lukas began, but they only laughed.

"Let's put him in the storage hut."

Chapter XX.

Ever since Saint-Gilles undermined its foundations, the Nicaean citadel had leaned at a crazy angle, apparently ready to fall at any moment. Yet with the breach he had created rebuilt by the Turks, there was no point attacking the citadel again.

This time, Saint-Gilles focused on the wall.

For an hour now his catapults and ballistae had kept up their barrage. This morning, the second of the massed assault, would be a repetition of the first: a withering bombardment interrupted only by the charge of storming parties, testing every inch of the city's wall.

Incredibly, despite the council's refusal to choose a sole leader, they had finally agreed on the coordinated assault he wanted. Yet still, the Turks held their ground. They still used their long iron hooks to snare the bodies of the Frankish dead: since yesterday, new corpses had joined the others hanging on the wall. Were they mad? Surely they must realise it was time to surrender.

Bishop Adhemar had command of the archers. To get his attention, Saint-Gilles slapped the side of the oxcart he stood on. "You don't know if Bessarion has returned, Adhemar?"

A shake of the head. "I haven't seen him."

Saint-Gilles gave a hiss of annoyance. He would have given good money to know whether his interpreter had been detained by the Greeks, or had defected to them. He shook his head. Now was not the time to ask such questions.

"Is it Terce yet?"

"Nearly."

"Signal the assault when ready."

As he turned to go, the bishop leaned down, putting a hand on his shoulder. "Raymond. Godspeed, my friend."

Things had been strained between them since the council, but Saint-Gilles' anger was spent now. He was so far from home, surrounded by so many strangers, and besides Galdemar, the bishop was the closest friend he had.

He gripped the bishop's arm. "Pray for us."

Adhemar smiled, looking relieved. "My priests have been at it since dawn."

Saint-Gilles returned to the front lines. "Hold yourselves ready for the signal! Achard, Raimbold, get those ramps stowed on the towers. Pons, ha! I promised you a knightly vengeance, did I not? There it is for the taking!"

The siege parties cheered as he passed and shouldered the massive wicker screens which Saint-Gilles hoped would shield them from bombardment as they crossed the kill zone. At the foot of his own siege tower, Galdemar waited, gulping some last-minute raisins and trading jokes with the men. When he saw Saint-Gilles coming, he lifted his fist with a cheer.

"God wills it! Saint-Gilles and victory!"

Over the cheers, over the deep *twang* of ballistae, the creak of tormenta and the far-off-*whump* of stones striking the wall, a scream of trumpets split the air.

They trilled out in the Provençal lines and fell silent, but the sound did not stop. On each side, the others took it up: the Greeks, the Germans, the North Franks.

Saint-Gilles mounted the siege tower, settled his helmet onto his head and strapped a kite-shaped shield to his arm. "Sound the advance."

A dozen brazen tongues shrieked together. One by one, the Provençal siege towers came to life with a shudder and then trundled forward as the men behind bent their backs to the wheeled platforms. All around Nicaea, machines inched forward to the wall.

Galdemar slapped Saint-Gilles' shoulder, crammed his helmet onto his head and clambered up the creaking ladder to where his men waited on the upper levels, huddled behind shields and screens.

With a sound like the first drops of a rainstorm, the siege tower began to take arrows. A first, a second, a spatter, and then a shredding deluge. A javelin found a weak point in the wicker shields and whistled through, so close to Saint-Gilles that he felt the wind on his cheek. Nobody was hurt; he only had a squire and two knights of his household on the lowest level of the tower with him. The others sweated outside as they muscled the tower forward.

Saint-Gilles grabbed an overhead beam for balance as the structure lurched more quickly across the pockmarked ground. Outside, someone screamed as a Turkish arrow found a target. Still, the Turks weren't returning fire with the same ferocity they had yesterday. Perhaps they were losing heart at last.

One of his knights tapped his elbow. "Look."

Saint-Gilles shouldered his way to the viewport at the front of the enormous, creaking structure. They were nearly to the wall, the ditch opening before them.

"Ease her up! Steady!" he shouted.

Now the immense ballistae on the towers flanking this segment of the wall began to fire. Massive darts and javelins rattled against the screens on either side. Saint-Gilles covered himself with his shield as his men outside threw their backs against the rolling tower and brought it to a halt on the very lip of the ditch.

"In with you!" Saint-Gilles beckoned, and they swung gratefully into the tower. Some swarmed up the ladder to the two higher levels. Others slipped into the ditch, armpit deep in the mucky water, to wrestle two great wooden ramps into place. Slowly, the two massive beams settled into position, spanning the ditch to the wall's foot. Sweat glistened on the men's faces as they worked, knowing they were vulnerable to whatever the Turks might throw from above.

His stomach knotted with tension, but Saint-Gilles forced the worry out of his voice.

"A gold *solidus* to every man of you," he called, but a yell from the upper levels drowned his voice.

"Beware above!"

Saint-Gilles glanced up to see a stone block teetering on the battlement above.

"Look out!" he yelled, throwing himself against the wicker screen. Too late.

Just as the second ramp settled in place, the stone toppled, shattering it to pieces and catching two of the knights holding it. One vanished under the water with a stream of ghastly red bubbles. The other slumped face-down in the water and stayed there.

A long iron hook swooped down from the battlements.

"No!" Saint-Gilles yelled, and one of the living men in the ditch lunged for the floating body. But it was too late. The hook caught the dead man's belt and lifted him over the battlements.

There was no time to stand and weep. That could come after. For now, he must take his grief and distill it into a cold and clear-headed rage.

"Bring up the spare ramp!" he called. Those that remained sprang into action, feeding a third beam into the ditch.

"'Ware oil! 'Ware oil!" came the yell from above. Above, Galdemar's men had their bows out, but they could do little about the great iron cauldron now being positioned between the battlements opposite them.

"Fall back!" It was a lightning-snap of a decision. There was no reason to lose more of them. "Get out of the ditch!"

His men scrambled for the tower. Only a handful of them made it in time. The others crumpled, screaming, beneath a rain of scorching oil. Then, as Saint-Gilles recoiled from the stench of burning flesh, came the fire.

Lit torches tumbled from the wall, wheeling in the air. A sheet of flame roared from the ditch. Soaked in oil, the ramps blazed and the wicker screens on the tower ignited with a crackle.

"Fire! Fire!" Saint-Gilles yelled. "Abandon the tower, form a phalanx, retreat!"

Saint-Gilles could only watch in horror as his worst nightmares played out before him. His men spilled from the tower, some of them falling in their haste. As they huddled into a shield-wall, Turkish missiles probed every gap in armour and shield. Their light arrows stuck harmlessly in the Franks' mail shirts, but the ballistae drove their bolts through shield and hauberk at will.

"Galdemar!" Saint-Gilles bellowed. "Get down here!" Even through his padded gambeson, he felt his armour heating to a branding-iron. The fire was scorched his hair as he jumped to the ground. His one eye made him a poor judge of the distance and he landed with a heavy stumble, nearly twisting his foot. "Galdemar! What are you doing?"

It was obvious what Galdemar was doing: he was waiting for his men to leave the tower before he did. The ladder was black with them as they slid hurriedly to the ground.

Suddenly, something gave way at the tower's base. Groaning, creaking, it pitched sideways. Flames roared, licking up the sides of the siege engine. Galdemar's men threw themselves from the ladder as the tower disintegrated.

Sparks and embers ricocheted from his shield, but Saint-Gilles was already charging into the wreckage.

"Galdemar!"

His friend's black shape had ridden the wreckage down, clinging to a long upright spar. Even before he had hit the ground, Saint-Gilles knew where to find him. Galdemar was there, crushed beneath a corner of the tower's roof, surrounded by flames.

Saint-Gilles' vision narrowed; he seemed to be looking down a long, dark tunnel. Galdemar's eyes were shut, blood seeping from a split in one eyebrow. Once or twice in his life, Saint-Gilles had heard of men given supernatural strength in a moment of desperation. It happened to him now. He crouched, dug his fingers beneath the fallen roof, and surged to his feet, throwing it aside with a howl of effort. At his feet, Galdemar's eyes shot open with a peculiar cry of pain. Saint-Gilles stooped again, lifted him as easily as if he had been a child, and fled into the safety of his phalanx.

His men held out their hands to take Galdemar from him, but Saint-Gilles had his sights set on the safe ground beyond his archers.

"Back!" he shouted. He was dimly aware of arrows stuck in the crevices of his armour, but he felt nothing. As they staggered away from the walls, the Turks poured a vicious stream of iron after them. On either hand, his men fell under stones and javelins.

Long after he thought it would never end, they crossed into the dust that marked the edge of the kill zone and fell to the ground with sobs and groans.

Saint-Gilles sank to his knees and lowered Galdemar to the ground. Slowly, the power seeped from his shaking bones. His heart was going like a hammer, pain trickling through his body as he felt the arrow-pricks and burns he must have sustained rescuing Galdemar.

Under the wall, his siege tower was wrapped in flames, his track marked by corpses. He doubted he had brought half his men out alive. Pierced, minced, or burned, they strewed the way behind, led into a firestorm by their own count.

With a howl, he threw down his shield.

Galdemar, at least, was alive and conscious, struggling to sit up.

"Lie down." Saint-Gilles scrubbed the tears from his face and bent over him. "Is anything broken?"

Galdemar prodded his ribs, wincing. "Bruised and burned, that's all. Saint-Gilles, you madman. That was *preux*. I thought both of us were dead."

Saint-Gilles sat back on his heels, staring at the wall in defeat. "Most of us are."

Saints, pray for their souls. Saint-Gilles felt guilt gnawing at his insides. Was this a punishment for his sins? Were his men suffering for his greed?

Of the other siege engines, one was in flames and another had broken down before even reaching the wall. None seemed to have achieved their goal. Yet, even as he scanned the progress of the siege, Saint-Gilles sensed a change in the rhythm of battle. A commotion of shouts rolled from the left, from the Greek lines. Was it—

Were they *cheering?*

Saint-Gilles staggered to his feet. To his left, Adhemar still stood atop his oxcart behind the line of archers, a shaking finger pointed to the citadel.

He caught Saint-Gilles' eye. "Look!"

Above the battlement, unfurling lazily in the morning wind, floated a great Greek chi-rho banner.

They had done it. They had taken Nicaea.

But how?

One by one, the ballistae on the wall fell silent. The sultan's banner above the citadel trembled in the air and slowly tumbled down.

"Call off the bombardment!" The bishop rushed to the edge of the cart, as excited as a child. "Get me a messenger—heavens above, Lukas Bessarion!"

Saint-Gilles turned and came face to face with his interpreter. The Greek boy was a spectacle. Covered in dried filth and particles of chaff, he almost looked as if he'd gone swimming in a latrine trench and then slept in horse-feed. He must have been fighting, too: he was developing a magnificent black eye, and held one arm protectively across his gut as though it pained him.

"My lord." Bessarion spoke faintly, grabbing the cart to steady himself. "My lord, the Greeks have been in Nicaea since last night. I saw at least a hundred of them go in by the water gate."

It took Saint-Gilles three long, sickening heartbeats to understand what he had just heard.

The bishop paled. "What are you saying, Lukas?"

The Greek turned to him. "Some landed from the ships with standards, and a division marched up from the camp. They all went into the city together."

Saint-Gilles understood. He pointed to the battlements. "Those standards."

"Yes, my lord. I think so."

"They've been inside the city since last night?"

"Yes, my lord."

His fists clenched. "Then our assault this morning was for nothing."

The Greek swallowed. "Yes. I'm sorry, my lord. Please believe me, I tried to tell you, but I was locked up all night."

"I don't blame you." Saint-Gilles gritted his teeth, carried away on a tide of rage that almost frightened him. "I blame Tatikius."

Chapter XXI.

I nside Count Raymond's pavilion, the air boiled with anger.
Still damp from his hasty scrub in the lake, Lukas hunched
against the canvas wall and hoped that if he made himself as
small as possible, no one would notice him. All the Franks present
were angry, but with his arms folded and a vein jumping against
the hollow of his temple, Count Evrard looked furious. The only
man who seemed perfectly calm was Tatikius, and that was no more
reassuring.

Two of the men in this tent were his enemies, the others were
in a scapegoating mood. All Lukas could do was pray they would
overlook him.

A pair of tall, blond Franks shouldered their way through the flap
of the tent.

"Count—Ah, my lords. To what do we owe the honour?" The first
blinked at them as he removed his gloves meticulously, finger by
finger.

"Holy Virgin, more blathering," the other growled.

Lukas did not know them, but the one-eyed count nodded to them
curtly.

"Duke Godfrey. Count Baldwin. I have to inform you that Nicaea
has surrendered to the Greeks."

"To the *Greeks?*" Godfrey put a warning hand on his brother's
shoulder.

"I knew it!" Baldwin threw off the duke's hand and stepped toward
Tatikius, his dark eyes narrowed and angry. "I knew you would

double-cross us! The agreement was that *we* should have the plundering of the city!"

Tatikius only looked at Count Raymond.

"Baldwin, please," said Godfrey. "God be praised, the way to Syria is open."

"Set God aside for a moment." Another of the counts spoke. "What about our booty, Tatikius? Are your people going to open the gate?"

"Good question." Count Raymond swung his head to scan the tent. "Now that everyone is here, perhaps the general will give us answers."

Tatikius' rings flashed as he fingered the glass ball he carried to keep his hands cool.

"What is there to answer? Naturally, since the Turkish garrison wished to surrender, they sent for the representatives of the God-led emperor, whom they know and can trust."

Bohemond frowned. "My lord, be reasonable. These men are not pleased to have Nicaea whisked out from under their noses. Tell us how you accomplished this feat. Where did you enter the city?"

Tatikius was silent.

"I can answer that." Count Raymond spoke coolly. "From the shore, my lords."

"So the Greeks have control of the city." Count Evrard's mouth tightened "Are they going to open the gate?"

"Whatever for?" Tatikius smiled. "The emperor's troops have taken command of the city. Your help is not required."

Count Baldwin lunged away from his brother and banged on the table with his fist. "Enough! Your wretched emperor promised us the booty from every city we take."

"Certainly, from every city *you* take," Tatikius parried. "*We* took this city."

"Only after we spent the best blood of France to reduce it!" someone shouted, and then the whole tent was in an uproar.

Abruptly, Count Raymond spoke again. "You had better leave, Tatikius. If you have reparations to make, they will be better offered to men who are calm."

"Then I will offer them to you."

Crash! The one-eyed count thumped the table with both fists. Glass and earthenware jumped.

"Should I be calm?" he bellowed. "The sword brothers I have lost today are men I raised from boys! Now they are dead because of your deceit! I ask you, *should I be calm?*"

There was a moment of silence. The Greek general blinked, then pocketed his glass ball.

"Very well. I will return later." As Tatikius turned to leave, his eyes caught on Lukas' face.

Recognition flared in his eyes.

Saint George. Lukas tried to swallow, tried to brace himself for the accusation. To his relief, Tatikius only smiled thinly and passed out of the tent.

"So they took the city," Baldwin snarled into the silence that followed. "What's to prevent us taking it for ourselves?"

Bishop Adhemar looked startled. "Any man who does so will be excommunicated!"

Count Raymond sank into his seat with a long sigh. "Nicaea has surrendered. She is a Christian city again. Furthermore, she is the emperor's city, and thus doubly sacred."

Count Evrard shoved forward, planting long bony fingers on the table. "It's easy for you great lords to say such a thing! What about lesser men? We do not have bottomless coffers. Without the spoils of war, our people will starve and die. Such unknightly timidity will destroy us all."

"Unknightly?" Count Raymond swung his head round to glare at him. "Should I break my oath for your sake, sir? I say I will keep it, and I will hold the rest of you to it if I must feed and equip your people from my own coffers."

Bohemond smirked. "I want to know how they managed it. Did the Greeks make a breach in the wall? Or did they use gold to oil the hinges of a postern-gate?"

"My interpreter can answer that question." Count Raymond beckoned. "Bessarion, come forward."

Tatikius was gone, thank God, but he still had to survive the rest of them. Lukas tried not to catch anyone's eye as he inched forward to stand at the foot of the count's table. It was hot in the tent under the pressure of so many eyes, and his face filmed with sweat. Somehow, he managed not to look at Count Evrard.

"Tell them what happened last night, Bessarion."

"I know this man." Count Evrard spoke harshly from behind. "He's nothing but a troublemaker and a liar, my lord."

"Count, please," said Bishop Adhemar.

The bishop's eyes held only concern and encouragement. Lukas found it easier to breathe when he looked at him.

"Last night after Vespers, my lord count told me that someone had seen a boat going to the Nicaean water gate. He sent me to learn what I could. I went into the Greek camp—" He caught himself just in time.

Devil take it.

He had gone into the camp and tried to sell them to the Greeks. He would have to explain that to the count somehow before Tatikius' return, but not now. A trickle of sweat ran down his back.

"I learned nothing from the Greeks, so toward Vigils I swam north to the water gate, where I watched a boat land from the Greek ships. By the light burning above the gate, I saw them carrying standards. They challenged me, but I was able to escape and hide among the reeds. Then a whole division of them marched up the shore from their camp and they entered the city together by the water gate."

There was a short silence.

Bohemond's eyebrow canted up. "This was last night?"

"Yes." Count Raymond's voice was brittle. "Isn't it obvious? They sat inside Nicaea this morning and watched us attack. They watched the Turks slaughter our people. For nothing."

Above the sudden hum of talk, Count Baldwin bellowed, "I knew it."

"Wait, wait." Count Stephen of Blois lifted his hands. "If this is true, why did the Greeks wait until this *morning* to raise their standards?"

"Easily answered," Bohemond said. "They wanted us to think they had stormed the wall and earned the city honestly." He smirked. "It's what I would have done. After all, Alexius knows he can't afford to anger us."

"Holy Virgin!" Baldwin jumped to his feet. "Why did none of us hear this till now?" He rounded on Count Raymond. "If you *knew* this last night..."

"I didn't."

In the silence, everyone looked at Lukas. Lukas looked at the bishop, pleading silently. *Please, don't let them hurt me.*

"I knew it," Count Evrard growled. "The Greek is in league with them!"

"Hang him!"

"Heretic!"

Heart pounding, Lukas whirled around, looking for escape. But the pathway to the flap was blocked in. Evrard loomed over him, hands clawed to bar his way out.

"What prevented you, Greek?" Count Raymond's voice was taut with anger, but Lukas sensed that he was not the target.

Reluctantly, he turned his back on Count Evrard. "My lord, I *tried.* You and the lord bishop were in council, and I went to the North Franks' camp to find you, but I was prevented."

"By what?"

He sensed his chance and took it. "By Count Evrard of le Puiset, my lord."

He actually heard the North Frank's gulp. "My lord! You ought to know that—"

"A *moment,* count. Why did the count of le Puiset prevent you seeing us, Greek?"

It was useless. It was only his word against Evrard's. Lukas' shoulders slumped.

"I don't know, my lord. I went to his tent first because it was lighted and I thought it might be Count Stephen's. I asked the servant, but I couldn't understand his speech. When I looked inside, the count beat me and threw me into a latrine. I tried to find you then, but some sergeants locked me in a feed hut. They wouldn't let me out until after the assault began. I came to find you the moment I could."

Next to him, Count Evrard had almost turned purple. "You never told me you had a message, Greek!"

"I did tell you, and you didn't believe me!" Lukas shot back.

"You should have told me *what* you saw! For all I knew it was chicanery!"

Count Raymond leaned forward. "So the Greek *did* tell you he had a message?"

A mutter ran around the tent. Very faintly, someone whispered the word, "Liar."

Count Evrard must have heard it too, for his breath caught and the colour faded from his face.

Lukas turned back to Count Raymond. "Should I have given him the message, my lord? The matter was secret, and I'm your man and no one else's."

Silence.

"So this is *your* fault, du Puiset," said one of the Normans, in a sour voice.

Evrard shoved Lukas aside and took his place at the foot of the table. This close, Lukas saw that his hands were trembling. "The fellow was insolent. He wanted chastising. No man of birth would have accepted the speech he used to me."

"Enough." Count Raymond spoke scornfully. "Stop trying to save face, count."

"My lord Stephen!" The young count turned to his overlord.

Blois threw up his hands. "What do you expect me do, du Puiset?

We've already paid a heavy price for a knave's chastisement. You should beg my pardon, not my protection."

Evrard drew himself up, his mouth firming to a white line. "I do beg your pardon, my lords," he said, very stiffly. "This is my fault."

Before he turned to leave, Evrard looked down at Lukas one last time, his gaunt fingers whitening on the tabletop. Lukas sensed he was receiving some unspoken threat, but exactly what, he dared not imagine.

With Evrard's departure, the tension bled out of the air as if he had taken the counts' wrath with him. They had found their scapegoat, and it was not Lukas Bessarion.

As they grumbled their last grumbles and took leave of the one-eyed count, Lukas realised that his knees were shaking with the intensity of his relief. He had done it. Somehow, by the mercy of heaven, he had survived them.

Now he had to find a way to survive Tatikius.

The bishop was the last of the guests to depart. Before leaving the tent, he beckoned to Lukas, who followed him outside.

"You have made yourself an enemy, Lukas Bessarion."

"I didn't mean to, my lord."

The bishop gave the ghost of a smile. "Who would? Evrard of le Puiset is noble, and rich, and proud. He will not like being humbled by a Greek serving-man."

Lukas could still smell the stench of the latrine on his clothes. How could he have guessed that he would have his revenge within the day? How could he have guessed how good it would feel?

He tucked his thumbs into his belt. "I'm not afraid of Evrard."

"You should be." The bishop's earnestness punctured his bravado at once. "Count Evrard is a powerful man, one not to be crossed lightly. Your best defence is humility. Do you understand?"

"I have told you that I am a nobleman's son," Lukas said sulkily. "The only reason the count thinks me insolent is that I treat him like an equal. Which I am."

The bishop shook his head. "Right now, your life depends on your willingness to serve. Bear that in mind." His voice dropped to a murmur. "Danger lies ahead of us, Lukas. This pilgrimage needs Watchers, not crow fodder."

Lukas looked away. "I'll bear it in mind."

"Good." The bishop straightened. "By the way, I have a message for you. Your young Turkish friend asked me to tell you that she is waiting for you by the lake, where you met the first night in camp."

"Kismet?" Startled, he realised that the bishop had said *she*. "Saint George, you know about Ayla?"

"All but her real name." The bishop put his hand on Lukas' shoulder. "Take care with that one, Lukas Bessarion."

"I can handle her. She's no problem."

"It's not the girl's actions that I worry about, it's yours." The bishop shook him, something between trouble and laughter in his face. "Remember, boy. Your life depends on your willingness to serve."

Chapter XXII.

Ayla sat on the mound among the reeds where she came to speak to Armen each night, her arms laced around her knees. There was a great hollowness behind her breastbone.

He was late.

She knew she should leave, that she shouldn't have sent for him in the first place.

You should be a lady. You should be a queen. Forsake them. The words still stung. She knew what they meant: *You're worthless. To everyone but me.*

God be merciful, she'd thought he was *different.*

She dipped into her pouch and rolled a pebble between her fingers. Why she had sent for him? She should have left—melted into the streets of Nicaea and never spoken to Lukas Bessarion again.

No. That was the one thing she couldn't do. She did not know whether she wanted to kiss him again or kill him, but it had to be one of the two. No half measures would do.

He was late. Maybe he wasn't coming at all.

The thought had barely crossed her mind before feet crunched in the dry grass at the top of the slope. Ayla slipped the pebble into her sling and rose into a crouch. He might have come with a band of armed Franks to capture the Turkish spy.

But he was alone under the shadow of trees at the top of the bank.

She stood, letting the sling dangle by her side. "You're late."

"Forgive me." He looked at her with eyes like a sick dog's. "Not just for being late, I mean. I shouldn't have said what I did last night. Of course you have to stick by your people. I don't know why I was so stupid."

Ayla tightened her fingers on the sling cord, but there was nothing she could do to move it. Already, the hollow in her heart seemed full again.

She huffed out a breath, tied the sling around her waist again, and stomped through the reeds onto the shore. "Me neither."

Now she stood here on the shore, she didn't know what else to say. Was this it, then? She could not kill him. She would not kiss him.

She would just take his apology and leave.

Lukas turned a palm up in a half-shrug. "If it's any comfort to you, someone threw me in a latrine trench last night."

"God is just," she said tartly.

"I'm late because the bishop was finding me a change of clothes."

He stepped toward her, and Ayla could barely keep from backing away. She could barely look at him. She had giggled like a fool when he kissed her last night. Was he thinking about that now? Did he think she kissed everyone like that?

"Your loyalty is with your own people. I understand that." He took her hand. "But you can't come back to the camp, Ayla."

"I know," she said huskily.

"What will you do?"

"Does it matter?"

He seemed to have difficulty answering that. "I don't want you to feel alone."

"Yeh, well, I can take care of myself."

"*Do you command the wind from the wilderness?*" he asked with a wry smile. "*Are you the mistress of fate, Kismet?* No? Then don't make any promises to me."

"I never claimed to be the mistress of fate."

"What, then?"

"If anything, fate's prisoner."

He did not speak his question, but still his eyes asked.

She scowled at him. "Don't pretend you care. I'm a heretic. You said so yourself."

"You're different," he began.

She spat a curse and yanked her hand away. "You can't, Lukas. You can't hate my people and pretend to like me. Don't you understand? We're at *war*."

There was a silence.

"I'm coming with you," he said.

"What?"

"These Franks…" He shook his head. "I've tried to learn from them, Ayla, but there's no place for me here. Let's leave. Let's go to Syria together. The count gave me some money as a reward for last night…"

"How much?"

Wordlessly, he handed her a pouch. Ayla peered in, and her heart fell.

"There isn't enough. This would barely buy a week's food, much less transport." And besides, in four months she would be dead. She was running out of time to find her vengeance, and serving Armen was now her only hope.

Already she could feel the void that would open when she left Lukas behind. He was the bones in her body. The sun in her sky. He was the only person in the whole world who would care when she died.

"Don't make me dream of a different life, Lukas Bessarion."

"But what will we do?"

"We? There's no *we*, Lukas. We were never fated to be together. You've got to stay with the Franks, they're your only way home." She dragged in a sticky sniff, rolling her shoulders back. "And me? Guess I'll stay right here. God have mercy! Never thought I'd end up on the streets in *Nicaea*."

"Don't." She didn't recognise his voice, it was so miserable. "I need you. How will I survive without you?"

She looked up in surprise, trying to kill the hope that scratched at her heart.

"I love you, Ayla," he said. "My guiding star. My fate-bound warrior."

Her heartbeat was deafening. She didn't know which of them moved first. The wave of euphoria that hit her at the touch of his lips blotted out all their surroundings.

All their past.

All their future.

He pulled back to catch breath. "I dream about you. Every single night."

"You should have told me," she breathed. "Why didn't you tell me?"

He moved to kiss her again, but she pulled back.

"This is insane."

"I know. But it doesn't matter. None of it matters except us."

"Wait. I have to tell you the truth." Saying this was madness, but she couldn't stop herself: she couldn't lie to him again. "I'm not going to stay in Nicaea. The road to Syria is open, and the Franks are going to Antioch. My mother is there, Lukas. I can't stop doing this. I have to work for my people. You realise that, don't you?"

His mouth twisted into a bitter smile. "Family is everything. Right?"

His words brought stinging tears to her eyes. "It's not everything," she whispered. "It's not *you*."

Smile wiped away, he reached out for her again. But she caught his hand. "Maybe it's not everything, but it's the most important thing. Otherwise you could come away with me. It wouldn't be hard. My people would take you in. You could stay in this time and have your home back."

He pulled away, folded his arms, and swallowed. For a while, he just looked at the white earth beneath their feet.

Then he looked up, and his eyes were troubled. "Ayla…it's not just my home. It's my family. I have to save them."

"Then this is farewell. When we meet again, we'll be enemies. Do you understand?"

He could't answer. He only touched his forehead to hers.

Ayla held his face in her hands, one last time. She didn't want him to let go, but he did.

It was the only way.

Chapter XXIII.

Saint-Gilles stood over the graves of his men and tried to pray. The road to Syria was open, but too many of his people would never travel it.

They had exchanged the earthly Jerusalem for a heavenly one. Perhaps he ought to envy them, but he still had too much of the knightly spirit. He was too much wrapped up in his ambitions to wish for death. At least they were holy ambitions: Travel to Jerusalem. Atone for his sins. And keep his people alive while he did it.

This made the second time that Alexius had thrown away lives for a whim. Saint-Gilles vowed there would not be a third.

Unlike many others, the count had not sustained serious wounds in the fighting that morning. By the time he returned to his tent, however, he was limping, every inch of his body aching from overexertion, burns or cuts. He took a bath to soak away the sweat and then, for the first time in three very busy days, he wrapped himself in a soft gown and crossed to his wife's tent.

Inside, one of Elvira's women was grinding something in a mortar. The other, bending over a basket of dirty linen, whispered with his chaplain, Peter of Narbonne. It took Saint-Gilles a moment to realise that something was wrong, before he caught the unmistakeable whiff of fever in the stuffy air.

"What is it, Father?"

Narbonne straightened his gaunt frame and turned. His eyes were tight and uneasy. Saint-Gilles' heart lurched.

"Is it William?"

"I'm afraid so."

As he shouldered through the partition, Elvira glanced up from the cradle, her face pinched with stress.

"Quietly!" she whispered.

Restless, exhausted little sobs punctuated the silence. Saint-Gilles bent over the cradle. William was swaddled up and flushed with fever.

"Why didn't you tell me? How long has he been like this?"

"Since yesterday. I was up all night with him."

"You should have told me!"

Elvira flinched. The next moment she broke down completely, hiding her face in her hands. Saint-Gilles' own shoulders slumped.

"Saints," he said tiredly. A pang of memory struck him. Philippa would have known what to do. But Philippa was long dead, the only woman who had been able to repay his tempers with interest. Now he must make do with this boneless child.

At last he touched her shoulder, schooling his voice to gentleness. "Don't cry. You've had an apothecary to see him?"

Elvira sniffed stickily and nodded. "He said to let the babe sweat it out. Juana is steeping coriander for a tea, but I don't know if he'll take it."

"You're exhausted," Saint-Gilles said. "Go to bed."

Her lips quivered. "But what if…"

"I'll wake you if anything happens. Sleep."

He could tell she hated the idea, but she lacked the spirit to contradict him. She crawled obediently into the bed, pausing only to kick off her shoes. Saint-Gilles sat by the cradle. After a moment, he glanced over and found her watching him with a worried frown.

"What is it?"

"You mustn't take your eyes off him for a moment. Promise me."

"I promise. Sleep," he said, and she closed her eyes obediently.

Silence fell in the room. To one side, the child's nurse lay sleeping on her own pallet. She, too, must have been waking all night. Saint-

Gilles reached into the cradle and picked up William.

His second living son.

Saint-Gilles laid the child across his knees and unwrapped the swaddling-cloths loop by loop. The apothecaries all said to sweat it out, but he had suffered the fever himself and had never taken any notice of what those charlatans said. There was nothing like cool air. As William lay mewling feebly in his lap, Saint-Gilles blew across the child's belly and prayed.

Saint Faith, pray for my son. Saint Giles, pray for my son.

Sir God, forgive me, for I have sinned. He hesitated, thinking. *I have been consumed by knightly pride. I have done an injustice to my niece—she who was the heiress of Toulouse. She did not come to claim the county, and for the sake of peace, someone had to rule it. Still, perhaps I ought to have ceded it to her when she did come, as Adhemar advised.*

Sir God, I acted only as any sinful knight would have.

But I am doing penance for it now. I have come east to fight for you and for the honour of your son. I want to atone for my sins and prove that I love you, and this is the only way I know how. I have people to look after, and my Lord, I'd make a terrible monk. I can serve you better by fighting for you than by anything else. I'm proud to be your man, my liege. And I'll fight and suffer for you as long as there's breath in this old carcass.

But visit my sins upon me, Sir! Not upon my people. Not upon my son!

The sweat dried from William's skin, leaving him hot and dry. Still he continued to toss and cry.

The partition moved and Elvira's maid Juana looked in, holding the steeped coriander in a bell-shaped glass. She hesitated when she saw Elvira asleep, but Saint-Gilles gathered the child into the crook of his arm and led the way out of the stuffy sleeping-quarters. In the front apartment of the tent, he motioned Juana to loop back the flap so that the air would move better.

Neither he nor the maid could make William swallow the coriander.

"Never mind." Saint-Gilles dragged a chair away from the table and sat down in what little breeze he could find. Juana brought

216

him a scrap of linen, and he used the rest of the lukewarm tisane to sponge the child's limbs. Exhausted, he let his head fall back onto the headrest of his chair and closed his eyes. Once again, he found himself praying. *I've lost so many today. So many. Please, don't take my son too.*

The next thing he knew, someone was lifting the tiny body out of his lap. Saint-Gilles started awake with a snarl.

"Shhh," Elvira hushed him. Her face swam into focus above him, serene and bright-eyed. "He's asleep. Look!"

Saint-Gilles climbed out of the chair to blink at his son. Only a scrawny little child, William was never impressive when half-naked. Yet his skin was no longer flushed, his eyes closed in healing sleep. Saint-Gilles laid a forefinger against the child's forehead and found it cool.

"He'll live." Elvira's eyes swam in tears. "You—you brought the fever down."

He cleared his throat, then passed an arm around her shoulders. "Common sense," he growled. "You learn a thing or two on campaign."

Elvira stiffened inside his arm. Then, amazingly, she yielded and rested her head on his shoulder. Saint-Gilles hardly dared to breathe.

"Not many lords would have known," she said softly. "Or cared."

She suddenly disentangled herself and carried the child behind the partition to lay him in his cradle. Saint-Gilles slipped out of the tent flap, feeling a great expansion in his heart. On the way back to his own tent, he sent a squire with three gold *solidi* to sponsor a mass of thanksgiving.

Upon entering his tent, Saint-Gilles found his worldly cares waiting for him with a vengeance. Decked out, as usual, in silks and gilded armours only slightly less gaudy than he had seen on Alexius himself, Tatikius and two others sat at his table refreshing themselves with wine, almonds, raisins, and cheese. Adhemar and a weary, battered Galdemar sat opposite them, but the thread of conversation snapped as Saint-Gilles entered.

217

Sprawled across the floor, the Greek's cheetah lifted a haughty face, as if to ask why he was intruding.

"Tatikius." Right now he only wanted to sleep, but evidently that was not an option. Saint-Gilles stepped to the ewer of water near the door and splashed his face before turning to meet the Greek's greeting.

"My lord." The gold-nosed general put out a thick hand to slide a package across the table: a gilded parchment with a massive gold seal on top. Saint-Gilles barely looked at it before sliding it back to Adhemar, who had the scholar's gift of reading.

"You'd better tell me what's inside it."

"This is a chrysobull from the God-led emperor."

"Evidently."

"The emperor bids you and your princes to attend him in Pelekanum."

"He does, does he?" Saint-Gilles' lips thinned. "Why?"

"He wishes to reward you for your faithful service. The emperor is well aware that he would never have taken Nicaea without your help. He would count it dishonourable to himself if you were the losers by your service."

Pelekanum was two days' travel on the road toward Constantinople. No messenger could have carried news of the city's capture to Alexius and returned with a chrysobull since this morning. Evidently, Tatikius had brought the parchment with him.

But that would mean…

"Alexius had all this planned from the beginning!" Saint-Gilles barked. "From the very *moment* we asked him for ships to float on the Askanian Lake!"

"Does the settlement seem unjust to you, count?"

"Devil take the settlement!" What did the settlement matter if Alexius was as slippery as a calf's tongue? He choked the words back. If he said that he would likely have a feud on his hands. As tempting as he found the idea, he had already committed himself to peace with the Greeks. Instead, he gritted his teeth. "Why does Alexius want to see us?"

Tatikius sized him up for a moment and Saint-Gilles could almost hear the man's debating thoughts.

"The emperor summons you to renew your oaths before you begin your journey to Syria. He wishes to confirm that he may rely upon you and your compatriots to keep your oaths."

"He ought to know better. My word, once given, is kept. I see no need to weary myself running at his beck and call."

"Alexius can help you, count. He knows the Turks. He knows the country. He has the supplies you need."

If this went on much longer, he would end up agreeing to it out of pure exhaustion. Anything to shut the man up. Saint-Gilles leaned his knuckles on the table, focusing bleary eyes on the general. "I undergo this pilgrimage for God, not for Alexius Comnenus. And God will get me to Jerusalem with my people. I neither want nor need Alexius' help. What I need right now is peace and quiet."

"Very well." Tatikius stood and chirruped softly to his men. "The emperor sends me to Syria with you to safeguard his interests on this campaign. Is that acceptable to you?"

"Are you trying to force a quarrel on me? I'm not interested in harming Alexius. If I was, I would never have sworn that oath. What are you trying to suggest?"

"Nothing, my lord. I only wish to understand you." Tatikius led the way out of the tent, drawing on his gloves. "Frankish ways are strange to us."

Saint-Gilles ironed his lips shut.

"Oh," the general added. "One more thing, count. Is that man a servant of yours?"

Saint-Gilles followed his gaze to where his Greek interpreter came strolling between the tents, thumbs stuck in his belt, gaze fixed on the ground. "Bessarion? Yes."

"You may wish to reconsider your choice," Tatikius said smoothly.

"He's a known heretic with a price on his head. Faithless, too. He came to me last night offering to sell information about you."

The Greek moved away, but it was the last straw for Saint-Gilles. "One moment, general." He lifted his voice. "Bessarion!"

The interpreter's head snapped up. When he saw Tatikius, the colour drained from his face.

"Bessarion!" Saint-Gilles roared again. A moment later the Greek boy was in front of them, looking mutely terrified. "Is there something you need to tell me, boy?"

"Saint George." Bessarion gulped. Then the words spilled out in a barely comprehensible flood. "I told you I was in trouble with the Greeks, but I didn't know how serious it was and when I tried to sneak into their camp I was picked up by the sentries and they took me to the lord general and I thought I could make a deal with them and sell them information about you so that they would let me go only they didn't and I managed to get free anyway so that's when I went to the water gate…"

"Stop yammering. What information did you give them?"

"I told them why you sent me into the camp." Bessarion slid a glance sideways at Tatikius, and swallowed. "Please believe me, my lord. I didn't mean…"

"I gave you the chance to leave my service." Saint-Gilles interrupted in a voice of cold fury. "Why didn't you take it?"

"Because I have to get home." His shoulders slumped. "I know I don't deserve a second chance, but…"

"You don't," Saint-Gilles snapped. "But fealty cuts both ways, boy. A man must serve his lord, just as a lord must serve his men." He swivelled toward Tatikius. "Wouldn't you agree, my lord? Oath-breakers should not be trusted."

Tatikius' eyes narrowed. "This man is subject to the emperor's justice, count. You'd best hand him over to us."

"No," Saint-Gilles said coolly. "Here's what you don't seem to understand, Greek. A lord who wants loyalty must *earn* it. By the saints, I ought to know. None of us can get our people to love us by bullying them into taking oaths. And certainly not by giving with one hand and taking with the other like has been done today at Nicaea. Bessarion!"

The interpreter jumped. "My lord?"

Saint-Gilles dropped a hand on the boy's shoulder. "Take your second chance. I only give it once. The next time you feel inclined to break your word, remember that I could have thrown you back to your people. And I didn't."

The boy swallowed, beginning to look hopeful again. "Yes, my lord."

"Have I merited your faith?"

"Yes, my lord."

"Good." As Bessarion ducked his head and scurried away, Saint-Gilles turned back to Tatikius. "Do you understand? You don't lead men by lording it over them. You lead men like Christ did. You wash their feet."

A look of disgust crossed Tatikius' face, the first emotion he had shown. "You suggest that the God-led and holy Alexius should wash your *feet?*"

Saint-Gilles could not help laughing at the Greek's scandalised look. "Think on my words. We are lords, not serfs, and if Alexius treats us no better, this alliance will never last."

Tatikius backed away, his eyes narrowing. "You should also think on mine, *Kelt*. You have no idea what you're about to face. Believe me, you should pray this alliance does last."

Chapter XXIV.

Ayla didn't see the shrine until she was almost upon it. Little remained of the ancient structure but four fluted columns that still supported a corner of the pediment. Weathered to a rich tawny colour, they were almost invisible against the dry grass of summer and the towering walls of the gorge in which they stood.

Yet there was no mistaking the meeting-place Armen had named. Apollo, he had said, and although the djinn who had once inhabited the place was long gone, and his statue rolled to smooth pebbles in the stream, the villagers who lived on the hill above still knew his name and could direct her to his shrine.

Ayla looked up at the pediment, closed her eyes, and let herself feel. Mercifully, no malicious presence touched her mind. The valley was clean and empty.

Suddenly the gorge felt less awful, its slanted afternoon shadows less frightening.

She kicked off her shoes and sat gratefully on a stone to wash her hot, blistered feet. Last night, when she had told Armen that the Franks had exposed her for a spy, he ordered her to meet him here. She'd walked all the way from Nicaea today, having left with the first light of dawn. She had no idea what to expect, but she doubted it would be good news.

Presently, the warm breeze transformed into a cold northern blast. With it, Armen came down the gorge riding a tiny, lithe horse the colour of a golden coin. A short bow of horn was tucked into one boot and a quiver of arrows rode at his hip. He swung out of the saddle, folded his arms, and spoke without greeting.

"How much do they know about you?"

Unlike Lukas, he truly did have a claim on her loyalties, and ought to know the truth. She climbed out of the stream and replied without resentment: "They know I am loyal to the Turks."

"But do they know about me? Do they know how we speak?"

"No."

His eyes narrowed. "None of them? What about the Greek?"

"Lukas?" Ayla shook her head. "He—he only knows I was trying to assist Nicaea, my lord. That's all any of them know."

The words were a mistake. Armen stepped forward abruptly. "You tried to assist Nicaea a *second* time?"

Ayla stood her ground. "Yes, my lord. I judged it was worth trying. The first time I warned them about Count Raymond's assault, they fortified the wall against him. If it wasn't for me, Nicaea would have fallen the very next night. I kept her standing two weeks longer."

"Two weeks! A triviality," Armen growled. "We have known for some time that Nicaea must fall. It was your presence in the Frankish host on which we relied for our *next* assault."

Ayla's jaw dropped. "I didn't realise—"

"No," he said grimly. "With Nicaea fallen, their way to Syria is clear. Either the sultan will destroy them in the mountains, or they will take back all of Anatolia. A whole generation of conquest, lost."

And Antioch would be next. "Look: I'll go back. If there's a plan to destroy them—if you need my help—then I'll go back."

"It's too late. If they catch you, they'll make you tell them everything you know."

"So I won't let them catch me." Her mind began to unravel a solution. "You've never seen such a host. It's like a city. It's like several cities. I can easily go back, slip into a different cohort…"

"*No.*" Armen interrupted without ceremony. "I will choose a more obedient tool."

She could only gape at him. Would he cast her off so easily? There was so little time now. Each heartbeat dragged her closer to death. She was an hourglass bleeding sand, and this was her one chance to make her life count.

Armen's laughter cut her like a knife. "What, girl! Did you think yourself irreplaceable?"

Ayla licked her lips. "I thought you wanted a spy, not a puppet. If that was all you wanted, you would have entered into a hawk or a dog, and spied on them that way."

"You *were* my hawk, my dog. Shall I keep you now that you have become insubordinate?"

Pride broke. She clasped her hands. "Give me another chance. Let me show my obedience."

He held out his hand. "The scrying-bowl."

Ayla felt numb as she dug into her bag and extracted the silver bowl. She wanted to fling it on the stones at his feet, but some whisper of fear held her back. Instead, she put it meekly into his hand, not raising her eyes to his face.

"Now go."

Ayla turned, looking up at the clouded sky. The wind had brought a thunderhead from the sea, and she shivered. "Where will I go?"

"You are no concern of mine," he said coldly. After a moment, however, his voice thawed a little. "You will find shelter before the road leaves the valley."

Ayla turned away before Armen could see the devastation written across her face, thankful for the strengthening wind that whipped her hair, hiding her eyes. Slowly she began limping up the road, her footsteps hastening as she sought the promised shelter.

* * *

Armen watched the girl leave as he took the bow of horn from his boot and braced it between his legs to string it. He took only one arrow from his quiver. With her back to him, the girl would be easy enough to deal with.

A shame. He remembered her father well. But Ilkay of Antioch had been a sentimental fool about his family. The girl had information which could put the Frankish Watchers on their guard, and if he could not make use of her, there was only one way to silence her.

He laid the arrow to the string. Shelter was coming. The dead do not fear the storm.

A cold blast of wind shrieked down the gorge from the north, spraying dust into his eyes. When Armen blinked them clear, *she* had come.

She perched atop the crumbling pediment and folded her black-as-night wings. "Slave," she rasped in her husky voice. "On your face."

Armen knew better than to argue, but as he prostrated himself, he spared a glance for the retreating girl. A few more steps and she would vanish behind the rocks. "My lady," he protested.

"Stay down."

His horse edged away from the shrine with a terrified whicker. It could not see her, but it could feel.

"My lady, your breath is my law, but what if the girl betrays us?"

"Unstring your bow," she rasped. "Ride after the girl. She must return to the strangers and spy on them for us."

He never understood her reasons, and she never gave them of her own accord.

"But my lady, why not send someone else?"

"Because of the *boy,* you fool. That girl is the only reason the Bessarion is still alive."

"Bessarion!" Armen jerked upright, squinting at the dark outline against the glaring clouds. "The *Bessarion* is with the Franks?"

"He needs her protection. You will send the girl back to the strangers." She spread her wings.

"Yes, my lady." He touched his forehead to the dirt again. When he looked up she was gone.

Bessarion. Armen touched his tongue to his lips. Well, by the Illuminator, this brought in a new age of the world.

The girl vanished beyond the rocks. As the first fat raindrops spattered across the stones of the shrine, Armen hauled himself into his saddle and raced after her.

Chapter XXV.

I t was still dark when the summons came.

Five days' journey from Nicaea, half the Frankish camp was pitched in a sheltered hollow, nestled amongst the straw-coloured hills. Behind, the ill-kempt road straggled down into a long valley bordered with trees. Plots of farmland, like a green tide of lowland fertility, washed up against the barren high plains of Turkish-occupied Anatolia.

All day yesterday Lukas had toiled up these long slopes, part of a silent, sweating river of men and beasts whose numbers still made him feel dizzy. Yet this was only a fraction of the whole pilgrimage. Somewhere nearby, Bohemond, Tatikius and a few of the other counts were travelling in a separate column.

As he had done every other morning, Lukas expected to help dismantle the count's tent and load the carts for the next stage of the journey. Instead, directly after Lauds, Count Raymond called him to a crest on the east side of the camp where he, Bishop Adhemar, and Duke Godfrey stood looking into the grey southern hills.

The count leaned heavily on his spear. In the two weeks since Nicaea surrendered, he had suffered a rough bout of fever, but his words were as much to the point as ever.

"We're sending you off to find the vanguard, Greek. They can't be far to the south—last night we picked up some of their stragglers." He worked a signet ring over a knobby knuckle and held it out. "Take this to Bohemond and tell him we've seen Turkish scouts in the hills. Best if we stick together from now on."

Lukas hesitated. Anyone who held the count's signet ring could speak in his name. After what he had done at Nicaea, this was a gesture of trust he did not deserve.

Bertrand moved forward, a deeper shadow looming behind the bishop. "It's dangerous, my lord, and a rider would move more quickly. I am willing to go."

Count Raymond shook his head. "We sent two riders last night. They never came back. It's the Turks, without a doubt."

"Sometimes a humble peasant will succeed where a lordly knight will not," added the bishop gently.

"We need someone who can pass as a native if he's caught. Best keep the ring hidden, Bessarion. Go on foot and take no weapons."

It's dangerous. Bertrand's words echoed in his mind, but Lukas squared his shoulders. "I'll do it, my lord. You can trust me."

"I believe it," the count rumbled. "Don't bother coming back unless it's safe. No need to risk a second journey."

Lukas added the signet ring to a bundle of almonds and dried grapes that he kept wrapped in a rag inside his pouch. He was refilling his water canteen at the stream when Bertrand's feet crunched in the dry grass next to him.

"I'll come with you," the squire said quietly.

Lukas stood, looking the gigantic young Frank up and down. Bertrand had peeled off his armour and weapons, leaving a simple homespun tunic and worn leather shoes. His skin was tanned from the summer sun and his hair, like many Provençals, was black. "You won't pass for a Greek. You're too big, and you don't have the language."

"So I'll let you do the talking. Come on. Two are better than one."

Lukas could not deny that the big Frank's company would be welcome. Regardless, he knew by now that men of Bertrand's rank could do as they liked. "Please yourself."

Lukas led the squire south and slightly west, keeping his eyes on the ground for any sign of the vanguard's passing. Bertrand loped easily next to him, his long stride swallowing up the ground.

"Where's Kismet these days?"

Every time someone asked the question Lukas' gut twisted. "Why do *you* care?"

The squire's eyebrows flicked. "The two of you were friends, right? I thought you would have gone with him."

"Wish I had."

Ayla's absence ached fiercely, like a lost limb. He told himself it was nothing to do with her. Torn away from his family, he had clung to Ayla to fill their place. Now that she was gone, it was them he craved, not the Turkish girl.

Perhaps sensing his discomfort, Bertrand changed the topic. "So you come from Palestine. Tell me about it. There must be many holy men living there."

Lukas angled a little further toward the grey east, aiming for a gap in the hills. "There are hundreds of monasteries and countless hermits."

"I once considered becoming a monk myself, since they are beloved of God for their great abstinence and poverty. But what about the laymen?"

"The same as anywhere else, I suppose. Some good, some bad."

"But to walk in the footsteps of our Lord and so many other saints, surely that must change a man. Make him holier. Even if he isn't a monk."

Lukas had never thought of it that way before. The reasoning would certainly explain why he was walking through Anatolia in midsummer with so many thousands of people. If the graves or the bones of a saint were able to work miracles, why not the very land where so many of them had lived?

"But surely," he said aloud, "if that was so, we would have been a different kind of people. Better. Holier. And there would be more Watchers."

"Watchers? I've heard of them. The bishop is one, I think. But what *are* they?" Bertrand's voice held a long-denied curiosity. "Where did they come from?"

"There have always been Watchers, since the beginning. They do righteousness and justice." Despite the earliness of the morning, the air was already warm. Lukas sleeved the sweat from his forehead. "You know the story of Sodom? Full of fornication and pride she was, idleness and oppression, so God decided to rain fire and brimstone on the city. But Saint Abraham begged him, if there were as few as ten righteous men in the city, to spare it."

"I know the story. So?"

"So Sodom perished. Because she didn't have Watchers." Lukas remembered the Varangian Messenger, and the message he had given. "Nor does Jerusalem, any more. Nor does Antioch."

He heard the grin in Bertrand's voice. "Just as well we are coming to save them."

"Better pray we outlive the day, Frank." The words came out of his mouth without thought. Saint George, now he sounded exactly like Ayla.

The sky was bright in the east by the time they came down into a wide, fertile valley that sloped upward: a clear trail into the Anatolian plateau. Here they found the unmistakeable signs of an army's march. Hoof prints and wheel ruts had churned the narrow path to a slough of white dust in which lay the inevitable litter left by tens of thousands of passers-by: bits of food, discarded clothing, broken and useless gear, dead animals. There was no missing the path.

Lukas beckoned Bertrand east on the pilgrims' trail. Ahead, the light grew. Day was coming, much too fast. If there were Turks about, they could be lurking anywhere in these hills, and with each passing moment Lukas felt more exposed.

A sound jerked him to a stop. Bertrand halted beside him and for a moment the two of them listened. For several seconds, they heard only the dawn wind in the dry grass and the trees scattered on the valley's slopes. He was imagining things.

"It's nothing. Tell me, how does one become a knight?"

They settled into a hurried lope. Bertrand's breath was coming short, but he too seemed glad of the opportunity to talk. "One's lord gives one the cuff of dubbing."

"So... the count could box my ear, and that would make me a knight?"

"It's not unheard-of for a nameless peasant to receive the cuff."

Nameless peasant. Lukas snorted. "Yes, that's the problem, isn't it?"

"Not the only one. It's costly, all the harness and gear. The war-horse alone is worth hundreds of sheep. And then the palfrey, to ride instead of the war-horse, which is a boneshaker on the open road. Then the squire, the household, the feed..."

"But you can be a knight even without those things, right?"

Bertrand huffed a laugh. "What do you mean?"

"If you lost your armour...or your horse was killed. Would you still be a knight?"

"Yes, but God forbid! Such a life would hardly be worth living."

They came over a rise in the hill.

"Bertrand." Lukas pointed ahead.

Here, beside the road, were the ashes of a tiny campfire and an old man lying in a handcart beside it. The old man's face was waxen in the morning light, his mouth open as if he had breathed out once and gone. Beyond the cart, two Frankish peasants were spreadeagled across the ground, their bodies hacked, their blood dry in the grass. All three of them were dead.

"Turks," said Bertrand very softly.

"They're killing stragglers." Lukas straightened, scanning the sides of the valley. Most of it was open ground, spotted by trees along the slopes. In the distance, small farms or settlements were tucked into the folds of the hills. In this terrain, it would be impossible to hide.

More than ever, he felt naked and vulnerable, marooned in open land.

Bertrand had been straightening the bodies, crossing their hands on their breasts and making the sign of the cross over them. Now he pointed to a smudge against the lightening sky a little to the right. "Look. Campfires. We could cut straight across to them."

"We could blunder straight into the Turkish camp, too." Lukas unslung his staff from his shoulders, balancing it in one hand. "Come on. We need to move."

He set the fastest pace he dared, pushing Bertrand into a steady dogtrot. Not much further on, Lukas wheeled aside, seizing on something that stuck up from the ground like a solitary black stalk of wheat. "Turkish arrow," he called to Bertrand.

Not much further on, they found the scouts: two knights riddled from the back with so many arrows that they looked like pincushions. There was no sign of their horses. As they approached, a bird unfolded its wings and clambered silently into the sky. A huge black vulture.

"Don't stop," Lukas panted.

"We can't just leave them—"

"The count will find them. Come on."

They made it to the crest of the next rise and ran into a shaft of blazing gold as the sun's edge broke above the hills before them and flooded the valley with light. Behind them, the moon still hovered above the horizon, a waning white globe.

Hoof beats echoed from the hills.

Lukas turned, clutching his staff. Under the pale moon, a black hooded rider raced toward them on a horse that glowed like a gold coin. He knew immediately that it was not a pilgrim. The horse was smaller and lither than the Frankish mounts, its pace a fresh and springy gallop.

"Sit down," he hissed, pulling Bertrand off the road. "Bow your head."

He stayed on his feet, prayers rattling over his tongue, his heart thundering in his chest. There was only one of them. Only one.

But one with a bow would be all it took to kill them.

The rider thundered closer, the cloak flapping like the wings of the vulture overhead. Lukas kept still, kept his eyes on the ground, like a fieldmouse waiting for birds of prey to drop from the sky. If only he had armour, a horse...

The rider was almost on them when the galloping pace broke suddenly.

"Lukas Bessarion?" It was the last voice he expected to hear. With a yank of the hood, Ayla revealed her face. "You cucumber! What are you doing here?"

He stared, speechless. Atop that beautiful horse, swathed in black silk with the golden light of morning on her face, she seemed to have been transformed into the princess he had always dreamed of making her. Worlds removed from the grubby urchin he had met in Myra.

"Ayla," he croaked, stepping forward to catch at her rein.

The golden horse danced away, rolling its eyes.

"What are you doing out in these hills?"

He had to give *some* explanation, and quickly, or she would guess that he was on some more important errand. "We're...straggling. It's Bertrand, he's not feeling well."

She barely seemed to hear. Her hands clenched whitely on the reins. "Turn around. There are farms in the valley where you'll find refuge. Turn around, Greek. You are dead if you go on."

She kneed the golden horse forward. He saw a flash of white within her hood as she glanced back at them. Then she was over the next crest and gone.

Bertrand was on his feet. "Was that...was that *Kismet?*"

Lukas did not know how to answer. "Come on."

At the next crest the column's tracks curved away to the left. A faint haze hung beyond the slopes in that direction. There was no sign of Ayla.

Lukas quickened to a run. Down the slope, across the tufty swamp grass in the valley's bottom, and up the facing hill—the Frankish vanguard, at last!

Someone barked something at him in Frankish. Lukas turned to find himself looking down the stock of a levelled crossbow.

His grip of Frankish deserted him. "Friend! I'm a friend!" he yelled in Greek.

"Stand down, we're Frankish," Bertrand gasped, bending double to catch his breath.

To his relief, the crossbow dipped. "All right, I know your lingo, Greek." The sentry was a big, rough-hewn Frank with a complexion already beaten brown by the sun. One of Bohemond's men? He spoke Greek with a thick accent: Lukas vaguely recalled that the Normans from Italy had fought in this part of the world before. "We were just about to leave. You'll find your lord and stick to him, if you're wise. There are Turks about."

Lukas extracted the count's ring from his pouch. "Our lord is behind. We've come from Count Raymond with a message for Count Bohemond."

The sentry motioned them through with a nod.

The camp was stripping down, breaking up and preparing for the march. As they made their way through the commotion to the central pavilion where Bohemond's blood-red banner fluttered, Lukas scanned the hills on either side. There was still no sign of Ayla and her gold horse.

Was she risking the same danger she had warned him against? Or was she herself the danger?

In the tent under the blood-red banner, Count Bohemond was eating breakfast. A chill crept up Lukas' spine as he recognised the two lords sitting beside the count. On his right was the count of Blois, Evrard of le Puiset's lord. On the left sat Tatikius himself, breathing the fumes of a cup of wine through his golden nose, with one of his Varangians at his back. Not the Messenger, Lukas noted with disappointment, but the one who kept his axe sharp.

It had made little difference in the valley, but he was grateful for

234

Bertrand's bulk at his back now. The Greek general beckoned to the Varangian and whispered something into his ear. Lukas felt the weight of both their eyes on him as he delivered the count's message in his still-laborious Frankish.

Bohemond leaned back with a laugh and exchanged some quick words with the men around him. He deftly tossed Count Raymond's ring back into Lukas' hands and spoke in broken Greek even worse than the sentry's. "Run back to Saint-Gilles, yes? Tell him better keep hosts apart. Better supplies, better—foraging. Yes?"

Lukas tried not to laugh at the count's atrocious Greek. Had he discovered something the illustrious Bohemond did badly? Instead, he spoke in careful Frankish. "But the Turks are going to attack. Maybe today."

"Pff!" Bohemond waved his comment aside. "We know the Turks. We deal with the Turks. We have all the knights we need. Run back to Saint-Gilles."

Lukas tried again. "On my way, I met one whom I know to be a Turkish spy. One who might be in the camp now."

"A spy more or less makes no difference." Bohemond got up, wiping his mouth. "We do not have walls to keep the rats out, either. Time to march."

The men in the tent filed out until only one remained. The man reached out a hand. "Bertrand Monteil, I think? We met before at the sparring."

The squire blinked a moment before recognition came into his eyes. "Count Robert of Paris. My lord."

"You met Turks on your way here? Is it safe to return?"

Bertrand glanced at Lukas. "Safe doesn't matter, my lord. Count Raymond should know where to find you."

"He can't be far. Let Bohemond send a fast mount for help when he needs it. You're on foot and helpless. You should stay here."

Bertrand pulled at his clean-shaven chin, his eyes shadowed with thought. "If anyone rides to get help, it should be someone who knows the way. Will you lend me a fast palfrey?"

* * *

Lukas never ceased to be amazed how quickly a camp could pull up roots for the march. This morning the pilgrims had formed a tight phalanx, with the non-combatants and baggage positioned between the mounted knights and foot-soldiers. Bohemond's red banner fluttered on the right wing, next to the Greeks. Duke Robert of Normandy and Count Stephen of Blois formed up on the left.

Evidently, the counts expected battle.

As the trumpets blew the advance, Lukas followed Bertrand into his place in the column. The squire had managed to borrow light armour and a good horse from the count of Paris, but of course, as a mere peasant, no one had offered anything to Lukas.

Sometimes a humble peasant will succeed where a lordly knight will not. Lukas cleared his throat. "I'm willing to go back on my own, Bertrand."

"No point. They're killing everyone they find, knights *and* stragglers."

Lukas was silent. If he let Bertrand do all the work, how would he prove his loyalty to the count?

Bertrand gave him a sideways glance, as if sensing his reluctance. "Didn't you hear the count tell you to stay? I'm just a fighting man, Lukas. I can always be replaced. You're something much rarer."

"What's that?"

"A man with the gift of tongues."

Lukas shook his head with a twisted smile. He just happened to be good with languages, that was all. Still, Bertrand was right; if he meant to prove his loyalty to the count, the last thing he should do was disobey his order.

Ahead, the land funnelled the pilgrimage upward into the hills. As the sun climbed higher, the dew dried from the ground. Already, sweat muddied the coats of the immense Frankish war-horses around him. The beasts plodded on miserably under their heavy packs, many with mangy tufts coming free from their thick, woolly coats.

Lukas wondered if any would survive the journey.

Someone in the host began to sing the *Non Nobis,* and soon it became a torrent of sound cascading from thousands of throats. The hair prickled on the back of Lukas' neck. This was the Frankish war song.

These Franks *wanted* to fight.

The minutes slid by and the march continued: valley, trees, empty land, dry mouth, aching feet. The valley rose higher still.

They had been riding for two hours when the expedition came to a wide green bowl of land with a narrow gorge opening out of it to the north and south. A river trickled through the lowlands, losing itself in a marsh at the lowest point of the hollow.

The column ground to a halt, a shudder rippling through it like the wind across pasture on a stormy day. In the silence, the sound of distant hooves pounded through the ground and faded.

Something had happened ahead.

Trumpets screamed. Riders galloped down the column shouting, "Down to the marsh, pitch camp, and saddle your destriers!"

Bertrand leaned down, slapping Lukas' shoulder. "I'm going to fetch the count. We'll come for you," he promised. As the army lumbered into chaotic forward motion, the squire reined away and spurred back down the valley.

Drums sounded in the hills, a racing pulse under the thunderous trample of the pilgrimage's feet. A vanguard of knights on horseback streaked down the forward slope to plant Bohemond's banner in the soft green ground that promised defence. Ox-carts quickened to a bouncing run, eager not to be left behind.

Above the hubbub of pilgrims scrambling for safety, the counts shouted orders to stick together, but still the column stretched out and thinned.

Far away, a shrill ululation began. The Turkish war-cry. All around Lukas, people broke into a panicked run. By now the column extended all the way from the lip of the hill to the green haven around Bohemond's banner. Some of the slower pilgrims began throwing their children aboard the oxcarts, or clambering aboard themselves. Every instant, the drums, the shrilling war-cry, rolled closer.

Panic flooded through Lukas, urging him to flee to safety. But he couldn't leave—not after seeing those dead Franks by the roadside. These people were in danger, and he was their Watcher. Lukas forced his rapid breaths to slow and turned, looking for someone—anyone—who needed help.

There. A man dragging a frame of three boughs lashed together. As the frame bounced over a stone, the lashings on one corner broke, scattering two children and their bundled belongings in the dust. Feet trampled on the bundles, splitting them open. One of the children began to wail.

Lukas shoved his way through the rout and scooped up the youngest child, pulling the other to his feet. "Take her," he said, putting the girl into the man's arms, and picking up the boy. "Run."

The man had no words for thanks. He paused only to catch up the nearest bundle. Then they were running.

Ahead, the Franks had backed some of their carts into a makeshift barricade. Inside, a ring of tents bloomed between the barricade and the river. Knights worked frantically, loosing the packs from their war-horses, buckling on saddles, donning helmets, grasping spears. Once equipped, they spurred to the ragged line of steel which now formed forward of the camp, facing the south gorge.

Still, the beat of drums. Hectic shrieks cascaded towards the Franks as they poured into the unfurling camp. Stragglers threw down their burdens and ran or hobbled for safety.

Beside Lukas, the Frankish peasant gasped for air. He had gone pale under his tan, gaunt and exhausted and coughing with effort. Lukas shifted the child to his left arm and grabbed the father by the elbow, trying to steady him. "Come on, come on, come on…"

He measured the distance to the camp. They could make it. They had to make it.

The Turkish war-cry rolled into a crescendo as their horsemen poured into view, bright tunics and elf-locks streaming in the wind, horn bows in their hands.

"Shields!" someone howled. The Frankish footmen hoisted their kite-shaped shields over their heads as the knights huddled into a solid block, pushing forward.

The wind hissed with arrows.

Ahead of Lukas, a man plunged to the ground as an arrow split his skull. All around, wailing filled the air.

The Turks were not shooting at the armed men. They were shooting the peasants.

Lukas skidded to a halt and hunched over the child in his arms. The world narrowed to the groans of pain around him, the stench of blood and death falling from the sky.

As quickly as it had begun, the volley of arrows stopped. Lukas straightened. Already the Turks were drawing to shoot again, this time at the Frankish knights.

A trumpet blew.

With a cry like thunder, the Franks charged. In two close-knit wings, they pounded directly into that inferno of noise and death, straight into a withering hail of iron.

Lukas grabbed the Frankish peasant by the arm. "Now!"

Chapter XXVI.

They said it was a new kind of war he was fighting, for a new kind of cause, but Robert of Paris had never imagined a whole new kind of foe.

Death striking from the sky. An enemy that babbled in shrill voices, repeating a devilish word he did not understand. A force consisting only of mounted archers with almost supernatural ability to shoot and manoeuvre at the same time.

Mobile. Swift. Deadly.

Nothing could have prepared him for this.

Shield up, head down, Robert pounded for the Turkish line. An arrow hissed toward him and stuck in his horse's shoulder, but apart from a shiver running through the beast's skin, his Couraigeux barely flinched. The Turks drifted closer and Robert tightened his fist on his spear, anticipating the moment that the Frankish charge would pound into them like a battering-ram through an alabaster window.

The moment never came. Instead of meeting their charge as a Frankish force would, the Turks parted their ranks, scattering like flies.

Trumpets blared and the charge lumbered ineffectually to a halt, unable to risk being cut off from the camp. Screaming Turks stormed around them just out of reach, pouring a constant stream of arrows into their ranks. *Whing!* One skipped off Robert's helmet. *Ta-tack!* Two more buried themselves in his already battered shield. Around him, knights sprouted arrows like human pincushions. Worse, the horses began streaming blood, not protected like their riders by multiple layers of chain and padding.

Caught in the midst of a useless block of knights, Robert ground his teeth. *Saint Genevieve.* This was like fighting smoke, or rain.

Motion on the far left caught his attention. Among the trees on the slope, the Turks were still busy hunting and slaughtering stragglers.

Our people, he thought furiously.

He was not a particularly selfless man. No knight was, by definition. But if Robert of Paris had ever taken pride in anything, it was his ability to protect the people who followed him.

No man, knight or not, could endure such bloodshed calmly.

"They're killing our people!" he yelled. "Who's with me? Odo? Henry? Come on!"

"Don't do it, you madman!" It was one of the Italian Normans, the one they called Tancred. "You'll get yourself killed!"

"You're not my lord," Robert howled, kicking Couraigeux into an unstoppable rolling gallop. Thunder from behind told him that others were following.

God was with him. The Turks fled before his couched spear. Their arrows tested his armour, rattling front and back, but none pierced the close-knit byrnie.

His focus narrowed on the path opening up toward the fleeing peasants. If nothing else, he would buy them time—

He felt the next arrow go in, not his own flesh but his horse's. Couraigeux gave an agonised shudder, clipped his gait suddenly, and then went down with a scream of pain. The iron had pierced between the bones of the animal's massive leg, crippling him. Robert yanked his feet free of the stirrups as the horse keeled over.

Just too late.

An agonising weight crushed one foot into the ground, then lifted as the horse struggled to rise. Robert pulled himself free and clawed his way to his feet. One leg could take no weight. His spear was gone.

He took a few excruciating steps before collapsing to his knees. Hoof beats thundered in front of him as Robert looked up, straight into the whistling flash of a Turkish sword.

* * *

As the Frankish charge ground to a halt, the Turks scattered. Lukas yelled a warning as a company of them peeled off and charged the ragged line of stragglers.

There was nothing they could do but run for safety.

The ground became soft and clinging underfoot, slowing their pace. Lukas struggled the last few steps, half-dragging the Frankish peasant and his children. As the Frankish footmen surged toward them, hands reached out to pull them in, enfolding them in the line of steel.

Lukas and his companion collapsed to the ground beneath one of the oxcarts, gasping for breath. Both the children were crying with fright; the eldest, Lukas realised, was only a boy of maybe four years old. He struggled out of Lukas' arms and crawled to where his father lay, wheezing and coughing for breath so hard that he could barely pull them close.

Saint George, Lukas thought tiredly. He had saved them for now, but how much longer would they last?

Suddenly, he could not face the thought of waiting to be thanked. He rolled out from under the cart and mounted its wheel for a better vantage point. By now, the stragglers who had not made it to safety were dead. Beyond the line of footmen, the Frankish knights huddled together, standing their ground at the eye of a whirlwind of Turkish archers. Again and again, the Franks tried to rush their tormentors, but the Turks either opened up to let them pass—or cut off the charge and annihilated it.

Lukas gnawed his knuckles. The best of the Frankish knighthood, and they looked as helpless as their own stragglers.

By the time help arrived, would anything be left?

Thwack. Lukas gave a yelp of surprise as an arrow sprouted, quivering, in the cart within an inch of his arm. He stared at it for a moment before whirling to look at the camp behind him.

Turks in the camp.

He dropped to the ground, the wet earth receiving him softly. Within the camp a cacophony of screams broke out: the shrieks of frightened women, the ululation of the Turkish war-cry, now closer than ever. The enemy must have circled them somehow, crossed through the marsh or the river to reach their undefended rear...

The camp was breached. It was over.

Lukas gritted his teeth. It *couldn't* be over, not like this. He had to get to Syria. He was not going to die today.

Beyond the barricade of carts, the ring of motley foot soldiers waited and watched, still oblivious to the threat in their rear.

"Help!" Lukas yelled, scrambling across the cart and dropping into the narrow lane between the barricade and the footmen. "Turks in the camp! Turks in the camp!"

His shout threw them into confusion and they reacted without thinking. Some plunged through the vehicle barrier into the camp, while others froze in indecision.

Footsteps sounded behind him and a hand fell on his shoulder.

"Stop panicking. Move."

Lukas turned. It was the Varangian bodyguard, the Messenger who had freed him. At his back was a detachment of tough-looking Greek infantry. Lukas flattened himself against the cart to let them past. They went up the pathway at a quick jog-trot, squeezed between two carts and headed into the camp.

Lukas unslung his staff from his shoulders and ran after them. If it was his day to die, let him die well, as a Bessarion should.

And if he was destined to live, he would have some questions for the Messenger.

He raced through the protective ring of tents and emerged into a clear area beyond, where the non-combatants huddled amongst the picketed animals.

It was pure chaos.

Turkish footmen swarmed through the crowd, shooting with their short bows or swinging their light swords. Blood and bodies were everywhere, and the Varangian Messenger was leading his men straight into the red quagmire.

Lukas was about to race to their aid when someone screamed nearby. A girl staggered out from between two tents and sprinted toward him. Behind her, two Turks spilled from the same opening, swords in hand.

The Frankish girl latched onto his right arm. "Help me!"

"Let go!" Lukas managed to detach himself with a shove that sent her staggering into the side of a tent. Free to move, he levelled his staff, feinted and jabbed the foremost of the Turks in the throat.

The man collapsed with an ugly choking sound. The other aimed a slashing blow at Lukas' head. He felt the steel breathe in his hair as he brought up the other end of the staff barely in time to catch it on the flat and deflect it high.

Momentum carried them past each other.

The Turk on the ground lay struggling for breath, clutching his throat with both hands. He had dropped his sword on the ground nearby when Lukas struck him, a slim, straight beauty of a weapon.

Lukas caught his breath and forgot that anything else existed. He threw his staff to the left hand and swooped down upon it, stretching his hand to catch the hilt.

Understanding flashed into the downed Turk's eyes. His foot lifted, flexed, drove forward.

Lukas took the kick on his staff and left forearm with a jar that shook every bone. Yet his right hand closed on the sword-hilt and he slashed blindly until he freed himself of the man on the ground.

He spun, staff and sword ready, conscious of other presences.

In the time it had taken him to pick up the sword, the other Turk had lunged for the Frankish girl where she sprawled amidst the wreckage of a tent. Now he dragged her to her feet and held her in front of him like a shield, sighting down the supple length of his blade at Lukas.

The girl's face distorted with tears and stress. The eggshell-blue dress, chain-mail shirt, and reliquary of gold and amber at her throat marked her as noble born. Whoever she was, Lukas was sure of a rich reward if he saved her life.

The sword felt odd, unfamiliarly balanced in his hand. It was both longer and lighter than the weapons he had trained with in the old days. Still, it had an edge, and that was the main thing. He slid into a fighter's crouch and inched forward, letting the sword point scrawl in the air as he loosened his muscles for action.

The Turk glanced to his left and stepped back, dragging the girl with him. To the side, a cohort of fifteen or twenty Turks appeared, sweeping along the perimeter of tents, waving stolen banners and torches, setting fire to the tents as they came. Some dragged young prisoners, women and boys. One drew an arrow to the ear, and Lukas dove aside just as the fletch sliced a runnel in his cheek. He caught his foot in a discarded rope and crashed to the ground.

A foot descended on his sword, pinning it to the ground. Lukas looked up. The Frankish girl stared down at him, her face blotched with tears. Behind her, the Turk drew back his sword.

This was how he died. On his belly. In the muck.

Yells interrupted them. The Turk glanced up, past him, and his eyes widened. Lukas let go of the sword and rolled away.

Between the gaps in the barricade of carts, Frankish knights stormed into the camp on massive horses maddened to the point of stampede. Panic or berserk rage, it was hard to tell what had them in its grip. As the tide rolled in, the Turks yelled and ran, dragging their captives with them.

Lukas knew he lay in directly their path, but he was unable to move, transfixed by the apparition that had appeared above the Frankish rout.

She flew in their wake, riding the wind from the wilderness. Her black-feathered wings spanned twice the height of a man. Her body was an abominable blend of woman and bird, with feathers for hair and claws for hands.

The creature swooped screaming down on the Frankish knights, her voice a tortuous shriek on the edge of hearing. When her eyes caught his she whipped a black bow up and loosed an arrow straight at him.

It hissed into the earth at his feet even as the maddened horses reached him.

Lukas pulled in his knees, wrapping his arms around his head, but the charge divided around him like a stone splitting a stream. On either side of him, inches from where he lay, the ground shook with the impact of hooves nearly as big as his head.

Lukas imagined, very vividly, what would happen if even one of those hooves hit him.

Then he found out, and his head exploded into a black dream of pain.

Chapter XXVII.

L ukas woke with his head throbbing. When he cracked his eyes open, the glare pierced his head, forcing him to close them again. Something was draped over his face to shade it, but it offered little protection from the merciless sun. Muzzily, Lukas tried to drag the cloth away, but he could not manage to move.

For a moment, he thought he was dying, but then more of his senses returned. He was soaked from lying on soft wet ground. The Turks were still yelling their war-cry, but apart from the occasional shout or scream, there was no sound from the Franks. As the pain in his head slowly retreated to a throbbing lump behind one ear, Lukas tried to move his hands again and felt the bite of hemp at his wrists.

Gingerly, he reached up with both hands, peeled the scrap of ripped canvas away from his face and probed the lump. His fingers came away sticky and the welt under his matted hair stung like fire, but he was relieved to discover that it was a bad knock, a glancing clip from a passing horse and nothing more. He sat, blinked his way through the resurgent pain, then forced his eyes open again.

Tall clumps of reeds surrounded him. Through them he glimpsed the white peaks of tents a little way off. Someone had moved him.

He had been tied up and dumped into the marsh between the camp and the river. No sign of the Turkish sword for which he had almost killed. Whoever had dragged him here was long gone, but they had laid his staff neatly beside him.

Feebly, he picked at the ropes. Whoever brought him here must know that if he woke, he would be able to get free quickly. It was

247

likely they had meant to return before that happened, and in his weakened state, Lukas did not want to stay to meet them. The last thing he needed was to fall back into the hands of Tatikius—or worse yet, Evrard of le Puiset.

What he *did* want was to track down the Messenger before something dreadful happened to either of them. Now the Greeks had a price on his head, he had not dared to sneak into their camp again to find the Varangian. The chaos of battle was his only chance to find the man, to ask the questions that burned inside him.

He got himself free at last, wet his feverish head with water and then crawled back toward the tents. The central refuge was even more crowded now. A congregation of blood-streaked war-horses was now packed in amongst the huddled people, tethered oxen and palfreys.

Lukas glanced at the sky. The sun was nearly at its zenith. He must have been unconscious for a while. Where was Count Raymond? Had Bertrand made it back to the other camp safely, or was he lying somewhere in the hills with a back full of Turkish arrows?

He pushed through another clump of reeds and nearly tripped over a corpse.

It was a Turk, lying face to the sky with a horrible wound in his head, perhaps inflicted by an axe. Hidden by the reeds into which it had fallen, the body had not yet been plundered. Lukas grimaced and set to work, sweating in the sun. There was no sword and the bow was not his best weapon, but under the red tunic the Turk wore a shirt of close-linked steel mail. Lukas stripped the body quickly and methodically, taking everything that looked useful and leaving the rest. It was not until he was trying to wrestle man's tunic over his head without getting too much blood on it than he realised what he was doing. Had it come to this, that he was robbing corpses like any desperate peasant?

Desperate, but sensible. Lukas climbed into the padded vest, the red silk tunic and the armour, wearing the steel shirt outermost as the Franks did. When he finally stood, he felt better defended than he had in months.

Lukas picked his way into the huddle at the centre of the camp where priests, women, children and the old sat miserably trying to shield their heads from the sun. Some prayed, some cried, some nursed wounds or sat silent in shock. Nobody paid much attention to him. Their fear hung over them like a blade, like the shrill battle cries of the Turks.

"Oi, you!" someone yelled. "Who's your captain?"

A Frankish foot-soldier standing at the perimeter waved him over. Head still humming, Lukas picked his way to the man.

"I have a crack in my head and no weapons," he said.

"Doesn't matter. If you're standing, you're on the line, boy. Don't let me see you hiding with the women!"

Lukas' face warmed. He was no coward, he was just not properly equipped. Still, he knew better than to try to explain himself. Instead, he picked his way through the ring of tents that defended the Frankish non-combatants from the Turkish arrows. Beyond them, in the space between tents and barricades, was a confused litter of the living and dead who could no longer fight. Beyond the barricades, the dismounted knights stood in a shield-wall of stubborn and silent iron. Archers and footmen reinforced them from the rear, providing a thin answering fire to the ceaseless hail of Turkish arrows.

Lukas scanned the shield-wall, looking for the Greek standard. There, just to the left of Bohemond's. As he looked, the arrow-hail ceased and the Turkish drums began to beat. Lukas clambered onto the nearest cart to see.

Beyond the shield-wall, a sharp wedge of Turkish riders quickened to a gallop. Down went the bows, up came swords and spears. In a glitter of lethal steel, they rushed the Frankish line. Ahead of Lukas, the knights set their shoulders and planted their feet, preparing to meet that lightning charge.

Someone called out in a high clear voice that carried a laugh. "If any of you wants to fight today, let him stand fast and play the man!" As the speaker glanced down the line, Lukas recognised him as Count Bohemond.

Then the Turks crashed into the line.

But the ritual requires blood and perversity, said a very calm voice inside his memory.

Suddenly he was trying not to throw up with the very weight of his fear. He remembered the snick of wings in the courtyard of Oliveta, the screams and the slaughterhouse scent of fresh blood filling the air. Lukas turned and sagged to the ground, shielding his head with his hands. It was not the Turks that sapped the strength from his limbs, that made him shake as if it was midwinter. It was what he sensed driving them, a malice not entirely mortal.

He opened his eyes to reassure himself that the sun still shone.

Instead, *her* shadow passed across it. The vulture woman swooped down, landing heavily within the barricade. Her black wings trailed behind her as she walked on the dead grass of summer, her hair a limp cloak half covering her feathered body.

As she passed Lukas, her shadow fell on a wounded man lying in the scanty shade of a tent. His laboured breathing stopped, and the man kneeling over him called his name in despair. In the vulture woman's wake, men shivered and died.

None of them saw her. Only Lukas.

The hair prickled on his scalp. Feebly, he touched his hand to his Watcher's Mark, but it provided no comfort. Nothing but the sudden conviction that here, now, was the enemy he had to fight.

The vulture woman paid no attention to him as she passed through the barricade and walked among the men of the shield-wall. Clawing after her on his knees, Lukas saw the shudder pass through the men as she went, the blood draining from their faces. He reached out to touch the black feathers of her wings, but they ran through his fingers like smoke.

Her weapon was fear. She had routed the Franks once, when they fled back to the camp. Fortuitously, it must have been that very influx of terrified, maddened men that saved them from the Turks. Yet the knights had rallied since. They had formed the shield-wall, and the Turks could not crack it.

Only fear could defeat them. Only despair. Only this.

Lukas swallowed, closing his eyes, trying to remember his mother's conjuration.

"The Lord rebuke thee." The words were only a whisper. *"He who has prepared for thee unquenchable fire, the unsleeping worm and the outer darkness unto eternal punishment: devil, the Lord rebukes thee by his frightful name!"*

A chill lifted every hair on his body. Lukas looked up, straight into the vulture woman's eyes.

She stood over him, able to touch him no more than he could touch her. But she drew her bow and croaked, "Keep silent, or perish!"

His voice grew stronger. *"Shudder, tremble, be afraid, depart, be utterly destroyed, be banished! Thou who fell from heaven together with all evil spirits: every evil spirit of lust, the spirit of evil, a day and a nocturnal spirit..."*

She bared her teeth at him and snarled.

"A noonday and evening spirit, a midnight spirit, an imaginative spirit, an encountering spirit either of the dry land or of the water..." Confidence mounting, he jumped to his feet.

And with a blink, the vulture woman was gone.

The Turks were in retreat, leaving the ragged shield-wall to reform.

She was gone. Lukas let out a shaking breath. He had done it. He had really *done* it. He had confronted something not of the mortal world and bested it in combat.

He had done the work of a Watcher.

"Here, I know you." The sentry he had met this morning elbowed his way between the barricade and the shield-wall. "What are you babbling about devils for? You're disturbing the men."

Lukas stopped smiling, but he stood taller. "Won't happen again," he said, and he raced for the Greek banners.

Tatikius was far off in the shield-wall with his men, and Lukas doubted that anyone else would recognise him. He bared his arm, showing his Watcher's Mark to a water-carrier.

"I'm looking for one of the Varangians. The one who led the charge against the Turks when they broke into the camp. Please..."

"You mean Kari. Third tent along."

Lukas hurried in the direction of the man's jerked thumb. What was the Varangian doing in a *tent*? He burst through the flap, smelled death, and knew.

"Kari?" he asked the started, bloodstained surgeon.

The man's eyes went to one of the shapes lying under the dim canvas. "He doesn't have long."

Lukas fell to his knees beside the Messenger. Kari breathed laboriously and blood soaked his side; a spear had punctured the armour and pierced his vitals.

For a moment, Lukas could not speak. Just knowing that there was a fellow Watcher who believed in him had been a comfort. After a moment, he realised the Varangian's eyes were struggling to focus on him.

"Messenger," he whispered. "It's me, Lukas Bessarion. Oh, Saint George! I'm so sorry..."

Kari's hand moved. "Bessarion...yes."

The surgeon left the tent, allowing them some privacy.

Lukas had so many questions. *Will I get home? And how? Will I convince Ayla to come with me?* But the Messenger was too feeble for any of them. He gripped the callused hand and simply asked, "Do you have any message for me?"

"Go to Heraclea. The last Watchers before the mountains. They'll help you." Kari spoke in quick, difficult breaths. "They'll help you when I can't. Tagaris. Next door to the apothecary."

"Tagaris," Lukas breathed. Heraclea was on the road to Syria. The pilgrimage would take him there—if they survived today.

The Varangian's hand tightened on his. "I saw Jerusalem filled with blood," Kari whispered. "They need your help. Even they..."

"I'll take care of Jerusalem. I promise."

"You will...at last. Go now."

Lukas opened his mouth to ask what the Messenger meant, but his eyes were out of focus again, his breath more laborious than ever.

"Go. Now." Kari's voice was barely audible.

The tent flap brushed open and the other Varangian entered. Tatikius' attendant from that morning. Behind him, the Greek surgeon.

The bottom dropped out of Lukas' stomach. He had said his name aloud to Kari. It was a mistake. Now the other Varangian had a sword pointed at him.

"In the emperor's name—" he began.

Lukas did not wait to hear the rest of it. His knife was already in his hand. Quick as thought he plunged it into the taut canvas behind him, ripped a long slash in the tent's wall and elbowed through before the bodyguard could reach him.

Outside, two Greek footmen faced him, spears ready. The closest one lunged, aiming to skewer him through the gut. But Lukas had been trained for this, and his staff was ready in his hand. With a sharp ringing *crack,* he parried the spear-point and side-stepped, getting the man between himself and the other Greek. Behind, he dimly heard the Varangian shouting—*Round the back and shoot him down!*

They meant to kill him.

Lukas reversed his staff, swept the Greek's feet out from under him, and ran, ducking between the tents. Hastily-shot arrows hissed into the ground at his feet, plucked at his loose sleeve. He found an opening between two tents and threw himself to safety.

They meant to *kill* him.

Lukas did not stop running until he reached Bohemond's blood-red banner and collapsed against the wheel of a cart in the Norman-held barricade. It would have been easy to deal with him. An arrow in the back, a spear in the gut, and they could lay him among the other dead.

But, saints, *why?* Just for being a *heretic?*

He leaned his head back against the wheel, scanning the camp. There was no movement. The Greeks did not seem to have pursued him; evidently, they knew they had missed their chance. After all, they would be weeks on the road to Syria together, if not months. They could afford to bide their time.

Slowly, Lukas realised that the rhythm of the battle was changing.

"Stand fast! Stand fast! Ready!" a voice shouted.

For once, there were no Turkish arrows in the sky. Lukas only had a moment to wonder why, before the noise of battle swelled and the Turks crashed into the shield-wall. The line staggered and reeled. Lukas heard the neighing of the Turkish mounts, the clang of their swords, and the deafening shriek of their war-cry.

The same voice shouted again, but Lukas could not hear a word of it. The line staggered forward again, and a phalanx of Frankish knights drove out from the blood-red banner.

Bohemond had charged.

Leading a spear-point of armoured knights, he swept forward from the Frankish line. This was not some suicidal charge led by two or three knights in blind desperation; it was a measured and lethal counterattack. In its face the Turks floundered, turned their horses and spurred out of range. Mounted and mobile, they quickly withdrew from the Frankish charge. Then, around they came, swords away and bows up.

Even as Bohemond pulled his men back to the line, a new volley descended. Lukas saw a discarded shield on the ground and dove for it, pulling it over his head as the arrows fell, rattling against the wood.

Tagaris, in Heraclea. He had to live long enough to find them. That meant avoiding the Greeks, and keeping the rest of the pilgrimage alive. Lukas slipped through the oxcart barricade and waded into the shield-wall, hoisting the shield above his head.

Another volley of arrows poured into the Christian ranks. Again, the Turks pelted for the Frankish line. Again, they crashed into the shield-wall, and again, Bohemond repulsed them.

It became a grinding pattern: arrows, charge, counter-charge. The Frankish line wavered under the blows, punch-drunk. Lukas' arms burned from the strain of holding the shield above his head, like Saint Moses in the wilderness. He had to stand strong, had to shield them. He had to be the Watcher.

But he didn't know how much longer he could last.

"It's getting worse," someone said in the sweat-soaked darkness below the shields. "Hark to them scream!"

"They know their time is short," said another.

Crash! Another charge hammered the line, throwing them back against the barricade of the ox-carts. Only the pressure of the bodies around him kept Lukas upright. This time Bohemond held his men in place. The Franks were tiring and they could not counter-charge forever. Even with the vulture woman gone, their strength still flagged beneath the glaring midday sun.

Lukas grimaced, trying to stiffen his shaking arms. Just *being* a Watcher did not save people. If it did, he could have saved Oliveta.

Crack! An arrow hit his shield and drove a crack end-to-end. *Crack!* With an awful splintering sound, the wood parted in his hands, bound together only by its leathern covering. *Crack!* The third arrow pierced the cover and slid through within inches of his eyes.

He closed them in a futile attempt to protect his vision.

Then, thin and far away—the sound of a trumpet.

At first it meant nothing to him, just another sound in the endless cacophony of battle. But as it blared, the arrow storm stopped and to Lukas' numb surprise, shouts of jubilation rolled up and down the Frankish line.

"Duke Godfrey!" they cried. "Duke Godfrey! Lorraine! Lorraine!

God wills it!"

Deeply embedded in the line, Lukas could see nothing, but his own joyful yells joined the tumult.

Even as their cheers shook the air, the Turkish war-cries swelled and hoof beats rolled away from them.

As the battle fled, Bohemond shouted. "Charge! Charge! Bring them in!"

Somewhere beyond the shield-wall, Godfrey's newly-arrived knights were already fighting for their lives.

Chapter XXVIII.

Even at this distance from the battle, the hellish sound of the Turkish war-cry reverberated in the hills. Behind Saint-Gilles, his men shifted and fretted, scanning the slopes around them like hounds waiting to be unleashed on the foe.

Saint-Gilles knew how they felt. Maybe, if he was not still debilitated from catching William's fever, he too would be willing to rush into battle with no thought of the outcome. Then again, maybe not. He had not become the richest count in Christendom through running his neck into nooses. He might not be much good at the devious intricacies of eastern politics, but Saint-Gilles knew how to fight.

"Saints above," he grumbled at Galdemar, "I *warned* Bohemond not to go on alone. Now I've got to save his neck somehow."

Galdemar chuckled from behind the apricot his men had foraged in the hills. "You're worried about the bishop?"

He was worried about all of them—even Bohemond, his unexpected ally. Saint-Gilles shifted in the saddle. "I don't like sending Adhemar off on his own like that. He doesn't do much fighting. He says it's unbecoming to a man of God. Saints! I should have gone with him."

Saint-Gilles stiffened as his scouts appeared over the crest of the hill in front. Each one bore his own heraldry, identifying the rider, but all the same, Saint-Gilles did not loosen his grip on his spear until they were close enough to show their faces.

When he did, he fitted his helmet on and beckoned them closer. "What news?"

Young Guy of Lastours slung his shield on his back. "Over this crest, the ground drops toward the river," he reported. "The whole Turkish army is between us and the camp."

"And the others? Duke Godfrey? Count Hugh?"

When the bishop's squire reached them with news of the battle, they had been packing up for the day's march. Within seconds, Godfrey had decided that the situation was too grave to postpone reinforcements until everyone was ready. He had left with the first fifty knights that were ready. Saint-Gilles thought it was an excellent way to get eaten piecemeal by the Turks, but it was no use saying so.

Thanks to the duke, the other counts had followed suit, racing off to the battle as soon as small bands of men could get ready. Saint-Gilles himself only had an embarrassingly small number of men in his following.

"Did the others make it?" he asked.

"I saw their standards in the camp, my lord."

"Still pinned down, eh?"

"They've raised a shield-wall and circled the camp with tents and wagons. The river protects them on the far side, but they're almost standing in it."

"And the Turks?"

"Attacking from the south."

"Good." That meant Adhemar was headed in the right direction.

Saint-Gilles turned to his men, not much more than a hundred mounted knights, and got to the point. "Forward slowly, and save your horses till the last moment. We'll have to charge through the whole Turkish host to get to the shield-wall, so don't fly before I give the command. God keep the right!"

He forced them to keep a walk as they crested the hill and descended toward the river. In a green depression bordered with reeds, the army of God nestled like the calm eye in a storm of death. On the higher slopes, Turkish scouts were waiting for them. They let fly arrows as they retreated, but Saint-Gilles did not take the bait. Only once the slope levelled out, making safer ground for the horses, did he signal his trumpet to sound.

His horse stretched out its neck and a cool gust of speed hit his face.

Saint-Gilles lifted a little in his stirrups, clamping his lance under his elbow in the new style that was so devastating to mounted enemies. Now it was just a matter of following the long ash-shaft through to the bitter end. "Saint-Gilles! Saint-Gilles!" he yelled. Other throats behind him took up the cry, and the hills responded with distant echoes.

As his cohort pierced their ranks, the Turks divided to let him through, then closed onto his flanks. A rattle of arrows glanced off his helmet and rebounded from the rings of his hauberk. The steel mesh was too well-woven to admit a point anywhere, save for a few inches of skin on the face, and Saint-Gilles had learned a long time ago to ride with his chin tucked to protect it. Unlike its rider, his horse wore no armour, and Saint-Gilles felt a shudder go through the animal as the sanctuary of the shield-wall reached out to welcome him. He heard the animal labouring beneath him, felt the fire in its veins flicker, the soft earth suck at its hoofs. It faltered and slowed.

"Once more, greatheart," he urged, and sank his spurs into its flanks. It heaved forward in one last effort. The shield-wall opened before him, and he and his men were safe.

Saint-Gilles reined in on a narrow patch of ground behind the barricade. Through the tents beyond, he caught a glimpse of a terrified huddle of women and priests, and his gut knotted. God and Saint Mary take pity, *why* did these people follow such a desperate pilgrimage? He had done his best to make them stay at home, but you could not lock up the entire population of France to keep them from following you.

He slid down from his horse and relinquished the panting, injured beast to a squire. Then he turned to watch his men swarm through the gap and dismount. On their heels, a band of Turkish riders swooped down in an attempt to exploit the open line. For a moment, it seemed as though they might succeed, but the Franks closed in, trapping some of the Turkish horses and wreaking a savage vengeance upon them. The others beat a hasty retreat.

"Where's Count Bohemond?"

"On the front line, my lord. To your left."

Hands pointed him down the line. Word must have reached the count that he was wanted, for Bohemond shouldered into view with a cheerful grin and open arms. "Count!" he yelled. "It's good to see you. There's been some heavy rain here today."

"And whose fault is that?" Saint-Gilles slapped Bohemond on the back, but his relief made him snappish. "Your men look terrible."

They did: skin pale and clammy with sweat, mouths slack with weariness.

Bohemond's mouth slanted in a wry grin. "It's this eastern heat, my lord. In Italy, you can always count on a sea breeze."

Saint-Gilles snorted. "From now on, the whole pilgrimage marches together."

"Can't say I disagree. Was there something you wanted to see me about?"

"Yes." Saint-Gilles swung to watch the south horizon. *Come on, Adhemar, where are you?* "Time to mount your men, count. As many as still have horses."

"A charge, eh?" Bohemond glanced at the enemy and a spark lit his eyes. "I reckon we can do it, too."

"Not at once. When the sign comes."

"How long? If I get my knights mounted up, the footmen will have to hold the line alone. They can't do it long."

"I know. Trust me."

Bohemond nodded, shouting for a lieutenant to take messages for the other counts. As the line thinned and the knights took horse, the Norman count swung back to Saint-Gilles.

"This sign we're waiting for?"

"The same as the Lord vouchsafed to the Israelites in the wilderness." Saint-Gilles pointed down the gorge to the south. "Watch!"

The sky showed blue in the cleft between the hills. Saint-Gilles lifted a hand to shade his eye from the sun. How long since he had parted from Adhemar in the valley above? Surely the bishop had had plenty of time, surely the Turks had no more reserves for him to fall afoul of.

There. A faint, dirty smudge against the sky. He turned to Bohemond, heart lightening. "Your eyes are younger than mine. What do you see?"

The count drew in a breath. "Pillar of smoke." He wheeled around, shouting at his knights to get into battle array, at his squires to bring his horse. "Stand fast," he called to them. "Trust in Christ and the victory of the Holy Cross. Today, if it please God, you will gain much booty!"

Saint-Gilles found a horse to borrow and mustered his men at the centre of the line, the Normans and Count Stephen on his left, Duke Godfrey with Flanders and Vermandois on his right. The smoke had thickened to a black cloud. The knights muttered and pointed, their horses fidgeting as they scented action, but Saint-Gilles held them in check.

Seeing the Franks prepare to charge, the Turkish archers drew off to regroup. Silence descended upon the valley: the calm before the final storm.

But the storm never came.

In the lull the Turks hesitated, looked behind and realised for the first time that there was trouble in the rear. Saint-Gilles knew it the moment their confidence broke.

"Le Puy! Le Puy!" he yelled. "The sword of the Lord and of Adhemar!"

He signalled his standard-bearer. The trumpets screamed. The shield-wall dissolved. Battered, bloody, but undaunted, the Franks pounded from their camp.

Chapter XXIX.

L ukas clung to the nearest oxcart as the ranks of footmen opened to let the knights through. A tide of horseflesh and iron swept by once more, making his head pound with remembered pain.

The Franks flowed across the open land and ploughed into the Turkish host. The enemy showed little resistance, weary from the blood and sweat they had spent that day. Perhaps they had lost heart as the Franks gained it. By now, they must have seen the pillar of smoke rising from behind them. Under the hammer-blow of the Frankish charge, they fled in as much terror as if the vulture woman herself was chasing them.

Lukas stared. Against all odds, they had won. The enemy fled, jostled, withered under the Frankish swords.

Today you will all win much booty, Count Bohemond had said.

Lukas dropped his broken shield and pelted after the charge, lost in the sea of shouting Franks that poured from the camp. Ahead, a few brave clusters of Turks rallied to fight, while others tried to escape through the narrow south gorge. Now they were crumbling, their wiry little horses running riderless in a panic across the battlefield. Lukas changed his direction and reached for the nearest. It shied away from him, but he caught the fluttering end of the reins, wrestled it to a standstill and swung into the saddle.

Now he was a Bessarion again.

Now he would prove himself to the Franks.

Lukas unslung his staff and quickened the animal to a gallop with little more than the pressure of his knees. The little horse was beautifully trained, light and fast. Despite the long months spent on his feet since Oliveta, Lukas might never have been out of the saddle. Within heartbeats he was among the Frankish charge, wielding his iron-shod staff like a spear.

Together they pushed the Turks back. Few offered much resistance. Toward them on the wind came the scent of smoke, stinking of things that were never meant to burn—leather, lacquer, and silk. Around a bend in the gorge they came upon the burning Turkish camp.

A wedge of Frankish horse peeled away from the camp and charged directly into the fleeing Turks.

Trapped between hammer and anvil, the Turkish flight stopped, rallied, and fought. On the far side of the battlefield, Lukas caught a glimpse of the banner of Le Puy. Beneath it, Bishop Adhemar rode, clad in steel like any knight, blood running down his broadsword.

As the charge slowed, a new melee developed. Lukas almost blundered into a slashing blow from a Turkish warrior, and parried it at the last moment with his staff. His heartbeat kicked up. He had no shield, no helmet, and no blade. All he had was a staff, a horse, and a mail shirt. Was he crazy?

Before he could do anything, two Frankish knights closed in on each side of him.

"Stay with us," one of them shouted, and together they drove into the crush.

The Turks did not mean to fight any longer if they could help it. As the Franks squeezed them harder, they slipped behind Adhemar's men and trickled away down the gorge like grains of sand speeding through an hourglass. Still the Franks pursued them, yelling their savage battle cries. Others descended upon the burning camp, rushing into the tents to salvage whatever valuables they could find. They emerged bloody-handed, draped in silks.

Oh, Saint George, Lukas thought. *Ayla could be here.*

The thought hit him like blow to the belly. Where else could she have gone after passing him in the hills last night? Lukas spurred his horse into the camp, shouting her name at the top of his voice. There were Franks everywhere. His gut twisted at the sound of a scream, and he wrenched his horse towards it. A brightly-clad figure lay on the ground, groaning in pain. Lukas almost fell off the horse in his haste to reach her. The black hair was matted with blood. He turned her gently, trying to hold in his horror.

The Turkish woman was older than Ayla, her eyes unfocused. Blood trickled down her face. Just a camp-follower. Just another one of these devils that had spent the best part of six hours—

"*Su*," she whispered, and to his horror Lukas realised he knew the word, had heard it many times on the ship. *Water.*

"*Evet*—yes," he said softly. He grabbed the waterskin hanging from his horse's saddle. She was too weak to swallow anything, but the water dampened her lips. She sighed, putting up her fingers to touch the cool moisture.

Stupid Franks! Could they not see she was harmless? Lukas laid her down again in the thin streak of shadow by one of the tents and stepped away, stomach heaving. *Oh, Saint George.* He knew the Franks were looking for revenge, he felt the same himself. But this woman deserved better than this. *Ayla* deserved better.

There was nothing else he could do for this woman, but Ayla—

He had to face the truth. If she had been in the camp he would never find her now, in the chaos of the sack. At least he knew she was no weakling. He closed his eyes. If he was Ayla, where would he go? What would he do?

He remounted, fleeing that awful scene of destruction, and came out on the camp's north side where the hills were smaller. Ayla must have ridden through here last night, she would know they were passable. He spurred for the nearest gap between the slopes and rounded a corner to see a pair of mounted figures disappearing around the next bend. Was it just the sun, or did one of them ride a golden horse? Lukas kicked his pony to a gallop and pelted after them. He rounded the hill and blundered into their midst.

Instead of two horsemen, there was a small company, as many as ten. None of them were Ayla. Strung out in a weary line between them was a little procession of perhaps forty Franks, their hands lashed to a long rope.

Prisoners.

Oh saints, he thought, as their guards turned to stare at him. All he had was a staff, a horse, and a mail shirt. Already the Turks were reaching for their bows. If he fled, they would shoot him down from behind. If he stayed still, he would be an easy target.

That left one choice. Charge.

He levelled his staff with a hoarse scream and kicked his pony into a gallop. The nearest two riders were unprepared. His staff caught the first under the breastbone, hurling the man off his horse.

"For Palestine!" he screamed as he yanked his horse around to swing at the other. The Turks, demoralised by the Frankish victory, did not wait for him. They dropped the rope and galloped for the hills. One of them loosed an arrow over his shoulder, but it flew at random and lost itself in the bushes. Lukas watched them go, his whole body beginning to shake as he realised what a close thing it had been. The Franks raised a cheer.

The man he had unhorsed lay on the ground with blood trickling from his nose. Lukas got down from the saddle, hoping that his suddenly wobbly knees would hold him up. Before anything else, he took the Turk's sword-belt and round buckler. The man was only unconscious, and Lukas could not help feeling grateful. He remembered too clearly what it had felt like to kill the Turkish captain.

He had always wanted to be a fighter, but to be a killer—that frightened him.

Shakily, he drew his eating-knife and went over to help free the prisoners.

At the head of the line, Lukas caught a glimpse of eggshell blue and stopped in amazement. It was the Frankish girl he had seen earlier that day.

"You," he blurted, and then felt his face heat. He had shoved her to the ground and then failed to save her. The last thing he should do was remind her of their previous meeting. If she was anything like the other Frankish nobles, she would want his blood.

Her eyes widened in recognition and Lukas winced, waiting for her wrath.

"By our Lady," she said shakily, "that was knightly done."

Lukas blinked.

The Frankish girl smiled and put out her hands so that he could cut the ropes. Feeling dazed, Lukas worked his way down the line. Drunk on freedom, everyone had a kind word for him.

"Well struck!" cried one knight.

"*Preux!*" said another.

He had finally done it. He had proved himself to the Franks in battle. The men clapped him on the shoulder, the women cried and hugged him. Everyone kissed his cheeks.

He had *done* it.

If Ayla had fled this way, he could not follow her now—he could hardly risk leading these people to her. Instead, he returned to the girl in blue and offered her his horse to ride back to the Frankish camp.

It was a long walk, and the girl in blue did not speak. She seemed shy, despite towering two or three inches above him with her feet on the ground. Lukas was too busy daydreaming to notice. With a horse and glory in his grasp, he might ask Count Raymond to give him the other weapons he needed. Or perhaps the Frankish girl's people would be grateful enough to take him into service as a squire. Maybe they would even give him the cuff of knighthood right away. He could spend the rest of the journey to Syria as one of them, no longer a despised outsider. He could receive training, and take home with him the deadly Frankish fighting style.

If only he could be sure that Ayla was safe.

The Frankish girl spoke at last. "What would have happened to us?"

Lukas glanced at her, then beyond to the other freed captives. "They would sell you as slaves, I expect."

She shivered.

Something, maybe the thought of Ayla, prompted him to add: "Of course, we would probably do the same to them."

He expected that to offend her, but instead she seemed surprised. "Would we?"

Lukas stared at her. "What else could we do with prisoners? The Greeks will have a use for them."

Her eyes were wide. Without terror distorting her face, she was pretty, in a fragile way. "Poor things. Do you think that's right?"

"It's war," Lukas said shortly. But he had been a captive himself, however briefly, and the girl's question ate away at his mind all the long way back.

By the time they reached the pilgrims' camp, the sun was sinking and the Franks had begun to return from the pursuit. Many came laden with plunder and leading captured horses. Meanwhile, the footmen combed the battlefield, looting the Turks and retrieving the Frankish dead.

Lukas did his best to pick their way through that red wasteland. Shattered corpses, ruined horses and fly-speckled pools of thickened blood littered the ground. It smelled like the shop of a mad butcher, but instead of the fragrance of lamb or the heartiness of beef, here the air was saturated with the gamey stench of horseflesh, the acrid rust of humanity.

"What ruin we have wrought on the world," the Frankish girl said very softly as they reached the edge of the camp and the other captives dispersed.

The observation struck too close to his own thoughts for comfort. He had thought of the Franks as battle angels, but after all they were just men. Frightened and vengeful and thirsty for blood, so long as it would buy them redemption. It was fair, Lukas told himself. If they were bloodthirsty conquerors, then so were the Turks. Maybe it was best if they destroyed each other.

Lukas looked up. "Where do I return you, lady?"

She tore her gaze from the battlefield with difficulty. "Oh…I see my brother's banner. That way."

He navigated them beyond the trampled, muddy ring that had been the camp's perimeter and led the horse in the direction she'd pointed out for him. By now more tents had been pitched. In front of one pavilion close by, a knight stood with his back to them, washing a gash on his horse's flank.

The Frankish girl pointed. "There he is. Evrard!"

Lukas froze.

The knight with the wounded horse turned. Evrard of le Puiset.

He did not spare a glance for Lukas. "Emelota," he said with haggard relief, limping forward as she slipped down from the horse. "Where have you *been?*"

Le Puiset. Of course it had to be le Puiset. Lukas forced himself to stand his ground. Today he had banished the vulture woman. He had stood in the shield-wall. He had singlehandedly saved a count's sister from her captors. He had no reason to run away.

Emelota pulled herself from her brother's hug. "The Turks took me. This knight saved us."

The count turned to Lukas, putting out a hand to thank him, but the words never came. Instead, the slow dawn of indignation.

"This…*knight?*"

Emelota glanced from her brother to Lukas, sensing the tension between them. "What's wrong, Evrard? He is a good youth. I've met him once before."

"When?"

"He helped me when the Turks broke into the camp. After, when they bound us together and tried to march us through the hills, he found us. There were ten Turks guarding us and he charged them, alone. It was very *preux*."

It was good to hear her praise, but it was even better to see the count's face working as she spoke. Lukas smirked.

Evrard flushed, but his lips were pale. "If this is true, then we owe him our thanks. But for the love of God, Emelota, if he has told you he is a knight then he has deceived you. He is only a Greek peasant."

Emelota was confused. "But look, he has a horse."

"Stolen," Evrard snapped.

Lukas put his hand on the horse's mane, flushing. "I had it as Turkish spoils!"

Evrard smiled in triumph. Emelota took half a step back. "Then you *aren't* a knight."

"I never said I was," Lukas responded wearily. "But it's true—I was born..."

The count cut him off, sticking a handful of gold coins under his nose. "It's as I said. We owe you our thanks, *peasant*."

Lukas had hoped for patronage, but the count had turned this into an insult. He suppressed the urge to strike the gold out of his hand. "Am I a lackey, to be paid for my services and sent packing? If you grudge my help, keep your gold. I don't need it."

"Evrard, for heaven's sake!" Emelota snatched the gold from her brother's hand and held it out to Lukas. "Please, Greek. Take this from me as a token of my thanks. Not in payment."

If it had been impossible to take the gold from Evrard a moment ago, it was impossible to refuse now. Mutely, Lukas put out his hand and the concave *hyperpyroi* dropped into it. But the moment he took the coins, he knew it was a mistake. A knight would never take gold from an equal like that.

Emelota nodded to him distantly and touched her brother's arm. "Come on, Evrard. Don't try to eat him for dinner."

"One moment." Le Puiset shrugged her off and snapped his fingers under Lukas' nose. "Here. Pay attention. You're a stranger, Greek,

269

so—"

"Syrian," Lukas growled.

"I beg your pardon?"

"I'm a Syrian. I'm not a Greek." It was a trivial distinction, one that he himself almost never bothered to make. But for the last few weeks it had become increasingly difficult to think of himself as Greek—and at this moment, he would have contradicted the count on anything.

"It makes no difference. You need to know the rules. Having a horse doesn't make you a knight, and being Greek doesn't make you part of this pilgrimage."

Emelota stared at her brother. "Evrard!"

He ignored her. "And above all, freeing my sister from the Turks gives you no right to speak to her. So keep out of our way, hmm?"

Some of what flashed through Lukas' mind must have showed on his face, because the count suddenly jerked back. Too slow. Lukas hit him in the jaw with a closed fist. Emelota gasped. Le Puiset staggered back two steps, hand to his face.

Lukas bared his teeth in a grimace of pain and victory. "That's for what you gave me at Nicaea."

The young count spat blood and worked his jaw. As he drew his sword, his voice was quiet and menacing. "Enough, by heaven."

The sight of the bare steel chilled Lukas to the bone, but he whipped out his Turkish blade and came on guard.

"Evrard!" Emelota backed away, putting both hands to her head. "Evrard, stop it! It's not worth it!"

Not worth it. The words stung him. These Franks were all the same.

"Stay out of this, Emelota," Evrard growled at her.

A voice Lukas did not recognise started chanting. "Fight! Fight!"

Lukas realised that everyone within sight was flocking to watch them. In a moment, they were surrounded by a ring of cheering onlookers.

"Greek, please," Emelota appealed softly.

"I'm sorry, lady, but…"

"What did I tell you Greek?" Evrard lunged at him. After a long, exhausting day, the count should have been slow on his feet. He was nothing of the kind. "Don't—speak—to—my—sister!" He surged forward, unleashing a blow with each word. Lukas could only duck behind his shield and retreat, but the light Turkish buckler was no match for the count's remorseless onslaught. In a moment, it was shredded to splinters.

As Evrard hoisted his next blow, Lukas tripped on a tuft of reeds and fell. The count struck again, and Lukas blocked it with his sword. *Crack!* Shock numbed Lukas' arm as the lighter blade shattered. Sword and buckler both useless, he threw them down and grabbed at the strap that bound his staff to his back. But he was lying on it. Evrard would kill him long before he could get up.

The crowd held its breath. In the silence, Emelota screamed in terror. As the count turned to his sister, Lukas rolled to his feet and unslung his staff.

Standing just beyond Emelota's reach, her eyes narrowed on the Frankish girl, was Ayla.

Her sling thrummed in the air. "Drop your sword, Frank. Or I'll kill her."

Chapter XXX.

Count Evrard did not hesitate. With a curse, he threw down his sword and kicked it toward a squire in the crowd.

Ayla's sling didn't slow as she transferred her aim to the count. "Leave, Frank."

Evrard grabbed his sister, shot a murderous glance at Lukas, and rushed her toward his tent.

Ayla stilled her sling and elbowed her way through the crowd toward Lukas. Her lips were white.

"What are you doing here?" she hissed. "I *told* you where to go!"

"Ayla," he said blankly. The silk cloak was gone, her black hair pulled back into a masculine tail at the back of her head. She was Kismet the cabin boy once more, but Lukas would never forget the sunrise on her face. "Ayla, where were you? I was terrified for you."

She grabbed his elbow, glancing at the dissolving ring of onlookers. "Let's go somewhere else. That Frank will cut your throat if we give him the chance."

Lukas collected his horse's reins and followed her toward the river.

"Holy George," he complained. "These Franks! I saved his sister from slavery and heaven knows what. What kind of man takes that as an insult?"

"No idea."

By now, the camp was swollen with an influx of people and tents—the other half of the pilgrimage had arrived. Lukas craned his neck for Count Raymond's banner.

"Just when I thought I was getting somewhere with these people!"

Ayla made a sound of disgust and let go of his arm. "God have mercy, Greek! Some of us have bigger things to worry about!"

"No! Don't go!" He rushed after her. "Ayla! I'm sorry. Tell me how you got here!"

She scowled at him. "Some idiot needed saving."

"Who?"

She rolled her eyes. "For someone so high-and-mighty, you certainly have trouble telling your right hand from your left."

"I'm sorry. I thought you were with the Turks…Wait, have you been here all along? Are you the one who hid me in the reeds?"

"Who else would help you out? Admit it, Greek, you're terrible at making friends."

"Why did you come back?" But he knew the answer, even as he asked the question. *I'll still be working for my people. You realise that, don't you?* He swallowed. "I thought we were going to be enemies."

"We are." She puffed out a breath and her shoulders dropped. "Can't seem to help myself."

He grabbed her shoulders. "You're spying on us again." His hands, his whole body was shaking. "Do you see all this death? Is this *your* fault?"

"*My* fault?" She slapped his hands away, but there were tears in her eyes. "God have mercy, Greek! How can this be *my* fault? Did I bring these Franks to the east?"

"Did you bring the vulture woman?" he challenged.

"The vult…" All the indignation went out of her in a breath of shock. "Lukas, what did you see?"

"A woman with black hair, black wings."

Then, a memory clicked into place.

Saint George. The harpy perched on Khalil's arm, that night in Oliveta.

He had forgotten her. So much of his memory of that night was missing, but she had been there. At the moment Paulus had smeared the sorcerer's sigil, she had kissed Khalil.

"Lilith," Ayla whispered. "The Poison Mother." Once more she whispered the strange words of her litany, her eyes fixing sightlessly on the sky.

Lilith. His sense of triumph vanished. He knew the name. The mother of demons, queen of darkness. The stories said she drank blood. Her arrows spread pestilence, and she stole children, suckling them with poison. Death walked in her wake.

Ayla's eyes were haunted. "Her time of power is the night, and she preys on weak-minded men. My father told me the stories and... I've seen her in my nightmares. Often."

I banished her, he meant to say. But if he told her that he might as well admit he was a Watcher. "She's gone now."

Ayla shook her head. "Don't fool yourself. She might have gone, but she'll return. She's at her weakest in the daytime."

Lukas did not need her encouragement to feel terrified. For months, he had lived in fear that Khalil would appear and ambush him, but this was something far worse. In a fair fight he might overcome a mortal man, but a demon? Lukas could not bear to imagine her power.

He would have to come up with a plan, but Ayla was the last person he could discuss Watcher tactics with. Instead he asked, "Who are you serving now? I have to warn them, Ayla. I'll tell everyone if I have to."

"Tatikius," she said. "Since last week, I'm a menial for Tatikius."

He ran out of words. Ayla tilted her head with a bittersweet smile. "Stole a march on you there, Greek. He's the one lord you can't tell."

Lukas made a bold face. "Count Raymond can warn him."

"Count Raymond will still make you face him. Do you really want to risk that?" She laughed. "Do you know Tatikius is half Turkish? He likes me to speak to him in his father's tongue. His big cat likes me too."

Lukas' mouth tightened. "He wants me dead."

The Greek general did not mean to let him slip away. One false move, and Lukas would disappear. Count Raymond was the only reason he still had his freedom, or even his life. And until he had proven to the count that he could be trusted, he could not afford to get anywhere near the Greek general. He would have to keep an eye on Ayla himself.

"You really did infuriate those Watchers, didn't you? It's one of the things I like about you." Ayla glanced over her shoulder, toward Count Evrard's tent. "Who's the girl?"

At first the question seemed pointless. When he realised why she asked, he couldn't help smirking. "Her name's Emelota. She thinks I'm *preux*."

"Knew I should have shot her."

By now he knew her well enough to know that if she was *really* jealous, she would already have hit him. Still, she was, just a little. Enough to make him want to kiss her again.

He should do it. Quickly. Before he remembered what a mistake it would be.

"Look at my horse," he said desperately. Hearing himself, he couldn't help wincing. *Suave, Lukas.*

Ayla shot it a level look. "Yeh. It's a horse."

"I took it from the battlefield."

"Wonderful. What are you going to do with it?"

He stared at her. "Ride it."

"Yes, but what will you feed it?"

"Oh." Lukas was a trained rider. He might as well have been born in the saddle, but he had never had to feed or physic a horse until he became Count Raymond's servant. By now he realised that it took constant foraging, expense, and care. "I'll find a way."

"Not on what the count pays you. You should sell it to someone who can care for it." Ayla put up a hand to smooth the velvety nose. "Speaking of which, the Greeks will be wanting me to help unsaddle."

He missed her so much. Their games. Their laughter. "Wait."

She crooked an eyebrow at him.

"I didn't thank you for saving my life. Again."

"You'd have done the same for me."

"Always. You know that, right? I would…" he swallowed. "I would do anything for you."

"Yes, I know," she said bitterly. "Anything. Except…"

They were on opposite sides of something much, much bigger than themselves. Something that had begun before either of them was born, and would go on long after both of them were dead. Something that not even love would conquer.

He reached out, slowly. All the generations of this war weighed on his back, and Lukas felt as ancient as the hills. Gently, he took Ayla's hand in both his own and pressed it to his bowed forehead. When he looked up, there were tears in her eyes.

Better to leave it all unsaid.

"Best you go," he said.

She blinked, nodded, and left.

Chapter XXXI.

As Saint-Gilles slid from his horse, a squire came forward to direct him to his newly pitched tent, but the count had more important matters to deal with. He could not yet take his ease.

"Adhemar," he called as the bishop came into view on a stumbling horse. "Are you wounded?"

The bishop winced, easing his shoulders. "Just a scratch from one of their arrows. God forgive me! I haven't fought in many a day."

"You saved us all with that flanking attack."

"Give God the glory, count."

Saint-Gilles smiled, tight with irritation. Adhemar was just like Duke Godfrey—always taking the high ground.

"And you?" the bishop asked.

"Ready to die of weariness. I don't know if it's age or sickness." It had been two weeks since he had caught young William's fever, but still he tired easily. The months of travel and fighting had worn him to a thread. "Still, best we make a circuit of the camp before we rest."

The bishop agreed with a groan.

The Provençals had pitched their tents a short way north of the battleground, among the trees that lined the river. Seeing Saint-Gilles and Adhemar making their circuit, Galdemar joined them. As the three of them approached the border of their camp, a handcart wheeled by piled with poor ragged bodies.

"What's that?" Saint-Gilles asked.

Galdemar turned. For once, his voice held not a hint of laughter.

"Stragglers, my lord. When the Turks attacked, many of the common folk were caught in the trees."

Beckoning the others with a nod, Saint-Gilles followed the hand-cart.

Under the trees that fringed the battlefield, bodies were lined up side by side, head to toe. Men and women walked between them, searching for missing faces.

Count Bohemond stood over them like a stone guardian.

Saint-Gilles slowed as he reached the silent congregation and took in the clammy faces as he passed. They were laid out by estates: first the pinched and worn faces of peasants, goodwives, and burgesses. They had walked hundreds of miles from their own fields and made it most of the way to Jerusalem, only to die in the first pitched battle. There must have been a few hundred of them, more or less armoured, all hacked to a violent death. Beyond lay a smaller gathering of priests and monks, caught unawares by falling arrows as they took confession or helped the wounded. Beyond these again lay the knights, rank after rank. There must have been close to a thousand.

Saint-Gilles stopped at the sight of a lady who lay among them, her linen dress and her starched veil blotched with blood.

"The women brought us water." Bohemond spoke for the first time, his voice ragged with grief. "Arrows caught some of them."

At the count's feet, his nephew Tancred knelt over one body, his face buried in his hands, his shoulders heaving. Saint-Gilles pulled Bohemond into an embrace.

Adhemar bent over Tancred. "Who is it?"

The young knight dragged in a sniff and glanced up with reddened eyes. "My brother."

Adhemar sighed. "I will sing a mass for them before I rest."

"These Turks!" Galdemar shook his head. "Where could you find braver or more skilful soldiers? I thought only the Franks were born to be knights."

"So much the greater our glory in winning this battle." But

Bohemond's smile was little more than a grey shadow of itself. His people had borne the brunt of the day's fighting.

Saint-Gilles was barely listening. "There are *children* here."

Bohemond's half-smile vanished. "Some of the enemy forced their way into the camp."

Saint-Gilles was used to the sight of violent death; he had caused much of it himself, but the longer he scanned the dead, the more priests, women, and children he saw. Even infants.

Why had these people come? Did they not understand that war was grim, and terrible, and cruel?

A hand touched his shoulder and he jumped. Adhemar.

"God take pity," Saint-Gilles said. "This was only the first battle."

No one replied. At last, Adhemar spoke. "You realise, don't you, that most of us will never see it?"

The hair prickled on the back of Saint-Gilles' neck. "See what?"

Adhemar spoke softly, as if he was afraid to be heard. "Jerusalem."

Chapter XXXII.

Tachys, the Greek general's cheetah, itched to stretch his legs. For two days' travel out of Iconium, he had sat on the pillion behind his master's saddle and now, just after sunset, he would wait no longer. Ayla smiled at the restless beast and released him from his harness. She paused to scratch behind the great cat's ears, then said, "Go." At her command, Tachys shot joyously into the desert.

His paws scrabbled across the hard salt ground and faded into the distance. In a sky still purple with the sun's last rays, a full moon the colour of old silver hovered in the east, above green plumes of aspen bordering the river. Ayla looped the leash into her belt and walked north until she left the sprawl of the camp far behind. Then she descended to the stream, filled her bowl with water, and waited for Armen to appear.

"You didn't meet me last night," he accused. "What happened?"

Would he ever stop finding fault with her? Ayla sighed. "Water shortage. Again. I'm sorry."

"Report."

By now she knew to only give the basics. "We're camped on the Wednesday Stream. There were more desertions before we left Iconium, but fewer than usual. The weakest have all fallen by the wayside."

The Franks had been crossing Anatolia for over two months now. Progress was painfully slow. After the great battle, the Turks kept their distance. News of the victory had spread, and the Franks advanced through city after city with ease. Again and again, the locals revolted against their Turkish garrisons and welcomed them as liberators. Meanwhile, the Turks retreated, pillaging as they went.

Since the battle, some of the Franks threw stones at her if she left the safety of the Greek camp. They knew she was a Turk. Before the battle, that had not meant much to them. It did now.

Though the Turks had retreated, the landscape itself had become an enemy. After the great battle, Tatikius led the pilgrimage into the dry and waterless plains of Anatolia, where for four miserable weeks they had toiled through scorching heat, dying of thirst and starvation. In the punishing midsummer sun, the magnificent Frankish war-horses, which had come uncomplainingly through the Turkish arrow-storm, sweated, pined, and died. By the time the Franks reached the cool green lowland of Pisidia, some of the knights were riding oxen and many were forced to walk. As they climbed into the high plains again, Ayla heard many of the Frankish knights wailing that they were no longer worthy of the name.

Since leaving Iconium, they had crawled like ants across a barren, sun-scoured salt desert, the white glare and drifting dust punishing their eyes. The local Greeks had advised them to carry skins of water to get them across the desert. Since so many of the packhorses had died, that left servants like Ayla to act as beasts of burden. For two days she had listened to the *slosh, slosh* of the waterskin strapped clumsily to her aching shoulders, aware that she would never get more than a few mouthfuls each day. Certainly not enough to fill a silver bowl. Not that Armen cared.

"I think the plan is to remain here for a day or two. The Franks are sending scouts to Heraclea in the morning, ten knights. They don't expect trouble."

Armen gave a dissatisfied grunt. "That's not good. Will their scouts enter the town?"

"Usually the people run out to meet them," Ayla said.

She didn't say, *The people rejoice and dance when the Franks come.*

She didn't say, *Why did you plunder and burn? Why did you make them hate you so much? Even I can make a wild beast love me.*

She said, "Is there still a garrison in the town?"

"More than a garrison."

Ayla sucked in her breath. An ambush. And the ten Frankish knights riding ahead of the others threatened to spring the trap before it could close on the whole army.

"Leave to speak, my lord? The Franks are not very clever. So long as the sultan keeps his forces hidden, there's a good chance none of them will suspect that you're waiting in ambush."

Armen only acknowledged her words with a grunt. "If it doesn't work, we'll have to try again in the mountains. Report again tomorrow."

"I'll try, my lord."

Salt clouded the water and settled, but as Ayla emptied the bowl into the river, she felt her scalp prickle. She was being watched. Ayla surged to her feet, grabbing for her sling.

The full moon showed a familiar shape standing on the other side of the narrow water.

Ayla swallowed. "Lukas, I…"

He plunged into the water and waded halfway before stopping. His voice was expressionless. "Ambush."

Oh, God have mercy. He'd overheard their plan.

Since the battle, they had spent weeks circling each other in wary vigilance. Every so often, in camp or on the march, she would look around to find Lukas staring at her from a distance. Every so often, she stole away from the Greek camp and loitered near the Provençals, trying to catch a glimpse of him

She told herself she needed to keep track of him, to make sure he did nothing to endanger her mission. Yet, each time she saw him, it took a weight off her mind to see him alive and well.

Now, she remembered what Armen had said at Nicaea: *One day, I may ask you to kill him.*

She knew her duty, didn't she?

This is war, and you are a soldier in it. Watch yourself. Do not let yourself feel.

Ayla swallowed, tried to buy herself time. "Why do you care about them? They aren't your family."

"Nor is *he* your family." His voice sharpened. "Is he?"

"Might as well be. He's my father's friend."

He pushed another step through the stream. Ayla picked up the silver bowl and retreated warily as Lukas used the staff to heave himself onto the bank. For a moment, he just knelt there. "I love you, Ayla. But I can't let you do this."

She should have taken her sling and killed him while he was still on the other side of the water. She should knife him now, while he knelt. Ayla touched the knife at her belt, but a memory flashed through her mind—the man she had killed in the battle outside Nicaea.

She'd killed one of her own people once already. She couldn't do it again. Not to Lukas.

Instead, she turned and ran.

The moon threw a faint shadow ahead of her feet as the grass thinned and gave way to hard desert ground. Where to go? Iconium was two days' journey across the desert, Heraclea was even further. The Greek camp was her only refuge.

Footsteps pounded behind her. Lukas was hot on her trail.

He grabbed at the back of her belt and Ayla wheeled away, drawing her knife. Lukas caught her wrist. Immediately, she twisted hard against the hinge of his thumb, but before she got free he reinforced the grip with his free hand and planted his feet.

For an instant, there was no sound but their breath.

"You're hurting me," she gasped.

His hands trembled, but he didn't let go. "Drop the knife, Ayla. And the bowl."

She gripped them harder. "Answer my question! Why are you helping them?"

"Because I have to," he said dully. "Because they're my people."

"They aren't your people."

"They're Christians." The word was wrung out of him. "This isn't about blood. They're Christians, so they're my people. I can't let you destroy them."

"Are my people worth so little to you, then? Am *I* worth so little to you?"

"Don't."

Ayla tried again to twist out of his grip, but he was too strong.

"We are at war, your people and mine," he said. "And so are we, while we belong to them."

"We don't have to belong to them."

"Then *leave* them."

Ayla didn't know how to answer. She couldn't afford to leave now. How many months were left? Two? "This life is only for a moment," she said wearily; "the next is eternal."

Tachys returned then. Lukas was opening his mouth to speak when the cheetah streaked out of the desert, a soft-footed, velvet arrow. The Greek boy glanced aside with a grunt of alarm, let go of Ayla's wrist and reached for the staff across his back. Too late. The beast sprang.

"Tachys!" Ayla screamed.

Lukas staggered under the great cat's weight and went down, throwing up both arms to protect his face. Tachys snarled, looking for something to bite. Ayla dropped knife and bowl, threw her arms around the cheetah's chest and hauled him back.

"To heel!" she panted.

Lukas sat up unsteadily`. Blood oozed from deep scratches on his chest. In Ayla's arms, Tachys surged forward with another growl, and she had to throw all her weight backward to restrain him.

"Heel, you brute! Are you hurt? I didn't—I didn't mean—he loves me, he thought you would hurt me..."

"I'm all right." Lukas seemed dazed with shock, but then his eyes fixed on the silver scrying-bowl lying on the hard salt earth between them. He looked back to Ayla.

Lukas knew her choices as well as she did. Tachys could kill him. All she had to do was let go. Slowly, watchfully, he got to his feet and walked over to the silver bowl.

Her only connection with Armen. Her only chance to make these last months of life mean something.

"Please," she whispered.

"I have to protect them, Ayla. I won't betray you, but I have to tell the Franks what I know." He couldn't look her in the eye. "You should leave the pilgrimage. It's too dangerous."

He flipped the bowl in his hands, then walked away. Tachys surged forward in her arms again with a frustrated growl. Lukas threw a watchful glance over his shoulder, then vanished into the shadows of the trees. She heard a splash of water as he put the stream between them, then he was gone.

Ayla loosed Tachys, straightening her aching arms, feeling the void behind her breastbone where her heart ought to be. She was supposed to destroy him. Why did it hurt so much when he told her to leave?

God have mercy, she was *confused.* She could have killed him. She *should* have killed him. Armen would be furious, and for good reason. Was this how she did her duty? Was this how she guarded her feelings? She had been *warned* about this. Now, because she had failed when it was most important, the Franks would learn about the ambush in Heraclea.

Either Lukas' blood would be on her hands, or the blood of her own people.

Worse: now she was in danger. Despite Lukas' promise to keep her identity hidden, the bowl was evidence of a Turkish spy in the pilgrimage. If his count showed the bowl to Tatikius, the Greek general wouldn't let nostalgia stand in the way of his vengeance.

Down by the stream, Tachys sniffed at the water and growled. Like any cat, he was dainty about water. When he returned to her with his hackles lying flatter now that he was sure the threat had gone, Ayla took his harness from her belt and crouched down, tickling him behind the ears until he began to purr. "At least *we* can love each other," she whispered as he rubbed his chin against her shoulder.

The next morning, the Frankish scouts crossed the river with not ten, but fifty knights. When a pair of them returned two days later, they reported a sharp skirmish followed by a Turkish retreat. Heraclea was in Frankish hands, and it was Ayla's fault.

Ayla was too despondent that evening to do more than swallow a little food, roll herself into a blanket and fall asleep, but she knew what she had to do. It might be too late to save Heraclea, but no matter what happened next, she had to retrieve the scrying-bowl.

Chapter XXXIII.

The church bells of Heraclea tolled for Nones. Outside the wall, in a high-backed wooden chair set in the shadow of sycamore tree, Saint-Gilles stretched out his legs and glared at the distant mountains.

The bells rang with a festive tempo, and no wonder—five days since its liberation, the city was just beginning to recover from the celebrations. Saint-Gilles shivered to think what a close thing it had been. Lukas Bessarion's information had proved true: the Turks *were* lying in wait for them. Yet when the Frankish scouts turned out to be a determined vanguard, the garrison had given up and fled.

Did that mean that everything the Greek said was true? Could the silver bowl really communicate with the Turkish sultan? Did they face devils and magic as well as mortal weapons? Baldwin of Boulogne's mad prophet had peddled some equally sinister tale.

Before he could decide what to think, Galdemar strolled up, peeling an orange and leaving the golden skin littering his path like confetti.

"You look comfortable," he said.

"It's for my health." Saint-Gilles pushed the problem of the spies and devils to the back of his mind. He had been ill again during the journey across Anatolia, nearly to the point of death. Even now he was still shaky on his feet. "I'm getting old, Galdemar. I'm going to die."

"Comes to all of us sooner or later."

"Yes, but I hope it comes to me while I can still hold a sword. I always vowed I'd die a knight."

"You could join a monastery."

"And do the Lord's work when I'm too feeble to do my own? If I were the Lord I'd be offended by that."

Galdemar chuckled richly. "Maybe that that's why you're not the Lord." He turned east, and Saint-Gilles followed his gaze to the hazy outlines of the Taurus mountains: a glistening, snow-covered rampart of stone. Somewhere between those peaks lay the famous Cilician Gates, the narrow pass that led to Cilicia. A fertile country on the coast, the Greeks said, and an easy road thence to Antioch.

"I wish we were taking that road," said Galdemar.

Saint-Gilles grunted. "So do I. But we discussed it last night in council, and…"

"And you decided on the north road?"

Tatikius had urged them to take that route. It was a road which even he admitted was twice the distance and no less difficult. Saint-Gilles had opposed it, of course. Their poor and infirm needed a quick passage of the mountains and then rest. Many would die on a prolonged northern journey—but the wrong tactical decisions might spell disaster for the whole pilgrimage.

"Bohemond argued for it. With a diversion north, we can liberate a larger hinterland. If Antioch resists us, if there's a siege, we'll want friendly country at our backs."

Galdemar squinted at the horizon. "Did you send scouts to clear the road?"

"No."

"Then who's that?"

Saint-Gilles struggled to his feet and stared at the riders making their way along the northeast road like a stream of black ants. It was moments like these that his lost eye bothered him most. "Saint Faith. Can you see their banners?"

"White, I think."

"Baldwin of Boulogne, as I live! What does he think he's doing? How many men?"

"A few hundred. Hard to tell."

Saint-Gilles grabbed the spear he was using as a staff. "This is because Godfrey can't say no to anyone. Where is he?"

The tall duke of Lorraine must have been making a circuit of his camp, for he stood leaning against his palfrey near the stream that marked its eastern border. Bohemond and Count Stephen were already with him. Saint-Gilles cut across their conversation.

"Are those your men wandering off into the wild, my lord?"

Godfrey gave a patient sigh. "Good day, count. I trust you are in better health—"

Saint-Gilles gritted his teeth. "Just give me a straight answer."

Another sigh. "Yes. It's my brother."

The duke himself was still weak from a hunting accident in Pisidia. He had injured himself with his own sword while wrestling a bear, having got between the animal and its prey, a peasant. It made him a hero to the commoners, but Saint-Gilles had no sympathy. A proper knight would have known what to do with his sword.

"Your brother? He'll be massacred! I thought we agreed not to split up."

"He's only taken five hundred men."

"Five *hundred?* Are you mad? Five hundred healthy men and horses, and you'll just throw them away? What on earth for?"

Godfrey stiffened. "You're demanding that I explain myself to *you?* They are *my* men."

"You still answer to the princes' council."

"Then I'll answer to them. But not to you."

"Good. Here are four of us already. I'll send for the others." But even as Saint-Gilles stepped back to signal a servant, Count Hugh and the two Roberts left the camp and came hurrying toward the stream.

"My lords!" Bohemond motioned them into the circle. "You come at an opportune moment. Now come, Saint-Gilles." The count flashed his most charming smile. "There's no reason to be at each others' throats. This could be good strategy! Now that we're all here, let Godfrey finish his explanation."

Before he spoke, Godfrey shot Saint-Gilles a sour look. Saint-Gilles suppressed a chuckle. He had actually offended the long-suffering duke.

"It's the Armenians," said Godfrey. "At Nicaea, my brother took one of them into his service. A knight with experience in the wars beyond these mountains. This man says the rest of his countrymen are like himself: brave knights and Christians. They're very numerous in Cilicia. While we take the north road, my brother will pass into Cilicia, raise the Armenians to revolt, and threaten Antioch from the west."

Bohemond nodded. "And then we come down out of the hills and pinch them from the east? I like it." He smiled winningly at Saint-Gilles. "I know you've had your differences with Baldwin, count. But you must admit it's good."

"Must I?" Saint-Gilles folded his arms. "We are in this pilgrimage together, my lords. He ought to have asked our leave. The *duke* ought to have asked our leave. With all due respect, Godfrey, you know how ambitious Baldwin is. You saw how he reacted when we lost the booty of Nicaea. If he gets Cilicia, do you really think he'll give it up again?"

Before anyone could answer, Bohemond cleared his throat and threw a meaningful glance toward the camp. Saint-Gilles straightened and stepped back as Tatikius arrived, holding the leash of his cheetah in one heavily beringed hand. Even after months of travel, the Greek general wore immaculately-laundered silks and lamellar armour with a golden sheen to rival the midday sun.

Ever genial, Bohemond stepped aside for him. "Welcome, my lord. We were just discussing this expedition of Boulogne's."

Saint-Gilles did not imagine for a moment that the Greek had left his own quarters in the town's citadel, and ventured into the Frankish camp for any other reason. Yet the general only lifted an eyebrow and said, "Expedition? Tell me about it, count."

Obligingly, Bohemond recited Godfrey's story. "As for me, I approve of it. If this Armenian is telling the truth about his compatriots, they could be vital to the siege of Antioch."

"And the name of this Armenian?"

Godfrey coughed. "Bagrat, my lord."

"The same Bagrat that was the emperor's prisoner until recently?"

Godfrey looked embarrassed. "I believe this is so."

Tatikius clicked his tongue. "This is painful to say, my lords, but Bagrat has a history. The Armenians are…independent people. Beyond these mountains, Syria is a patchwork of petty warlords, fighting Turk and Greek alike as the whim takes them. Such was Bagrat. If he intends to carve out another lordship for himself, will your brother restrain him?"

There was no uncertainty in Godfrey's voice. "Count Baldwin will conduct himself like a man of honour."

Saint-Gilles was tired of the sidling way in which Tatikius approached his goals. "What do you want, general? Come to the point."

"You wish me to speak plainly?"

"Please," said Godfrey.

"Well, then." A hard edge crept into Tatikius' voice. "You have all sworn to return the emperor's lost territories to him. Naturally he lays claim to Cilicia. Why did no one tell me this expedition was planned? I would have gone with him, or sent men to garrison the Cilician towns."

"My brother thought it best if he took a small force," Godfrey began.

"Did he also think it best to keep his departure secret?" Saint-Gilles interrupted.

Godfrey's expression admitted that it was true. "Spies," he began.

Saint-Gilles overrode him. "Did *nothing* about this smell rotten to you? For once, I agree with Tatikius. Baldwin's only in this for his own gain."

Godfrey opened his mouth and closed it again, looking harried.

Bohemond regarded Tatikius with growing curiosity. "What's Cilicia like?"

"Fertile, well defended by the mountains, and full of Armenians. He could hardly have chosen a better country."

Bohemond grinned. "No wonder he asked for secrecy."

"Will you order him to return?" Tatikius asked.

"I don't see why we should." Hugh of Vermandois cut in with his high, nasal voice. "It's a sound plan. Strategic. Saves the rest of us some trouble."

Tatikius' mouth ironed shut. "And the emperor's claim to Cilicia?"

Bohemond shrugged. "Baldwin is bound by two oaths. One to serve the emperor, another to visit Jerusalem for the love of Our Lord. He's not proven faithless to either."

"So you mean to do nothing." Tatikius glared at Saint-Gilles.

The other counts silently exchanged glances until, at last, Count Stephen spoke. "We stand by Count Baldwin, my lord. For now."

At that, Tatikius lost his calm. Although his voice remained level, it cut like a whip: "Fools! The emperor will hear of this! Don't you realise he's your only hope of survival? If he withdraws his aid, who will come to save you?"

He snapped his fingers at his entourage and stormed back to the city.

Chapter XXXIV.

There were two apothecaries in Heraclea.

The first was a small shop just inside the city wall, not far from the gate. Next door was only a warehouse. The second apothecary took up the ground floor of a more affluent tenement just before the town square. On one side was another tenement, on the other a large villa with a gate that opened onto a central courtyard. When Lukas knocked at the gate, it came unlatched and swung open with a slow, agonising creak.

"Good day?" There was no answer, so Lukas ventured through the gate, feeling like an intruder. The courtyard was empty, the house silent. The only movement was a curtain flapping at an open window in the loggia above. "Good day?" Lukas called again, and waited, listening.

Again, nothing but silence. He should ask at the apothecary next door. Lukas turned, and jumped. A man stood in the open gate. Black-bearded, short, and tough, he looked Lukas up and down suspiciously.

"What are *you* doing here?" he asked.

Lukas swallowed. "Master Tagaris?"

The man did not blink. "What do you want from him?"

Praying that it wasn't a stupid risk, Lukas pushed up his sleeve, showing his Watcher's Mark.

The man with the black beard straightened in surprise. He yanked the gate shut and bustled toward the main door of the house. "Come with me."

Lukas had to run to keep up. "Are you Tagaris?"

For answer, the man only threw open the door and stood back, gesturing to Lukas to enter. Hesitantly, Lukas ventured inside.

It looked as though a whirlwind had been there. The furniture was overturned, curtains yanked to the floor, pottery smashed, books torn.

"It was the Turks, curse them." Behind, the man's voice was scratchy with emotion. "They took everything before they left. They burned our crops, rounded up our animals, took the children as slaves, even stripped the gold and silver from the churches. And they took my poor master and his family."

Lukas felt nothing. It was as though the words made no sense to him, yet he heard himself speaking, as if from a distance. "You were the servant of Tagaris?"

"I'm the only one left."

"Where will they take them?"

The Greek shook his head, defeated. "I don't know. Into the East. Anywhere."

As the pilgrimage had advanced across Anatolia, they had found the whole place terribly ravaged by the Turks. They seemed determined to destroy anything that the Franks might find useful. Lukas felt a helpless sense of rage. He ought to have seen this coming. He ought to have done something to stop it…

"What am I going to *do?*" he murmured.

The servant clutched his arm with surprising strength. "Master Tagaris was the last Watcher we had. Stay with us, so that we are not destroyed."

"I can't. This isn't my home. *You* must be the Watcher now."

The servant stared at him, his mouth open in shock. "Me? But I'm only a servant."

"And I'm only a stray dog." Lukas shook off his hand. "You know this town. You served a Watcher. You should know how it's done." He had to get away from this man and *think*. He started back across the courtyard.

"But I don't have a Mark."

Lukas turned. Tagaris' servant stood on his master's threshold, his hands hanging slack by his sides in despair.

"Then *get* one. Being a Watcher isn't about having Marks or being part of a council. It's about justice and mercy, and anyone can do that."

He walked out into the street and leaned against the wall of the villa, suddenly exhausted. *Oh, God in heaven, what now?* Kari the Messenger had died. Tagaris had been enslaved. By all accounts, there were no more Watchers left beyond the mountains. The Greek Watchers wanted him for heresy.

And Lilith. Black vultures still haunted the pilgrimage. Try as he might, he could think of no way to stop her if she seriously wished to kill him.

Even if he returned to Syria, how would he find his way home? Who would help him?

He considered, for a moment, trying to track down Tagaris and his family. But Ayla had said that the sultan of Nicaea had assembled his army from a patchwork of nomad tribes, and Tagaris could have been taken by any one of them. It was more than five days since the main body of the fast-moving Turkish army had withdrawn from Heraclea, and the Watcher could be anywhere by now, from the slave markets of Aleppo to the mountains of Georgia. Finding him might take years—if either of them survived the journey.

He just wanted to go *home*.

Lukas pulled his hood well forward to exit the city gate, anxious to avoid being recognised. He need not have bothered: the Greek sentries barely glanced his way. Outside the gate, a path led north to where the Franks were camped by the side of the stream. Lukas turned the corner and found himself looking straight into Tatikius' eyes.

The Greek general must be on his way back from a visit to the

Frankish camp. A small entourage rode at his back, his cheetah padding by the side of his horse. For an instant, Lukas was frozen in place, waiting for the order he knew would come.

The general had only opened his mouth when a welcome chatter of Frankish interrupted him. Lukas spun around. Bertrand and four other squires were exiting the gate, talking and laughing.

"Ho, Bessarion! Didn't know you were here," Bertrand called.

Saved. Wordlessly, Lukas fell in with them. Tatikius' mouth twitched in a wry smile and they passed each other in silence. Yet the escape gave him no feeling of relief. He was in danger here. What if he was stranded in this time for good, at the mercy of Lilith or Tatikius or Evrard or whoever else might take offence at him?

They arrived at the Provençal camp to find it full of commotion. A tent had caught fire somehow and the wind had spread the blaze to another nearby. Those who were not tripping over each other, trying to stop the blaze with water and rugs, were standing on tip-toe to watch. Bertrand and his friends ran to help, but Lukas was just grateful that the rest of the camp was empty and silent. He needed to think.

Wait.

Lukas narrowed his eyes at the count's tent, bells ringing in his mind. Count Raymond's tent was deserted. Every servant and guard that usually waited in its porch was gone.

Just like that, he knew how the fire had started.

Lukas slipped inside, walking as quietly as he could. At first, he heard nothing. Then, from beyond the sleeping partition, there came a faint rattle.

He twitched the tapestry soundlessly aside.

In the dim sleeping-quarters, Ayla knelt in front of the count's three treasure-chests. Behind her, scattered across the carpet, were three picked locks and a whole treasury: all the count's gold and silver plate, bags and bags of coins. Her breath was quick, rattled. With a grunt, she heaved a bag of gold Byzantine *hyperpyroi* out of the third chest, dumped it on the floor and flattened her hand desperately against the empty bottom.

Suddenly, she whirled, drawing her knife.

Lukas lifted his hands slowly, showing her they were empty. Her blade was shaking. Lukas did not miss the relief that washed through her at the sight of him. If it had been a guard…

The thought of what might have happened next knotted his gut. He still had nightmares about Ayla.

"Are you looking for this?" he whispered, bending to pick something from the carpet. A featureless bar of silver. He tossed it toward her and Ayla caught it with her free hand. She blinked for a moment, feeling the weight. Then, sick despair filled her eyes.

"You *melted* it."

He swallowed, unable to meet her gaze. "I had to."

* * *

"I knew you'd visit. I've been waiting for you." It was the saddest smile she had ever seen. It was the smile he kept only for her, but today it only maddened her.

Ayla clenched her teeth, enraged by his betrayal. "What did you tell the count about me?"

Lukas dropped to his haunches, gathering up the coins to repack the chests. His back was toward her. Somehow, he still trusted her. "Nothing, except that there's a Turkish spy with the pilgrimage."

Her bowl was gone. Her link with Armen severed, and with it her hope of getting across the knife's-edge bridge without falling into Lilith's hands. It would be so easy to kill him. And *just.* He'd thwarted her at every turn, denying her every chance to save her soul before she died.

This is war and you are a soldier in it.

He was locking the second chest now. In another moment, he'd be on his feet and facing her. *Without the bowl, I'll die a nobody. And it'll be Lukas Bessarion's fault.*

The knife was still in her fist. She reached out her hand to grab the dark, wavy hair. A yank back. A slash across the vein in the neck. He'd bleed out quickly. It would be painless.

Beyond the partition, light moved and voices trailed into the tent. Count Raymond had returned. Ayla snatched her hand back as Lukas swivelled and jumped to his feet.

"You'd better go," he whispered. "Come on, I'll see you out."

He'd already spotted where she'd entered the tent—a slack section of the canvas wall, unpegged at the bottom. Lukas slid through it and held it up for her to wriggle under. As he helped Ayla to her feet, passers-by stared. The fire must have died down, since the camp was no longer deserted. Ayla swallowed hard, expecting pointed fingers and shouts. Lukas followed her glance, then reached into her hair, pulled it free of its tail, and leaned forward so that his lips brushed her cheek.

"There," he whispered, "now you look like someone who's been dallying in a tent."

The stares slid incuriously away, but the panic stayed, like a thread twisted around her throat. Ayla pushed him in the chest. "Don't touch me!"

He stepped back, surprised. Oblivious to the fact that she'd almost killed him.

Ayla gulped. *"You melted my bowl.* Do you have any idea what you've done?"

He just stared at her for a moment. Then his face hardened.

"No, Ayla. Wrong question. Do *you* have any idea what *you've* done?" He threw out a hand, pointing toward the city wall. "Your people have destroyed, enslaved, burned and plundered their way across all of Anatolia. And *you're helping them do it.*"

His words hit her like arrows, but she couldn't let him see that. "And when your people make it to Antioch? They'll, what, teach us all to play polo? Do you dare to look me in the face and tell me that my mother, my sisters have nothing to fear from these people?"

"My last hope of finding a way home was a man living in this city. Now, if he's *lucky,* he and his family are slaves somewhere in Turkish territory."

Ayla swallowed raggedly before she could speak. "Were they Watchers?"

"Ayla..."

"They were, weren't they? They were damned sorcerers." She folded her arms, relieved to find some way of suppressing the guilt his words had evoked. "Well, they deserved it."

He shook his head at her, pain shadowing his eyes again. "Ayla...how could they deserve it? These people can't have had anything to do with your father's death, any more than yours had to do with mine. The Watchers..." his voice trailed off. "The Watchers of Antioch wronged you. They were never supposed to be like that and I'm sorry for it. I would set it right if you'd let me, but—"

"How? By turning my back on everything my father believed?" She backed away from him, shaking her head, her insides a knot of grief and anger and raw, bloody fear. "We aren't fated to be together, Lukas Bessarion. Trust me. I know."

Chapter XXXV.

Whats all the commotion?" Saint-Gilles asked as Galdemar hurried into the pavilion after him.

"One of the tents caught fire. It's under control." Galdemar wiped soot off his feet and took a seat at the table on Saint-Gilles' right hand.

Bohemond slouched in the chair on his left. "Worried about Tatikius, count? You were oddly silent during the meeting."

After the gold-nosed general had stormed back to Heraclea in disgust, Saint-Gilles had asked the Norman count for a private word. Now he pinched the bridge of his nose and sighed. "I never wanted to swear to Alexius. I knew it would be trouble."

Bohemond's white teeth flashed in a smile. "Don't pull such a long face! Tatikius is making a great theatre out of a small thing. Baldwin won't succeed in holding anything that Alexius wants, and as long as we wield this mighty army, he'd be a fool to try it."

Saint-Gilles shook his head. In his mind he still saw the dead laid out after the great battle. The Greek was right. Perhaps they needed allies. Perhaps there was a way to placate Tatikius.

Bohemond's eyes narrowed. "What's on your mind, count?"

Saint-Gilles leaned back, drumming his fingertips on the table. "Do you remember that mad ascetic of Boulogne's?"

"The one who saw angels?" Bohemond shrugged. "For a while he gave me entertaining prophecies at breakfast. Offered me the kingdoms of the east as playthings. But I wouldn't go to war with the Greeks, and so he moved on. I think he and his black angel went to Tatikius, in fact."

Saint-Gilles snorted. "Inciting him to strife with us, no doubt. I wonder. Tatikius knows Alexius better than we do. What if he's right? What if the Greeks do abandon us?"

Bohemond hitched a shoulder. "So? We'll be less two thousand men."

"Tatikius himself is nothing," Saint-Gilles retorted. "Do you feel how far we are from home? How surrounded by enemies? How difficult it is to find enough food and money? I hate to admit it, but we need the emperor's goodwill. Out here, he's our only ally."

Bohemond smiled faintly. "I thought we had God on our side."

"That's no reason to act like fools."

"I thought that was the idea." Bohemond sounded almost contemptuous. "God rescues the foolish. Or do I mistake the whole point of this journey?"

"Maybe you do, count."

The Norman count shook his head, the corner of his mouth twisting in a smile. "You have a plan?"

"If all else fails, I do. Baldwin can't get far before nightfall. We could send a messenger and order him to stay put until Tatikius can join him."

Bohemond laughed. "Baldwin won't take orders from you or me. Only Godfrey."

"And Godfrey's wrapped around his brother's little finger." Saint-Gilles slammed a fist on the table. "We should have picked a commander. It should have been a condition of the journey that all of us vowed obedience to one man. Now a second-rank count is holding all of us hostage to his whims."

"My sentiments precisely." Bohemond leaned forward. "I have a plan of my own."

Saint-Gilles gave a thin smile. "I was counting on that. Do tell."

Bohemond's teeth flashed. "Baldwin plans to be king of the beasts down there in Cilicia. At the head of five hundred knights, he holds all the power. At one stroke, I can halve that power and neutralise him completely."

"Go on."

"Create a balance. Send someone else in with a comparable force."

Saint-Gilles leaned forward. "Who?"

"Not one of *us*. The Greeks would never stand for it. Someone Baldwin's own size. Tancred would be ideal."

"Your nephew? But he's so young."

"He's my best. And forgive me for saying it, but that makes him the best in the whole pilgrimage."

Saint-Gilles considered it. He could possibly send one of his own men, Raymond Pilet or Galdemar, but Bohemond was right. Young as he was, Tancred had a reputation, and reputations didn't come cheap among the Italian Normans. A mission like this could go horribly wrong. Tancred had the best chance of survival.

Besides, if something *did* go wrong, then his own Provençals were better off out of it.

"Are you willing to send him tonight?"

Bohemond pursed his lips. "It'll cost. In your ear, I don't have a lot of money left."

Neither did Saint-Gilles. Still, if Bohemond was providing the men, the least he could do was part with some gold.

"I'll see to the funds."

"Then I'll send him at once." Bohemond smiled cheerfully and their hands clasped across the tabletop.

Saint-Gilles supplied the Norman count with money and saw him off, before heading to his sleeping quarters with weariness thrumming in his bones. If he pushed himself any further, he would have another bout of fever. The next step would have to wait. Before collapsing into his bed, Saint-Gilles sent a courier into the town to let Tatikius know that he would visit in the morning.

As Terce approached, the Greek received him behind a desk in the cabinet that had belonged to the city's previous governor; a room whose scarred marble and faded silk bore witness to long-exhausted wealth. With his hands clasped across his soft belly and his gold nose winking in the light, Tatikius looked more like a vain and prosperous merchant than the ascendant star of the Greek army.

"Count," he greeted, getting up. "I'm glad you came."

Words had been on the tip of his tongue, but the Greek's greeting stopped them. "You are?"

"I wanted to speak more about your interpreter." Tatikius' eyes were hard. "There's a price on his head. The boy has already betrayed you once, you can have no reason to shield him from the emperor's justice."

Saint-Gilles blinked. "Bessarion is useful to me. What has he done?"

"He's a heretic. A dissident."

"A *dissident?*" Saint-Gilles repressed a snort of contempt. The meeting had not even started, and Tatikius had already managed to get him on the defensive. As petty as the Greeks might be, however, he was not here to antagonise them further.

"The boy's not doing any harm as my interpreter—"

"First Baldwin of Boulogne harbours the Armenian Bagrat and now you are shielding the heretic Bessarion. Whose side are you on, count?"

Teeth gritted, Saint-Gilles rested both hands on the marble desktop. "On yours, my lord. I have spoken to Count Bohemond. We agree with you as to Count Baldwin's real motivations."

Tatikius smiled acidly. "From memory, so does everyone."

"Yes, but Bohemond and I have done something about it. We can't recall Baldwin, but we can introduce a new factor, something to keep him from ruling the Cilician roost."

"I'm listening."

"We've sent Tancred of Hautville after him with a cohort of Bohemond's best. He'll keep an eye on Baldwin, make sure the count keeps his attention where it belongs—fighting the Turks—and off the Cilician towns."

Tatikius' eyebrows lifted. "Tancred of Hautville? You must be joking."

Saint-Gilles blinked. "On the contrary. I'm perfectly sincere."

"This is the young man who refused to swear homage unless he was filled with gold, yes? The young man who assaulted Paleologus in the emperor's *very presence* at Pelekanum, yes? And you expect me to trust this man?"

Holy Virgin.

"I didn't attend Pelekanum," Saint-Gilles said slowly. "What did Tancred do?"

Tatikius stared at him skeptically. "Alexius asked all the counts, even the lesser lords, to swear homage to him. Tancred refused and then with unbounded insolence, demanded a tent full of gold."

"Did he swear?"

"Only after grappling with one of our officers. They had to be pulled apart. And I'm supposed to be satisfied that this man will guard the emperor's interests?"

Saint-Gilles gritted his teeth. He had evidently missed that detail. Still, Bohemond was right: Tancred was the best man for the job.

"Look, I came here to mend things, not to make them worse. With power in Cilicia balanced between Baldwin and Tancred, neither of them can do anything. It's the best I can offer given that I'm not commanding this pilgrimage."

"And Bessarion?"

The boy was sworn to his service, but then, so were thousands of Provençals who had followed him halfway across the world, perhaps to their deaths. He owed them penance just as much as he owed it to Christ. If he had to choose between them, he would sacrifice the Greek every time.

But he did not have to choose between them, not yet. Until that time came, he would keep his word to both.

"In Francia, we treat our followers like family. We don't hand them over to their enemies."

Tatikius narrowed his eyes. Finally, he stood and circled the desk.

"Raymond Saint-Gilles, I believe you are a man of your word. But I don't trust Baldwin, and I don't trust Tancred. Once we cross the mountains, the game will change. You will be on the borders of the Holy Land, the place you came to fight for. The temptation will be strong for your followers to keep what they gain."

"So?"

"So I give you notice that the holy emperor claims both Syria and Palestine. Alexius is willing to support you, but only if you perform your vows to the letter. If not, I have full discretion to withdraw his support." Tatikius put a hand on Saint-Gilles' shoulder. Although the Greek was the smaller man, there was steel in his grip. "Don't think I'm not keeping tally. You wouldn't take the oath the emperor asked. You wouldn't hand over the heretic Bessarion. And now Cilicia. I'm loyal to my emperor, count. I won't let him sink endless money and resources into this venture without a guaranteed return. It would be best if all of you remembered your oaths."

With any other man, Saint-Gilles would be angry. But everything had changed the day that a Turkish army nearly wiped out half the pilgrimage. He would never forget the sheer number of the dead. Now they were alone in enemy territory, weeks from help. As little as he liked to admit it, their survival was entirely dependent on the goodwill of Constantinople.

Little as he trusted Alexius, they needed his help.

"I will not forget, Tatikius, neither will I forgive." Deliberately, Saint-Gilles removed the Greek's hand from his shoulder. "But joy or sorrow, I'll do as I swore."

Chapter XXXVI.

After picking himself up from his third fall of the afternoon, Lukas became convinced that the mountain actually hated them.

North of Heraclea, the road had not been too difficult. Food and forage were scarce, but at least the blazing edge of summer had been blunted. At Caesarea, however, they had turned at last toward the snow-streaked mountains. The road sloped up across the shoulders of the Taurus, dwindling to little more than a narrow footpath with barely room for three horses to walk abreast. The weather had thinned and chilled. Wind and water hummed through the narrow gorges and between the stunted cypress. For miles on end the pilgrimage had strung out into a line of footsore travellers slipping and clambering across the rocks.

Even so, the worst had been reserved until the final leg of the mountain road, three weeks out from Heraclea. The already narrow road became a thread looping between grey, craggy peaks and zig-zagging down brutally steep slopes. The pilgrimage had slowed to a crawl, skirting the edges of precipices in single file. By this time, most of the oxcarts had already been abandoned, the salvage bundled onto weary travellers' backs or lashed to the surviving animals.

Lukas' own horse was long gone. Within weeks of the great battle, he had been forced to admit that Ayla was right: he could not feed the animal. Eventually, rather than watch her starve, he had sold the horse to Raymond Pilet. So much for claiming his place as a knight. His only consolation was that as a wiry Turkish pony she had more chance of surviving the journey than the Frankish behemoths.

The afternoon air was purple and stuffy. Lightning flickered at the edge of the clouds. Ahead, a single file of men and the occasional ox plodded doggedly down the slanting path, heads and backs bent beneath their burdens.

Lukas stumbled and lurched against the man in front of him. Cursing, the man shoved him upright again. Wondering what had tripped him, Lukas turned and saw the splayed legs of an exhausted traveller, slumped onto the path with his back against the rock wall.

Immediately behind Lukas, a pack pony shied at the unexpected obstacle, veering too far from the rock wall. Its hoof slipped on the edge of the path and a stone crumbled from the brink. The pony gave a whinny of fright.

Slowly, heavily, it began to sideslip. Its driver yelled, dragging on its leading-rein. Lukas started forward.

"Cut the rope!" he shouted, but there was no time, no space. The pony screamed in alarm, scrabbling to right itself, but more of the path crumbled beneath its feet. Then it fell, its leading-rope burning through the Frank's palms. "Cut the rope!" Lukas yelled again, but it was already too late. The pony was the first of a train of five animals, linked by a rope. The fall of the first dragged the others to the brink—the second, neighing in pain and terror, slipped to the edge and followed it—and then the others were dragged off their feet and plunged after.

The stones below were grey, jagged, and merciless. For a moment, the mountains resounded with the *thud, thud, thud* of falling bodies.

Then silence.

Lukas recoiled against the cliff, holding a hand over his mouth. The driver stood on the edge of the path and looked down, his face slack and pale with fear.

"Imbecile! Fool!" A knight panted up the path to seize him by the scruff of the neck. "Our food and fodder! Holy Virgin!" The knight's voice cracked into a wail, and he lifted his hands helplessly to his head. The knights following him fell to their knees in abject misery. One of them, with a groan, threw his shield into the gorge after the ponies. Another turned to Lukas and held out his helmet.

"Threepence and it's yours."

Lukas hesitated, then dug into his pouch and handed the money over. When he refused to buy the knight's mail hauberk, it followed the shield into the gorge.

The man sitting in the path had neither spoken nor moved the whole time. Lukas crouched down to touch his face. It was like touching wax. The body was still warm, but the spirit was gone. He had been a knight too, Lukas realised, seeing the padded leather jerkin and empty sword-belt. Like the others, he must have sold or thrown away his belongings in the hope of surviving the murderous pass. His shoes were worn through. He must have lost his horse long ago. Now loneliness, poverty, and sickness had finished him off.

Pity stabbed Lukas' heart. It seemed wrong to leave the man where he was, underfoot. It seemed equally impossible to pitch him after the fallen animals. Lukas cleaned three silver coins out of the knight's money-pouch, slid the signet ring from his finger, then hailed a passing peasant for help getting the dead load onto his back.

After Lukas had walked a mile under that terrible weight, the path finally emerged into a valley. Gratefully, he stepped off the path and laid the dead Frank in the grass. Even if he found ground soft enough admit a grave in these hard mountains, there was nothing to dig with. Instead, he simply covered the knight's face with his ragged cloak and weighted him down with stones.

More Franks dropped out of the shuffling, weary column to rest on the green verge. Most collapsed wordlessly onto the grass but two of them, seeing his efforts, crawled over to help.

It had been a still and cloudy day. Although it was mid-afternoon, it seemed as dark as evening. By the time the Frankish knight was no more than an oblong heap of stones, the sky was almost black.

Lukas sat back, wiping his hands on his filthy pants and watched the procession toil past. When Lukas had first joined the pilgrimage, the column had resounded with singing, chanting and laughter. No one sang now. No one even spoke. They were too desperate to reach camp before the skies broke. He turned to look up the slope behind, and looked directly into Ayla's eyes.

She was sitting on a grey stone, watching him with her chin propped in her hands. Since Heraclea, she had not come close enough to speak to him, although from time to time he still caught her watching him from a distance. He got up and blundered through the mid-afternoon dusk toward her.

She stood watching him until he had halved the distance between them. Then, instead of rejoining the pilgrims, she jumped from her perch and raced up the green slope toward the jagged grey ridge. Lukas scrambled after her on hands and feet like a spider.

"Ayla," he called, "I only want to speak to you!"

She glanced back over her shoulder and waited for a moment, but before he got close she set off again, clambering up over boulders toward the grey sky. The wind picked up, blowing his hair into his eyes. By the time his vision cleared, Ayla had vanished.

Lukas made it at last onto the narrow, stony crest. Great striations of stone scarred the hillsides on each side. Mountains marched as far as the eye could see, a land as tormented as the winter sea. Light pulsed in the clouds and a rumble of thunder followed.

"Ayla!" he shouted again. Then he saw her: a flash of colour among the rocks lower down, heading into the next valley. Lukas plunged recklessly after her. "Ayla! Stop!"

He caught up with her halfway down the slope and grabbed her by the elbow. Instantly she whipped around, throwing all the weight of her body against him. Down they went, and her knife tickled his chin.

Saint George, he thought, *she's actually going to do it.*

Say something. It's the last chance you'll ever have.

"You're beautiful," he said.

She bit her lip until it went pale. "Don't try to flatter me."

"Then prove it doesn't work. Kill me."

It was a stupid thing to say, but she spat into the grass next to his head.

"I will if you touch me again without my leave." She got off him. Sheathing her knife, Ayla raised her voice to shout over the rising wind. "Come with me. There's someone you need to meet."

Lukas glanced at the massive clouds, then back at Ayla. "Someone out in these God-forsaken hills? Who?"

"Someone who can help you go home!" She turned and scrambled down toward the valley's depths.

Home. It was too good to be true, but if she was luring him away to kill him, she would have done it already. Still, something made every hair on his body stand on end.

Danger. Danger.

The wind howled in an icy torrent. A gigantic drop of rain burst against his cheekbone.

Someone was watching him. Lukas turned, but the valley was empty.

Ayla's shout blew on the wind. "Hurry!"

A few drops had turned into a downpour. Lukas moved toward Ayla, but once again, every sense flared.

Danger.

He stopped in his tracks. This was ridiculous. What danger? Anyone caught out in a storm like this should be crowding into shelter, not lying in wait—

In his mind's eye, he saw the bent backs and silent despair that had descended on the pilgrims. The handwringing knights. The man sitting dead by the side of the road. The fear.

Lilith.

"Saint George," he muttered.

Ayla yelled at him as he scrambled back up the valley wall, but whatever she said was lost in the hammering of sleet. Particles of ice rang on his helmet and stung his hands. On top of the ridge, the wind was nearly strong enough to knock him over. Lukas crawled among the rocks, finding a vantage-point where he could see the road. Below, the long string of pilgrims had come to a halt, huddling under cloaks and shields to escape the storm.

Hailstones grew to the size of pebbles and the landscape whitened. He could hear nothing over the rattle on his helmet. Still the downpour showed no sign of stopping. The pilgrimage was totally exposed. If the stones got any bigger, people would die.

Lukas put an arm up to shade his eyes, scanning the clouds. No sign of Lilith or her vultures. Was he crazy?

He scrambled down toward the road, racing against a wind that seemed determined to hold him back. Suddenly, a rock came loose beneath him, throwing him against the jagged stone of the hillside. The skin on his fingers split as he hooked them into a niche and halted his downward slide.

The wind screamed through the valley and, in desperation, Lukas screamed back. *"Peace! Christ bids you be still!"*

The downpour ceased as abruptly as a snuffed flame, the violent wind hung motionless in the air. In the wake of that ear-splitting roar, the silence was just as deafening.

Lukas clawed for another handhold and wedged his toes into the rock. If he let go, he would drop onto the Franks below, pale terrified faces turned up to see him splayed against the precipice. He clung to the rock for dear life and squeezed his eyes shut. In the silence, his mother's prayer returned to him.

"Lord, stretch out Thy mighty hand and send down upon us a peaceful angel, a mighty angel, a Watcher of soul and body, that will rebuke and drive away every evil and unclean demon. For Thou alone are Lord, Most High, almighty and blessed unto ages of ages."

A rumble of distant thunder muttered in the sky, but there was no more wind. Instead, a soft rain began to fall.

* * *

Hidden under the lee of the rock, Ayla was still almost dry when the downpour stopped, as if someone had closed the windows of heaven. Within arm's reach, hailstones the size of her thumbnail were heaped against the rocks. Smooth and heavy and almost big enough for a sling. Ayla reached out and picked one up, her mind whirling down impossible paths.

If it doesn't work, we'll have to try again in the mountains. It was the last thing Armen had said to her before Lukas took the scrying-bowl. Was this what he meant?

The Vowed had strange powers. Her father had used his to heal people. Could he have done something like this too? She could not bear to think of her father raining stones on his enemies, but Armen? She could almost believe it.

The pilgrimage. *Lukas.* With the thought, she dashed from the shelter of her rock and scrambled up the hillside, afraid of what she might find beyond.

Ayla did not know whether to weep or rejoice when she reached the crest. The pilgrimage seemed largely unharmed, their last stragglers passing below. Lukas himself sat among the stones watching them, nursing cut and bleeding hands.

He didn't look at her. "Lilith."

Ayla's skin prickled. "Did you see her again?"

The voice from her nightmares echoed in her mind. *You are mine, girl. Don't think you'll make it across the chasm. I'll be waiting.*

"I felt her. I know she was here. This storm was her doing." Lukas spoke with quiet and utter certainty. "Whoever you're working for, Ayla...whatever they might be trying to do for your people...*this* is who they're in league with."

Ayla's gut clenched. "They would never...That's impossible! Lilith is the Poison Mother, pure wickedness! Am I a demon-worshipper, to do her bidding?"

For a moment, he watched her, his eyes guarded. Then he let out a sigh. "It wouldn't be the first time good intentions were corrupted. When the Watchers met in Constantinople, a black vulture was roosting in the trees above them."

Ayla snorted. "See? I knew it."

"All right. I shouldn't make accusations I can't prove. I'm sorry." He got up, wiping his hands on his clothes. "You said you were taking me to someone who can get me home."

She glared at him. "Only because you're pathetic and I was feeling sorry for you. *Was.*"

The strain on his face cracked, letting a smile slip through. "I'll behave like an angel. I'll be as pathetic as you like. *Please,* Ayla."

Despite the laughter, he did look pathetic. Ayla glanced at the sky. It was impossible to see where the sun stood, but the afternoon was certainly progressing. "We'll have to travel fast," she muttered.

She didn't want kill Lukas, but he had proven himself too great a risk to stay. They had butted heads again and again since Nicaea, and so far, he was winning. She had to get him away from the Franks before this double life of hers fell apart, and the only way to do that without bloodshed was to send him back where he belonged. They weren't fated to be together. And if she could not love him, then at least she could protect him.

At the top of the next ridge, she found the path. It looked like a goat-track, but as they followed it, they found first one, then another ancient milestone. For miles, it led them along the crest of the sharp ridge, looping and zig-zagging to avoid the steep valleys.

It was like walking on the world's roof.

They had been travelling for hours when the sun dipped below the purple dome of clouds, painting the hills gold and splashing long black shadows at their feet. Ahead, the ridge broadened into a high grassy plateau crowned with standing stones.

Ayla stopped. "Do you hear that?"

Lukas glanced at her, then stiffened as a thin sound reached them, a melodious piping that rose and fell with the wind.

"Sunset at the Singing Stones," Ayla said, and pointed. "Look! She is here."

* * *

At first, Lukas could not see what Ayla was pointing at. Closer, he realised that what he had mistaken for a smaller stone was a woman in a grey cloak, sitting cross-legged on a smooth boulder at the centre of the circle. Closer still, he realised that the circle embraced a crossroads.

It was the stones themselves that made the melody. Someone long ago had bored holes through the unhewn rocks. Now they thrummed in the wind, making a formless and eerie music.

The woman was old, her eyes a blind and milky blue.

Ayla bowed, pressing her hands together. *"Salaam aleiki!"* She spoke entirely in Turkish, and beyond the greeting Lukas did not understand it.

To his surprise, the woman replied in Syriac, the language he had grown up speaking with his brothers and sisters.

"Do you have payment?"

Lukas dipped into his pouch to touch the silver he had found in the dead man's pouch. "Payment for what?"

"Answers to your questions. One silver groat per answer." She thrust out a wrinkled brown hand.

Ayla glanced at him. "I have enough for both of us."

That decided him. "No need."

Quickly, he dropped his own coin in the old woman's hand. Her wrinkled fingers brushed each side of the coins, weighed them, and found them satisfactory.

"Who first?"

Lukas nodded to Ayla and left the stone circle.

With the sun low on the horizon, the air became bitterly cold. On

314

the edge of the hilltop, Lukas rubbed his arms and wondered what Ayla might be asking. It was impossible to hear their hushed voices over the stones' singing. He glanced over his shoulder. Ayla stood before the woman with her head bent.

Was she asking how to destroy the pilgrimage?

Was she asking about him?

What if she found out he was a Watcher?

A chill ran through him, but there was nothing he could do. He had shown her all the gentleness, all the love he could. If she learned the truth about him, he must trust to those to plead his case.

A little longer, and it was over. Lukas watched her face closely as she emerged from the stone circle, but the twilight veiled her expression until she came close enough to speak.

"Your turn."

"What did you ask?"

"Does it matter?"

She sounded tired, looked sad. If only he could kiss the smile back to her lips—but she would not allow it, and he knew better than to try. Instead, he walked between the rocks and faced the seer.

"What's your name? Who are you?"

"These are your questions?" The old woman snorted with contempt.

"Did Ayla tell you my name?"

"Three questions already, and none of them worth answering."

"All right." He tried to summon his thoughts. *Will I find my way home?* No, too vague. He needed a person. *Who.*

"Who will show me the way home to my people?"

The sightless eyes seemed to look far beyond him. "The girl will tell you."

Lukas blinked. "Ayla? *Ayla* can send me into the past?"

"One answer for a groat. You've had your answer. Do you have more coins?"

"No, wait. She *knows* I'm lost in time. If she knew anything, she'd have told me."

"Would she?"

Lukas opened his mouth, then closed it again. After all, they were supposed to be enemies. Ayla owed him nothing, especially not the truth. Even so, he was surprised how betrayed he felt.

Why would she not help him?

"This answer surprises you?" The seer chuckled. "Angers you, maybe?"

Anger? All the emotion had bled out of him. He was tired, that was what he was. He was tired, and he wanted answers, not more riddles. Lukas dipped back into his purse for another silver coin. He could not afford to spend more, but he had to know. He tossed it into her lap and watched her fumble for it between the folds of her faded red skirt.

"Is there any hope for us? Can I take her home with me?"

She lifted the coin, stroking the surface. She did not turn her blind eyes toward him, but her voice was clear over the humming rocks.

"You and she are bound by fate."

Chapter XXXVII.

As the sun set, all other light and colour leached out of the world, leaving only a glow of narcissus yellow in the west. Little by little, even that light failed. Neither Lukas nor Ayla said anything as they picked their way back up the crest path.

Finally, Ayla broke the silence. "We'll break our necks in this dark. We should stop until morning."

Lukas' feet had hardened during the last three months, but after the day's hard travel, he was ready to stop and rest. Together, they clambered down a green hillside. Stunted pine-trees clung to its slopes, hissing pricklishly in the wind. They gathered fir-cones as they went and found a level, dry place to bivouac under a rocky overhang. While Ayla worked with tinder and flint to light the fire, Lukas felt his way further down the slope until he came to a spring where he could wash his hands and refill their water-bottles.

There was no food, but they had both become accustomed to hunger by now.

Fire lit, they huddled into their cloaks, feeling the welcome heat drying their still-damp clothes. Ayla stared into the blue-green pine flames.

"So. Did you get an answer?"

Lukas nodded.

"S'pose you'll be leaving soon."

It took him a moment to realise what she meant. With his whole mind consumed by the seer's second answer, he had almost forgotten her first.

Ayla knew how to get him home.

Ayla and he were bound by fate.

None of it made sense, and he felt trapped in a snarl of contradictions. How was he going to get what he needed to know? How could they be bound by fate?

He cleared his throat. "Ayla. Tell me what you know about the Watchers."

She touched her tongue to her lips. "I told you, they're sorcerers. They killed my father."

"But why?"

"They need a reason?"

"In Constantinople they run *hospitals.*"

"Yeh, well." He thought she would not go on, but she did. "Maybe they thought he was pricing them out of the market, healing people. I don't know."

"Tell me about the day it happened. Please."

She closed her eyes. "He'd been into the mountains again. He did that all the time. He'd be gone for weeks. That time, while he was gone, the Watchers came. They locked all of us into my mother's room—the wives and all the children. Then, for three days, they worked."

"Worked? At what?"

"Peculiar things." Ayla frowned. "Most of them copied manuscripts. Some of them repaired leaks in the roof. One of them spent the whole time weeding and pruning and re-potting the garden. But all the time they wore swords.

"My father's first wife said not to worry, that Father would see his own fortune and steer clear of us until the Watchers went away. But he didn't. When he came home, they were waiting to surround him. It was like a court hearing, except that they didn't let him speak. Then…"

Ayla laced her fingers into each other. "From the window, we heard everything. We saw everything. There was nothing we could do. My mother put her hands over my eyes. But after they had gone, I saw him lying in the courtyard with his head on the stones next to him and his blood was…thickened. Like tapioca."

If there was one thing he had learned in the last six months, it was that Watchers were, like any men, capable of great evil. "I'm sorry," he said.

Ayla shrugged, reached into her pouch and unwrapped a small package of almonds and dried apricots. She held them out to Lukas. "Wasn't your fault, Greek."

He took a handful of the food and ate it one nut at a time to make the most of the nourishment. "So there were still Watchers in Antioch when that happened."

"Yeh."

"What happened to them?"

"We happened to them." Ayla's voice dropped to little more than a breath. "My father had friends and relatives all over the city. Some of them powerful. All of them angry. One by one, the Watchers disappeared. Anyone who was left began concealing their marks."

The food turned to ash in Lukas' mouth.

In front of him, the fire continued dancing as if it did not care.

The destruction of the Syrian Watchers was done by Ayla's family?

Or by unjust Watchers to themselves, a voice added in the back of his mind. Slowly, painfully, he swallowed.

"There are still Watchers in Antioch, living in secret." Ayla's voice was dark as the night around them. "We drove them deep underground, and we'll keep them there where they can never hurt anyone again."

We?

"You were only a child when they killed him."

"Couldn't do anything to avenge him then. My fight is still in the future." She threw another pinecone onto the fire and huddled closer, rubbing her hands. "Why are you so worried about those devils, anyway?"

"I hoped they could point my way home." He studied her fire lit profile. "But the seer told me it was you who knew that secret."

For the first time since they had left the singing stones, Ayla looked him in the eye, completely bewildered.

"Me? How would I know?"

He knew her well enough by now to know her confusion was sincere. The realisation washed over him, irrationally relieving.

"Think," he said gently. "Perhaps it's not you. Perhaps it's someone you know of."

She frowned. He was still watching when her eyes widened, her forehead smoothed.

She knew.

Instead of telling him, she bit her lip. "Do you want to know what she told me?"

Puzzled, Lukas nodded. For a moment, she would not meet his eye, her hands twisting nervously in her lap.

"She said we were bound by fate."

Instantly, his mouth was dry, his heart was stuttering. "She told me the same thing."

"If I tell you how to find your way home, you'll leave me."

"No. Never. Ayla, you're my destiny. My Kismet. I want you to come home with me."

Once, she would have refused even to consider it.

Don't make me dream of a different life, Lukas Bessarion.

Now she looked up at him with candid eyes. "You're different to the rest of them, Lukas. I trust you. Go into the mountains of Syria, to the dead city, that once was named Oliveta. If the answer is anywhere, it's there."

"Oliveta," he breathed. Of course. Ever since Heraclea he had known—and dreaded the thought. But if Ayla was with him, he could face it. "What's in Oliveta?"

She bit her lip. "I've already said too much. You can't—Lukas, you can't let anyone else know about this."

You and she are bound by fate.

"I'll never betray you, Ayla, and I'll never leave you. I swear it. Promise me something in return."

Her eyes were enormous, twin fires burning in their depths. "Anything."

"Set me as a seal upon your heart, as a seal upon your arm. For love is as strong as death; jealousy as cruel as the grave."

"That's beautiful." She looked dazed. "But what does it mean?"

"It means I want you to be my wife."

Her hands tightened on his shoulders. "My people will kill both of us if they find out."

"Then we don't tell them. Many waters cannot quench love, neither can the floods drown it. Promise me."

"I do," she breathed. "I will."

* * *

Ayla woke as the fire burned low and the cold began to nip. Under the same cloak, Lukas lay asleep beside her, an arm thrown over her waist.

You and he are bound by fate.

She reached out to their pile of unburned pinecones and tossed another one onto the dying embers, but it rolled away. She knew she should get up, tend the fire.

How easy it was, in the end, just to break down the walls and surrender. Despite the enmity between their people, there could be peace between them. It was fated. She only had to let it happen. She only needed the faith to see it.

Reluctantly, she slid out from under the cover of her cloak and rebuilt the fire.

She had so little time left. Days, unless she was mistaken. Yet for the first time, she began to image a better future. She had always believed in her father's foretelling, but what if he was mistaken? What if she was destined to leave this time, to travel into the far past and find peace?

What if she could live?

Ayla had told Lukas the seer's words, but she hadn't admitted that, like him, she'd paid for two answers.

"Mother," she said, *"I have tried so many times to stop this Frankish army. Why does nothing work? How will I stop them devouring my people?"*

"You wish to destroy them?"

Tears stung her eyes. "I have to destroy them. There's no other way."

"Then you should look at the boy."

It seemed like useless advice at the time. She'd looked at him so many times before, but now, in the firelight, she could look again. Ayla pulled her knees to her chest and stared into his face. There was nothing there, she was sure.

Even in sleep he looked tired, his cheekbones cutting sharply through sun-darkened skin. The arrogance he used to wear like a cloak was almost completely gone now. His breathing caught and he shifted, reaching out his naked arm as if feeling for her. Ayla took his hand. The fingers clenched around her hand and then relaxed as his breath evened again. As Ayla lifted the arm to creep back under, she saw the mark on his forearm.

A rimless wheel, *I* and *X*.

A Watcher's Mark was written on his skin.

Chapter XXXVIII.

Ayla was still staring at the mark when Lukas opened his eyes. "You're a Watcher," she said thickly.

Instantly, he was awake. He snatched his arm from her grip, eyes wide. "Oh, Saint George! Ayla, I forgot. I meant to tell you, I just..."

"You *forgot?*" Her voice hitched up a register. "Six months we've known each other, and you *forgot?* Watchers killed my father, and you *forgot?*"

"I didn't want it to come between us!"

"Are you going to kill me, too? Is this how I die?" What month was it? What day? The foretelling had said she would die at the hands of a Christian. God have mercy, why had she not seen it sooner?

She fumbled in the folds of their cloaks, trying to find her weapons.

"Ayla, no! I would never—"

Sling. Pouch. Her hands were shaking too much to aim. At last, she found her knife. She disentangled her clothes from the damp pile on the grass, pulling the tunic over her head, struggling into the trousers.

"Did you really think I wouldn't find out?"

"We were friends! You said yourself I was different—"

"I *trusted* you!" The words ripped from her throat, unleashing her tears. "I—I—"

The vow he'd made. The peace she thought she'd found. All a lie. But there was worse.

"I told you about Oliveta." She jerked the knife from its sheath. Her

father's most prized secret, and she'd handed it over to the enemy. How could she face him in heaven now?

Only if the secret was safe.

Only if Lukas Bessarion was dead.

Ayla struck.

Lukas fell backward with a yelp of alarm, throwing up an arm to block her. Ayla landed on top of him, pulling back the blade for another blow. He tried to grab her wrist, but only succeeded in catching her loose sleeve. At once she drove her arm forward, aiming for his throat. With a convulsive jerk, he avoided the blade and heaved, toppling her into the grass. She slashed blindly with her knife, eliciting a yelp of pain. He wrestled himself free of her and jumped to his feet, grabbing his staff.

Blood spilled from a jagged cut across his cheek.

Ayla rolled to a crouch and coiled for another leap. Lukas didn't wait. He turned his back and fled from the light. On the edge of the dark, Ayla halted, straining her eyes.

Silence. He must be near, or she would have heard his footsteps.

"Greek!" she yelled. "Greek! I know you're there! Face me, you coward!"

No answer.

"Face me! Or I'll tell everyone you ran from a woman!"

Still, no answer.

"She warned me, you know! She told me you were the reason I couldn't stop them! I should have killed you when I had the chance!"

"Then why did you marry me?"

The voice came from her right. *Got him.*

"Because I'm a fool!" She plunged blindly into the dark.

The shadow of a juniper tree loomed above her. A darker shape rolled away from it, got around her, and pelted back to the campfire. Ayla was hot on his trail, but Lukas moved faster, stopping just long enough to gather up his belongings.

With a kick, he scattered the campfire, snuffing what light remained in the valley.

Then his footsteps, his panicked breath, trailed away from her up the slope. Ayla pelted after him, but her foot turned among the rocks. She barely caught herself before slamming into the ground.

Ayla lay groaning among the rocks, listening to the night, but Lukas was gone.

And he'd taken her secret with him.

* * *

The moon did not rise for hours. When finally it peeped over the horizon, Lukas left his cold, rocky perch on the hillside and picked his way carefully back to the path on the crest. The moon was only a sliver at its last quarter, but he looked down into the shadowed valley longing to see some sign of life.

During the long, cold hours, he had wondered if it was the wind in the pine trees he could hear, or the sound of Ayla crying. Was she still looking for him, knife out, ready to finish what she had started? Either way, he could not risk being here when the sun came up. He could not fight her again, nor watch the betrayal pooling in her eyes. Maybe that made him a coward, but it didn't matter.

Maybe he should have let her kill him. It would be better than what he felt right now. Lukas had always assumed that when he married, it would be for life, like his parents. Yet he had not even managed to make it through the first night. It was as though the promises they had made just hours ago were no more than a youthful infatuation. Sheer impatience and appetite.

Saint George. Was that all it was? The thought was like swallowing a lump of fire.

In the thin moonlight, it was just possible to see the path. Lukas walked slowly, testing each step with his staff, his whole body still aching from the previous day's journey. By the time night yielded to dawn, he could see across the ridges to the main road and—thank heaven—the litter of the massive camp in the valley.

He stopped then, leaning on his staff. He knew now that the time had come to leave the pilgrimage, but Oliveta was still days away by road. He would need food, his bedroll.

He started toward the camp again, but with each footstep his heart sank. Was that the end of it? Was he going to leave Ayla betrayed and crying in the mountains?

What would he say when his mother asked about the cut on his face?

It would be like cutting off his arm, like ripping out his own heart. But what else could he do?

Fool, fool, *fool* that he was to have rushed in where he ought to have crept. He had told her the truth: the moment that the seer had told him they were fated to be together, he had forgotten all about the mark on his arm, forgotten the depth of her injuries. He thought she would accept him.

How could they find peace when everything they believed, everything they hoped for, stood at such stark odds?

Exhausted and footsore, Lukas was picked his way through the Frankish camp toward Count Raymond's banner.

"Lukas Bessarion!" At the door of the chapel tent, Bishop Adhemar waved him over. "Count Raymond was looking—good angels protect us, boy! Where have *you* been?"

Lukas was in no mind to make excuses this morning. "I got married."

The bishop glanced at the clergy standing next to him, then waved them away. "You need to confess yourself? Come in. Bertrand, get a surgeon."

"I don't want to take up your time, my lord." Lukas touched the gash. It hurt even to speak.

"We're in Syria now." Inside the chapel tent, the bishop studied the cut on his cheek. "We need interpreters more than ever. We need you stitched up and in your right mind, Lukas."

"You said the count wants me?"

"Rumour has it the garrison of Antioch has fled, so he's sending an advance force of five hundred knights to secure the city. They're leaving at Terce. He was *going* to send you with them."

Lukas stiffened. With five hundred mounted knights, he would travel fast and be in Antioch within days. From there it was only another few days to Oliveta. If all went well he might be home within the week. Home, with his family, where he belonged.

Ayla had tried to kill him. He had ruined his life and hers, and now he did not want to face her again. He only wanted to run.

Lukas backed toward the tent flap. "I'll go with them."

"Not so fast. You said you were married. There are other interpreters—"

"My wife tried to kill me."

The bishop loosed a snort of incredulity that almost dissolved into laughter. "She must have had a good reason for that."

His breath puffed out in defeat. "It was because of this, my lord." He pushed up his sleeve. "Turns out it was her people who killed the Syrian Watchers. When she saw my Mark, she thought I'd deceived her."

"And did you?"

"It was folly," he snarled. "Haste and appetite. That's the only reason I made those vows. I see that now."

There was pain in the bishop's eyes and tears in his own.

"It's over, my lord. Now I just want to go home to my family."

"Stop," the bishop said. For a moment, he seemed at a loss where to start. "You made vows to this woman?"

"Yes."

"As a representative of Holy Church, I must forbid you to break them." Although the words were harsh, the tone was gentle. "They may have been made in folly, but the only path of wisdom is to keep them if you can."

"But…"

"She is your wife. You cannot go home to your family: she is your family now. Go back to her and make peace."

Lukas could not look the bishop in the eye. "But that was my mistake: thinking there *could* be peace. What concord has Christ with Belial? What has the true faith to do with heresy? She's a Turk, my lord. I love her. I need her. But there's no common ground between us, just an endless chasm. I was a fool to forget it."

The bishop sighed. "Yes, there is a wide gulf between you. But we are Watchers, Lukas Bessarion. To us is given the message of reconciliation. Between Rome and Constantinople, between Jerusalem and Athens, between Christ and the children of Belial. Go and make peace."

"Reconciliation."

A memory scratched at his mind. *We could have reconciled them through love, but we persecuted them through fear. Is it any wonder that they turned to destroy us?*

She might still refuse his attempts. She might kill him. But…

She is your family now.

He had no other choice.

Bertrand stuck his head into the chapel tent. "My lord, I have the surgeon."

"There are still two hours until Terce," the bishop said with a smile. "I am going to see the count now. What should I tell him?"

If he left now, he would never see her again. But if he stayed…he had the secret of Oliveta. Ayla would come looking for him. All he had to do was wait.

Lukas swallowed. "Tell him I want to stay."

Chapter XXXIX.

O n the second day after the storm, the pilgrimage reached Marash.

Tucked behind the shoulder of a mountain and defended by a river, the city itself was invisible from the road, but Saint-Gilles heaved a sigh of relief when he spotted the looping blue water. The nightmare mountain crossing was over. Syria lay before them, and according to the Greeks, Antioch was now no more than a week's easy journey.

So long as they had no trouble with Antioch, they could be in Jerusalem by All Saints', just two months from now. Later than he had planned, but acceptable given the complications of the journey. Best of all, the fever that had haunted him since Nicaea had vanished at last in the cold mountain air, leaving him fit and strong enough to lead an advance guard to Marash.

Their force was made up of both Provençals and Greeks, with Lukas Bessarion as interpreter. The Greek had rendered irreproach-able service for the last few of months, and from the nervousness he showed each time Tatikius glanced in his direction, Saint-Gilles could guess why.

The gold-nosed general rode on his left hand, nestled into a purple cloak lined with orange fox-pelts. As ever, the grime and hardships of camp life seemed to have passed him by, leaving him as plump, as tidy, and as smug as ever. After three months on the road together, Saint-Gilles had stopped looking down his nose at the man. To remain so healthy and sleek through the purgatory of Anatolia and the Taurus mountains demonstrated a physical and mental toughness that equalled any of the Franks.

As they descended the mountain road, Tatikius kneed his horse closer to Saint-Gilles. "Have you considered my request?"

"Saints above," he said, irritated. "All this fuss for a boy. Doesn't your emperor have more important things to worry about?"

"Bessarion is nobody." Tatikius fluttered his fingers dismissively. "But Alexius Comnenus is the vice-gerent of Christ on earth. It's a matter of principle. If one nobody of a heretic is able to defy him and live, how will the great and the ambitious respond? The stability of the throne rests on such questions."

Saint-Gilles only smiled, but all the rest of the way into the valley he chewed on the meaning behind the words. If Alexius would not tolerate the dissent of a single sulky peasant, what would he do to an army of wayward Franks? He breathed a prayer of gratitude that he had never done the homage Alexius demanded. A man of spirit should never bind himself to such a lord.

It was just past noon when they forded the river. Olive groves and orchards lined its banks, and the dry grass of summer already showed green at the roots. Where the horses' hoofs struck holes in the turf, a rich red soil showed beneath.

"This is good land," Saint-Gilles observed to Tatikius. "But where are the people?"

All across Anatolia, cities had opened their gates and peasants had swarmed out, laden with food and flowers, to greet the liberators. As the Turks retreated and their garrisons fled, they had ravaged crops and herds. Yet there was no sign of war in Marash.

"No one has burned the olive groves," Saint-Gilles observed as they climbed up the bank. Beyond, a line of cypresses cast thick cold shadows over the road. "It's as if the Turks had never been here."

"No." Tatikius narrowed his eyes. "They've been here for years. It's as if they never left."

Another ambush? Or a determined stand? Saint-Gilles called for five men to scout the bend in the road ahead. They trotted forward, lances and crossbows ready, then turned and beckoned Saint-Gilles.

"Nothing?" he growled. He exchanged glances with Tatikius. "I don't like this."

He set a faster pace down the road, signalling the scouts to move on ahead, staying within eyesight. The road curved around the foot of the hillside and came to a crossroads. To the right, the south road snaked away down the long valley to Antioch. To the left, the walled city of Marash nestled beneath the mountain.

Its gate was shut. No banners showed on its limestone wall. Only the blue haze of smoke rising from the city's chimneys betrayed the presence of any inhabitants at all. Saint-Gilles knew the look of a town that did not want guests.

"I'm done here, Tatikius. Let's go back to the river and wait for the others to arrive."

"A moment." Tatikius reached into his cloak and shook out a large, immaculately white silk kerchief. "Let us see if anyone will speak to us at the gate. Your lance, count?"

"Sounds like an excellent way to get an arrow through your ribs."

"I am not afraid," said the Greek.

After that, he could only lower the lance and allow Tatikius to knot the kerchief to the staff. Saint-Gilles beckoned his interpreter to follow. Together, they rode up to the massive oaken gate.

Tatikius' voice was high but clear. "I come as the personal emissary of his God-given majesty Alexius Comnenus, emperor of Rome! I seek conference with the governor of this city!"

Saint-Gilles squinted his one good eye at the battlements. There was no sign of life. No—there were men on the walls, but they were keeping out of sight. He prayed this parley would not turn into an ambush.

Tatikius waited, then called again. "The God-led emperor claims this city! Open your gates to make your submission!"

Again, nothing.

Tatikius leaned from his saddle and thumped his fist against the gate. "If you will not open to the emperor's troops, then we will open them for you!"

"One moment," Saint-Gilles hissed. "Let's not commit to a siege before we know what we're dealing with."

Tatikius retreated, dusting his gloved hands against his knee as if the gate had dirtied them. "Don't forget, you're here to liberate the Christian people of Syria, count. If the Turks—"

There was a sound from the other side of the gate: the grating noise of a bar being lifted.

"Fall back!" Saint-Gilles yelled to the men, loosening his sword in the sheath. "Crossbows ready! Wait for my signal!"

The massive doors ground open a crack. Beyond, a splash of colour resolved itself into the figure of a man on foot.

He emerged from under the shadows of the gatehouse: a well-made man with a beard greying magnificently against his smooth olive skin, his cloak a vivid red-and-gold exclamation over his hooded black robe. Saint-Gilles had met enough of them on the other side of the mountains to know that he was looking at a clergyman of the Armenian church.

As he spoke, Lukas Bessarion translated his words. "My lords, you are welcome. I am Grigor, the bishop of this town. I come to offer our thanks and blessings for liberating our city. When the Turks heard of the coming of your people, they called together their garrison and fled. Now Thatoul, Prince of Marash, welcomes you to his city and promises every aid in his power."

Saint-Gilles looked at Tatikius. "Thank him for his warm welcome," he said dryly.

The interpreter and the bishop exchanged words again.

"Thatoul bids you to make camp in the meadows beyond the river. Our people will bring you food and other supplies which you may purchase. Meanwhile, he invites your leaders to visit him in his own palace, so that he can thank you in person for your services to his city."

"I'm delighted to hear it." Saint-Gilles butted in between the translation of the Armenian bishop's last words and his indrawn breath for another speech. "But if the Turks have only just left, how does Marash have a prince?"

"Alas! Our God-led prince has been forced to accept Turkish suzerainty these last few years. Now you have restored him in his own honours."

"Thatoul," Saint-Gilles said in an undertone to Bessarion, "is that a Greek name?"

"Armenian, my lord."

Tatikius spoke in fluent Armenian, and Saint-Gilles snapped his fingers at Bessarion, impatient for the translation.

"He's demanding Thatoul open the gate to us, my lord."

The Armenian bowed. "My lord, I beg to tell you that I have no authority to admit an armed force. But if you have anything to discuss with the God-led prince, he invites you to visit him in person, with a guard of no more than four warriors."

"Tell him we'll certainly do that." Saint-Gilles spoke hurriedly, to forestall Tatikius. To his relief, the general made no objection. As the gate opened to readmit the bishop, he glimpsed the shine of steel from within. It confirmed his fears: Marash was ready to resist.

"Come on." Saint-Gilles kneed his horse back toward the road and this time, Tatikius followed.

Saint-Gilles chewed fiercely on the question as they returned to the river ford. Politics here in the east was more complicated than he had imagined when he set out from Provence. It was not simply a case of heathen Turks and Greek Christians, the former as enemies and the latter as allies. Things were ticklish enough with just two Christian factions on the pilgrimage. Add a third, local power and things could get messy.

"This Prince of Marash," he said to Tatikius in an undertone, "this man is not to be easily cowed. It's not just going to be a matter of installing our people and moving on."

"No doubt."

"Look." Saint-Gilles swung around in his saddle to watch the Greek's face. "Look, this town may be best left in the hands it's in. What Alexius needs is a foothold, not a plethora of backwaters. Antioch, for instance."

Tatikius lifted his eyebrows, but said nothing.

"This Armenian has just got rid of the Turks. What makes you think he'll take Greeks?"

"Why shouldn't he? He's evidently accommodating, and he ought to expect it. The Empire claims this land and always has."

"And if he refuses?"

"If he refuses, we have the greatest host since the dawn of the world, camping outside his gate."

Saint-Gilles gritted his teeth. This was exactly the kind of entanglement he had imagined when he first refused Alexius' oath. He had sworn to fight for *Christ's* patrimony, not Alexius'. He refused to be a club in the emperor's hands, wielded to enforce Greek domination. More than that, on such a pilgrimage, it was not just wrong to attack his fellow Christians here in the east. It was unthinkable.

Saint-Gilles opened his mouth to say all these things, but then he remembered leaving the camp that morning, looking back on it and seeing the tents that speckled the high mountain valley.

His mouth had gone dry. *So few.*

He estimated that his own Provençals had dwindled by at *least* a third since they first departed their homes on that autumn morning a year ago. Perhaps as many as half of them had melted like the snow. Desertion. Disease. Starvation. War.

He did not need to swallow his anger. It dissipated of its own accord, leaving a hollow fear to replace it.

Tatikius spoke quietly. "It is as I said. If one prince can defy the emperor, what will the others do? In the game of crowns, weakness is death."

"I'll go and speak to him, Tatikius. I'll do what I can to persuade him."

A flicker of triumph showed in the Greek's eyes, there for a moment and gone again. "You are a man of honour, Saint-Gilles. You are different from the others."

That might be true, but it was not what drove him in this moment. It was only that he could see a little further into the future.

Chapter XL.

Ayla hadn't slept in days. Night after night she watched the moon hovering above the horizon, dwindling first to a sliver, then to a black shadow in the sky. The last moon she would ever see. When the moon began to wax again, in the first days of Zulqida, she would die. Days from now, maybe even tomorrow.

She tried to make herself care, but she felt like an egg shell inside, scraped dry and empty. For months Lukas Bessarion had deceived her, hiding his Watcher's Mark to make sure she never suspected the truth. He'd used her, worming his way into her affections, until the time was ripe and he could wheedle the truth out of a girl too infatuated to know better. Then, once he had what he needed, he had left her to die. It was a fitting punishment for disobeying the law of her people, for marrying a Christian.

Lukas Bessarion, with his story about being lost in time. Lukas Bessarion, with his promise of taking her home. Nothing but a cold ruse to get at the secret of Oliveta.

He had only made one mistake. He should never have left her alive because now, at last, she knew what she must do. She must secure the secret. She must rob the Franks of their sorcerer, their guardian, their Watcher.

This, at last, was her life's purpose: before she died, she must kill Lukas Bessarion.

For two days, she followed the Frankish army through the Syrian hills. When they reached Marash and made camp, Lukas was still with them, trailing after Count Raymond, reading messages or liaising with the merchants who flocked out of the city to set up their market on the riverbank.

Ayla retreated into the hills. There was still no moon. She had time to practice.

There were calluses on her fingers from using the sling. In the streets of Antioch after her father died, she'd been forced to master the weapon or starve. Rats, dogs and conies would not wait to be caught. And the bullies and slavers that took an interest in street brats only spoke the language of pain. That day, Ayla hurled stone after stone at distant targets until she was satisfied that it was a language she, too, would speak with precision and force.

When evening came, she lay watching the sky until it appeared: the first, slim light of the Zulqida moon. For no good reason, she found the sight reassuring. Everything was going according to plan. That night, she slept soundly. The next morning, she walked down into the valley to kill Lukas Bessarion.

Trees in the valley north of the Frankish camp provided cover. Ayla slid down the riverbank, removed her clothes, and plunged into the cold water. If she was about to die, she preferred to be clean when she met her end. When she'd rubbed the dirt away and run through all her prayers, she plunged her hands down into the stony bed, sorting through stone after stone, looking for the shapes that would fly true. One by one, she plucked them from the streambed, examined them, dropped them again.

None were quite right. She straightened, rubbing her back, squinting at the climbing sun. This was taking forever. She needed to hurry.

She still didn't want to kill him.

With the realisation came a multitude of other excuses. Maybe he was telling the truth. Maybe he just wanted to get home. Maybe he was different to the other Watchers.

Maybe he really loved her.

No. She could not afford to have doubts. No matter whether he loved her or not, he was still a Watcher, and so long as he was with the Franks, they could never be stopped.

"None of them can ever know about Oliveta," her father said. *"If the Watchers ever knew where our power comes from, they could destroy the Vowed forever."*

Ayla closed her eyes. This was war. Better to go on thinking him a liar.

Nestling the imperfect stones into her pouch, Ayla waded to the riverbank. As she grabbed a tree root to pull herself up, a sweet sound thrummed between the hills.

A hunting horn.

Some of the Christians must be hunting. Ayla's clothes stuck awkwardly to her wet skin as she yanked them on. Nearer, little hooves drummed through the forest. She crawled up the short, steep slope from the river and peered through the trees.

A mountain gazelle sprang into view, red nostrils flared, neck straining for escape. There was no sound of pursuit, just a liquid streak of tawny, speckled fur. The gazelle whipped around, black-and-white horns levelled at the Greek general's cheetah. Tachys bounded to a stop, snarled and flattened for the pounce.

Then the cheetah stiffened, turned, and looked at Ayla.

Further down the valley, galloping hoof beats heralded Tatikius' arrival.

Ayla slid down the bank, trying to hide. *No, no, no...*

With a trill of delight, the cheetah dropped over the edge of the bank, greeting her with lashing tail, rasping purr, and a bump of its eyebrows. It was like being embraced by a small thunderstorm.

"Tachys," Ayla whispered in desperation, "hush, hush, there's a good boy."

She got her arms around him and scratched his ears till he subsided into a happy daze. A glance over the bank told her that the gazelle had faded into the shadows again. Then the hunters poured by, Greeks in magnificent cloaks with bows of horn. She huddled under the bank, praying the cheetah wouldn't betray her.

But Tachys paid no attention to the rushing horses. As soon as the hunters vanished between the trees upriver, Ayla pushed him off her and scrambled back up the bank. The animal followed, gazing at her adoringly.

What to do? She made him lie down, tickled his ears, then got up and moved slowly south. The masked face rose inquiringly as she tiptoed away. Ayla edged behind a bush and picked up speed. With a whisper of paws, Tachys rejoined her.

"Your master wants you," she whispered in frustration. "Go away! I don't work for him anymore!"

He wouldn't stay, and would not be shooed away. She dared not linger too long; the Greeks would quickly realise they had lost both quarry and hunter, and circle back to find them. Ayla huffed out a breath. With a great cat at her heels, anyone who encountered her was sure to remember her. Maybe it didn't matter. She didn't plan to outlive the day, anyway.

"Come on, then," she said, turning downriver.

It was good to run through the forest on a sunny autumn morning with the great, beautiful beast at her side. Forest gave way to olive groves, olive groves to meadows and the Frankish camp.

Ayla wormed into the grass at the edge of the olive grove, pulled Tachys down behind her, and scanned the camp. Lukas would be with the Provençal camp, but she could hardly stroll in with a cheetah on her heels. She needed him to come to her.

Maybe she could find someone to act as messenger. She slipped a hand into her pouch, but found it empty. She had paid her last coin to the old seer at the Singing Stones days before.

For a moment, she was completely at a loss.

Then, motion in the camp caught her eye. Count Raymond and Count Bohemond emerged from between two tents astride their best palfreys, followed by a small entourage. Lukas Bessarion rode a small Turkish pony by their side and at the sight of him Ayla felt the strangest mixture of relief and dread. She'd put a purple gash across the left side of his livid face. He looked terrible.

They were too far away to take a properly-aimed shot, but there was a windbreak right next to the ford. Ayla slipped through the olive grove, sliding into the scented shadows of a cypress and shrinking against the massive trunk.

Hoof beats clacked nearer. Ayla fumbled for a stone and loaded her sling, focusing on the mechanical problems of the ambush. She'd wait for him to come closer. She wouldn't move until he passed within a few feet of her, close enough to speak to.

She leaned against the rough bark, closed her eyes, slowed her breath.

Horses passed.

Ayla stepped smoothly away from the great tree, winding her sling into motion. She saw Lukas' profile, leaned forward for the release—

The string broke.

Her carefully-selected pebble cut into the ground behind her, and the sling twined uselessly around her arm.

Ayla threw herself behind the tree again, cursing behind her teeth. How had this happened? She'd *checked* it last night, when she finished target practice.

Oblivious to her presence, the Franks rode on. By the time she'd yanked the sling free of her wrist and knotted the string, they were halfway across the ford, too far to make a sure target.

Then Tachys rose to his feet, his hackles a cloud of stiff, suspicious fur.

Ayla followed the animal's gaze. Across the river, a single traveller stood watering his donkey and watching the Franks pass by. When they had gone, he glanced back to Ayla and signalled her with an imperious crack of the fingers.

Ayla swallowed. She'd had no word from her overseer since Lukas stole her scrying-bowl outside Heraclea.

Now, Armen had come to find her.

Chapter XLI.

After the barren highlands of Anatolia, the Syrian hills were a paradise: cool, green, and fertile. Saint-Gilles loosed a sigh of contentment as he kneed his horse up the Marash bank of the river.

"Thatoul's people are not hiding in their city these days," he observed to Bohemond as they passed a Syrian shepherd herding his flock toward the market which had sprung up on the river's east bank. "Seems that he's relaxed his vigilance."

Some of the stall-owners waved and cheered as the Franks passed toward the city. Bohemond heard them and made his horse dance, raising still more cheers at his display of horsemanship.

Saint-Gilles shook his head as the Norman count rejoined them. "Braggart," he said affectionately.

Bohemond laughed. "What are they saying?"

Bessarion cleared his throat. "They're calling in Armenian, my lord. They say, 'Long live the Kelts.'"

"Kelts?"

"It's a name we have for the Franks, my lord."

Saint-Gilles chuckled.

"How little they really know about us," Bohemond said.

I suppose we know equally little about them, Saint-Gilles thought. Aloud, he asked, "How is it you know the Armenian tongue, Bessarion?"

"My parents had me taught."

"They wanted to fit you for a career as an interpreter?"

"No, my lord." Bessarion pressed his lips together. "They wanted to fit me to rule."

Saint-Gilles stared at the young man. To all appearances, he was perfectly serious. What if it was true? Did Bessarion have valuable connections in the East? If so, he might be invaluable, and not just as an interpreter. He would have to learn more when he had the chance.

As they rounded the shoulder of the mountain, Marash came into view. "That's a nice little place." Bohemond scanned the defences appreciatively. "Rich enough to be worth owning, too small to threaten greater realms."

Bohemond was right. Marash was no great power and Thatoul had no serious hope of fighting off the Frankish army. He would lose everything if he tried. "So what is he doing refusing a garrison? Is he bluffing, or is someone coming to help him?"

"Or is he simply a fool?" Bohemond grinned. "That's also a possibility, you know."

A small delegation waited in the gatehouse to lead them to Thatoul's citadel. Beyond the wall, Marash was a bustling little town with streets so narrow and crowded that the Franks had to pass through them in single file. Like the waving peasants and merchants at the market, the people inside Marash were pleased to see them. Windows flew open and people craned their necks to cheer. A tiny bunch of alyssum fell into the mane of Saint-Gilles' horse, and when he looked up, he saw a laughing girl at a window. As he met her eyes, she snatched a veil before her face. Absurdly pleased, he picked the flowers out of the palfrey's mane and tucked them into the pin of his cloak.

The citadel was the largest single building in the city, a towering block of stone built on a high and ancient mound. Thatoul himself stood waiting to meet them inside the walled courtyard that surrounded the fortress. A handsome, slight man with the apparently perpetual youth of his people, the prince wore a silk cloak of iridescent green over his breastplate of lamellar armour. It was the hands that Saint-Gilles looked at, however, and noted approvingly that they were bulky and callused from swordplay.

"Welcome, my lord," Bessarion translated. "Your followers will be entertained in the garrison. Please enter my house and refresh yourselves."

Saint-Gilles expected Thatoul to lead them to the citadel, but instead he bypassed the rugged stone tower for a low house built nearby. The entrance-hall led directly into a small inner courtyard decorated with a fountain and lush greenery. Saint-Gilles, Bohemond and Bessarion followed the prince around a pillared portico to a low marble-topped table surrounded by folding chairs of polished wood, softened by dyed sheepskins.

Saint-Gilles sank into the offered chair with another sigh of contentment. "Your house is like a stream of water after the desert, Thatoul. It does me good to be here."

"You have no such places in your own country, my lord?" he asked when Bessarion had translated.

Saint-Gilles stifled a smile with his hand. "We have many comforts, naturally. But for the last year we've lived as nomads, travelling through deserts and over mountains, in battles, in sieges, and always in fear."

"Too long at war," Thatoul replied, "and men forget what really matters."

A door opened on the other side of the courtyard and silk whispered across stone. A woman's voice murmured. Saint-Gilles caught a glimpse of a smooth young face under a headdress of gold and scarlet silk. He began to feel as though he had walked into a dream, that this landscape was not quite real. Everything about this place was enchanting him. In response he sat forward, suddenly distrustful of the prince and everything in his city.

"I've come a long way, prince, and I'm new to Syria. But perhaps we can help each other."

Thatoul put a hand on his heart. "You've already helped us, my lord."

"The other princes you've seen must have told you about our quest."

"Your pilgrimage to Jerusalem?"

"That is one reason. The greater aim is to make war against the Turks for the liberation of the holy places."

"So I hear. You are all in the emperor's service, I believe."

Saint-Gilles hesitated. "To put it simply. Yes."

"I am familiar with such journeys," Thatoul said. "The emperor often hires western mercenaries to guard his borders. Though I've never before known him to employ such a vast army."

"Mercenaries?" Saint-Gilles lifted an eyebrow as the word was translated.

"Perhaps he means vassals," Bohemond suggested.

They both looked at Bessarion. The interpreter shrugged. "It's more or less the same thing here, my lords. Service has more to do with gold than with oaths or loyalty."

"Good, good. Translate this: Since we have come all this way for the aid of the eastern Church, we ask if you will aid us in completing our pilgrimage and fighting for Christ's holy places."

Thatoul spread out his hands. "You can rely on me to assist in any way I can, my lord. Your people need food, shelter, and medicine. We can provide those for the usual kind of price. You can also rely on us to help with any local disturbance, whether from the Turks or other Christian cities." Thatoul shook his head. "I know they are my own countrymen, but don't trust any of the Armenians too readily, my lord. They'll stab you in the back as soon as look at you."

Saint-Gilles felt his smile become wooden. More infighting among the locals. More complications. "I'm on a mission for Christ. I'm not here to fight Christians. You or anyone else."

Bohemond lifted a finger. "Don't translate that, Bessarion. Count, we can't tell him that if we've got to bluff him into surrender."

Saint-Gilles folded his arms. "Very well. Bessarion, ask him where he derives his authority from."

"From the emperor. I am *protonbelissimos* and *archon ton archonton,* prince of princes, scion of royal Armenia which is gone."

"Ah." Bohemond seemed enlightened. "Those are Greek titles. He's claiming legitimacy from Alexius himself."

"Then why doesn't he open the gate?" Saint-Gilles turned back to Thatoul. "We have sworn an oath to the emperor, prince. Alexius made it a condition of crossing his dominions and receiving his continued aid that we should install Greek garrisons in the cities we subdue."

Thatoul's face did not change. "Well, my lord, seeing that I already rule as the emperor's representative, it cannot apply to me. Marash is already a Greek city."

Bohemond chuckled appreciatively.

So that's his argument. Saint-Gilles watched the Armenian closely as Bessarion translated his reply: "I quite understand. Nonetheless the Greeks with us are eager to reinforce your garrison with a cohort of their men."

"The emperor is very generous," Thatoul said dryly. "All the same, I have a full garrison of my own and no particular need for more. With your lordships making war in Syria, there's no reason to waste good men on an unimportant mountain garrison."

That made good sense. The Armenian was obviously no outlaw or rebel, and he was friendly enough to his fellow Christians. He just wanted the freedom to rule his own city without Alexius holding a blade over his head. Saint-Gilles could sympathise with that.

"I understand, but if Marash refuses a garrison, the emperor will hold us in violation of our oaths."

The Armenian prince unclasped his hands with a lazy gesture. "Why should he do that? I am a Greek subject already. My city is the emperor's city, my men are the emperor's men. Please assure the general of my humble obedience, my lord."

Saint-Gilles leaned forward. "Prince, this *is* the obedience the emperor requires. What will you do when it is demanded at the point of fifty thousand lances?"

Thatoul linked his hands again, his elbows wide and relaxed on the arms of his chair. "You just told the count here that you were not here to fight Christians. Did you mean it?"

He spoke in Frankish.

He must have been listening to their muttered asides all along. Too late, Saint-Gilles remembered that Frankish companies often came east to fight in the emperor's service. Thatoul must have learned the language from them.

No more bluffing. Saint-Gilles sat back in his chair, took a deep breath. "I meant it. We are not Alexius' enforcers and we will not besiege you. That is Tatikius' job."

"Then let Tatikius visit me." Thatoul looked up and signalled to the servants hovering at the far end of the portico. "As for us, let us eat and speak of other things."

Chapter XLII.

L ukas felt drained once the meal finally came to an end. Although the conversation ran more smoothly once Thatoul proved to know a little Frankish, the Armenian and the two Franks still required his help as they traded hunting stories and discussed where to buy hounds and hawks to replace the animals that had died on the journey. To distill the shades of meaning in one language with which he was barely familiar, into another that he had only begun to learn in the last few months, taxed his mind to exhaustion.

And if that was not enough, since he had last seen Ayla, the mere effort of drawing breath seemed enough to drain and kill him.

He realised, too late, that Count Bohemond was looking at him expectantly.

"I'm sorry, my lord. Did you say something?"

Briefly, the Frank's brows knitted, but he repeated his words and Lukas fumbled through a translation, breathing wisps of anger. Could they not see that he was hungry, grieving, and tired from hours of unfamiliar work? Yet he could not hold onto the old resentment for long.

Ayla.

He felt raw with the loss. Yesterday he had paid a Frankish harlot his last coin to go into the Greek camp and ask for her, but Ayla was not there. Tatikius' other servants were no wiser than himself. *How should we know where the brat of a Turk has got to?*

The Franks bade their farewells in the courtyard, remounted their horses, and rode for the gate. Lukas followed, his mind still consumed by worry. Would she come looking for him? How many days had it been now? Why was there no sign of her?

They descended the mound, passed through the gate and emerged into the town's small forum, a level paved space with a public well in the centre and a few stalls whose owners had chosen not to migrate to the market by the river. Once again, locals and passers-by crowded close to stare at the travellers.

The hair on the back of his neck prickled. As they crossed the forum, Lukas glanced over his shoulder. Under the citadel wall, right beside the black arch of the gate, was Ayla. The moment their eyes met, she turned and pushed her way into the crowd.

Without a second thought, Lukas slid down from his borrowed horse and plunged into the crowd after her.

"Bessarion!" Count Raymond shouted.

Lukas paid no heed. Right now, Ayla was the most important thing in his world, and he couldn't risk losing her again. He fought his way through the thickest part of the crowd and glimpsed her short dark hair bouncing as she sprinted for one of the narrow streets leading off the square. He lunged in that direction, collided with a baker's boy and went flying. Loaves littered the stones around him. Lukas pushed himself to his knees.

Was she gone? No, she was peering around the corner of the street at him. As he surged back to his feet, she vanished.

Trap. His senses jangled, as insistent as they had been in the mountains. *She's waiting for you. She wants you to follow her. She's going to kill you. Trap.*

It didn't matter. The bishop was right: he *had* deceived her. He was not his own man anymore. He owed her revenge if she wanted it, and his love and service if she did not.

He fumbled in his pouch for a coin for the baker's boy, then realised it was empty. All he could afford was an apology and pair of clean heels. He swung around the corner and made it into the lane before the baker himself could appear.

Limestone walls rose high on either hand. Ahead, the buildings reached out to span the street, forming a tunnel with only the faint blue glare of daylight at the other end to light it. There was no sign of Ayla.

He gripped his staff and moved forward, slowly now, watching the other end of the street for a sign of the girl.

He was in the darkness of the tunnel when a door opened in the wall behind him and he sensed her in the dark.

Lukas froze. There was no sound but her breathing.

"Aren't you going to kill me?" he asked when he could bear it no longer.

Instead, something snagged his ankle and he fell heavily, slamming into the stones underfoot. A weight descended onto his back, pinning him down. As he gasped for breath, someone thrust a bowl of embers under his nose.

Lukas inhaled a cloud of bitter-smelling smoke. He coughed and gasped and coughed again, desperately trying to get his face away from the fumes, but the weight on his back pinned him down. Then the smoke took hold of him, lifting him off the stones to float in endless warmth, with every worry far removed.

He made a sound in his throat of perfect contentment. The daylight at the end of the tunnel was getting closer. No, not daylight. It was a woman. She wore a tunic of purple silk the colour of crushed berries. The clasped shoulders left her arms and neck bare, like the goddesses on an ancient frieze. There were black wings on her back, a bow in her hand and arrows on her hip. Her feathers chattered like knives as they fanned in the hot air that blew her toward him.

Lilith.

In the darkness she shone like a moon, the most beautiful woman he had ever seen.

She leaned down to him, her breath hot, her teeth pointed.

"Lukas Bessarion. Worship me."

He could not reply, could not think.

"Worship me," she whispered, "and the girl is yours."

The girl. Ayla.

"Worship me," she said a third time, "and I will send you home to your people."

He wanted to go on looking at her for an eternity, that was all. No mortal woman ever had such red lips, such long sooty lashes, such translucent, shining skin.

"Pay attention." She slapped him in the face and it felt like being kissed by an angel. "Tell the girl that Lilith wants you. *Alive.* Tell her I'll eat her heart if she fails me."

Then slowly, everything faded.

Lukas slept.

Chapter XLIII.

L eave him," Saint-Gilles snapped to his men as the Greek shoved his way through the crowd. "Bessarion isn't important."

What was important was getting back to the camp to speak to Tatikius as soon as possible.

As they made their way through the narrow streets to the town gate, Bohemond edged his horse forward till they were riding knee by knee. Softly he said, "He was bluffing."

"I beg your pardon, count?"

"We have the answer to our question. He doesn't have powerful friends, and he isn't a fool. Thatoul was bluffing."

"*Was?*"

"Well, he isn't now, of course. You promised him you wouldn't attack. He has no reason to submit now. I hope you know what you're doing."

Saint-Gilles had no idea what he was doing anymore. The count who had faced Alexius in Constantinople would have had no trouble defying the emperor's lackey. But Bohemond had been right: this was the east. Things were different here, and he was out of his depth. The Turks were a fiercer enemy than he had ever dreamed, their mounted archers mobile, deadly, and fearless. The crossing of Anatolia had been punishing—every single day the pilgrimage was whittled down. Now, although they had reached Syria, he should know better than to expect anything to be easy. Before leaving France, he had arranged with the Genoese, as Robert of Normandy had arranged with the

351

English, to send supply fleets to meet them at the ports of Syria. Still, two fleet-loads of supplies would not go far. It was Alexius, and only Alexius, who could dependably provide them with the men, the siege engines, and the food that they would need.

Bohemond sounded thoughtful. "We are distant from Constantinople now, and the emperor's name means less than it did at Nicaea. Perhaps it's time we focused on nearby allies like these Armenians."

Saint-Gilles shook his head. "Thatoul doesn't have the resources to supply this pilgrimage. Only Alexius can do that."

Bohemond smiled.

"I know," Saint-Gilles said irritably. "I know I am singing a different song to the one I sang at Constantinople. But Tatikius was right. So far from home, this alliance with the Greeks could make the difference between life and death. Not just for me, but for all my people. For my *family*."

"Then why promise to support Thatoul?"

"Because my oath to Christ is more important than my oath to the emperor."

All the same, was it more important than the lives of his people? If he did what Tatikius wanted, he could keep them alive, but he would be forced to attack an innocent city. He would be forced to lay more mortal sins on his conscience.

Bohemond's laughter broke into his thoughts. "Count, are you sure you didn't miss your vocation? You sound like a monk."

Did Bohemond doubt his ability to lead, the audacity of a good knight? "A knight may do good and keep his vows, just like a monk," he growled. "I know I can make Tatikius see reason. He'd be a fool to abandon the whole alliance over a single Syrian town. And that man is no fool."

"No indeed." Bohemond fell silent, still thoughtful.

Their small entourage exited the Marash gate. Straight ahead, the south road led toward Antioch and Cilicia. Riding up the road toward them came a black mass of men riding under white banners.

Saint-Gilles squinted at the banners and whistled softly. "Baldwin of Boulogne, as I live."

"And all his men." Bohemond smirked. "I told you my nephew would keep him from getting a foothold in Cilicia."

Saint-Gilles slid him a sidelong glance, remembering what Tatikius had told him about Tancred. "Have you received any news from your nephew, my lord?"

"Not a peep." Bohemond seemed unconcerned.

"I wonder if Baldwin knows that his wife is ill."

"She is?"

"At death's door, I hear." Elvira had mentioned this to him and the news had stuck in his mind. The harsh journey across Anatolia in the heat of midsummer and the gruelling passage of the mountains had pared everyone to a starveling. He thought of William, still just a few months short of his first year, who had been born on this journey and had nearly died on it. Now they had come to Syria, he would have to make sure Elvira and the child had every luxury he could provide.

As Count Baldwin's army approached the crossroads, three horse-men trotted ahead of the others to meet them: the count himself and two knights of his household.

"Boulogne," Bohemond greeted. "What news from Cilicia?"

Baldwin's eyes were dark and cold as stone. Riding on his fist was an immense black vulture so tame that it needed neither hood nor jesses: a kingly bird with intelligent eyes.

"A word with you, Taranto," he snapped. "And you, Saint-Gilles."

Intrigued, Saint-Gilles signalled to his followers to drop back. Side by side, the three counts rode on with the others following at a distance.

"It was you who sent Tancred after me?" Baldwin growled.

Bohemond exchanged a guarded look with Saint-Gilles. "I did."

"We both did," Saint-Gilles cut in. If Baldwin was going to be angry, let him be angry with both of them. "We believed it was best if Cilicia was not left in the hands of one man."

"Holy Virgin! When did I ever pay homage to you, my lord? Who gave you the right to interfere?"

"You paid homage to Alexius," Saint-Gilles shot back.

"What does that have to do with Cilicia?"

"Alexius claims Cilicia."

"Alexius claims the whole damned world!" Despite Baldwin's agitation, the great bird merely unfolded its wings for balance. "Godfrey knows why I went to Cilicia: the Armenian strategy. Isolate Antioch from the west, get the local Christians on our side. Your precious Greeks were the ones who advised it. It was sound. It *would* have been sound, if it wasn't for the pair of you."

The words were ominous. "What happened?"

"We fought." Baldwin smoothed his bird's feathers. "Tancred blamed me for an incident at Tarsus—he got there too late and found that I had the city, and when I turned the Turks out of the garrison, they fell on his men and hacked them to pieces. I told him I couldn't be responsible if he wouldn't post proper sentries, but he was out for blood after that. He attacked me outside Mamistra."

Saint-Gilles' gut turned. The knights of God, spilling each other's blood? "How many dead?"

"At Mamistra? A handful, and prisoners taken on both sides. I don't know how many the Turks killed at Tarsus."

"And now?" Bohemond asked.

"Tancred has Cilicia." Baldwin spat. "After what happened, there was no question of us remaining in the same region any longer."

Bohemond was not smiling now. "What can I say, my lord? I would rather cut off my own right hand than be the cause of any discord within the army of God!"

"Save your breath," said Baldwin. "You knew what you were doing. Can *you* restore my lost men?"

Saint-Gilles lost his temper. "You also knew what you were doing, count. You were willing to risk those same men conquering Cilicia.

Is it them you grieve for, or is it the chance to lord it over these Syrians?"

"And if I do?" Baldwin reined his horse to a halt, his eyebrows lowering over his dark eyes. "Someone is going to have to defend these places once they have been taken. You can be sure it won't be Alexius."

"This is why you instigated not one, but *two* attacks on fellow Christians?"

"Holy Virgin! Why take *me* to task? Tancred is the one enjoying the occupation of buxom Cilicia! Do you think he has *any* intention of giving it to Alexius?"

"I'll answer for my nephew," Bohemond interjected.

"Let Tancred prove his intentions when the time comes," Saint-Gilles said. "What I want to know is this, count. Do you have any intention of keeping your oath to the emperor?"

Baldwin gave a short, sharp laugh. "Since you ask, no."

Saint-Gilles took a sharp breath, shocked by the blunt admission.

"Don't preach at me," the count added. "As far as I'm concerned, Alexius broke his oath at Nicaea. He has no right to expect anything more from us."

"Then you're a fool, Boulogne, and the blood of all these people will be on your head. Can't you see our position? We aren't in France anymore! No help will come if Alexius withdraws his support. No money, no lancers, no siege engines, no local information, nothing. Pick your next deed right and you might even convince Alexius that we're more of a threat than the Turks." Saint-Gilles' horse tossed its head, and he realised he was gripping the reins too tight. Slowly, he released them. "I hate the thought of licking Alexius' boots just as much as you do, but this isn't about what our rank deserves. This is about living to the year's end. Alexius may treat us like dirt, but I have the lives of thousands of people on my hands and I intend to keep as many of them alive as I can."

Baldwin only snarled. "Stay out of my affairs, count, and I'll stay out of yours."

Launching his great bird into the air, Baldwin spurred his horse to a gallop. His two attendants overtook Saint-Gilles and Bohemond, and as they passed, one of them glanced over his shoulder. Saint-Gilles caught a glimpse of an olive-skinned Eastern face. Boulogne's tame Armenian.

"He's going to try again," Bohemond said quietly.

"That fool is going to destroy the alliance." Saint-Gilles clenched his jaw. "Tatikius can wait. I have to speak to Godfrey."

Chapter XLIV.

L ukas woke with a dry mouth and a pounding headache. He must have been out for hours, but he felt exhausted, as if he had spent the whole night keeping vigil.

He cracked his eyes open and found himself sitting on a flagstoned floor in what seemed to be a storage cellar. Big sealed jars and the waxy scent of olive oil filled the room. A faint yellow glow filtered in at the edges of a curtain that hung at the top of a flight of stairs.

Lukas shifted. Chains rattled. It took a little searching before he located his hands, each hanging at shoulder height from a length of chain that passed through a staple in the wall above his head. He might rot down here before anyone found him.

"Ayla!" he called in a moment of panic. His voice was too scratchy, too hoarse to carry. *"Ayla!"*

The curtain above moved, letting in a bright glow, as though a star had fallen to earth. Lukas flinched back, closing his eyes. Footsteps descended the stairs and brought the piercing light closer. He forced his eyes to open again and tried to focus on the shape behind the lamplight.

"What did you give me?"

"Poppy-juice." It was Ayla, her voice distant and impersonal. "Didn't want you running off again."

"Are you going to kill me?"

Her voice fell to a whisper. "Give me one *single* reason not to."

I love you. But after the other night, he knew that the words would only make her laugh.

She grabbed him by the jaw and turned his head so that she could whisper into his ear.

"You tricked me into telling you my father's secret. You lied to me and you lay with me. There's only one cure for that."

He swallowed, trying to work some saliva into his dry mouth. The effort made him cough again. "So why not do it in the alley?"

"Oh, I wanted to." She gave a laugh that went through his skull like an arrow. "You should be glad he wants you alive."

"*He?*"

"Armen. The Vowed. Remember in Constantinople, when I said was looking for my uncle? Armen is my father's brother in heart, if not in blood."

His head pounded, as if he was trying to go through a door without opening it first. But piece by piece, the truth fitted together. Ayla's friends had destroyed the Syrian Watchers. The Presbyters in Constantinople had whispered of sorcerers. Ayla's father had foretold the future, healed the sick.

"Sorcerers," he whispered. "The Vowed are sorcerers."

"Lies!" She slapped him. This time it felt nothing like being kissed by an angel. "Listen, Armen is the only reason you're still alive. So if I were you, I would be very, very careful what I said to him."

She left the lamp on the floor just out of reach and went back up the stairs again. This time, she held the curtain back for a man in a rusty black cloak, who looked like a beggar but carried himself like a king. At his heels padded a cheetah with a jewelled collar. Not just any cheetah: Tatikius' cheetah.

Ayla followed the two of them downstairs and tethered the animal to another staple on the opposite wall. It turned and rubbed its head affectionately against her leg. Lukas grabbed his chains and tried to stand, but the Vowed waved him to the floor again.

"Sit." The Vowed settled himself cross-legged on the stones, where the simple oil lamp lit him flickeringly from below. "I am Armen of Kars, and I can give you your heart's desire."

358

Ayla had her arms folded, her eyes on the floor. Lukas looked back to Armen.

"Only one person can give me my heart's desire." *And she wants me dead.*

"You want to bring back past years. It can be done."

Oh, he thought stupidly, *that heart's desire.* "How?"

"There is a price. Destroy the Franks for us and we will tell you what we know."

Lukas almost laughed. "Destroy the Franks? That's impossible. The Sultan of Rum couldn't do it and neither could the Poison Mother in the mountains. Who am I? Just a beggarly hireling."

"That is why you have power. The Franks cannot be destroyed with the raw might of armies. Only with the knife of a trusted servant." Armen leaned forward, palms together. "You serve the count of Saint-Gilles. The count of Saint-Gilles leads the largest part of the Frankish army. When he is killed by his own Greek servant, his men will take out their anger on the other Greeks. As for the Frankish princes, some will choose one side, some another. The pilgrimage will tear itself apart. So divided, they can be destroyed."

"Kill the count?" Lukas ran his tongue over his lips. "How will that get me my heart's desire? They'll tear me to pieces."

"I can keep that from happening," Armen said. It did not sound like a boast, merely a statement of fact.

The hair prickled on Lukas' scalp. "No."

"You will never see your family again." Armen's voice remained quiet. "You will die in this cellar and here your bones will rot."

Who was Saint-Gilles, anyway? An upstart barbarian who thought the cosmos revolved around him. But there were some things he could not do, not even for the sake of his family. He could not murder the man who had kept him alive all the way across Anatolia, much less a pilgrimage of thousands. "I won't do it."

"Then you will die." Armen stood up, drawing a knife.

"No! Wait!" Lukas moistened his lips again. Ayla was looking at him, but when he met her eyes, she dropped her gaze.

No matter if she believed him, he still had to say it.

"Ayla, I was wrong. I came to tell you that I'm sorry. I'll pay any price you like. All I ask is your forgiveness."

She looked up at him and her eyes glittered in the lamplight.

Armen said, "Girl, leave."

"I'm staying," she said coldly. "I want to watch."

She was looking at him now. Lukas swallowed. "I understand if you want me dead. But strike the blow yourself."

Ayla pushed away from the wall. "I can do that."

"Stand back." Armen lifted a hand, halting her in her steps. He turned back to Lukas. "Know that if you refuse us, we have another way prepared. Your sacrifice will gain you nothing."

Lukas swallowed, then snatched at his last chance. "Lilith has a message. She wants me alive."

The Vowed stilled. Ayla's eyes widened in shock.

"I saw her while I slept. I know it was Lilith, I recognised her from the battle near Dorylaeum." Had the vulture woman saved his life then, protecting him as the Frankish knights fled back to their camp? Questions rattled in his mind, but he set them aside, focusing on the man in front of him. "She said, *Tell the girl that Lilith wants you alive.*"

"Let me do it! Let me kill him!" Ayla drew her knife with a shaking hand. "He's in league with Lilith—"

"I told you to leave, girl," Armen said tightly.

Lukas struggled to his feet, gripping his chain for stability. The hailstorm in the mountains that began when he left the Franks and stopped when he returned. Ayla, constantly appearing to drag him away from danger. The facts snapped in place one by one, as easily as a strap in a buckle. "Lilith was *never* trying to kill me. She's been keeping me alive...But why? What does she need from me?"

"Your blood." Armen's voice was soft and menacing as he weighed his blade in his hands. "Bessarion blood. Lilith may need you alive, but she doesn't need you whole. She doesn't need your eyes, your ears, your tongue."

A chill overwhelmed him. They would make him a helpless beggar to the end of his life. As good as dead, yet still living. Lilith's tool, helpless to resist whatever it was she wanted him for. He looked at Ayla. Beyond Armen, her face was sick and white, her knife dangling forgotten by her side.

"You know I can't live like that. Better if you killed me."

She did not even look at him. "Is it true? Armen?"

"Is what true?" Armen reached into his sash, withdrew a second knife.

All at once, Lukas had the dreamlike sensation that he had been here before. It was like remembering the future: he knew what was going to happen next, even his own part in it. Even though he had no way rational way of knowing. When Ayla spoke again, his lips also moved.

"Is it true that you serve Lilith?"

"Power must come from somewhere." Armen shoved the lamp aside and turned toward her. "Now leave. Get out of the house. You don't have the stomach for this."

She blinked at him, seeming to recover her wits. Her voice was harsh, certain. "Answer my question. *Is it true that you serve Lilith?*"

From its place tethered to the far wall, the cheetah sprang to its feet and snarled.

Obedient to the sudden compulsion of his foretelling, Lukas moved before Armen could strike. The chain tethering his wrists rattled as he slammed one palm against the wall next to the staple, doubling the reach of his other arm. He grabbed for Armen's belt just as the Vowed lunged toward Ayla. The other man was bigger and heavier than Lukas, and the chain between his wrists snapped tight with a bone-crunching jerk.

But his fingers held.

Lukas yanked Armen backwards and got his right arm around the man's neck. Armen swore, jabbing behind him with his left-hand

361

knife, but the blade ground uselessly against the rings of Turkish mail.

It was only a matter of heartbeats until the bigger man got free or found something unprotected to stab at. "Ayla," Lukas breathed.

She had crouched into a defensive stance, knife up, when Armen attacked. As Lukas called her name, Armen reversed his grip on his right-hand knife and scythed up, stabbing for his unprotected face. Lukas jerked his head aside. The blade stung his ear.

Then Armen's head smashed back into his cheekbone. Vivid patterns of red and gold burst against Lukas' vision and he slid down the wall under the weight of a heavy body. A hot salty trickle ran from his nose, but he kept his arm locked around the sorcerer's neck, holding on for dear life until he realised that the man had gone limp.

Lukas blinked his vision clear and looked up.

Ayla lowered an oaken staff—his own staff. She must have hit Armen in the face with it, knocking their skulls together. Beyond her, the cheetah yanked wildly against its harness.

Ayla dropped to a crouch, twisting the knives out of Armen's slackened grip and throwing them against the wall, where they dropped discordantly out of sight behind the massive jars of oil. Then, together, they rolled him off Lukas and laid him on his back where the flickering lamplight could play across his bleeding face. Ayla checked his pulse.

"Alive," she said, and then looked at Lukas. "He would have killed me. How did you know?"

He was shaking with the realisation. "I have my mother's gift. I'm a Messenger. I…"

He had compulsions he couldn't explain. He could see Lilith when no one else could. He knew when danger was near.

"I have a power," he whispered.

At that, her eyes narrowed and she said in a voice as hard as flint: "You too, hah? From whom? From Lilith?"

She stood, pulling the knife from her belt again.

CHAPTER XLIV.

Upstairs, with a splintering crash, the door broke open.

Chapter XLV.

We have found your interpreter. Come and collect him. That was the gist of Thatoul's message. At first, Saint-Gilles did not understand why the prince insisted he come personally. A squire would do just as well, surely, and he still had to see Tatikius this evening. Nonetheless, the prince's messenger insisted in broken Frankish.

"Thatoul will see *you*, Saint-Gilles."

Saint-Gilles had stared at him for a moment before realisation dawned. "Oh. Well, why didn't you *say* he wanted a confidential meeting?"

It was a day for confidential meetings. Godfrey had been very polite about his brother, as always. He had even agreed that the pilgrimage should keep its oaths and avoid angering the Greeks. Yet he had refused to issue an ultimatum.

"My brother is a count in his own right," Godfrey had said. "Moreover, he's a man of spirit, my equal in worth if not in rank. I'll speak to him, but I can't command him."

Saint-Gilles had returned to his own tent thumping his spear vindictively into the ground with each stride. This was exactly why the pilgrimage needed a strong leader.

With night descending, the Marash citadel loomed above the sleeping town, a patchwork of shadow and fire. Saint-Gilles dismounted in the courtyard and beckoned his two knights to follow him as Thatoul emerged from the shadows of his portico.

"Thank you for meeting," he said solemnly in accented Frankish. "I

364

have questions for you."

Mystified, Saint-Gilles followed the prince into what must be the audience-hall of his house. With its elevated chair and immense Pantocrator icon, he recognised a very small imitation of the Chrysotriklinos in Constantinople where he had met Alexius.

A captain in armour met them in the room and said something to Thatoul in their own language. The prince dismissed him and turned to Saint-Gilles. "Your man will come soon. But first, I think you are unknowing that I have received second visit today from the other count."

"From Bohemond?"

"He says to open gates to the Greeks. Or he will attack."

"Bohemond?" Saint-Gilles repeated stupidly. "Did he give any reason for this?"

"Special arrangement with Emperor Alexius," Thatoul said. "He intends to be Grand Domestic of the East. Syria, Armenia, Palestine, all of it his. He said: *Prince, I am about to become very powerful man. Do not burn bridges.*"

"Impossible," Saint-Gilles began, but then he caught himself. It was like the wind suddenly catching a banner, unfurling it so that for the first time, the whole thing was visible.

For all his talk of the Greeks' distrust, Bohemond was the one who had manipulated him into swearing the oath to Alexius. At Nicaea, Bohemond was the one who oversaw the Greek supplies, set up the markets, and profited from the sales. All the way across Anatolia, the Greek troops marched side-by-side with the South Normans. It was odd behaviour for former enemies. What if Bohemond *did* have a special understanding with Alexius? He had always had ambitions in the east; having failed to conquer Constantinople from the west, it made sense to bypass the emperor's domain and construct something of his own out in Syria. Peace with Alexius, a war for his fighting men and finally, the inheritance he never got from his father.

I flatter myself Alexius does have some interest in my welfare.

Saint-Gilles closed his slack mouth. "Saints above. I'll wager it's true."

Curse him, he had thought they were *friends.* They had spilled blood together, defended Cilicia together.

No.

Saint-Gilles' gut contracted, realising how thoroughly he had been played. Bohemond had used *his* money, Provençal money, to fund Tancred's conquest of Cilicia. And he had done it in the name of Alexius. Holy *Virgin.*

This is the east. Men have subtle minds here.

"Will he do it?" Thatoul asked, worried.

"Devil take him, no!" Saint-Gilles gritted his teeth. "Make himself overlord of the whole East? King in Christ's own city? Take homage from *me? By my holy dame, no."*

Thatoul levelled a patient look at him. "And Marash?"

"Let me think." Saint-Gilles pressed a fist to his mouth and paced the room.

The worst of it was that he could not *tell* anyone. Apart from Bohemond, none of the other princes had enough foresight to grasp the necessity of the Greek alliance. If they found out that Bohemond had secretly arranged with Alexius to make himself their ruler, then that alliance was as good as dead. Saint-Gilles understood better than anyone why the alliance had to continue. Unlike Bohemond, he actually cared for the pilgrims' welfare. That made him the only leader among them who could keep the people alive.

But at what cost? Putting Bohemond on the throne of the east? Helping him make war on the very people they had come to liberate?

Those questions could wait. Saint-Gilles swung back to Thatoul and put a hand on his shoulder.

"We came to build the kingdom of Christ, not the kingdom of Bohemond," he growled. "I'll do what I can, prince. You have my word."

"And you have my thanks." Thatoul climbed the low step to his dais and settled on the carved chair, signalling to the guards at the far end of the room. "Now we will see the prisoners."

Chapter XLVI.

At least Tachys was free.

When Thatoul's soldiers broke the door open, the cheetah had snapped his leash and bounded up the stairs. Startled, the men had shouted and lashed out, but Ayla doubted they managed to hurt him.

With any luck Tachys would find his own way home. Or better, he would slip away into the Syrian forests and spend the rest of his life chasing the stripe-horned gazelles. It would be a lonely life, a life with no love, but then a life with no disappointments either.

Lilith. The Vowed got their power from Lilith. Her *father* had got his power from Lilith, and at what cost?

You are mine, girl. The thought scored pain through her gut. No, it was impossible. Her father would never have traded her soul to a demon in return for power.

Once they were brought into the citadel, Lukas was spirited into the prince's house, while she and Armen were locked in holding cells within the fortress.

Armen spat. "Even now, girl, you are doing the will of the Poison Mother," he growled.

"I did this for my father, for Ilkay of Antioch. Not for you or anyone else!"

"Quiet!" A guard thumped the bars.

Another moment back there in the cellar, and she would have done it: she would have served justice on Lukas Bessarion. She would have restored her honour, struck one last blow at the Watchers and made her father proud. She didn't want to see Lukas tortured and crippled. She would have given him a good death.

Her father. God have mercy.

You are mine, girl.

Why would Lilith have any claim to her?

Why else would her father know the exact day of her death?

You are mine, girl.

The hair prickled on the back of her arms. The citadel was unbearably cold.

No. Even if her father had traded her soul to Lilith, it was only to heal people. Perhaps an eternity in hell was worth that. She should be proud to make the sacrifice.

Yet what kind of father would sacrifice his eldest daughter like that? If family was everything to him, why didn't he make the sacrifice himself? Whatever lay in store for her on the other side of death, she would gladly accept it. But was her father God, to sell her to such a doom?

They must have waited an hour or so before Thatoul's captain came to get them. When they reached the house, Lukas was waiting in the porch, his nose swollen and a few stitches decorating his earlobe, in addition to the welt across his cheek where she'd slashed him three nights ago. Someone had given him a clean tunic. Its short sleeves left his arms bare and his Watcher's Mark was clearly visible. He got to his feet when he saw her.

"They're going to try you," he said in urgent Frankish. "If you want to live—"

The captain barked something in Armenian. With a wave of his hand, he had his men shepherd the prisoners further away, where they couldn't speak to each other.

Ayla turned her back on the Greek, but her stomach writhed as though it was full of snakes. A trial. Maybe this was how she died.

Why was he still trying to save her? *Why?* She wanted to turn and yell the question at him, but no sooner did the urge strike her than the answers came. He hadn't run to Oliveta even when he had the chance. He'd followed her even though he must have known it was a trap. He'd nearly died pulling Armen off her in the cellar.

Because he really did love her.

For one terrible, lovely moment she let herself imagine that he really did mean to keep the promise he'd made her in the hills.

Then they were summoned into the prince's audience chamber.

Thatoul sat on a dais at the far end of the room under one of the big, creepy pictures the Christians liked to hang in their churches. Next to him, hands clenched tightly on the spear he used as a staff, was Count Raymond himself. It was probably as a courtesy to the count, not herself, that the audience was mostly carried out in a language she understood.

"I think this is your interpreter," Thatoul said in Frankish.

"Yes, yes, this is the one." The count pointed to Lukas, but glowered at Ayla. He evidently recognised her. "Must we remain for the trial?"

"I am afraid yes. Apart from the prisoners themselves, your interpreter is the only witness. But we will be quick," Thatoul assured him. "Captain?"

"These two had him shackled in an oil cellar, my lord."

"Who are they?" Thatoul asked Lukas. "Did they come with the Frankish host? Tell me how it happened."

Her life was in his hands now—as it had been for months now.

Lukas reached out to touch her, but stopped before his fingers brushed her shoulder. "The man is a Vowed, if that means anything to you. But this woman is my wife and when your men arrived, he was attempting to kill her. I'm grateful to you for saving her life."

She felt his earnestness, heard the plea he'd left unspoken outside on the porch. *If you want to live, play along with what I say.*

"She's my wife," Lukas repeated with more of an edge in his voice. "Why don't you take those chains off her?"

Thatoul pointed at Armen. "And this man?"

Ayla reached out and sunk her fingers warningly into Lukas' wrist.

If he could save her, then he could try to save Armen as well. But either he didn't understand, or he chose to ignore her.

"The man is a Vowed, a servant of the Poison Mother. He has offered me a reward to murder the count of Saint-Gilles, so that the Greeks can be blamed and the alliance destroyed."

Ayla let go of him, schooling her face to stillness.

Count Raymond grunted in surprise. "Ha! Did he?"

"That is capital offence," Thatoul said quietly.

"The Greek is lying!" Armen erupted. "The girl was in it with me!"

"I did not lie! She is my wife, and you did try to kill her."

"Keep silence," Thatoul said. "Kidnapping, murder, these are capital offences. But I cannot hang a man on the words of one witness. Perhaps he is telling a lie to murder the accused. That is capital offence, too. Only solution is, another witness to say which is lying and which is telling the truth." The prince looked straight at Ayla. "Which is it? Which man deserves death?"

She wished that anything had come to her, anything but this choice. Why did she still want to protect Armen? He had told her himself that he was in Lilith's service. But if she admitted it was so, then she admitted that he deserved to die. If she admitted it was so, then her father and the Vowed had deserved their fate. What would she have to show for her life then?

Armen looked at her, faintly smiling. His words echoed in her mind: *Even now you are doing the will of the Poison Mother.*

Lilith's will? May God forgive her. That would *not* be her legacy, even if it had been her father's. If he was a good man, she would meet him beyond the chasm. If he was not, then she did not want to meet him at all.

She had spent her life pleasing those who had gone before. Today she would do something which those to come would remember.

"Lukas Bessarion is telling the truth," she said.

Thatoul smiled slightly. "Armen of Kars, do you have anything to say?"

"Should I call down my vengeance?" he said scornfully. "It makes no difference."

"Then take him away. He dies at dawn."

As Armen was hurried from the room, Count Raymond descended the dais, feeling the step with his spear-butt. His eye missed nothing as he swung his gaze from Lukas to Ayla and back again. "Your wife, eh, Bessarion?"

"Yes, my lord." He didn't look at her, but his voice was firm. "Bone of my bone, my lord."

As the guards unlocked her chains, Thatoul spoke in Greek. "You are a wise man, Lukas Bessarion."

"I don't know, my lord."

"It takes a wise man to get the love of any woman. Or man. If your other Watchers had understood this, perhaps they would still be alive today."

"Perhaps."

"Marash could do with more Watchers. Stay here with me and you may have any post you care for. You'll no longer be a servant."

Ayla saw Lukas stiffen. She knew what this meant to him, but he shook his head.

"I'm sorry, my lord. I'm going home with the pilgrimage."

"Home? There is no home with the pilgrimage." Thatoul descended from the dais and put a hand on Lukas' shoulder. His voice dropped. "These Franks have no idea what they have woken. They think they've fielded an army big enough to take Jerusalem? They know nothing. The Turks rule Asia, the Ishmaelites rule Africa, and both of them claim the Holy City. Each commands millions of souls, and wealth enough to pave the sea with gold. They could make crow-fodder of ten times your numbers and not notice the loss. This pilgrimage is doomed, Bessarion. It's only a matter of time."

"Then they're in more need of Watchers than you are." Lukas let out a gusty breath. "I know my destiny lies in the south. Please excuse me."

The prince scowled. "Go, then. If you survive, return."

Chapter XLVII.

One solitary torch burned in the citadel, but it gave ample light for Armen's purposes. He waited for the guards to bed down on the flagstone floor outside his cell before easing the piece of chalk from his shoe.

He worked fast, but took care to draw each figure correctly. When he had finished, he settled in the centre of the sigil, took a pinch of powder from his pouch and laid it on his tongue. He closed his eyes, waiting for the bitter particles to dissolve.

When he opened them again, he looked out of the cheetah's eyes.

At first, he did not completely overpower the cheetah's consciousness. That would be risky, for the animal's reflexes were quicker than his, its ability to read scents and shadows more sophisticated. Still, it was not difficult to keep control of the creature's faculties.

Let it not be said that Armen of Kars died without striking a final blow.

He blinked through the great cat's eyes, trying to interpret what the creature was seeing. Ah. It had found its way over the Marash wall and was slinking through the outbuildings of a farmhouse, following the scent of—

Food, he thought, feeling the beast's hunger. Sheep? Chickens?

Come and I will feed you other meat, he told it.

He got his bearings, spotted the dark mass of hills against the north horizon, and forced the animal into a bounding lope toward the river. The sound of hooves on the road hinted that the count of Saint-Gilles was still on his way back from Marash, but Armen took no notice. In armour and flanked by his knights, the count was too well protected. His was not the servant's knife.

As they approached the water, the cheetah tried to rebel, but Armen tightened his grip on its mind. The longer he inhabited the beast, the better he was able to control its muscles without help from the creature itself. A helpless passenger in its own body, the animal slid through the water and up the far bank.

With the exception of a few brightly lit tents, where men sat drinking or talking the night away, the camp was dark and silent. No part was darker or more peaceful than the Provençal camp. Armen forced the cheetah into a low crouch and slunk among the tents, searching for the central banner that marked the count of Saint-Gilles' tent.

Over the last months, he had spent hours probing Ayla on the details of the count's household and living arrangements. Now, rather than going into the big pavilion where a lamp burned to welcome the count home, he angled toward the smaller red-and-gold tent nearby.

Despite the darkness, the cheetah's sensitive eyes led him easily through the tent's outer partition. No one stirred. Seeing a gleam of light, Armen nosed cautiously into the space beyond. Here it was warm and filled with sleeping bodies; a dim lamp burned next to the camp bed where the countess of Saint-Gilles was lying.

Next to the bed was the cradle where the count's young son slept.

Again, the cheetah tried to rebel, knowing that a small space filled with people and light was dangerous. Armen forced the animal's weak consciousness into total hibernation.

Then he sprang for the cradle.

The box toppled with a crash. Someone screamed, but the child did not make a sound.

Bite, and hold.

The small body jerked and went limp. His jaws were still locked on the tiny form when a blade rammed through the cheetah's spine at the back of its neck.

In the citadel at Marash, Armen of Kars jerked, spat blood, then toppled forward onto his chalk diagrams like a puppet with its strings cut.

Chapter XLVIII.

Having crossed the river, Saint-Gilles went straight to the South Norman camp, sat down in the vestibule of Bohemond's tent, and would not shift. Some kind of commotion was occurring in another other part of the camp, but an army of tens of thousands was bound to see disturbances sometimes.

Within the partition there was a slap and an indignant feminine yowl before the count emerged from his sleeping-quarters still grinning.

How typical, Saint-Gilles thought, but he would not allow himself to be distracted. Right now, he had to get some sense out of the count. He drummed his fingers on the tabletop once and said tightly, "I have been speaking with Thatoul."

"Oh." Bohemond wrapped a furred gown closer around his body and collapsed yawning into a chair.

"He tells me that you're preparing to attack him."

Bohemond shrugged. "Tatikius makes it a condition of his support."

"You can't do that. Marash is a Christian city. Thatoul is not the enemy!"

"Obviously. But neither is Alexius, and I'm trying to keep it that way. I thought you understood."

Saint-Gilles looked at him for a moment, considering his next move. Trying to pin Bohemond down was like wrestling sand, he should know that by now. What was his best weapon?

"This is expressly against the Pope's wishes. He's trying to reunite Christendom, not fracture it beyond repair. Adhemar will have you excommunicated."

"Not if he thinks about it rationally." Bohemond smothered another yawn. "The breach that needs healing is the one between Rome and Constantinople, not Rome and the middle of nowhere in Syria. Thatoul is nobody. Focus on the real power, Saint-Gilles."

"I tell you this is *wrong*, Bohemond. Please. I entreat you."

"I heard a wise man say, *I hate licking Alexius' boots, but this is about living to the year's end.*" Bohemond's lip curled. "You should listen to your own advice, count."

"Why, so that I can put *you* on the throne of the East?"

Bohemond looked at him expressionlessly for a moment. Then he smiled. "Why not, if I'm the man for the job?"

"I can't believe this." Saint-Gilles shook his head. "I thought you were my *friend.* Back in Nicaea, you supported me to lead this pilgrimage. You were happy to follow me then."

A smile tugged at the corner of the count's mouth. "Only because it's easier to take power from one man than from a council of seven."

"Saints *above.*" He leaped from his chair, knocking it over.

Before he could go on, Adhemar pushed his way into the tent, breathless and pale.

"Raymond. Thank God I've found you. You must come at once."

The look on the bishop's face acted like a gutting-knife. Adhemar never looked like that unless something was horribly wrong. Saint-Gilles' mouth went dry. "What is it?"

"It's William."

He snatched his spear and stalked out of Bohemond's tent without another word. His horse was still waiting outside. Saint-Gilles did not wait for the bishop.

Elvira's tent was lit like a lantern. There were people everywhere, but they fell back as he approached. Some of his knights had cordoned the tent's entrance from onlookers.

Galdemar put a hand on his shoulder. "Prepare yourself, Raymond."

Raymond. Galdemar never called him that.

The vestibule was full of weeping women. Beyond, in the sleeping-quarters, Elvira sat on the edge of her bed, rocking back and forth, holding a bloodstained bundle to her heart. More blood stained her hands. At her feet, a cheetah's body lay stretched out with a knife embedded in its spine.

He recognised the animal instantly; the lapis-studded collar was unmistakeable.

Saint-Gilles held out his hands. "Give him to me."

Elvira seemed not to hear.

"Give me my son!" His raised voice made her flinch, but she let him take the limp body from her arms.

Saint-Gilles stood very still, looking at the dead child. So tiny. So fragile. So irretrievably broken. For an instant he was overwhelmed by his failure. He had done everything he could. *Why* had it not been enough?

It was bitter to find that he was not, after all, the master of fate. That he could not always save the people he loved. He should know this by now—but the knowledge never became easier to bear.

"Who killed the beast?" he asked, when the silence threatened to suffocate him.

"I did." Elvira whispered through tears. "I woke up and saw it and..."

He would never have imagined Elvira finding the strength to kill a kitten, much less a beast of prey.

"My friend?" It was Adhemar calling from the other side of the curtain. Saint-Gilles laid his son's body in the cradle and twitched the curtain back to admit him.

"I know who did this," Saint-Gilles breathed.

The bishop looked at him, then Elvira, in concern. "Not the Greeks, surely?" he whispered.

"No. Someone who has already been condemned to death." He might not know exactly how the renegade Armenian had managed it, but Bessarion had said something about magic, and the idea was obviously the same: sow discord between the Greeks and

Provençals. "Someone who is trying to destroy the pilgrimage. Stay here, Adhemar. Watch over my son. And don't let anyone know what happened here." He bent down and unbuckled the jewelled collar from the cheetah's spotted ruff.

"What are you going to do?"

Saint-Gilles lifted the blue stones to the light. "I'm going to save the alliance."

Unlike most of the Franks, the gold-nosed general was still awake. Saint-Gilles found him in his tent at a writing-desk, filling page after page with tiny writing.

Saint-Gilles lifted the collar to swing and flash in the lamplight. "Are you missing something, Tatikius?"

"You found Ta—?" The Greek cut off when he saw the blood on Saint-Gilles' hands.

"Yes," Saint-Gilles said with deadly calm, "I found him in my wife's tent. She had just taken the body of my son from your beast's jaws."

Tatikius swallowed and reached out for the collar, but Saint-Gilles jerked it back, closing his fist. "Not so fast, Greek." Saint-Gilles almost spat the last word. "You owe me *something* for this."

"The animal has been missing all day." Tatikius spoke in a soft, controlled voice. "Are you blaming me for its actions?"

"Not personally, no." Saint-Gilles rattled the linked stones in his fist. "I have good reason to believe what you say. This evening, I learned of a plot which would have arranged my death so as to throw suspicion on you. It was Bessarion who uncovered it, by the way. I think he's proved his worth, don't you? I am still alive, and I know you're not to blame."

He did not miss the infinitesimal loosening of the Greek's tense shoulders. "But that's not what I'm going to tell the other princes," he added. "Not unless you meet some conditions."

"Conditions?" Tatikius was incredulous.

"Give up the high ground, my lord. Do you think this is a matter of an alliance parting ways? This is my son's *blood* on my hands. If you don't listen to me now, it will mean war. And if there's a war, then Alexius can bid farewell to you, your men, and all your possessions in these lands. Your empire in the east is a dream. Baldwin and Bohemond both have plans of their own, and believe me, neither of them intend to let you interfere."

He wondered if the Greek would laugh at him. But now, at last, Tatikius was listening. "Well?"

"First: stop telling me which members of my household I may or may not keep. From now on, you'll trust my judgement and my fidelity. Second: call off Bohemond's attack on Marash. Thatoul assured me this morning of his loyalty to Alexius, and I'm willing to vouch for him. Third: forget Bohemond. If anyone should be lord of the east, it's not him; it's me. You know that I keep my oaths and you know that I put my people first, not my own purse or glory."

A flicker of disbelief crossed Tatikius' face. "My lord, you cannot be serious. Should I go to the count and tell him that I am taking back what the emperor promised?"

"Not at all. You need say nothing to him. All you need to do is help me get control of the pilgrimage. I can take care of Bohemond."

"How?"

Saint-Gilles had the answer at the tip of his tongue. "Money. That's all I need. Money for food, for horses, for armour. Give me money to spend and watch how fast these haughty lords come to eat from my hand."

Tatikius laughed. "Saint Michael, count. Did you stop to bury your son before you came here to trade on his body?"

It was an ugly blow, but Saint-Gilles was a man of cold tempers. "Let the dead bury their dead. I have thousands of the living to think about."

Tatikius looked at him for a few more heartbeats. Then, slowly, he took the most recent page from the slope of his writing-desk, crumpled it into a ball, and threw it into the nearby brazier. "Very well, then. Let Bohemond continue to think of himself as the emperor's favoured prince. But you will have your gold."

Chapter XLIX.

Ayla and Lukas stood at the crossroads outside Marash. The moonless night was so dark that she could barely see his face, but even under the cover of darkness, Ayla did not want to be the first to speak.

Lukas had taken her hand as they left the citadel. Now, with an awkward laugh, he said, "If I let go, will you stay?"

She felt very tired. "I don't know. Try it and we'll see."

He let her hand slip away from him and then, curiously, she felt unmoored. Drifting in a world of darkness in which Lukas was the only fixed point. After a moment she reached out again and found his hand in the dark.

His fingers tightened fractionally on hers. "You're not angry with me anymore?"

"I don't know who to blame," she whispered. "Everything that's happened, all this fighting, all this injustice… I just know this for certain: there is real evil in the world, and Lilith is a part of it. And no one who aligns with her is worth my love." She swallowed. "The Syrian Watchers murdered my father, and maybe they had a reason, if not a good one. Armen would have murdered me. But you…tonight I saw God in you, Lukas Bessarion."

In the dark came a huff of startled laughter. "Then he should depart from me quickly, for I am a man of unclean lips!"

"Not news to me."

"I'm sorry," Lukas said after a moment. "I'm sorry you had to condemn Armen for my sake."

"Not for your sake," she said fiercely. "For mine. For all the people he lied to and used. For all the people he would have destroyed. I thought he was serving *God* and all along it was the Poison Mother."

Then, finally, she saw it and her heart almost stopped with wonder. *"This* is what I was born to do. *This* is the legacy I was meant to leave. Justice for the last of the Vowed."

"Ayla...I'm sorry."

"Don't be!" She closed her eyes and breathed in the scented night. "I was always afraid of Lilith before, but now I don't have to be. Whatever claim she had on me is gone. I can feel it. I could die in peace now."

"Saint George, why so grim?"

Why, indeed? She remembered the hope that had come to her that night in the mountains: "Or maybe I could go home with you."

Lukas' breath hitched and he grabbed her other hand. "Ayla, are you sure about this? Even with Armen gone, I'm still a Watcher, and I still want freedom for my people. Even when I take you home, there'll still be a war. And I'll still believe it's worth fighting."

The war. That was another problem she would have to solve. She still could not stand idly by as her people suffered.

Somewhere, there had to be an answer, even if she was not the one to find it.

"Wars don't just end with victory, Lukas." She pulled him closer, slipped a hand up to his cheek, and kissed him. "They can also end with peace."

Peace.

Maybe this, right now, was the only place in the world that knew peace. This little circle that was themselves. This breath of warmth in the night. It was a start. Even if she died tomorrow, it was a start.

"I'll take you to Jamnia, where my father has his country estate," Lukas told her as they strolled to the ford. In his excitement, the words spilled out of him. "We used to spend every summer there, eating ourselves sick in the vineyards, when we weren't swimming or climbing trees. My sister Marta was always fearless about heights. Once she climbed in an upstairs window to bring us some grapes which a traveller had brought to my father. We ate them all. Of course, it was only afterward that we learned they were a rare breed my father had bought to improve our stock." He laughed, pulling her closer with an arm around her waist. "You'll like Marta."

"Lukas, there's something else. Something my father foretold years ago." Ayla hesitated and changed tack. "This power you have. What do you see in my future?"

"I…" He bit his lip, as though he was waiting for something, but then looked disappointed. "I don't know. It only comes in flashes."

"If you know something, tell me. Even if it's something terrible."

"No. There's nothing. It doesn't come at will. But the seer said that we're fated to be together. I believe in that."

She let out a soft breath, surrendering to hope. "Then I believe in it too."

The sound of hooves on the western road shook her back into the present. Short or long, life was fleeting. She moved closer to him, knotting her fingers into his tunic. "So you truly can't predict what I might be about to do?"

"No…"

"Thank God," she said, "I can't stand to be predictable." She pulled his head down and kissed him again.

They were still standing there when the riders approached. Lukas grabbed her hand and pulled her to the side of the road below the shadows of the cypresses. All the same, the riders stopped. One of them shushed the tipsy laughter of the others.

"Hey!" he called, lifting his torch. "Who goes there? What are you doing skulking around at this hour, eh?"

Franks. They'd clearly been tasting the wines of Marash.

"We're friends," Lukas called, putting up his hands. "We're heading back to the camp."

"Look, it's the Greek peasant," said a familiar voice. "I thought so."

Lukas stiffened. Ayla thought her heart would stop.

As Evrard of le Puiset rode forward, Lukas pushed Ayla behind him, his voice a hurried whisper. "Go."

She'd already spent too much time estranged from him. Tonight, and for the rest of her life, she'd stand with him. "Never again," she hissed back, and her hands stole to the pouch where she kept her sling.

The riders pressed closer, gradually surrounding them. Evrard's mouth was set in a humourless line, but Ayla sensed his triumph. "What's this? We saw the two of you on the highway. Does Count Raymond know you're out whoring, Bessarion?"

Lukas reached for the staff at his back, but Evrard lifted a crossbow from his right knee. That explained the count's relative sobriety: he was here to make sure his friends got safely home.

"No weapons, Greek. Keep your hands where I can see them. Let's have an explanation."

There was nothing he could say, nothing he could do. They both knew du Puiset was only looking for an excuse to let fly, and that bolt could drill right through the mail shirt Lukas wore.

Not while she stood there. Ayla dipped into her pouch, drawing out a stone.

"Well?"

Lukas' throat worked. "This is my lawful wife."

The torches were close enough to light their faces. The count glanced at Ayla, and recognition narrowed his eyes. "This is the Turk who threatened my sister."

It was like a nightmare that she was powerless to stop. In front of her, Lukas took a step back. Ayla loaded her sling, but the knotted cords felt unreal as they slid through her fingers, ready for action.

"So you've been lying with a Turk, Bessarion." Evrard slid down from his horse and stalked forward, crossbow ready. "That's a hanging offence."

"Please," Lukas began.

"Get on your knees and keep your hands up," Evrard barked. "Take their weapons, Roger, and be careful. The girl is dangerous."

Ayla took a breath, ready to wind the sling into action, but Lukas reached back, grabbing the strings.

"Drop it, Ayla," he whispered urgently.

Too late. One of the knights saw it first. *"She's got a sling!"*

"No!" Lukas screamed.

The count jerked his crossbow up and pulled the trigger.

* * *

The bolt hit Ayla between the eyes with a sound like an egg cracking. Lukas turned and saw the light snuffed out of her eyes even before he got his arms around her.

His voice wouldn't work. Dead silence screamed his horror as loud as a shout.

No, no, no. He lowered Ayla to the ground, touching her cheeks. He had no idea what to do. There had to be something. The five knights circling him began to react with shock as Le Puiset lowered his crossbow. The count tried to look grim, but something like fear lurked behind his eyes.

A wave of recognition hit Lukas. The grass under his knees, the scent of cypress, the glare of torches. The red star across Ayla's forehead and the thick bolt protruding from where the bridge of her nose used to be.

It was a dream. It happened this way each time. Relief surged through him. Any moment now he would wake to the comforting knowledge that it wasn't true.

He could hear his voice as if it was coming from a long way away. "No, no, no. Ayla. No. Wake up." He slapped himself, trying to jolt his eyes open. But he did not wake, and Ayla was still lying there.

It all seemed so real, but then it always did. More real than any dream he had ever experienced before. He could remember what was going to happen next:

"Devil take it, count, did you *have* to kill the girl?"

"That's *Greek* livery…are you sure…?"

The Frankish voices were much more sober now. Count Evrard shouldered his crossbow and sucked in a long breath. "That's enough. Let's go."

They rode away and took the light with them. Lukas sat in the grass, holding Ayla to his heart, feeling the warmth ebb away from her moment by moment.

They were bound by fate.

Just not forever.

He had foreseen Armen's attack. Why had he not foreseen this one? But of course, he had: in his dreams.

Peace, she had said. *Wars can end in peace.*

Yet it only took a single crossbow bolt to destroy the peace they had found. That was the cold, hard truth at the bottom of all the sweet words Ayla had said, all the good and well-meaning things his father or Adhemar had tried to tell him. You could only bring peace to the peaceful at heart. Some people had no desire for peace at all. Some people were only good for vengeance.

By the time the light was strong enough to see her face again, Lukas was numb with cold. Stiffly, he got to his feet, gathered Ayla into his arms, and carried her back across the river, wading through the freezing eddies.

He could not take her back to the Franks. Instead, Lukas turned to take her up into the hills. She would like it there.

"Lukas! Lukas Bessarion!"

Lukas did not stop until the pounding footsteps were almost on him. Then he lowered his burden to the ground, looked up to see Bertrand.

"Kismet," the bishop's squire said in hushed shock as he recognised her.

Fate.

You and she are bound by fate.

"Her name was Ayla," Lukas said faintly. "We have to bury her."

"I saw you passing and I knew…" the squire seemed to run out of words as he focused on what Lukas had said. *"Her?* Holy James. I'm so sorry."

Not your fault, Frank. That's what Ayla would say, but Lukas was too bitter to say them.

Bertrand helped him carry her into the hills. They found a green east-facing hillside, and as the sun rose, they built up a cairn of stones to cover her.

When it was finished, Lukas stood over the mound, twisting his fingers together, wishing Bertrand would go away. He wanted to say something over her, pray for her, but Ayla had died a heretic and he dared not hope the Frank would understand.

Before he could decide, Bertrand cleared his throat. "May God have mercy on her soul."

The words made something inside him crumble. Blinding tears stung his eyes. "May God have mercy," he repeated. And then, because it was the best he could do for her, he cleared his throat and spoke the burial prayers of her own people.

"In the name of God, the infinitely Compassionate and Merciful. Praise be to God, Lord of all the worlds. The Compassionate, the Merciful, Ruler on the Day of Reckoning. You alone do we worship, and You alone do we ask for help. Guide us on the straight path, the path of those who have received your grace; not the path of those who have brought down wrath, nor of those who wander astray. Amen."

Bertrand cleared his throat, putting a hand on Lukas' shoulder. "Amen."

"God forgive her, God forgive her. To God we belong, and to God we return."

"Lord, have mercy," Bertrand said.

It was the *Kyrie.* Lukas replied almost automatically: "Christ, have mercy."

"Lord, have mercy." For a little while, they stood looking down on her grave in silence, listening to the cold wind. Then Bertrand squeezed his shoulder. "Come back to camp, Bessarion. You should eat."

"Not yet."

Bertrand touched his shoulder once more, then left him to weep.

Later, he thought. He would stop only long enough to collect his gear and his bed-roll, and buy food for the journey. Then he was done with the Franks. There was nothing left for him here.

Chapter L.

When they reached the crest of the hill, Galdemar Carpenel reined in his horse and gulped the bite of apple he was chewing on. "God take pity on us. This is *Antioch?*" Saint-Gilles grunted. "Well, it's not Paris."

Four days on the road from Marash had brought the pilgrims down the river-meadows of the Orontes to Antioch. Although summer was only a fading memory, the fields surrounding the city were green with new growth. Despite the midday sun, a bleak autumn wind promised that winter was not far away. Barring a miracle, they would be spending it in front of the walls of Antioch. That much was obvious.

The rumours that had reached them in the mountains were false: Antioch's Turkish garrison remained entrenched behind her defences. And such defences! On the west, the immense city was girdled by the Orontes river and the marshes that flanked it. On the east, her towering walls left the plain and zig-zagged sharply up craggy hillsides to crown the peaks of the city's twin mountains. Perched atop one of them, remote from the city itself, the citadel was little more than a black knob against the sky. The sight alone almost made Saint-Gilles dizzy. He dared not imagine what it might be like trying to scale those heights for an assault.

The wall itself, massively strong and studded with towers, rushed down the crags like a silent avalanche and looped its way from mountain to river and back again. Seen at this distance, it was clearly more than twice, maybe even three times the length of Nicaea's walls, and the river and mountains would prevent them from surrounding the whole city even if they could find the manpower to do it.

Galdemar voiced the doubt at the back of his own mind. "This is insanity, Saint-Gilles. This city will never fall."

"It has in the past and it will again."

After centuries of Turkish rule, the Greeks had managed to retake Antioch more than a hundred years ago. Then, just twelve years previously, it passed back to the Turks. Both times by bargain or treachery.

"It had better, or we'll most certainly die trying." Galdemar flashed a half-hearted grin, and munched another bite of apple.

Saint-Gilles clucked to his horse and led his army onward, down the old Roman road toward the monstrous city. Ahead of them, the city's main gate stood shut and barred against them under a massive gatehouse that bristled with defenders. Before that gate, the camp of the army of God was already blooming like spring flowers.

The blood-red banner of Count Bohemond flapped in the chill wind directly opposite the great gate.

Galdemar chuckled. "Someone's eager to get in."

Saint-Gilles grunted again. He knew why. If Bohemond planned to be lord of the east, Antioch was the logical capital city. Though holy, Jerusalem was strategically unimportant. Antioch was larger, closer to the Greeks, and more defensible.

Galdemar was still complaining. "This is going to be a miserable and expensive winter, Saint-Gilles. Remind me why we aren't sitting it out in the comfort of the local fortresses like Tatikius suggested?"

"Better to keep the army concentrated on its job. Jerusalem is still miles away. If we scatter to the local castles, who knows if we'll ever manage to assemble an army again?"

At least, that was how he had convinced the other princes. He did not tell them that he, too, foresaw a miserable and expensive winter. When the rest of the army ran low on money and Greek gold kept flowing from the Provençal coffers, the other princes would soon run tame to his call. Divided, they would never stand. But united, they just might reach Jerusalem alive.

As they approached the city, Bohemond himself emerged from the camp, waving Saint-Gilles to a halt. "Count. It's good to see you again." He smiled from the depths of his fur-lined hood, lifting his voice to be heard above the wind. "There's a place for you around the wall to the south. We can't encircle the city but by heaven we can annoy them."

"I'll take a look at it," Saint-Gilles said.

Bohemond put a hand on his horse's neck. "How are you faring, my lord?"

Saint-Gilles recoiled at the look of sympathy the count gave him. He wished people would stop asking him that question. Each time they did, it was like tearing the scab off a wound. More to the point, he wished Bohemond would stop pretending that he cared. They were not friends. They had never been friends, and he was a fool not to see it sooner.

"I'll fare better once I have my people under shelter," he snapped, intentionally mistaking the count's meaning. "Come on, Galdemar."

He turned his horse and led his people on toward their camp. Yet he could not still the flicker of disappointment as he turned his back on Bohemond. He could have loved the man as a friend, but he would never serve him as a vassal. If that meant they must be enemies, then so be it.

Chapter LI.

Oliveta.

Lukas almost did not recognise the town. Little was left of it but the empty, ruined shells of some of the larger buildings. Although the shepherds he had met on the road warned of ghosts and demons, the ruins called to him. Lukas climbed over tumbled blocks of stone to reach a derelict and neglected-looking wall covered in scrawls of graffiti in Syriac and some other tongue he did not know. Above the reach of idle hands, a narrow stone border of twining acanthus leaves girdled the wall, a piece of delicate and defiant beauty.

At the centre of the acanthus belt, nestled among the leaves so humbly that he looked for a while before noticing it, was a small round medallion bearing the six-spoked wheel, an *I* superimposed upon an *X*.

The Watchers' Mark.

Lukas touched the wall as if it was an old friend, before he scrambled down again and ventured on.

The wind blew cold on the mountaintop. Stunted, gnarled old olive trees dotted the red hillsides among tumbled white stone. There was very little else. The grey sky above and the red earth below was empty and lonely. Not even a footprint marked the ground.

Closer to the centre, stone villas stood gaunt and eyeless, their dead trees blackened by ancient flames.

His father used to tell of visiting the ruins of Egypt and Persia, the skills and beauties that could be learned and reproduced through sketching the aftermath of destruction. Now he was looking at the ruins of his own people. Their own vanished glory.

Lukas wandered through the city. The bath-house was no more than a line of foundations, but he remembered taking a bath there on the afternoon before the Watcher's Council. He drifted through the marketplace where he had discovered, for the very first time in his life, that he did not have enough money.

It was strange to remember that even before the night of the council, even with his whole family around him, they had been fugitives from an invading army.

The villa they had stayed in was now a fragile shell of walls pierced by arches, its internal walls and floors collapsed into a morass of rubble. As his footsteps disturbed the sand, he found tiny, coloured chips of glass mixed into it, and from time to time his toe dislodged cube-shaped tesserae from a long-vanished mosaic.

He wondered what would happen when he returned through time. He had left amidst destruction. Was he going back only to find the corpses of his family? He closed his eyes for a moment, thinking of a grave in the hills. Did he have the courage to bury more of his people?

Yet so long as any of them were left, he had to find them. So long as he had the chance to take his revenge—on Khalil, on all the heretics—he had to return. This time, he would not be helpless. All his worst fears had already come true. He had nothing left to lose.

There was one more place to see: the basilica. Lukas turned back to the centre of the town. As he walked through the streets, the cold wind thrummed through the stones, wailing a little in the chinks and crannies and blind arches of the ruins.

He saw the basilica long before he reached it. The domed roof had fallen, but all four walls were still intact and so was the courtyard.

The wind sounded almost like a voice wailing.

The hair prickled on his head. This was where it had happened. This was where it began.

He reached the courtyard opening and clambered across a fallen archway. Beyond, the tessellated pavement was strewn with dust and fallen rubble, but the outline of its geometric knots and labyrinths was still faintly visible.

Elsewhere in the city, grass had taken root among the stones. Not here. There was nothing that lived in this courtyard; nothing except—

In the centre of the pavement, shrouded in a dusty and ragged black robe, a man sat hunched and cross-legged, shaking in the chill wind and rocking his upper body to and fro with small keening cries. His black hair and beard had grown so long that they almost brushed the floor. As Lukas approached, he saw that the figure's clenched hands and the skin of his forehead were both covered in horrible raw sores.

Lukas moved as quietly as he could, but his foot caught against a piece of rubble. At the sound, the figure's head snapped up to look at him.

Lukas froze. He would know that face anywhere.

Khalil.

At first they only stared at each other in silence. There could be no mistake. For Lukas, it was not much more than half a year since he had last seen that thin hawklike face, and it would take him far more than a lifetime to forget.

For a moment he thought Khalil recognised him too, but then the heresiarch hunched his body over his clenched hands again and went on rocking himself back and forth with feeble moans.

"Leave me! Be gone! Cease tormenting me with visions!"

Heart pounding, Lukas inched closer. "Khalil," he said.

The sorcerer flinched but did not reply. The pavement around him was still scarred with the outlines of the sigil he had drawn so long ago.

Closer now. Despite the chill wind, Lukas felt sweat beading his forehead. How was this man still alive? Had he, too, travelled through time?

Whatever the answer was, Ayla had known. This was the secret she would have killed him to preserve.

"I am not a vision, nor a ghost. I am Lukas Bessarion."

The wail cut off without warning. Slowly, slowly, the matted head turned, and Lukas saw glittering eyes and blistered skin through the matted elf-locks.

"Water," he croaked. "Food. For the love of God."

Lukas shook his head. "I have none." He had taken a cluster of ripe figs from an orchard early this morning, but had eaten all of them. It was on such scrounging that he had managed to live these last few days. Instead, he dropped to a crouch to peer into the madman's eyes. "Why are you still here, Khalil?"

The sorcerer stared at him. "I was waiting for you."

"You knew I was coming?"

"Give me water."

That, he did have, in a canteen on his hip. But the man was dangerous. Lukas got up and backed away again.

"First answer my questions. Or get your own water."

Khalil began to laugh until he subsided into a weary cough. His dry and blistered lips cracked, and a trickle of blood ran down his chin. Then the heresiarch dragged aside his black robe and said, "Now do you understand?"

Lukas stepped back, his eyes widening. From the waist down, Khalil's body had been turned to black marble, the high sheen of the stone still capturing each pore in the skin, each stitch of the rich trousers that he had been wearing beneath the robe.

Lukas swallowed, noticing how the stone pavement was swept clean and worn down around Khalil for an arm's length in every direction, placing him in the centre of a polished, ring-shaped hollow.

No wonder he had not moved since Lukas appeared. No wonder he was so ragged and weathered, so blistered and raw. In this courtyard, no shadow would ever fall on him. Nothing would protect him from wind, rain or sun.

"How long?" Lukas whispered.

With a madman's smile Khalil shrouded his half-petrified body again. "I do not know, Watcher. I thought it was years beyond count. I thought I had endured a hundred summers and twice a hundred winters. But now you return and are still a youth. Perhaps I have gone mad indeed."

This man had hunted his family, had destroyed an entire town with a casual word of command, but at this moment Lukas could not help pitying him. As he took the tin water-canteen from his waist, Khalil's eyes flickered savagely.

Only a few weeks ago, he might have done what pity prompted. Now he subsided into a low comfortable squat, setting the bottle on the dull stones just beyond the sorcerer's reach. Khalil licked his lips and stared at it.

"Answer my questions first. Why aren't you dead? No man lives four hundred years exposed on a mountain."

Khalil muttered something in his own language. "Four hundred years?"

"It is now the year of Our Lord one thousand and ninety-seven."

"Four hundred and ninety by our calendar." Khalil wiped the smear of blood off his lower lip, staring into the distance.

Lukas' curiosity got the better of him. "Who did this to you?"

Khalil refocused. "You were there. You saw it. The child blurred the lines."

"Paulus." Lukas remembered his terrified little brother crawling away through the chalk sigils, smearing them.

"The ritual fell apart. With the line broken, the lesser djinn could get in. But they were meant to fall on *you.* Not me. What was protecting you?"

Some protection. Lukas ignored the question. "So they turned you to stone? What happened to me? Why did I wake in Myra four hundred years later?"

A flicker of interest from the sorcerer. "You woke up in this time?"

"I've been here six months."

Khalil made a sound of realisation. "You were still within the diagram when the line broke. The ritual was not complete. I was partly bound to Lilith already, so they could not kill me. But there was power gathering; when the djinn attacked it spilled out and took you with it."

"Through time?"

"To a sorcerer, time is meaningless. We seek to exist above and beyond time, like God himself. For a moment, so did you."

"Wonderful. Now how do I go back?"

There was a silence. "The water first."

Lukas picked up the canteen and took a drink. Three swallows, sweet and cold, shocking wakefulness into his veins. He shook the bottle. "Not much left. Tell me how to go back."

Khalil stared at him murderously. "Call on the Poison Mother. Tell her what you desire."

Lukas put his hand on his knife. "Answer me!"

"Or you'll do what?" Khalil levelled a black gaze at him. "Kill me? Torment me?"

Lukas drew his knife, the blade trembling in his hand.

"Give me the water. That's all I ask. A mouthful." Suddenly, he lunged and Lukas jumped back in alarm. Khalil strained forward, his hands scrabbling futilely against the stone.

Lukas was trembling "You have no power anymore. The djinn saw to that. But you've had visitors, haven't you? The Vowed, for example. You've taught them what you know."

Khalil stared at him through stringy black hair, his eyes sick and despairing.

"Someone else will bring you water. Otherwise, you can wait for the rain." Lukas picked up the canteen and stepped back.

"God have mercy!" Khalil lifted both hands to his head in despair; they were little more than bone and shrunken flesh. "All I ask is a mouthful of water. It is not much to a man who is only half a man."

Lukas had his pity well in hand now, crushed deep down inside where it would never see the light. "Then it is not much to withhold." Resolutely, he turned on his heel and made toward the fallen arch.

Khalil's voice rose to a scream. "No! No, don't leave me! Give me water and I'll tell you anything!" He clawed at the pavement, teeth bared in a desperate grimace, his stone legs pinning him in place. "Do you know why they call this the Dead City, Lukas Bessarion? Not because it is ruined, but because dead things *live* here."

Lukas turned, a shiver crawling his spine. "What do you mean?"

"I mean the goats and winds, Watcher. I mean the Horrible Croucher and the Terror by Night. I mean the brothers Flame and Pestilence."

Lukas' skin crawled. "Don't speak their names!"

"Too late for that. They are already here. For four hundred years they have been my companions as well as my captors." Khalil pulled himself upright with a sickly grin. "They whisper to me in the night, how I might be freed. Only if one of my four sacrifices should return and offer me a drink in the name of mercy. Then, at last, I will be free of my torment."

So this was why Lilith wanted him alive.

"You want *me* to free you?" Lukas' voice was scratchy. "After all you've done?"

Khalil scowled at him. "What else can you possibly offer me? I will accept your terms. I will tell you how to return across the aeons of time. But you must swear by all you hold sacred that you will set me free."

"Free to complete your ritual? To make war against my people?"

Khalil shrugged. "What lies in the far future is not your concern, surely. You will return to your home, live to a ripe old age, and die. I will remain here during your lifetime, bound and helpless. What damage could I possibly do?"

He could do damage once he was freed. But to whom? To the Franks? Lukas thought of Ayla. Loneliness washed over him again, together with the sickening grief that had haunted him all the way from Marash. He had no reason to love the Franks. Let them suffer.

He shifted his knife to his left hand and placed the water canteen on the ground just within Khalil's reach.

"I swear. Tell me how to return to my own time, and by Saint Luke, the Holy Virgin and my hope of heaven, I will release you."

The sorcerer ran his tongue over blistered lips. "It is neither natural nor easy to transcend time. You must create the same conditions that brought you here in the first place."

"What do you mean?"

"I mean a sacrifice. Not just one, nor four, but many. A whole city. You must slay them for the Poison Mother and ask for your desire."

Lukas stared at him, aghast.

"When I am free I will help you myself." Khalil lunged for the water.

Lukas knocked it away. It tumbled clattering across the courtyard and lay still. The sorcerer gave a howl of rage, and Lukas stepped back again, shaking.

"No. *No.* That's no answer."

"You swore!"

Lukas pointed his knife at Khalil. "There's another way. There *must* be."

"I told you what I know. Now keep your oath!"

"You're lying!"

"Why would I lie to you?" Khalil hunched over his bleeding knuckles. "I lived four hundred years to reach this time. I can *never* go back. But you can. Why would I not send you back if I could?"

Slowly, Lukas lowered his knife. If what Khalil said was true, he could never go home. Not even his family was worth that much.

The purpose that had kept him on his aching, blistered feet through the perils and hardships of the last six months was gone. He felt himself spinning in a world without direction.

Ayla's voice came to him from long, long ago. *Then you ought to avenge them.*

"Yes," he said huskily. "Yes, I'll free you."

Khalil had been staring at the water-bottle, but Lukas's voice made him look up with a question in his eyes.

Lukas' hands were shaking. His knife was shaking. He passed the hilt from hand to hand, wiping the palms on his tunic. What was wrong with him? He had killed before, hadn't he? He took a firmer grip and reversed the blade in his hand.

Khalil saw his purpose now, but he only smiled and closed his eyes.

Lukas struck.

The blow should have torn the sorcerer's throat open. It did not. Lukas felt the flesh part under the blade's edge, but the only sign of a wound was a thin red scar.

Khalil put a hand to his throat and rubbed, swallowing. Then he looked up at Lukas, his voice soft and his eyes full of bitter despair:

"Do you think, boy, fixed here as I am, that if any mortal weapon could free me from this body, I would not have used it?"

He thrust out his shrunken arms and turned them over. They were a mass of scars, as if a wild beast had gnawed them open again and again.

Lukas dropped the knife and sank back onto his heels. For a moment, the nausea almost convinced him he would faint. "They made you invulnerable too."

"Their punishment would hardly have been complete otherwise."

Saint George, even this purpose, this last starveling hope was gone. Even revenge was beyond his power. Khalil, his greatest enemy, his greatest fear, was a broken shell.

"No." Lukas spoke drearily, seeming to hear his voice from a very long way away. "No, and for me, it still is not complete." He sheathed his knife, went over to pick up his water canteen.

"I meant my offer," Khalil called. "Free me and you could go home. You could find your family. You could do as you liked in the knowledge that I was bound. What does this age have to offer you? You must be little more than a beggar!"

402

Lukas stood, reattaching the canteen to his belt. "My father left something for me in Antioch. A weapon of some kind."

"A spear." Khalil's voice hushed. "A spear with its own power. Unbeatable in battle. Did your father tell you he stole it from me?"

Lukas stared. A weapon so powerful that Khalil would level a whole town to the ground for the chance of regaining it? He could think of any number of reasons why such a weapon might have fallen into his father's hands. As the spoils of war, for instance.

He did not ask himself how an invincible spear might *become* the spoils of war.

"You would never tell your disciples about such a weapon," Lukas said after a moment. "Unless my father was able to recover it himself, that spear must still be in Antioch."

He frowned. What about Father and Marta? When Paulus broke the line, they were in the same place as him: inside their sigils. Were they also scattered through time? Were they out there, somewhere in this enormous, lonely world, looking for him and each other?

The thought gave him hope, and the glimmers of a new purpose. "Here's what I'm going to do, Khalil. I'll be four hundred years too late, but better late than never. I'll get that spear. I'll take it south to Palestine and I'll fight. Turks, Egyptians, Franks, *anyone* who wants to lord it over my people. No more foreign conquerors."

Visions marched through his brain. He saw himself riding at the head of an army with the Spear in his hand. He saw himself challenging Evrard of le Puiset to combat for the sake of justice for Ayla. He saw himself sitting in a graceful peristyle, holding a city or a string of cities or even a whole province against all contenders.

He would be a warlord. He would be a prince. He would be a king.

Lukas turned. "Farewell, Khalil."

"You swore an oath!" The sorcerer's voice hitched, bordering on the edge of panic. "I know about you Watchers! I know you must keep your oaths!"

"Well, I choose not to keep this one."

He almost held his breath. Almost waited to be struck dead. But nothing happened, and he smiled a small, hard smile at Khalil. "You see? Suffer another four hundred years and more, heretic."

He walked across the courtyard and climbed over the fallen stones at the gate. When his feet were on the grass again, a feral wail broke from the stone captive. Lukas listened, and deep inside, his heart was hot with cruel delight. Four hundred years of winter's cold and summer's heat, thirst and hunger.

It was not *his* revenge, but it was the only revenge he would find against Khalil.

In the face of the thin chill wind, Lukas smiled bleakly and took the road that led to Antioch.

Epilogue

High in the upper air, the black vulture circled.
Watching.
Waiting.

The Syrian Watcher was a tiny dot, crawling antlike along the north road. Behind him, on the tessellated pavement of the desecrated church, the half-stone sorcerer lay with his hands stretched out in useless supplication.

His spirit was only a feeble, despairing flicker. For centuries, her power had sustained him, a constant irretrievable drain on her strength, and for what? The half-finished ritual had bound them together, but there was no use she could make of him while he was trapped on this mountain. He had sent her acolytes—the Vowed—in a pathetic attempt to win her favour. She had accepted them, but she had not wasted her time on the sorcerer himself.

Ah…but now, there was a chance to free him. To use him. Perhaps, even, to complete the ritual.

Lilith released the bird and descended.

The half-stone creature sensed her coming. His heaving shoulders stilled; then, slowly, he peeled his shadowy face from the ground.

"*Now* you come to me." His voice rasped painfully over a long-dry throat. "Tell me you can end my life."

She knelt before him, adopting a form the children of earth found desirable. "It is not my pleasure to end your life. But I will begin it, if you like."

He laughed raggedly. "I expect you will make me pay."

"Once I was a goddess. They made offerings to me in blood. I would like to taste blood again, Half-Stone."

"There is only one God. I could not put you in his place even if I wanted to."

"True. The children of earth have grown wise of late, and have driven us out of their temples. But if they can no longer be deceived, they can be corrupted. They will butcher each other for God's sake, and I will drink and be satisfied. Be my prophet, Half-Stone. Lead your people to war for my sake."

The sorcerer looked on her with loathing. "What a fool I was, to call on you."

"You needed me then. I need you now."

"As your ally? Or as your slave?"

Her voice sharpened to a hiss. "Double-tongued knave, I know you well. You never intended to serve me; you meant to be my master, and have a djinn as your servant. But *I* will be mistress, one way or another. Kiss my foot and I will make a king of you. Defy me, and I will torment you forever."

His shoulders slumped. "Can you release me, then?"

"No. But I can bring you the Bessarion."

"He has already been."

"Then I will corrupt him utterly, and when he is moulded to my will, I will bring him back."

She spoke with serene certainty and the sorcerer could not help but believe her. He did not speak, but the flicker of his spirit grew brighter.

Lilith smiled. "Do not be afraid, Half-Stone. I will not ask you to spill the blood of your own people. Look, I have brought an army from the west. They are too strong for me now, but I will corrupt them, and when they have become weak, we will slaughter them together. Do we have a bargain?"

The half-stone sorcerer laughed, the hard, bright sound of a soul shattering into fragments. "Yes. We have a bargain."

S.D.G.

Lukas Bessarion will return in
  A Conspiracy of Prophets

Wondering what happened to the other Bessarions? Marta Bessarion's
story will begin in
  The Lady of Kingdoms

Historical Note

Perils and embarrassments lie in wait for the historical novelist bold enough to claim historical accuracy. While I would not claim total accuracy, I can, nonetheless, claim to have done a certain amount of study on the history of the First Crusade.

Obviously, I've embroidered upon the history by including a number of characters and events with no historical foundation. Khalil, Ayla, the Bessarions, the Watchers, and the Vowed are more or less my own invention. Others, like Saint-Gilles, Bohemond, Adhemar, Emperor Alexius, Tatikius, Godfrey, Baldwin of Boulogne, Galdemar Carpenel, Evrard of le Puiset and many more were real historical people, although the chronicles give us little information on their personalities, motivations and relationships.

The Prologue to this novel focuses on the situation in Palestine and Syria in the aftermath of the Battle of Yarmouk in AD 636. Heraclius, the emperor of the Eastern Roman Empire, had just emerged victorious but exhausted from a costly war with the Persian Empire. It was then that the Muslim Arabs, then viewed by the Byzantines as another heretical sect of Christianity, began their wars of conquest under the brilliant leadership of Khalid ibn al-Walid, who defeated the forces of Rome decisively at Yarmouk in August of 636. One factor in Khalid's victory was the defection of Monophysite Christian cavalry troops from the Romans, a motif that recurred throughout the history of the conquests. Again and again, religious dissenters who had lived through miserable persecutions under Heraclius turned against him to welcome the Arab invasion.

Early in this book, I imagine what might have happened in the background to Alexius Comnenus' negotiations with Raymond of Toulouse in April of 1097, when "the emperor of the Greeks" (as he was known to Westerners at the time) tried to force him into swearing homage. Alexius' daughter, the historian Anna Comnena, claimed that Alexius' relationship with Raymond was very chummy at this time, and that both of them were suspicious of Bohemond, the South Norman count who had tried to conquer the empire on two previous occasions. However Frankish historians, including the count's chaplain, Raymond of Aguilers, tell us that Saint-Gilles was enraged by attacks on his people as they crossed Greek territory and refused to swear the oath Alexius demanded.

There's also excellent historical evidence that, at this time, Bohemond was following in the footsteps of other family members in offering his service to Alexius in exchange for lands in the east, though his ambitions were (typically) far more grandiose. The scene in which Bohemond attempts to persuade Raymond to attack Constantinople with him is completely fictional, though it was inspired by a rumour that he had made a similar offer to Godfrey of Bouillon. Certainly it would not have been beyond him. Bohemond always was an opportunist.

The siege of Nicaea developed more or less as depicted. After Count Raymond's attempt to undermine the wall failed, the Frankish princes took counsel and asked Alexius to send ships overland to the lake. I have invented the council scene itself, with Raymond's attempts to gain control of the whole pilgrimage, although he may very well have believed himself entitled to the leadership of the expedition, based on a previous meeting with Pope Urban. When the Greek ships arrived outside Nicaea's walls, the Turkish garrison quickly surrendered to the Greeks. Anna Comnena describes in detail how this was done secretly at night, to prevent the Franks getting control of the city.

Next, we see the battle of Dorylaeum and the journey across Anatolia. Again, I have attempted, though not necessarily realised, historical accuracy. The battle itself is difficult due to the many differing accounts of it. Nobody knows for sure exactly where it took place, but I have followed John France's expert harmonisation of the known details. While none of the crusaders seem to have recorded seeing apparitions during the battle (these became common later in the campaign) I have tried to follow the chroniclers in describing the intense terror and despair which they felt both during the battle and later, in the crossing of the Taurus mountains. John France points out that the Turkish battle strategy depended on breaking the Frankish resolve early in the engagement. In fact, this came very close to happening: having been savaged by the Turkish archers, the Frankish knights fled back to the camp in terror at the pivotal moment, enabling them to save the non-combatants who were being attacked from the rear. It was sheer stubbornness that then allowed them to stand firm until help arrived.

Chroniclers record that, after an abortive ambush at Heraclea by the Turks, Baldwin of Boulogne and Tancred Hautville set out into Cilicia. Historians argue over whether this was part of an "Armenian strategy" to establish friendly relations with the Christian Armenians of Cilicia, or whether it was simply two ambitious lesser princes setting out to grab lands for themselves. I tend to agree with John France that the evidence favours the "Armenian strategy", simply because there is otherwise no good reason why the main body of the pilgrimage should have undertaken the much longer and equally difficult route north through the modern Kayseri. By splitting up, the pilgrimage was able to approach Antioch in a pincer movement from north-east and north-west, having cleared the enemy from its hinterland and freed the northern Armenians. France believes that if there *was* an Armenian strategy, the Greek general Tatikius was its most likely architect. However, this is speculation, and it suited the dramatic purposes of this novel to imagine the strategy taking form in a more ad-hoc manner, partly driven by ambition, partly by strategy, and not entirely according to Tatikius' wishes. While I have taken liberties with the expedition's motivation, the eventual outcome is the same. Meanwhile, although the journey through the Taurus mountains was gruellingly difficult for the majority of the expedition, the storm is my own invention.

The final part of the book, which sees the crusade resting at Marash, contains a great deal of speculation and invention. It is likely, for instance, that the Greeks had already briefed the Franks on the complicated nature of politics in a Syria which was ruled partly by Turks in the service of the sultan at Baghdad, and partly by a patchwork of Greek, Armenian, Syriac, and even Frankish warlords. There is reason to assume that Marash was ruled by Thatoul at the time, although the chroniclers do not record his existence till three or four years later. There is no reason to assume that Thatoul would have refused to accept a Greek garrison, or that Raymond ever discovered the true nature of Bohemond's relationship with Alexius at this or any other time. Additionally, the evidence suggests that when the siege of Antioch began in late October of 1097, Raymond still viewed the Greeks with much suspicion. However, Raymond spent money freely throughout the siege. Nobody has ever explained where his apparently inexhaustible treasure came from; the most probable source would have to be Alexius, and it's possible that if this was so, his association with the Greeks began much sooner than the spring of 1098.

Raymond's son William, and the events surrounding his short life, are mostly speculation on my part. We do know that Raymond's third wife Elvira of Castile gave birth to a son at some point during the journey, and that the child did not survive for long, but we know nothing else about him. I have taken the liberty of naming him after Raymond's brother and predecessor as count of Toulouse.

Throughout this book, I have attempted to accurately depict the mindset and motivations of the crusaders as currently understood by modern scholars. Once more, I will not claim a high standard of historical accuracy, but I will say that I have done my best to achieve it. One concept that was very important to the crusaders was the notion of liberation. Pope Urban's message at the Council of Clermont, when he preached the crusade to the assembled nobility, was self-consciously a message of liberation of the eastern church and the holy places of Palestine from occupation and exploitation. It is certain that the majority of the population of Anatolia and Syria at this time were still Christians of various different sects, and although there is debate on this topic, this may have been the case in Palestine as well. For these people, the crusaders were indeed liberators. By depicting the Turkish retreat through Anatolia as ruinous to the native population, and by depicting the local peasantry as welcoming the Franks with jubilation, I am sticking close to the eyewitness accounts given by Frankish chroniclers. Both Franks and Muslims would later record Frankish war crimes against Muslim populations, but not while the crusade was in majority-Christian lands.

I would like to thank my beta readers for their time, patience, and invaluable feedback: Schuyler McConkey, Christina Baehr, David Noor, and Courtney Gilliland. I'm particularly grateful to my Muslim readers, Leila Ammar and Razan Ewisat, and to Intisar Khanani for graciously finding me the help I needed. Finally, warmest thanks are due to my wonderful editor, Lucy Holdsworth, and my cover designer, Jenny Zemanek. You have all helped to make this story what it is.

Suzannah Rowntree

October 2018

Further Reading

In preparation for this book and series, I have spent (so far) four years reading up on Crusader history. Generally, I have not relied upon Sir Steven Runciman's landmark history of the Crusades, except in a limited way for the seventh century events discussed in the Prologue. Runciman's work is now very old and almost completely superseded by better scholarship. For the history of the Eastern Roman Empire, I found John Julius Norwich's *A Short History of Byzantium* helpful in giving the overall outline and Judith Herrin's *Byzantium: The Surprising Life of a Medieval Empire* fleshed out some of the everyday details, while her *The Formation of Christendom* helped provide the seventh century backdrop. I also consulted a range of other materials, including Marcus Louis Rautman's *Daily Life in the Byzantine Empire*. For the history of the First Crusade itself, I enjoyed the very readable *The First Crusade: A New History* by Thomas Asbridge, although Jonathan Riley-Smith's *The First Crusade and the Idea of Crusading* and John France's *Victory in the East: A Military History of the First Crusade* are more scholarly and detailed studies. Christopher MacEvitt's *The Crusades and the Christian World of the East: Rough Tolerance* contained indispensable details on the local Armenian and Syrian political situation in 1097, and how the Franks reacted to it. John France's *Western Warfare in the Age of the Crusades* was my go-to for military background, and Carl Stephenson's *Medieval Feudalism* was an excellent general handbook on that institution with more distilled information than available in Marc Bloch's *Feudal Society*, which I have also used as a reference. Jonathan Shepard's article *When Greek Meets Greek: Alexius Comnenus and Bohemond in 1097-1098* was

413

vital to figuring out the interpersonal dynamics between Alexius, Bohemond, Tatikius, and Raymond.

The medieval chroniclers themselves have provided some of the most readable crusader literature currently available. Anna Comnena's *Alexiad* provides a not-always-trustworthy spin on the history from the Greek perspective. Christopher Tyerman's Penguin Classics compilation of *Chronicles of the First Crusade* was my constant companion, including selections from the *Gesta Francorum* and the chronicles of Fulcher of Chartres and Raymond of Aguilers, with some excerpts from Muslim and Jewish sources. William of Tyre's *History of Deeds Done Beyond the Sea* was also helpful as it provides a synthesis of earlier accounts. Malcolm Barber's compilation of *Letters from the East* includes many missives from the crusaders themselves. The chanson de geste *The Song of Roland,* which was most likely written down in its current form shortly after the First Crusade, possibly by someone who experienced it, was very helpful in trying to appreciate the mindset of an eleventh-century crusader. Finally, Tim Severin's *Crusader: By Horse to Jerusalem* is a wonderful travel book discussing the difficulties and technicalities of long-distance horse travel, medieval style, along the same route taken by the First Crusade.

About the Author

Suzannah Rowntree lives in a big house in rural Australia with her awesome parents and siblings, reading academic histories of the Crusades and writing historical fantasy fiction that blends folklore and myth with historical fact.

Printed in Great Britain
by Amazon

41641990R00251